This book is availab  ᴧ
Amazon.com. You may fin .
Please leave a review and ₃
author. Feel free to ɪᴏᴏᴋ ɪɪɪʏ ᴅᴏᴏᴋ up ᴏɪɪ ɡᴏᴏᴅʀᴇᴀᴅs
@https://www.goodreads.com/book/show/18306100-warzone and leave a
review.

Karen,
Thanks for the encouragement.
Best Regards,
Morris E. Graham

WARZONE: NEMESIS

A Novel of Mars

By Morris E. Graham

Dedicated to the men and women around the world in our military, who serve this country, and who fight for freedom and democracy for both the USA and the world.

PREFACE

The space race was a lie, and the cold war wasn't as cold as you thought. While we were playing spy versus spy, conducting an arms race and a space race on Earth, things were heating up in the solar system.

In 1959, an alien vessel crashed on the Navajo reservation, ushering forth a colonial space race in the solar system between the two superpowers. The prize is the mysterious metal known only as alloy-x and the alien technology that promises to make one nation or the other the dominant superpower in the arms race. The American commander finds himself fighting with the toughest antagonist of his career. He had finally met his nemesis. The stakes are high. Losing the struggle could tip the balance of power on the Earth, giving the Soviets the advantage in Earth's cold war.

Acknowledgements

To Jesus Christ, the "author and finisher of our faith."
To my wife Edie for all her love and support.
This was written under inspiration of the video game Battlezone, created by Activision®, currently owned by Atari® Interactive.
The Art of War quotes are from translation by Thomas Cleary, Shambhala Publications.
Star Trek© presently has two owners: TV - CBS Television Distribution, CBS Paramount Network Television, Movies - Paramount Pictures, Viacom.
Sonic Drive-In© 2012 America's Drive-In Brand Properties LLC.
San Geronimo Lodge Bed & Breakfast Inn is owned and operated by Charles Montgomery and Pam Tyler of Taos, NM.
McDonald's™ is a global franchise retailer, selling food in 119 countries.
Mandina's Restaurant of New Orleans is owned and operated by Cindy Mandina.
The song of the Navajo shepherd children is a traditional Navajo folk song, author unknown.
Fencing terms defined http://www.synec-doc.be/escrime/dico/engl.htm and http://en.wiktionary.org/wiki/derobement
The explanation of "there is no sex in the Soviet Union," is quoted from Russiapedia online.
Other quotes from Wikipedia
Quotes from martial arts legend Bruce Lee.
References to "A Piece of Steak," a short story published in the book *Boxing Stories* by Jack London.
Also I wish to express thanks to the world's best research assistant, Google.
"Bad, Bad Leroy Brown" was written and recorded by Jim Croce.
"Bad Moon Rising" was written John Fogerty and recorded by Credence Clearwater Revival.
"Cecelia" was written by Paul Simon and recorded by Simon and Garfunkle.
"Evil Ways" was written by Clarence "Sonny" Henry and made famous by the band Santana.
"Good Hearted Woman" is a song written by country music singers Waylon Jennings and Willie Nelson.
"Johnny B Good" was written and recorded by Chuck Berry.
"Sweet Caroline" was written and recorded by Neil Diamond.
"The Charge of the Light Brigade" is an 1854 narrative poem by Lord Alfred Tennyson.

Cover art by Jordon Riser, http://www.jordanrdesigns.com.

Special thanks to Jim Decker, Jim Lambright, Ladonna Hargis, Jon Sowden, Meredith Smith, Don Hall and Dave Smith for helping me edit this. Special thanks to former servicemen, who helped me "keep it real," Bob Heitman, Jim Decker, Jim Lambright, Jerril Smith, Isaih Jernigan, John Garrett, Darrel Tucker and Greg Schleintz.

Also thanks to members of the Battlezone Club, Dx. for his technical support, and Blunt Force Trauma, proof read the early manuscript. Finally thanks to Guido Henkle for his tutorial on formatting eBooks.

Special thanks to Victor Marx of ATP (All Things Possible) Ministries, who graciously allowed me to write in his father, Soke Karl W. Marx, founder of Keichu-Ryu Karate, and my former judo instructor into the story in a fictional setting.

Boxing Terms Glossary is a compilation from different sources:
Ringside By Gus [http://www.ringsidebygus.com/boxing-terms.html] website by Gus Petropulos:
Sports Pundit website, [http://www.sportspundit.com/boxing/terms]:
Boxrec website, [http://boxrec.com/media/index.php/Category:Glossary]:
the Merriam-Webster online dictionary [http://www.merriam-webster.com/dictionary].

Special thanks to Sergey Zuhair for consulting about Soviet military and Russian culture. Most of all, thanks to Walter Parchomenko for his enthusiastic encouragement and invaluable assistance in helping me finish this project.

Disclaimer

There are three glossaries in the back, Navajo terms, military and other terms, and boxing terms.

TOP SECRET

THIS IS A COVER SHEET
FOR TOP SECRET INFORMATION

ANY INDIVIDUALS HANDLING THIS INFORMATION ARE REQUIRED TO PROTECT IT FROM UNAUTHORIZED DISCLOSURE IN THE INTEREST OF THE NATIONAL SECURITY OF THE UNITED STATES.

HANDLING, STORAGE, REPRODUCTION AND DISPOSITION OF THE ATTACHED DOCUMENT(S) WILL BE IN ACCORDANCE WITH APPLICABLE EXECUTIVE ORDER(S), STATUTE(S), AND AGENCY IMPLEMENTING REGULATIONS.

(THIS COVER SHEET IS UNCLASSIFIED)

TOP SECRET

805-K02
STANDARD FORM 785 (04-86)
ASD 8201-2-128-3728
PRESCRIBED BY ASDC/SECURITY
48 ASDC 1985

TABLE OF CONTENTS

UFO CRASH—NAVAJO NATIONS

July 5, 1959

The explosion in the engine room rocked the alien vessel orbiting Earth. The three engineers standing closest to the engine were killed instantly. Chief engineer Ba-Torah threw up a containment field to seal off the engine and prevent it from continuing to leak poisonous gas into the engineering bay. He was able to vent out enough of the poison gas to give enough time for the crew to put on their oxygen masks. The engine failure was just the beginning; they were now experiencing cascading failure to multiple systems. They were in serious trouble. The Chief engineer telepathically relayed the news of their troubles to Captain Ik-tah.

"Status report!" the captain barked telepathically to his first officer.

"Multiple system failures, life support fifty percent and dropping, complete primary engine failure, impulse power thirty percent and falling. We've broken orbit and are losing altitude."

"Impulse drive, reverse full," the captain ordered.

"Sir, impulse drive, reverse full," repeated his helmsman. The lines on his face hardened as he prepared for the loss of his ship and the deaths of his crew. It was times like this the discipline the Ktahrthians used to keep telepathic *noise* down was dissolving. He could "hear" the fear and confusion from his crew.

"Discipline! Control your thoughts, all of you! Lieutenant Ak-beiha, start the vessel's self-destruct sequence to engage if no life signs from the crew are detected."

"Sorry sir, that system is offline."

"Start the wipe of the entire computer system in the event all hands are lost!"

"Sorry sir, that system is down, too."

Unable to control his thoughts, the captain cursed telepathically, then composed himself and braced for impact. The alien vessel tore through the tops of the juniper trees on the Navajo Nation's Chuska mountain range, forcefully hitting the ground in a grassy clearing. What was left of the impulse engines on full reverse was the only thing that kept the vessel from being destroyed.

First officer Rik-Bar couldn't feel his legs due to a broken back. He knew he also had multiple internal injuries. Bluish-green blood gurgled in his throat and trickled down his face from his mouth. His first thoughts were of the vessel and his mate Lo-Bin, the communications officer. He could "hear" various crew members crying and moaning telepathically from their own injuries. "Status report!" he urgently commanded. Lo-Bin was dying but could still move her head.

"Captain Ik-tah is dead, and most of the crew are either dead or unconscious. I love you, Rik." The death rattle in her throat was the only audible sound before her body stiffened and then relaxed as she took her last breath.

One by one the telepathic moans and cries ceased. Rik-Bar's duty was to destroy the vessel. The shame of his failure eclipsed his grief over the death of Lo-Bin. Waves of intense pain from his internal injuries washed over him while he waited to die alone.

TWO HOURS EARLIER

"Good morning, sleepy head. By the time you wash up, breakfast will be ready."

Twelve-year old Benjamin Begay rubbed the sleep from his eyes. His mother was singing softly to the music of the sizzling Navajo fry bread cooking in the cast-iron pan on her wood stove. The smell of sweet piñon sap his mother used to start the morning fire perfumed the air, but it was the fragrant aroma of the frying bread that moved the boy into action.

"Yes, mamma." Ben stretched and hastily threw on his clothes. The cool water from the rain barrel felt good on his face, and he drank in the beauty of the summer dawn. The boy was starved and he made short work of the fry bread and warm sheep milk. He liked eating breakfast at home; it tasted a lot better than anything they served at the mission school. His mother would feed his two little sisters breakfast as soon as he finished eating and was on his way to the grazing lease.

Ben was born into the Coyote Pass People and born for the Bitter Water People. His maternal grandfather was from the Towering House Clan, and his paternal grandfather was from the Water Flows Together People. Before the white men put them on a reservation and sent them to school, Navajos only had one name and were identified by their matrilineal family line. It was not Navajo custom to call the family by the husband's name, but adapting to the white world under the reservation brought changes. As a result of those changes, all children of the same family were given patriarchal last names, often created by the white men that taught school. Therefore Ben was called after his father's last name after the custom of the white man, Begay, and still identified with his mother's clan, the Coyote Pass People by traditional Navajos. His father, Henry Begay was presently working away from home, breaking horses for a white rancher in Colorado. Ben's maternal grandfather, Joseph Yazzie, had died from cancer after breathing the dust in the uranium mine he had worked in for twenty years.

10

Ben's job was to herd the male goats and sheep away from the female flock, so mating didn't result in winter births. The male goats and sheep were in a sheep pen outside of the hogan. Their sheepdogs Max and Betty greeted him with wet tongues and wagging tails, in anticipation of breakfast and another day of adventure on the mountain.

After feeding the dogs, Ben greeted Dawn Boy with a song and blessed the day with corn pollen from the medicine jish hanging from a leather thong around his neck, and a pinch of corn meal from his mother's kitchen. Bucks and rams were harder to herd than the female flock, but he had proved time and again to his uncle that he could handle it. Besides, Max and Betty would help with herding the flock and keeping away the coyotes. Navajos didn't keep dogs as pets; they kept them to help tend their flocks. To Navajos, sheep was life, woven tightly into the tapestry of their lives. Tending their herds was the way young Navajo children learned grown-up responsibilities. The meat from the flock fed them, and the women spent painstaking hours weaving rugs, blankets and clothing from wool and goat hair.

The times were struggling to change them from stock herders to something else. The Navajos were caught in changing times with no vision of the future. Ben had already spent one year at the boarding school run by Baptist missionaries and would be returning in the fall. He was a handsome and good-natured boy, in good health with dark skin and eyes, thick black hair and high cheekbones.

Councilwoman Annie Dodge Wauneka had convinced Mary Yazzie, his grandmother, that it would keep tuberculosis and pneumonia away if they didn't sleep on the earth floor of the hogans. Ben's uncle George Etsitty, in compliance with his mother-in-law's wishes, bought each of them a cot from the Army surplus store in Farmington. In the Navajo culture, the matriarch is in charge.

The sheep pen had four-inch diameter piñon poles that served as a gate. Ben slid the poles to open the gate and released the male goats and rams. He picked up his staff, lunch bag, water bottle and flute as he bade his uncle and aunt goodbye. He and the dogs headed for the pasture on the family grazing permit where he would keep the male flock today. Uncle George's two daughters, Ophelia and Esther, would take the female flock to another pasture after he left. The girls were quite capable and Uncle George's dogs Skip and Millie were more than able to help them guard the flock.

It was the cool of the morning, and the damp soil was cool beneath the feet of the young boy. A "male" rain had occurred in the night and cooled everything off, and settled all of the dust, but would be forgotten by late morning. Its arrival was fast, very noisy and superficial, yielding no permanent benefit, rushing down the dry washes without the ground soaking up much. It contrasted with what the Navajo people called the "female rain," which was slow and gentle, lasting a while and soaking into the ground, giving life.

The morning smelled of the perfume last night's shower left behind. Ben drank it in, thinking it was good to be alive.

Usually Ben walked along with the sheep and goats in the morning, and rode back on a tame ram. Today he was feeling playful on the way out to pasture. Besides, the patch of blue grama grass he would lead the sheep to this morning was at the same elevation, just south of them, so his ram wouldn't fall with him on its back. He grabbed the hair on the back of the neck of the most docile of the big rams and hiked his leg over for a ride, laughing as he rode him down the trail.

He sang a traditional song of the Navajo shepherd children...

"Na'nishkaadgo ch'éédishááago, deenísts'aa'ga' yiistso'
Áádóó tóó shi naaldlooshgo bee na'nishkaadgo é'é'áá
Ná'níshka' go deenísts'aa'ga' honishchingo bee shénálkah
Sh££' yówe danidii'nííné dashiníígo shich'anídahashkee."

Translated into English...

When I herd the sheep and become tired,
It is discovered that I rode the ram because I stink,
And they scold me when I return home.

Ben was happy to tend the male flock in the summer. His uncle was full of the summer hogan stories of the Navajo people, and he knew of the outside world and spoke of it sometimes. But some stories of the Diné were only supposed to be told in the winter, and Ben was always away at boarding school then. Like all of the children sent to boarding schools run by white people, he was learning to read and write but only about half of his culture.

His uncle's name was George Etsitty, and was married to Ben's mother's older sister, Elsie Mae. They had two twin girls, age eleven, and a baby boy. He had served with honor in the Fourth Marine Division in some faraway place called Japan, but he never spoke of what he did there. He did, however, talk of great oceans of water as far as the eye could see and beyond, flying machines that took men above the clouds and lands that were green and wet. Uncle George spoke of travelling on boats and planes, which gave wings to young Ben's imagination.

The only bilagaana (white men) Ben had ever seen were the teachers at the Baptist school he boarded in, but his uncle said they were as many as the stars in the sky, and more strange races in faraway places.

It seem strange to Ben that many of the Navajo men went to war, yet when they returned, none of them had the cleansing ceremonies—the Enemy Way or Ghost Way chant—done for them by a hataalii. (Navajo holy man) To do so would mean they would have to say what they'd been doing, and none of them would. Instead, these men remained without being returned to *hozho*, not to be in harmony or to walk in beauty, not quite being whole. His aunt told him once she thought it had something to do with the bilagaana.

Ben moved the sheep and goats through the piñon-juniper woodlands at an elevation of eight thousand feet to the patch of grass where he would graze his sheep this morning. A humming noise was moving from higher elevations toward the stand of grass where he was moving his flock.

He arrived at the grass field to the excited barking of the dogs and the noises of his unsettled flock. The intensity of the humming increased to nearly intolerable levels as a large spherical object made of metal came crashing through the branches of the juniper trees surrounding the grass field, settling down hard on the grass which had been meant for the flock's morning grazing. The dogs responded to the intruder by sounding their *threat alarm* with short, low-pitched sounding barks, standing their ground between the object and the flock. Some of the goats had gone back down the trail, but the sheep stayed put and looked confused. *Sheep are real stupid*, thought Ben. In his young life he'd never seen anything like this. As Ben approached the vessel, the dogs stayed close by his side, showing their teeth and growling. The growling increased in intensity, and the hair on their backs stood straight up as they approached the vessel. Ben shared the dog's distrust for the object—his heart pounded in his chest like a runaway horse and every nerve in his body was on high alert.

He cautiously approached the vessel with his two guards and his staff in hand. The vessel had a door slightly ajar, so Ben peered inside. His eyes met Rick-Bar's, who was barely still alive. The ship's first officer gazed into the young Earth man's eyes with his pain-filled yellow eyes, and recognized that he had a good heart.

"Yá'át'ééh," the sky traveler greeted him in Navajo. Or did he? His lips never moved. Bluish blood trickled down the being's mouth. Had he truly spoken to him, or was Ben dreaming? If he was speaking Navajo and was not one of the Diné, was he Yei? (a god). Ben remembered his manners.

"Yá'át'ééh," the boy answered.

The being was dying and was greatly out of harmony. He shared his burden with the boy, not unlike a parishioner making his confession to his priest. This sky traveler was in great pain, but his tears were for his dead wife and the shame of failing to do his duty.

Ben felt empathy for the poor alien. The dying first officer felt that empathy, and it gave him comfort and courage to greet death. Ben's eyes remained fixed on Rik-Bar's until the clear yellow eyes glazed over and stared into the void, unseeing. Ben decided that he was not a god, for everyone knew that gods did not die.

Ben did not have any answers concerning who this was. Neither the hogan stories nor the Christian school stories explained this. He found himself in conflict concerning his life view but strangely in harmony. His comforting of the sky traveler while he died gave him a personal involvement that transcended his conflict about his life's view. He would sort it all out later. He came to himself and then remembered the sheep.

The boy's first responsibility was the flock, so he got the dogs to break off from the object and led the flock back home. He would have to take them north of the family's hogans, and he would stop by and tell his *little father,* as maternal uncles were called.

Arriving at his aunt's hogan, he found his uncle preparing to ride his sorrel mare down the mountain to Sheep Springs to trade for some needed supplies.

"Why have you returned?" George Etsitty thought the boy had run into some predators and decided to come back to go north, beyond where his cousins were tending the female flock. If the dogs were not sufficient to drive them off, he knew he might have to take his rifle and go back.

"Uncle! You have to come see this!" he breathlessly replied.

"What is it?"

"I don't know, I've never seen anything like this, it was flying and fell to the ground. There are beings in it, and they are all dead. I got there just in time for one of the beings to talk to my spirit as he died."

"Beings? You spoke with one of them?"

"Yes, Uncle. He was greatly out of harmony. I stayed with him until he died."

"What did he say?"

"He felt ashamed and was crying for his wife."

"Was he in a hogan?"

"Perhaps. I do not know what their hogans look like."

"Did you enter that dwelling?"

"No, Uncle."

"Tell me about the beings."

"They're not Navajo, human, or animal. Could be skin walkers or Yei Bechei." George studied the boy carefully. Ben was not a fearful boy. He'd seen him hold off black bears and coyotes with nothing more than a staff and two dogs. Whatever he had found disturbed him, but strangely, he did not appear out of harmony.

"Put the flock back in the pen and we'll go look." The flock hadn't been grazing yet, but Ben put a handful of corn in a bucket and placed it in the backside of the pen. When the goats saw it they went in and the sheep blindly

14

followed. Ben put the pole gate back up and joined his uncle. His uncle considered it for a moment and decided it was probably a helicopter crash from the Bureau of Land Management, Bureau of Indian Affairs, or one of the other government agencies.

He climbed into the saddle of his horse, and with one motion pulled Ben up into the saddle behind him. Arriving back at the crash site, they dismounted, and puzzled, approached the vessel. It had quit humming and what appeared to be a loading ramp's door seemed to be cracked open on one side. Ben's uncle motioned to the boy to stay back as he looked inside the vessel. His uncle was both amazed and horrified by what he saw. The fate of his nation bore its entire weight on George's shoulders. Not since Iwo Jima had he felt so out of harmony. He had no intention of telling the authorities about Ben's "conversation" with the strange beings; lest someone misunderstand and accuse the boy of being a witch. What happened next could be disastrous if it were handled wrong.

Sergeant Michael Roanhorse of the Navajo Tribal Police was travelling south on HWY 666 on patrol. Standing five feet, eight inches tall, he was lean and well-built with narrow hips typical of Navajos. He had very dark eyes and hair, high cheekbones, and eyes shaped more like an Asian's, which he inherited from his Anasazi ancestors who'd crossed over the Bering Sea.

He was a man of modern and traditional beliefs, and unquestionably loyal to the Navajo Nation. Earlier this year, the Navajo council had finally gotten their voice heard and formed the Navajo Tribal Police. But, it came with a price. Each NTP officer was also deputized in all of the counties his district covered, and when in that capacity—under white men's authority. The odd thing was most of these counties were totally swallowed up by the reservation. Major crimes like drug running and murder were officially under the jurisdiction of the FBI, or as the NTP officers called them, the "Federal Bureau of Ineptitude." A former marine, Roanhorse decided not to re-enlist when he was offered a position as sergeant in the NTP. For him, this was a dream come true.

He had returned home to the sacred Four Corners Reservation. He was single at twenty-six and lived with his mother in a rented house in Shiprock. A Many Goats Clan woman, she was on the lookout for a suitable wife of the right clan to keep him among his people forever and bring her grandchildren. Michael seemed amused by her efforts but assured her he was not in a hurry and wasn't leaving the reservation.

Roanhorse stopped by the Sheep Springs Trading Post for some tobacco and cigarette papers. The owner had a pot of coffee on and offered him a cup, which he accepted, with sugar, no cream. He swapped reservation news with the owner for a while, then rolled a Bull Durham cigarette which he smoked while finishing his second cup of coffee. After finishing his cigarette, he pinched out the amber on the end, and wiped off his nicotine-stained fingers on his pant leg. It was time to get back on patrol. There had been some reports of cattle rustling toward Two Gray Hills. Putting on his Stetson hat, he walked back to his car. Roanhorse recognized George Etsitty riding up on a horse and leading a second horse behind him.

"Yá'át'ééh, Sergeant Roanhorse."

"Yá'át'ééh, Uncle." He overcame his curiosity and practiced proper Navajo manners with the elder man by waiting for him to speak.

Holding the lead to the second horse, the elder man offered it to the young policeman. "I have something to show you."

"Is there trouble? Do I need help?"

"No crime committed. Trouble maybe, but help probably not needed." *Help probably not needed* didn't fit the expression George wore. He looked like a man who'd seen an evil spirit, or maybe suffering from ghost sickness.

"George, what's bothering you? You look like a man out of harmony."

"There was an accident on Mary's grazing lease. A flying machine crashed. There are many dead on the mountain; it's not just the dead but who they are."

"Who are they?"

"I have no idea. I thought you might help me figure that out."

Roanhorse's immediate concern was that George might be afflicted with ghost sickness. "Did you touch any of the bodies, or enter the vessel?"

"No."

"Okay." Roanhorse called into his dispatcher Gladys Chavez and advised he would be going up to Mary Yazzie's hogan up on the Chuska Mountains west of Sheep Springs to look at something with George Etsitty. He followed George to the Sheep Springs Chapter House. Retrieving his shotgun from under the dash, he locked the car and made arrangements for someone to see that no one messed with his patrol car.

Roanhorse accepted the reigns of the black stud and they rode five miles past where HWY 32 reached the foot of the Chuskas. Both men rode the long climb to the Yazzie hogan and arrived about two pm. It was good manners to stop and speak with Mary Yazzie.

"Yá'át'ééh, Ama' Sa' ni?" (Hello, is it good, grandmother?)

"Yá'át'ééh. (Hello, it is good.) I made some mutton stew and coffee; come and eat." He'd skipped dinner, and was starving after the ride up the mountain. He looked at George, who nodded his head. What he had to show him could wait.

Mary Yazzie was about fifty years old. She wore a red velvet blouse adorned with silver buttons and pins on the yoke and sleeves, and a crimson colored velvet skirt, with a squash blossom silver pin in her long, dark-black hair. George was blessed with a good natured mother-in-law. Sometimes the son-in-law wasn't treated well, as with all cultures, but more so in a matrilineal culture. She had two daughters living and one son, whom she lost in Korea. His widow lived near her mother's hogan with her two daughters. The handsome young policeman recited his family lineage upon introduction. Mary's daughters were both married and her granddaughters were not old enough for her to explore the possibilities of this young policeman's single status. *Pity*, she thought. *He is a very handsome man, and employed.*

George hadn't discussed with the women what he found at the crash site, saying only that a flying machine had gone down and that he had to go get the lawman. He solemnly charged Ben to speak of the crash site to no one, and to take the herd to the north to graze.

The women didn't ask SGT Roanhorse anything about the crash because he hadn't been there yet. The women asked the policeman about the news of the Diné (Navajo people). He chatted with them politely and gave them updates of general reservation news. He refused a second bowl of stew claiming he couldn't ride very well on two helpings, but he did accept a cup of coffee. He and George rolled and smoked a cigarette after dinner and then decided it was time to leave.

The two men mounted their horses and rode to the crash site.

Roanhorse was puzzled and uneasy when he beheld it. There in the clearing, in the stand of blue grama grass, was a large metallic disc. *This can't be anything but trouble*, he thought. If it was a military prototype of a new fighter aircraft, then the government had to be alerted. Even if it, this could cause a backlash with the local shamans. They could make some kind of religious thing out of it, resulting in a curse or witching of the mountain. He hoped it was the military. If it wasn't, and the shamans found out, it would be worse. He dismounted and approached the craft, noticing that a door like a loading ramp was partially opened. He peered inside and sharply inhaled… Nothing could have prepared him for what he found. This was trouble, big trouble. He composed himself long enough to address George.

"Uncle, can you use your knife to cut juniper branches and cover this up so it cannot be seen from the sky?"

"Yes. Do you know what they are?"

"No. I have never seen anything like them. When you are through, go back to the hogan and wait for me. I have to go back to my car and call Captain Fowler, and I will be back in the morning. Speak of this to no one, particularly the women, and do not let anyone come back here. Do you understand?"

"Yes, but Mary will want to know more." Roanhorse ran his hand through his thick black hair, considering.

"Tell her a flying machine crashed and all its crew is dead. She knows Navajos do not have any aircraft, so she will assume it is bilagaana. Allow her to think this. Tell her to keep everyone away, because of the dead bodies and the chindi. She will dutifully take charge and no one will come here. Advise her we will have the bilagaana come get their aircraft, and we will have the pilots buried."

In Navajo metaphysics, contamination by a corpse can cause ghost sickness, which would require a Night Way or Ghost Way chant by a shaman at great time and expense to the afflicted. The ghost sickness is brought about by the person's chindi, which is released upon death. A chindi is all the dark parts of a person: the avarice, hate, lust, malice, greed and all things ugly in the human spirit. Contamination by exposure to the person's chindi could result in becoming *ghost sick* and losing hozho, harmony. It was a good bet Mary Yazzie would keep her clan away from the site.

George went to work cutting juniper branches with his bowie knife to cover the odd vessel, while Roanhorse took the horse back down the mountain. He made sure not to get careless riding downhill. He wasn't willing to risk an accident by trying to get there too fast. It was late afternoon by the time he reached the Chapter house where his car was parked. He turned on his radio, keyed the mike and hailed the dispatcher.

"Gladys?"

"Yes, is that you Mike?"

"Yes, I need to speak with Captain Fowler."

"Okay." In the background, he could hear her calling for his captain.

"This is Fowler."

"Captain, I need you to come down to the Sheep Springs Chapter House in the morning, along with Lieutenant Nez and Chairman Jones if he is still in Shiprock."

"He is, but what is going on?"

"I cannot discuss it over the air, and the Chapter House does not have a phone. Please bring a horse trailer and three horses. You are going to need them."

"All right, we will be there very early in the morning."

"I'll spend the night here at the Chapter House."

Captain David Fowler of the Navajo Tribal Police was almost fifty years old. He'd spent time breaking horses for the white ranchers and doing the rodeo circuit before he enlisted in the Marines' Code Talker program. His mother's clan was the Black Streak Wood People, and his father's clan was Chíshí, part of the Chiricahua Apaches who had been rounded up, mixed together with the Navajos and sent on the Long Walk to Bosque Redondo. He'd served in the Marines as a code talker in both Japan and Korea. He left the Marines when his enlistment ended because the council had received government approval to form the NTP. He gladly accepted the position of captain of the Shiprock District. A tall man over six feet, he was built like an ox, but starting to put on a few pounds now that he had a desk job. A large nose dominated his face, accented with high cheekbones and dark eyes with long, jet-black hair tied in a ponytail, peppered with a light graying at the temples.

A horseback ride up the mountain would do him good, he thought. It would be good to see his fellow code talker George Etsitty again. He wondered what was so serious that required Chairman Jones to be present. Roanhorse hadn't alluded to any crime having been committed. What could be so important that the three of them must come, and he wouldn't even discuss it on the radio?

This didn't fit the pattern of what they normally dealt with: domestic violence related to alcohol, theft of livestock, and violence related to suspicion of skin walkers. The latter was nasty business. Skin walkers, Navajo witches, also called wolves, were reputed to have the power to change their form into birds or animals, fly, and to witch someone with corpse sickness. It was this belief that caused trouble. Fowler wasn't sure he even believed in skin walkers. The trouble was that all the traditional Navajos did. Stories of skin walkers were deeply woven into their religious stories and folklore. It was easier to believe that skin walkers were responsible for a tragedy like cancer or mysterious illness than to have no explanation. In Navajo metaphysics, there was certainly a cause and effect for everything. This calmed the people's spirits and helped them to *walk in harmony*. All it took was a sick person and whispers of a skin walker, and a normally peaceful person might be provoked to kill the offending witch. This was the ugly side of the traditional Navajo beliefs that in most other ways encouraged them to walk in truth and beauty, in harmony with their world. Fowler hated anything stupid or senseless blamed on the "skin walker nonsense," as he called it. The first Navajo chairman, Henry Chee Dodge, had started the campaign to eliminate skin walker related violence, yet it was still a problem today.

The newly formed NTP was still figuring out its role in local law enforcement. Unlike local law enforcement elsewhere, the FBI had jurisdiction over murders on the reservation. The NTP was always the first to arrive after a murder had occurred. They were sometimes able to discern a motive that baffled the white FBI agents.

Fowler informed both Chairman Paul Jones and Lieutenant Frank Nez of the trip in the morning. He also arranged for a truck, horse trailer, and three horses for the drive down to Sheep Springs. He made sure to pack his Polaroid Land Camera, which processed black and white pictures in about a minute, without needing to process the film through a commercial outlet. It might be useful to get pictures without sending them through a photo shop.

The three horses were loaded into the horse trailer early the next morning, along with their tack, bedrolls for the men, canteens, rifles, and jackets in case they got caught on the mountain after dark. Of course, they made sure to bring their all-important coffee thermoses. By seven a.m., they left Shiprock for Sheep Springs, arriving at the Sheep Springs Chapter House just before eight o'clock. They found Officer Roanhorse talking with two men on horses in front of the house. Nez pulled the truck and horse trailer up to the parking lot, put it in park and shut off the engine as Roanhorse approached the truck.

"Yá'át'ééh, Chairman, Captain, Lieutenant."

"Yá'át'ééh, replied Nez, and the other two men nodded."

"Well, what brings us all here so early?" asked Fowler.

"A flying machine crashed on the mountain on Mary Yazzie's grazing lease. I never saw anything like this in the military. I did not enter the vessel, but all the crewmembers I saw were dead. They were not human."

Captain Fowler turned to Chairman Paul Jones, who had remained silent so far. "How do you want to play this, sir?"

The chairman was curious about the description *not human*. "Sergeant, you did not call us out here to look at dead animals. What do you mean by not human?"

"Looks like something in a science fiction movie. They are small beings, hairless, no ears or eyebrows, pale skin, not like the bilagaana." Chairman Jones pondered the implications. His parents had been traditional Navajos, but he learned to read in a missionary school. To find beings not from this world was an idea that would disturb anyone's religious beliefs: Navajo, Christian or Mormon. He suspected it was probably worse for the traditional Navajos.

"Was there any evidence of foul play?"

"No, sir, it looked like a crash, probably mechanical failure."

Chairman Jones paused to consider the best course of action. Navajos did not consider silence to be awkward. Since Jones was rightfully in charge, the men all waited for him to speak again. The chairman seemed to have figured out what he wanted to do, and broke the silence. "Who are these men with you?"

"Sam and Pete Dooley, Salt Water Clan," Roanhorse answered. "They live about ten miles toward Nava, and they are Mormons. I drove over to their house last night and asked them to ride up here on horseback with picks and shovels today to bury the sky travelers. (Navajos who converted to Christianity or Mormonism were not concerned about getting ghost sickness. It was preferred to get a nontraditional Navajo to handle burials.)

"We need to see this for ourselves. Sergeant, you are right about the burial. If they are bilagaana, the government will want to collect the bodies for burial. But you say they are not... Ride with the Dooley brothers and go directly to the crash site and wait for us. Do not bury anything until we get there, and do not stop by Mary Yazzie's hogan. I do not want her to know about the burial until we see the site."

"Yes, sir."

Roanhorse rode along with the Dooley brothers while the chairman made arrangements to look after his truck. The chairman locked his truck, and the three men mounted their horses and headed out to the Yazzie hogan.

The Sergeant had already been to the crash site and would be escorting the Dooley brothers there. The chairman and the two policemen would go to Mary Yazzie's hogan first and George would guide them to the crash site.

The chairman, Fowler, and Nez made it to the hogan by ten thirty, dismounted, tied their horses to the sheep pen and greeted George Etsitty.

"Yá'át'ééh, George," greeted Captain Fowler.

"Yá'át'ééh, my friend." He nodded respectfully to the chairman and Lieutenant Nez.

"Mary has been expecting you." The matriarch didn't know who was coming, but with the aircraft crash, she knew there would be more than just one policeman. The men knew they should respect the matriarch, so they entered the house and greeted her.

"Yá'át'ééh, Ama' Sa' ni?" asked Chairman Jones.

"Yá'át'ééh," responded the matriarch. "I have food and coffee for you all."

"Later when we return, we will sit a spell and visit, and have some food. Now I have to get George to show us the bilagaana flying machine. They say the ship crashed, and all are dead. If they are bilagaana, it is probably a military ship, and they will want the bodies and ship back. Keep the coffee on and the stew warm. We will be back."

"I will," she promised.

George saddled his horse and led the men to the crash site. *This is a beautiful day for a horseback ride,* thought Nez. *It is a shame that this kind of business is ruining harmony of it.* The men arrived at the clearing of grama grass where the object rested. None of the men had ever seen anything like this. They approached the craft, and Nez pried the door further open with a wind broken branch of an oak tree as a lever. All three men looked in, and their worst suspicions were confirmed. The craft smelled as though something had died, but it was no smell they recognized. The beings looked unlike any race they had ever seen. Their lifeless bodies were hairless and earless, the color of campfire ash. They were the size of ten-year-old children. No one said anything for at least two minutes. Each man was speechless, sorting out in his mind what the existence of these beings implied in his life's view. The police captain had deferred to the chairman, as this didn't appear to be a police matter. Chairman Jones spoke.

"This could be very bad. If this is made common knowledge, we will have skin walker or Yei Bechei stories, possibly even curses or witching by tomorrow. This is fertile land. Our father Barboncito called the Chuskas, the 'goods of value range.' I do not want any skin walker or dead Yei Bechei talk cursing this mountain. I also want to control how and to whom we tell about this vessel. The worse thing that could happen is some shaman might decide these were Yei Bechei, *holy beings*, and George or Mary witched them, and they died. I think I can get the government to trade us something for it, but if we report this to the local authorities, they will just come take it, and not too quietly.

I assume we are all in agreement that no laws have been broken?" All the men nodded in agreement. The chairman continued. "Since these are not human, there is no law that says we have to report this accident. Captain, may I have your camera?" Captain Fowler retrieved his camera from his saddlebag and handed it to the chairman. "Could you men uncover the flying ship?" asked the chairman.

George and the two officers worked to remove the juniper branches covering the top of the vessel. The chairman had the Dooley brothers remove two of the dead crew members, and stretch them out on the ground. The chairman took pictures of the aliens and the vessel from several angles until he had no more film. One by one, he peeled off the backing of each picture and handed it to Captain Fowler, who in turn, wiped the photos with the print coater appliqué and laid them out on a rock to dry.

"Now would you men please cover the vessel back up?" asked Jones. To the Dooley brothers he said, "They have no relatives, and they deserve to be buried. Please bury all of them with respect in a secret place and speak of this to no one." He pointed to the dead bodies. "I know that this is particularly disturbing, but this could be trouble to the Diné if it were made public." He handed each brother a twenty dollar bill from his wallet, and they assured him they would comply with both requests.

Satisfied the pictures came out all right and were dry, Jones handed the camera back to Fowler, put the pictures in a manila envelope he brought and put it in one of his saddlebags. "I think I like this camera of yours. It can develop pictures without leaving a negative behind, and without the help of an outsider." The men had already finished covering the vessel.

"I think we should go back to see Mary Yazzie and reassure her that everything is all right," said Nez. Turning to the chairman, Fowler asked, "Exactly how much do we tell her?"

The chairman looked thoughtful. "Tell her as much truth as we can, but nothing to incite her imagination." He inhaled, and then exhaled slowly, carefully choosing his words. "We tell her this. A flying ship like nothing we've ever seen before has crashed, and all are dead. We think the government will want this vessel, and we intend to give it to them. The crew of the ship did not look like soldiers, so we arranged for their burial, to prevent predators or skin walkers from taking their bodies. We will ask her to make sure no one goes up there until after the government has removed their vessel."

The men all nodded in agreement.

"I like it. All you said is true, and we will not tell her anything about these beings," commented Fowler.

"Chairman, what do you think these beings were?" asked Nez, asking the question they were all thinking. All of the men except Chairman Jones were ex-military and policemen. None of the men were given to fearful displays of emotion, but they were all in shock. All eyes were on the older man. Instead of answering right away, he asked a question.

"Captain, George, when you went to Japan, had you ever seen Japanese before?" Both men shook their heads no. "Were they gods?" Again they shook their heads no. "Just because you had never seen them before, did not mean they were gods. They could be some other mortal race we have never seen, or Yei Bechei. I do not think they are skin walkers. From what I have heard about them, they do not need a flying machine to fly. Even if we turned them over to the bilagaana, our land would not have rest from crazy white people, all wanting to see where they landed. In any case, they are all dead. They deserve to be buried, not left for the coyotes to eat, or skin walkers to use their corpses for witchcraft."

The four men mounted up and rode back to Mary Yazzie's hogan, and it went rather well. She was not suspicious they were withholding anything. The men all looked uneasy, but that was normal for Navajos after viewing death. The men ate lunch and drank a couple of cups of coffee, observing the right amount of socializing that good manners required. The chairman charged Mary to keep everyone away from the wreck for the sake of the chindi, and to speak of it to no one. She solemnly promised to do so and the chairman was relieved. It was five o'clock by the time the men had reached the Chapter House. Roanhorse put George's horse in the corral behind the Chapter House, where George would retrieve it later.

Captain Fowler addressed the chairman. "I guess this one is all off the books, right?"

"Yes. I'll drive down to Gallop area office of the Bureau of Indian Affairs tomorrow in my pickup truck and see if I can negotiate a trade for the ship. The reservation is in need of many things."

Chairman Paul Jones left Shiprock before daylight the next morning, arriving in Gallop around sunrise. He'd skipped breakfast, so he stopped at a local diner and had the special of sausage, eggs, hash browns, a biscuit and hot coffee. The tribe's lawyer offered to come, but Jones wanted as few people knowing about this as possible, so he refused. Besides, he was a very shrewd negotiator, and was not afraid to speak with the BIA Chief alone. He was remarkably fit for a man sixty-eight years old. He wore his gray short hair in the style of the modern world, which helped in dealing with outsiders. Dressed in a dark suit and tie, he was ready for the meeting with the bilagaana BIA Chief. Finishing breakfast and a second cup of coffee, he paid his tab and drove over to the bureau's office. BIA Chief Hal Wallace was going over his budget and estimating projected spending for the next quarter, when his secretary buzzed him.

"Chief, Chairman Jones is here to see you."

"Thank you Betty, send him in." Chief Wallace rose to meet the older man, and greeted him in customary fashion as one would a business associate.

"Good morning, Chairman Jones." Chief Wallace never tried to honor the Navajo leaders by learning their customary greetings or social manners. It was mostly because of the bureau's attitude that the Navajos were best served by being assimilated into American mainstream culture. He wasn't malicious in his thinking. He honestly believed Washington's policy that replacing the Navajo culture with modern American culture was good for them.

"Good morning, Chief Wallace." The men exchanged courtesies, shared local news, and discussed the weather. Finally, the elevator talk exhausted, and Wallace knew it was time to get to the point.

"Chairman Jones, to what do I owe the pleasure of your visit?" Jones retrieved an envelope from his shirt and slid it to the younger man. Chief Wallace removed the contents, studying each photo carefully. He looked up at the older man, ran his hand through his thinning hair, carefully considering.

"Looks like a military prototype. The government will want it back."

The Navajo retrieved a second envelope from his shirt and offered it to the agent, who examined each photo. As Wallace studied the photos of the aliens' bodies, the realization dawned on him this was something more—much more than he'd anticipated.

"This is no military prototype. I'm sure the government will want it, though," the chairman stated.

"Where did you find it?"

"On Navajo land," he flatly stated. "Salvage laws favor us, but then the whole thing would be hard to keep quiet if it went to court." The tribe had a lawyer to handle lawsuits, but the Navajo came alone, without his lawyer. Wallace knew the government would not want this to be made public. Jones wouldn't be here unless he wanted to deal. The question was not if he wanted to deal, but how much would he settle for?

"What do you want for the ship?" Jones made an offer, and Wallace knew he was going to need deeper pockets than he had to close the deal. It was time to play his ace card. Wallace had spent a lot of money to get his only son into an Ivy League school, where he majored in government studies. Jesse lent his youthful energy and enthusiasm to the Eisenhower presidential campaign and was rewarded with a white house job as an aide to the president himself.

"Chairman Jones, would you excuse me while I make a call? I don't have the authority to agree to your asking price."

The older man smiled, took his hat in hand and walked to the front office. Betty offered the chairman a cup of coffee, which he accepted. The White House switchboard put the Chief through to his son.

"Hi, Dad, how's God's country?"

"Jesse, an alien spaceship crashed on the Navajo reservation. The Navajo Council Chairman is in my office and wants to sell it to us. I need authorization to negotiate a price."

"Okay, Dad, hang on." His father waited for a few minutes.

"Chief Wallace, this is the President. Is this real, or a hoax?" He recognized the president's voice from television.

"It's real, sir. I've seen the pictures, and the chairman has never lied to me. In any case, we'll not pay them unless our experts verify the disc is genuine."

"Okay, but keep a lid on this and report only to me. Try to get a good deal on the disc. I need men to work for me who are loyal and discreet. When this business is concluded, I'll have a job lined up for you here in Washington."

"I appreciate it sir, but bestow any favor upon my son."

"Very well, I'll find a good job for Jesse that will last beyond my administration."

"Thank you, sir."

"Goodbye and God bless." Wallace thought of walking to the front of his office and personally inviting the chairman to accompany him back, but reconsidered. Negotiating was sometimes as much posturing as anything else. His desk was his symbol of authority; he would have the Jones approach the seat of his power.

"Betty, send Chairman Jones in."

"Yes, sir." To the chairman she said, "Chief Wallace will see you now."

Two pots of coffee later, at noon, they stuck a deal. The white man had never negotiated with anyone who drove so hard a bargain. He tried once in the negotiation to stall some road improvement projects on the reservation, but it didn't faze the Navajo a bit. The elder man held all of the cards, and he knew it. It was a sweet deal for them. It cost them only forty dollars so far to bury the sky travelers, and it held great value to the bilagaana government. The government would authenticate the find, transport it out, and then pay the council. The price was four backhoes, twelve GMC pickups, well-drilling equipment for each district, road improvements for the reservation, and twenty college scholarships to a United States college of their choice. A mutual agreement of secrecy was agreed to by both sides. Neither the Navajos nor the government would profit from public disclosure. Ben continued to have recurring dreams of space and aliens, but told no one.

CODE NAME DESERT JEWEL

GEN Carter F. Colson, the commanding officer of Presidential Nuclear Command Center 4 in southwestern Utah, had been summoned to see President Eisenhower. He thought he might be given new orders concerning his facility. One of the fighter aircraft covering his facility flew him into the nation's capital. The general arrived in his dress greens and was escorted to the Oval Office.

"The president will see you now, General," said the president's secretary, a cute brunette with big brown eyes and a heart shaped face, pert and very polite.

"Thank you, miss." He opened the doors to the Oval Office to find his old army buddy standing to receive him. He clasped his old friend's arm warmly. "General, how have you been?"

"Good, how's Mamie?"

"Good, as always."

"And John?"

"He's as well as can be expected. He never liked the restrictions his military career took on once I ran for president. He's now serving in division headquarters. It isn't easy being a soldier when your father is the president."

"Well, he's still serving his country, and you both know it can't be helped."

"I know. How are Esther and your daughters?"

"Well, thank you. I'm a grandfather now for the fifth time." The two old friends visited for a while, reliving their glory days as young officers, then settled down to business.

"Mr. President, you didn't call me here for a social visit. What's on your mind, old friend?"

The president walked over to his desk and retrieved a file marked *Classified* and handed it to him. The cover read TOP SECRET–OPERATION DESERT JEWEL. The general opened it up and looked through the material, stopping to examine the photographs of the aliens very carefully.

"I have a large disc that needs transported discreetly to your command center, and I do not want any outside paper trail. It's probably a spacecraft of an alien race. America cannot afford to have its public engrossed with an extraterrestrial infatuation. We have enough trouble worrying about the possibility of the Soviets developing a nuclear bomb. The object is too large to drive down the highway in a crate, and I don't want any other military involved in its transport. It will be taken to the edge of Navajo land through the Shiprock district. You'll need to assist the transport vehicle to cross the San Juan River west of Bluff, Utah. I want you to use a tank to tow the flatbed and crate through the desert, avoiding any contact with people if possible.

"That's a lot of land to navigate across quietly."

"If you need assistance closing down any roads or highways, we will assist you, though we'd prefer to do so at night. You must, of course, arrange for refueling along the way, and you'll need aircraft from your facility to provide air security for the trip. Other than that, I don't want this discussed or reported to anyone save me. You'll take possession of the disc for study and possible repair. Only necessary eyes should view the disc. If you can salvage any technology of any value to help us against the Soviets, let me know. As of now, I'm decommissioning Presidential Nuclear Command Center Four. Your main function there will be to study the disc and keep it secure and secret. The new name for the center will be the Alpha One Test Center, maintained as a top-secret and high-security facility. You'll answer and report only to me, and only through dispatched courier with sealed letters. This file must be kept under lock and key, and any correspondence is to be destroyed."

"Understood, Mr. President."

The two men chatted about the implications of the file's photographs and the possible trouble if the information reached the wrong hands. GEN Colson left the Oval Office with a new job and purpose.

Captain Fowler oversaw the crew of white men that took the spaceship down from the mountain. They had to cut a few trees at the crash site, put the disc on skids and pulled it with log skidding mules to a dry wash. From there, they used twelve teams of mules, six in front and six in back, to pull the disc down the wash to the base of the mountain. The mules in the back of the disc controlled the sliding in places so the disc couldn't run over the mules pulling in front. More white men were waiting at the base of the mountain, where they had a very large trailer with large tires and high clearance. The mules pulled the disc up the ramp, where the white men constructed a large crate around it and strapped it down to the trailer. They hooked up a large tow truck to the trailer, likewise built high off the ground with huge tires. The NTP closed the roads in front of the procession and they hauled it north to the Utah border.

THE REAL SPACE RACE
AP news release—Oct. 17, 1959

Both Soviet and American scientists are investigating a meteor shower off of Alaska's coast which covers an area from Alaska's Seward Peninsula to Poluostrov, USSR. No details are known at this time, but the material is thought to be a man-made alloy.

PASSING THE TORCH

Washington D.C.—June 12, 1961

This was GEN Colson's first trip to Washington since Ike had left office. He was unsure of his mission now. The disc they'd been studying for almost two years had yielded many technological secrets, but there was no material to construct a new engine core. They had been able to repair the disc's power system, and access the ship's computers. The hull and engine core were made of an alloy of unknown composition. The alloy had an element not in their elemental charts, something they referred to as *element x*. The computers revealed a wealth of information, including the construction plans for a new engine core, but they had none of the alloy with which to build it. Ike was gone, and supposedly the test center had been a secret. The young new president from Massachusetts had summoned him. He was picked up at the airport by presidential limousine and driven straight to the White House. Upon arrival, the president's aide escorted him to the Oval Office. The young president greeted the older general and warmly shook his hand, motioning to the general to sit down and to his aide to close the door. After the formalities were over, the general spoke.

"Mr. President, how may I be of service to you?"

"Good, straight to the point. I like it," he said, smiling the broad, warm smile that got him elected. "GEN Colson, recent events have unfolded that the cold war with the Soviets may be heating up soon. Vice-President Johnson just returned from his fact-finding tour to Vietnam. His findings were clear. If we do not intervene in Vietnam, communism will spread throughout Southeast Asia and then the nations of the earth will fall one by one, like dominoes. But, that's not why I've called you here today. After I was sworn in, Ike came to my office. He handed over to me a top-secret file of an alien disc his people had recovered, but had kept secret from congress and the intelligence communities. It was code-named Desert Jewel. Ike advised me to contact you."

The president showed GEN Colson the file marked DESERT JEWEL, proving the secret was also his. The general glanced at the file and waited for the young president to speak. The president continued. "A recent meteor shower in 1958 that fell on Alaskan and Soviet soils revealed a treasure beyond our wildest dreams. At first we didn't pay it much attention. The material from meteor showers have always been studied by our scientists, but have never before been of any military importance—until now. Our scientists, as well as Soviet scientists, collected a few tons of meteorites and took them to study. Ike's notes in this file indicated the composition of the disc. This appears to be the same material we're studying from the meteor shower. It is now hoped that we may finally repair the alien spacecraft at your facility.

As you know, I'm not particularly popular with the CIA since the Bay of Pigs fiasco. As for the FBI, ever since I came out for civil rights for blacks, J. Edgar Hoover has had it in for me. Ike had already kept your program from the intelligence communities, and so have I. This was assumed to be a routine collection of rocks anyway, so neither agency should be suspicious. The reports from the scientific team confirmed that the metal was of the same composition as the disc in this report. Ike's original report said that the disc might be reparable if they had more alloy-x. I want you to confiscate all the alloy-x being studied and shred all evidence of its existence. The only record of its existence will be yours alone. Please transport the alloy-x to the Alpha One Test Center to be stored there.

The Soviets have also salvaged alloy-x of their own. It is of the utmost importance that we act quickly, with as much secrecy as possible. Once you've accomplished this, I'll give you further orders. This has to be kept secret from the American public. I don't want to alarm them with the uncertainties of alien beings that are more advanced than we are. In our struggle with the Soviets, it is imperative that the American public believes that Americans are the most advanced race in the universe. If they believe that, we will prevail." The young president awaited a response from the older man.

"I am your servant, Mr. President."

"Good. Keep me informed. You don't have to call or come to Washington. Ike used couriers, so will we. I have the locked attaché case you and Ike used, and the key." The two men finalized the details and GEN Colson returned back to Utah to begin work.

June 16, 1961

President Kennedy admitted the courier into his office. The president rose from the resolute desk and moved forward onto the Truman carpet. He had always admired how the presidential seal was represented monochromatically in the varying depths of cut pile. The young officer saluted the president. Kennedy said "at ease" and motioned for the attaché case. The young man waited without speaking until the president opened the locked bag and retrieved the letter. It read...

From GEN Carter F. Colson, Alpha One Test Center
To the President of the United States

Mr. President, I've transported all of the alloy-x to the secret test facility. We will attempt to repair the disc and conduct flight tests.

GEN Carter F. Colson
Alpha One Test Center

The president sent a note back saying he'd received the letter, locked the attaché case and handed it back to the courier. The young man stood to attention, saluted the president, and after being dismissed, returned to Utah.

The president received another courier the following week.

From GEN Carter F. Colson, Alpha One Test Center
To the President of the United States
July 25, 1961

Mr. President, we've been able to fix the disc and have conducted flight tests with it. In our first test flight, the disc's antigravity drive worked flawlessly. The antigravity drive is too large to be used for smaller fighting craft. A smaller scale of the antigravity device along with some conventional fuels can power hovercraft vehicles for exploration and combat on Luna or Mars. We found that small hovercraft ships made of the alloy-x run very well with a scaled down antigravity unit and a carbon based liquid fuel. However, it is limited to maximum speeds of thirty-five meters per second, with limited lift from jump jets. We were also able to manufacture amazing weapons for these small vessels out of the alien technology and alloy-x. We will have transport vessels with troops and supplies ready to launch for the moon soon.

GEN Carter F. Colson
Alpha One Test Center

The president asked the courier to remain at the white House in one of the guest bedrooms until the next day while he wrote an answer. Before lunch the next morning the president had crafted his response and sent for the courier. He placed the letter in the attaché case and locked it securely. The courier left Washington that afternoon post haste to return the message. Upon arriving at Alpha One Test Center in Utah, he was ushered into GEN Colson's office. The courier surrendered the attaché case and the general unlocked it. The letter read as follows...

From the President of the United States
To GEN Carter F. Colson, Alpha One Test Center
July 28, 1961

I'm commissioning the creation of a secret agency known as the American Space Defense Corps, which will be responsible for building posts on Earth's moon and anywhere in our solar system alloy-x may be found. I'm shifting enough funds from NASA, the CIA, and other government agencies to your new organization, which is enough to get you started. I advise you to develop a network of operatives within other agencies to be able to share intelligence and resources without undue scrutiny of future government investigators. You will need to develop an independent financial structure to safeguard the ASDC from undue government interference.

For security reasons, you should seek to have staff members who're willing to make long-term commitments. Only those who are working on the disc project should ever see it. This must be kept strictly on a *need to know* basis. All personnel including you, who've seen the disc or have knowledge of the center's true purpose should leave the Army to join your new organization. Upon your retirement, you'll head the military and research part of the organization as the ASDC's first commanding officer. You'll need to recruit ex-military personnel to fill the vacancies with men whom you can trust. Ike had Nuclear Command Center Four decommissioned and records of its existence destroyed. The post has existed as private property on former public lands in southern Utah. That property will be deeded over to you to ensure the organization's full independence. You'll also be responsible to provide checks and balances within your organization to prevent it from becoming a monster more hideous than communism.

As for the citizenry, my greatest concern is that traitors to our country, and those with less wisdom who do not see the need to win this conflict in the solar system. And then, of course, every war produces *conscientious objectors*, who believe they're doing our country a service by opposing any armed struggle. You're well aware the space race with the Soviets has become very competitive and the nation's eyes are on its every development. We're engaged in a public space race to the moon with a goal of having a man there by the end of the decade. I want you to use the alien technology and the alloy-x to land an exploratory team on the moon to search for alloy-x. If you find any, build an American post there and begin salvage operations for the material. This is very important. It is imperative that if any alloy-x exists, the Soviets get none of it.

Future presidents and government officials will know nothing of the existence of the ASDC. You'll be on your own. May God be with you.

President John Fitzgerald Kennedy

The general digested the order, took the letter and locked it in his safe. His orders were clear. This would be the beginning of a new military organization.

The Kremlin: Moscow, Russia USSR In a meeting between GEN Mikhail Andropov, Army of the USSR and Nikita Khrushchev, First Secretary of the Communist Party of the Soviet Union.

"Comrade General, please sit down." The general complied, removing his fur hat and holding it in his hands. "Would you like some tea?"

"Yes, Comrade First Secretary, thank you."

The first secretary's aide poured the general a hot cup of tea spiced with oranges, cinnamon and cloves.

The general blew the hot tea to cool it, and inhaled the fragrance from the citrus and spices. He took a sip of the hot liquid and held the cup in his hands to chase Moscow's winter from his cold fingers.

"We have good news," the first secretary began, "our infiltration of the secret American facility where the disc is being studied is complete. An American scientist on their research team is willing to sell us information. He'll give the information in the form of microdots to a security guard at the facility. The guard will smuggle the information off of the post and to our agents. The Americans are using the public space race as a ruse to build on the alien technology for the real race. Their goal is to be the first to harvest the precious alloy-x in the solar system. This must not be allowed to happen. We have enough alloy-x to build what we need to compete with the Americans once we have the technology to do it."

"Excellent! I have always believed greed is the weakness at the very core of capitalism. We can buy anything we want for a price."

"Yes, for a price, but his betrayal did not come cheap. However, combined with the equipment from the crash site in the Urals of the alien vessel, we should be able to get the disc flying again. Too bad the computer's hard drive of the alien vessel was wiped clean in the crash. The aliens no doubt had the presence of mind before dying to format the hard drives of the ship's computers."

Conversation between COL Wilson Edwards, Chief of Security, ASDC and GEN Carter F. Colson, Commander, ASDC

"GEN Colson, we found a leak at the facility. Dr. Arlen Stafford and one of the security guards were working for the Soviets. We can only assume most of the technology we've gotten from the alien craft has been sold to the Soviets. We found the guard with a microdot containing information we got from the disc project and interrupted a meeting with his contact. Under interrogation, he implicated Dr. Stafford, and we found incriminating evidence in his quarters. Both of them have been discreetly removed from service here. I'm sorry to report Dr. Stafford had a heart attack and died this morning and is being replaced as department head by Dr. Jan Eichmann. The guard died in an accident while on patrol in the desert."

The general's eyes widened. "How much information was compromised?"

"We can only assume he's been able to smuggle information out for the last two years. All of it, I assume."

The general swore under his breath. Pandora's Box had been opened wide.

To GEN Carter F. Colson, Commander, ASDC
From Dr. Jan Eichmann
August 7, 1961

GEN Colson, let NASA have their public space race. They offered me the position of Chief aerospace engineer, but I turned them down when you made me a better offer. While the eyes of the world are focused on this charade, I'll be coordinating the real space race. By the end of the decade, we will have an American post on every rock in the solar system. Before others go down in history as being the first to fly into space, I'll be standing on Olympus Mons. Theirs is a "dog and pony show." We will see about the real business of colonizing the solar system."

Dr. Jan Eichmann
Dept. of Research and Development,
Alpha One Test Center

The president's secretary buzzed the president, who was finishing up some notes for a speech. He was scheduled to meet this afternoon with a group of supporters.

"Yes, Janet."

"A courier is waiting to see you with a message from GEN Colson, sir."

"Send him in."

"Yes, Mr. President."

The young officer entered and, surrendering the case, assumed his waiting stance. The president unlocked the case, retrieved the letter, and started to read...

To the President of the United States
From GEN Carter F. Colson, Commander, ASDC

Dear Mr. President, COL Edwards has discovered and removed a Soviet mole here. We can only assume the Soviets have all of the information we have. Until now, they were able to keep an eye on us from the inside. Security has been increased significantly, and we shouldn't have any more trouble there. It was as you've said. We have sufficient enough technology to complete the assignment and also the means from the commercial development of the other technologies to fund our organization independently as you requested.

GEN Carter F. Colson,
Commander, ASDC

The young president frowned and rubbed between his eyes to relieve the beginning of a headache. He sighed and shredded the paper. The space race was on, not just the public one, but the real one.

To GEN Carter F. Colson
From the accounting office of Newberg, Klein, and Hoffman

Mr. Colson, the corporation and its subsidiaries have been established under the name of the Investco Corp as you requested. Your organization is in good condition, being in the black with no outstanding debt at start up. Since this is a privately owned company, I assume you'll be appointing your own staff and board members.

Respectfully yours, Joseph Klein

From Rear Admiral Perry Dubois, USN
To GEN Carter F. Colson, Commander, ASDC

GEN Colson, I accept your offer to head the Investco Corporation. I also understand the importance of making this work for our country. I assure you that lower level management will know nothing of our true purpose. This corporation will essentially be run to make a profit like any other well-run business. My retirement from the Navy will be in effect at the end of the month. I'll then be fully able to devote my time to the business at hand. I have many connections within the government to be able to get bids for us on defense contracts. If what you're telling me about having a steady stream of advanced technology to market is true, we should have no problem becoming very profitable to fund our war effort.

Respectfully,
Rear Admiral Perry Dubois, USN

The courier by now was getting accustomed to these trips to Washington. His main qualifications were that he didn't talk unless he needed to and was very discreet in discussing his work. He also understood the contents of the case were above his pay grade. It was a need to know kind of thing, and he was satisfied he didn't need to know. He once more stood before the most powerful man in the free world. It was getting pretty much routine by now: salute, hand him the case, and wait for an answer. The president unlocked the case and read the letter.

To the President of the United States
From GEN Carter F. Colson, ASDC

Dear Mr. President, we're on schedule with our project code name Desert Jewel. I've established a corporation which will provide independent finances. All the board members are good men who understand our cause and the cause of freedom. The corporation's structure makes it impossible to turn it into a dictatorship. Power is shared among the board, which is comprised of career military officers, and legal and financial counselors. As we're a capitalist country, you can see the irony in the checks and balances in our organization existing at the financial level. Lenin and Marx should roll over in their graves.

GEN Carter F. Colson, ASDC

Inside the Kremlin office of the First Secretary of the CPSU First Secretary Khrushchev greeted GEN Andropov. The general had a worried look on his face.

"Comrade First Secretary, our agents within the secure American facility were discovered and killed, but not before a wealth of technical information was received by us. It is a pity that we will get no more information from them."

"Comrade General, it does not matter. Our source sold us the research the Americans had collected for nearly ten years. The damage to the Americans' exclusive ownership of the information is irreparable. We will proceed as planned and start our colonization of the cosmos. It is of little importance if we're first in that race. We must be the first to establish production facilities on the moon if alloy-x does indeed exist there. We must get to the Moon as soon as possible in a disc large enough to transport equipment and an expedition team. If we find alloy-x there, a post must be built. Once we have a military post there, we should destroy the Americans and take full possession of the Moon and all of its resources."

Courier dispatch from GEN Mikhail Andropov to First Secretary Nikita Khrushchev.

To Nikita Khrushchev, First Secretary of the CPSU
From GEN Mikhail Andropov, Army of the USSR

Comrade Secretary, I am reporting today the successful formation of the SCA - Soviet Cosmonaut Agency). With the technologies our operatives stole from the Americans, combined with the alloy-x we've harvested, we are poised to win the struggle. We should be able to build transport space vessels to transport our troops and equipment to the moon to establish our permanent post within a few months.

The SCA shall remain completely secret to keep the Chinese in the dark. Our greatest concern is the Chinese may somehow be able to join us in this race and become the dominant Marxist superpower. I advise the "public space race" continue, and the real one main secret. Our agents discovered that President Kennedy is the only government official that knows about the disc and the secret test center's existence. Our sources stressed that even the vice-president does not know. President Kennedy's failure at the Bay of Pigs invasion and his executive order to withdraw from Vietnam has earned him many enemies within his own military and the CIA. Our mole within the CIA Black Operations assures us it would be possible to motivate the CIA to eliminate him on their own. Kennedy should be killed before the Americans have a chance to establish their space organization to compete with us. This in itself may be enough to give us the momentum to beat the Americans to the moon to establish our post first.

Please advise,
GEN Mikhail Andropov, SCA

The First secretary wrote his response and placed it in the locked attaché case and gave it to the courier to return to the general, who was on Army business doing an inspection along the Chinese border. The courier took the first plane to the Army post where the general was staying. He surrendered the case to the general, who eagerly unlocked it. The Soviets had never assassinated a sitting United States president before. He was concerned the first secretary would consider the plan too risky. He read the response.

To GEN Mikhail Andropov, SCA
From Nikita Khrushchev, First Secretary of the CPSU

Comrade General, I approve of your plan to assassinate President Kennedy. It is imperative no evidence of Soviet involvement be discovered. As soon as the mission is accomplished, our agent within the CIA should conveniently have a fatal heart attack, so no link to the Soviet Union should be discovered in any investigation sure to follow. I understand he has had a history of heart trouble, so this should not arouse any suspicion.

Nikita Khrushchev
First Secretary of the CPSU

General Andropov was pleased with the response. It was time to plan the American president's demise. He'd thought of nothing else since the Cuban Missile crisis and the Bay of Pigs incident. It is time to stop this arrogant young man dead in his tracks, the operative word being *dead*.

Memorandum from Dr. Jan Eichmann
October 8, 1963
To: GEN Carter F. Colson

General, we will launch the three discs we replicated from the alien disc in T-24 hours, at zero eight hundred hours MST. We're also able to make twelve transport vessels out of alloy-x to transport troops and supplies to set up our post on the moon. There's going to be a clear blue sky, so we painted all of the discs and transport vessels sky blue. We've set up security to clear all civilians from the area and have arranged for satellite blackouts during the launch time. We're going to set up a rash of false UFO sightings all over the west, so most serious people will ignore our launches. We've enough water, food, fuel, equipment, and a recycler to start up our post. When the American public celebrates the public moon launch in a few years, we will already be standing on the moon.

Dr. Jan Eichmann
Dept. of Research and Development,
Alpha One Test Center

Arriving at the white house, the courier checked his locked attaché case again. Even though silence was considered golden, after his many trips to the White House, he was on a first name basis with the president's secretary. Janet smiled at him.

"Dan, the president will see you now." He smiled a shy smile.

"Thank you, Janet."

The young courier opened the door and closed it behind him and then saluted, relinquished the case to the president, and waited for a response.

From GEN Carter F. Colson, ASDC
To the President of the United States
October 12, 1963

Mr. President, we landed the expedition team this morning and found the moon is indeed rich in alloy-x. We will have a secure post constructed and a reclamation facility and begin salvage operations within two months. Our team reported the Soviet team also arrived mid-afternoon. I assume they're planning the same thing we are. We're also making the building of post defenses and offensive hoverships a high priority as soon as we have our post built.

GEN Carter F. Colson,
Commander, American Space Defense Corps

The young president wrote a quick response of *message received*, placed it in the case, and handed it back to the courier. "Lieutenant, there's no rush in sending this response back. I think you should stay in Washington tonight. I have it under good authority Janet doesn't have any dinner plans," he confided, flashing his trademark smile.

"Yes, sir. I'll look into it."

Phone call to Nikita Khrushchev, First Secretary of the CPSU, from GEN Mikhail Andropov, SCA

"Comrade First Secretary, Our expedition team landed on the moon this afternoon and found the American team was already there, by about eight hours. We're quickly moving to build a post and alloy-x reclamation facility. Our plan is to construct adequate defenses and offenses out of the alloy-x. Then we will begin our war with the Americans in an attempt to destroy them quickly before they can establish a dominant position here."

"Dah, very good."

AP news release, November 22, 1963

In Dallas, Texas, three shots were fired at President Kennedy's motorcade in downtown Dallas. President Kennedy died at 1:00 P.M. Central Standard Time, two o'clock Eastern Standard Time.

The young Soviet courier delivered his message to the general. The general opened the case and retrieved the letter.

To GEN Mikhail Andropov, SCA
From Nikita Khrushchev, First Secretary of the CPSU

Comrade General, the timing of President Kennedy's demise would have been better had it occurred before the American post's construction. However, it will still serve our purpose. We have sent inquiries though all of our operatives within the CIA, the State Department and other agencies. We concluded this is a covert operation their congress and military are not aware.

Our listening device planted within President Johnson's office monitored his calls and visitors after Kennedy's demise. We are convinced he knows nothing of the ASDC. With Kennedy dead, all government support should dissolve, and the ASDC will not be able to function.

Nikita Khrushchev
First Secretary of the CPSU

General Andropov crafted his response, placed it into the locked case, and dispatched the courier back to the First Secretary. The courier dispatched to the Kremlin delivered his locked case to the First Secretary. The First Secretary unlocked the case, and read the letter.

From GEN Mikhail Andropov, SCA
To Nikita Khrushchev, First Secretary of the CPSU

Comrade First Secretary, concerning the American president's demise, our agent within the CIA black operations has conveniently died of a heart attack this morning. Ironically, the CIA is trying to blame the assassination on us by using an unstable former US Marine. They claim he had ties to Cuba and to us. We stopping using him because we discovered he was a double agent and untrustworthy a few months ago. Meanwhile, we will continue to fight with the Americans on the moon until we've vanquished them. I trust we have the resources within the American press and government to blame this on the CIA.

GEN Mikhail Andropov, SCA

The courier was admitted to the office of Perry Dubois, the chairman of the Investco Corp. The chairman opened the locked case, and read the letter.

To: Chairman Perry Dubois, Investco Corp.
From GEN Carter F. Colson, ASDC
November 23, 1963

As you know, the president, our Chief benefactor was killed yesterday. Please convene a board meeting of Investco to determine our financial status and structural independence. Our post on the moon is complete and we've begun salvaging alloy-x and fighting openly with the Soviets. Fighting there is fierce, to say the least, and we need to know if we can operate as the president wished. A member of our staff who worked for the president obtained access and destroyed the only copy of project code name Desert Jewel the president possessed.

GEN Carter F. Colson, ASDC

The chairman dismissed the courier, and called his secretary to contact the board members to convene a meeting. The courier was received from the Investgo Corp by the general at his post in Utah. He received the case and read the letter.

To GEN Carter F. Colson, ASDC
From Perry Dubois, Investco Corp
November 26, 1963

GEN Colson, after examining the books and the infrastructure of the Investco Corporation, the board has concluded we're well able to stand-alone as you instructed. The recent *reverse engineering* will be extremely useful to expand our financial base and secure more inroads into other businesses and corporations.

Perry Dubois, Investco Corp

Rotten business, the president getting himself killed thought the general. At least we can operate as the president wished.

Secure radio transmission to Luna—July 12, 1969
Memorandum from GEN Carter F. Colson
To COL Darrel Cavender, ASDC Commander, Luna

Colonel, I'm pleased to hear the American position on Luna is strong. Soon the American space program under NASA will be putting on a dog and pony show for the world to see. I want you to coordinate the cleanup of alloy-x in the area surrounding the Eagle Lander's landing site. The priority is to make sure there's no alloy-x anywhere near the site. Our people on NASA's team will let you know the exact lunar landing site in advance. Make absolutely certain the only *moon rocks* the astronauts find aren't alloy-x. Also brush out any footprints we may have left near the landing site.

GEN Carter F. Colson,
ASDC

LOG ENTRY:
June 16, 1969
2LT Paul Smith, ASDC

After leaving the Naval Aviator Academy, I served my four years as a cold war fighter pilot. My father served as a naval aviator in the Korean War, and never returned. I'd have liked to have known more about his death than *missing in action*. I was young when I last saw my father, but my memory of him has been a guiding light. I followed in his footsteps.

For four uneventful years, I served. We came close to a conflict with some Soviet fighters once or twice over the Sea of Japan, but we never had an incident. I had a bright future after the Navy as a commercial airline pilot. My tour of duty drew to a close and I started the paperwork of processing out. We all felt as though the clash between the superpowers would happen during our tour. I felt as though what I'd been trained for was being wasted. Soon the only wings I'd be wearing were of an American Airlines pilot.

My plans were interrupted by *the visit*. The government had various different covert ops that sometimes recruited, so the visit was no surprise. What did surprise me was they wouldn't tell me what I would be joining. Once they found out my loyalty to our country was absolute and I had no conflicting commitments, they made me an offer. I signed up for a military outfit without even being told its name, with whom or where we would be fighting. I was sent to a top-secret training center. I had no idea what I was training for, and the training was more grueling than anything I'd ever experienced. The drill instructors pushed us beyond our limits and back again. The only encouragement the instructors would offer us was we'd be actively fighting the best the Soviet military had to offer. That was enough for me. I sucked it up and made it to the end.

Graduation came, and I was finally to learn of my mission. We were to leave on a space vessel to start a post on the moon, where I'd be actively fighting Soviet pilots flying hovertanks. The gloves were off, and the cold war wasn't cold anymore. The contest between the superpowers had begun. I had a choice; I could leave now, or stay and fight. I was born for this. Communism is a disease that threatens liberty around the world. I accepted my commission. I chose to stay and fight for freedom—it is my destiny.

CPT Paul Smith died during the Soviet offensive on Eagle 1 post on Luna; July 13, 1970.

LOG ENTRY:
April 5, 1969
1LT Vitaliy Grigorovich, SCA

I was a member of the Soviet Air Force when I was chosen. It was a great honor to be selected, but it was even a greater honor to pass training.

Only five percent of the trainees were selected. Although my father was not told what unit I was fighting in, he was very proud when my commander told him I would be serving in the Soviet Union's most elite fighting force. Later I learned I would be serving in space, fighting the hated Americans. The Americans want to spread their poisonous system of government and force it on us.

Our society is orderly. Gangsters do not run free on our streets carrying guns. Criminals are not let loose on society over legal technicalities, to repeat their crimes by preying on the innocent. Our leaders do not amass wealth and live like czars, like the rich Americans, while the rest of the world starves. It is for the common good and the Soviet motherland I fight until every last American is destroyed from among the cosmos. Then we can bring the war back home and finish the job there. Only then will there be security for the Soviet peoples. Soon it will be evident how corrupt and worthless their democracy is. There is no greater honor for me than to fight for justice and the Soviet peoples. All Power to the Soviets!

An American sniper on Mars killed MAJ Grigorovich; August 5, 1971.

THE FALL OF EAGLE 1

"COL Wycoff, please sit down," said GEN Colson, motioning to the seat before his desk. The colonel sat down in the chair directly in front of the general's heavy oak desk. COL Wycoff eyed the map behind the general's desk of the far side of the moon with markings indicating the American and Soviet posts near the D'Alembert and Fabry craters.

Behind his desk was displayed a map of the far side of the moon, with markings indicating the American and Soviet posts near the D'Alembert and Fabry craters.

"Colonel, there's been a change of plans. You won't be leading your landing force on Mars to set up a post there." The Americans had hoarded the precious alloy-x material for the last six years to help build next post on Mars.

"Sir, am I being relieved of my command?"

"Nothing like that, read this." The general handed him a printed copy of the commander's log from Luna. COL Wycoff accepted the white paper printout and started to read...

Eagle 1 Post: Black Dogs Battalion, Luna; July 10, 1970
Commander's log, COL Darrel Cavender

The fighting with the Soviets over the last three months has shifted the balance of power to the Soviets. It began after we sent the lion's share of our alloy-x reclamation to Earth to provide the material to set up the Mars post. We didn't have reserves of the precious material and we started to lose ground with a slight loss of two ships in a skirmish. The Soviets were able to hold the battlefield and recover the alloy-x scrap. Each time we met them in battle, they had greater fleet strength, and each time they became bolder in battle. When it was clear that their fleet strength was superior, their strategy was to shut down our alloy-x reclamation. We were unable to defend our scavenger crews and the alloy-x supply dried up.

At this writing, we have only five offensive units left. We can't send scavenger teams out to harvest any alloy-x because we can't defend them. Our defensive grid was already partially dismantled to recycle for building tanks. I estimate the Soviets will bring their artillery and all of their offensive units soon to begin the siege of our post. ASDC command has informed me that reinforcements won't be ready to deploy here for at least four days. With no hope of reinforcements, we will fight to the last man. Sidearms and rifles have been issued to noncombatant personnel, including the mess crew. When a security leak to the Soviets compromised the personal information of many of my men's families, the Soviets used the threat of harming them to break our morale. I recommend to ASDC Command that all personnel who serve on frontier posts use call signs only.

COL Darrel Cavender
Black Dogs Battalion, Luna

A dark shadow crept over the colonel's face as he digested the report. The idea that they were losing because of the alloy-x freighters he was packing for his post on Mars cut him to the quick. He could do the math. They weren't ready and wouldn't make it there in time to defend Eagle 1. COL Wycoff put down the paper.

"What are your orders, sir?"

"How soon can your team be ready to leave for Luna?"

"One week, sir."

"You have three days. Even so, Eagle 1 may have fallen before you get there. You'll direct your landing team to reinforce Eagle 1 on Luna. If the post has fallen by the time you get there, dig in and establish a new post. I cannot stress enough the importance of this mission. There is no more alloy-x to supply another team should you fail, and failure is not an option. If Eagle 1 has fallen, you must establish your landing zone at Landau Crater, which will give you ample time to dig in and build a post before you have visitors. The distance between the Soviet post at the Fabry Crater and the Landau Crater is 3,933 kilometers. Make the landing zone at the beginning of their satellite blackout window to gain an additional hour and fifty minutes before the Soviets know you've landed. You never know when the extra time may be critical. Speed in setting up your recycler, defensive grid, artillery, armory, and factory is imperative. If you can't raise anyone alive on radio at Eagle 1 when you arrive, don't attempt to go there. Any questions?"

"None, sir."

"Here is the file on your mission," he said as he handed him a file stuffed with documents. "There will be only a small window for you to construct your post and get prepared to defend her. Once the Soviet satellite blackout is over, you have approximately thirty-nine hours before all of the tanks the Soviets possess will come knocking at your door, followed by their artillery pieces approximately three days later. You must have your defensive grid in place, and enough tanks built by the time the Soviet tanks get there to hold them off. You must have your own artillery constructed before theirs arrives."

"Understood, sir."

"I believe COL Cavender was right. From now on, all personnel on these frontier posts will be referred to by call signs only. What will yours be?"

COL Wycoff thought a moment, and then showed his teeth.

"Red Fangs, sir."

"Very good. Launch time has been moved up to three days from now, at seventeen hundred hours."

"Yes, sir." Rising to his feet, the general shook COL Wycoff's hand and wished him luck. He had every confidence in COL Red Fangs as he was now called. He was a hard charger and had filled his team with hard chargers and the best technical people he could find.

The Americans worked around the clock to ready the expedition of sixteen ships for the trip to Luna. They would sleep on the sixteen hour trip, then hit the ground running and work sixteen hour days until the Soviets arrived. The men had endured grueling training to learn how to function with little sleep or food when the need called for it. It was time for their training to pay off.

COL Red Fangs couldn't bring all of his personnel on the first trip. His priority, on the first trip, was to transport essential equipment and supplies. The equipment included electronic and surveillance equipment, the recycler, heavy equipment for the oxygen extraction and steel mill, meager medical equipment and supplies for a sick bay, food, water and fuel.

His personnel would be his command staff, the construction crew, one doctor, one clergyman who was cross-trained as a nurse, a few support staff, and three shifts of tactical operation technicians. All but five of the transport freighter pilots were also his combat pilots. CPT America, who had the lead ship, the pilots of the two fuel tankers and the two water tankers weren't part of his crew. His pilots who would remain were all cross-trained to work in the oxygen extraction and steel mill or the factory that they would construct to build artillery pieces, work and combat vessels. The construction process used a lot of fuel and water, so as soon as one water or fuel tanker was empty, they flew back for a refill at top speed. His construction crew was cross-trained as his artillery battery. More personnel, food, supplies, and equipment would be would be arriving with each vessel returning. One small vessel was left behind for shuttling any emergency spare parts for equipment breakdowns. It was faster and lighter and could make the trip from Earth to Luna in only twelve hours. A total of one hundred and twenty men would be on the first trip. His construction battalion was ready to lift off.

July 13, 1970—Seventeen Hundred Zulu

"Colonel, all preflight checks are complete. All systems are go: all cargo loaded and accounted for, and all personnel ready to embark," reported his executive officer LTC Judgment Day.

47

"Very good, load up." His XO gave the order for all personnel to enter the ships. Luna was a sixteen hour trip. The first one hundred and twenty men would sleep most of the way there. This would get them ready for the grueling pace of setting the new post up before the Soviets attempted to lay siege to it. Six of the freighters would be unloaded and return quickly to pick up more equipment, supplies, and another one hundred and twenty men. It would be another thirty-four hours after they landed before they were relieved. The American fleet of sixteen transport freighters, one by one lifted off from their secret post in Utah. They were painted sky-blue to limit the amount of possible UFO sightings. It was imperative civilians didn't see their ships. All civilians had been removed from a one hundred square mile area, under the pretext that the EPA was checking for radiation leakage from some old uranium mines. *It was good to be connected*, thought the colonel.

"Captain, get us there ASAP," COL Red Fangs ordered.

"Aye sir, full speed it is."

So it was on the third day, at seventeen hundred, the American fleet left for Luna, unsure of what they would find there. CPT Walker recently had undergone a name change as per orders. He was now referring to himself as CPT America, and his transport freighter the America was the lead vessel. COL Red Fangs regarded the name as a good omen. The colonel hated this part of any assignment. The waiting was unsettling, especially knowing his good friend COL Cavender and all hands may be dead by the time he arrived.

LUNA—July 13, 1970 Nineteen Forty-Two Zulu

COL Red Fangs was reading the file's documents for the tenth time. The summary on the last page contained the physical parameters that defined how they would conduct their mission. Summary… 'Luna has no atmosphere. Its gravity is 16.6% of Earth's. To keep their cardiovascular system healthy over a long period of time, the men were required to exercise by carrying weights to overcompensate for the weak gravity. The Lunar month is 27.225 Earth days, half of which has around the clock intense light and heat, reaching temperatures up to 265 °F/129 °C, while the dark period gets as cold as -170 °F/-112 °C. Because daylight and dark periods are nearly two weeks long, post operations will keep Earth Zulu time and date, and operate on twenty-four hour days, seven day weeks to keep the men on the bio-clock they're used to. Time zones are irrelevant on Luna, so we refer to time in relation to how much light or darkness is left until the state changes, and regard marking time for records by Earth Mountain Standard Time, Zulu. Whenever possible, Sunday will be observed as a day of rest and church services will be available for all men. Luna has roughly three trillion craters. The far side is more heavily pockmarked with craters than the near side. The hoverdrives on all vehicles use antigravity technology for hovering and use conventional liquid carbon-based fuel for propulsion.'

"Your coffee, sir, hot and black." COL Red Fangs looked up from his reading.

"Very good, Corporal." He blew on the hot liquid, to cool it and took a sip, refocusing his attention to the file he'd been reading. 'Luna has no water, but some ice is on the poles. Luna only has igneous rocks, rich in oxygen, formed from molten rock. Oxygen will be supplied by these rocks in an oxygen extraction process, key to the post's survival. The men's flight suits and ships had rebreathers, but there wasn't enough room to bring enough oxygen tanks to fill all of the buildings. The moving line of darkness is called *the terminator*. The edge of the terminator that separates light from darkness advances about ten miles per hour. Should the American post have fallen at the D'Alembert crater, then you'll construct the new American post at the Landau Crater, on the far side of Luna for security reasons.'

He would have liked more time to put his team and equipment together, but if there was any chance of saving the American post and his old friend it would be worth it. He had the best team on Earth. He had confidence that his team would get the job done if they had to help reinforce Eagle 1 or set up and defend a new post. He smiled slightly when he considered that the men could carry heavier weight due to the weaker gravity. The weaker gravity would be a bonus when they were unloading the ships. The lead ship picked up a satellite transmission from Eagle 1, six hours after lift-off. The transmission was laced with static, but the voice was understandable.

"COL Cavender, we have Soviet tanks and bombers on radar, sir," the voice cross- reference was identified as belonging to 1LT Westbrook.

"This is COL Cavender. Form a line behind the east guntower, and in front of the post HQ. All noncombatant personnel report to the post HQ, where you'll receive a rifle and side arm from Chief Higgins. The combat officers have elected not to surrender. I'm leaving the noncombatant personnel under the command of CPT Lacey. Should we fall in the attempt to defend our post, CPT Lacey will confer with you all to decide whether or not you'll surrender. May God be with us all." The colonel exhaled and steeled himself for the attack to come. He laughed at the irony of the situation. Four generations of military officers in his family and his end will have to be modified to show he died in Vietnam: to have a public funeral with military honors. None of his family would be told the real truth, but that's the way this war was.

Eagle 1 Post: Black Dogs Battalion, Luna
Personal Log, CPT Neil Lacey
July 13, 1970

"COL Cavender and all of the remaining combat officers have elected to fight to the death and not surrender. He's left me the burden of leading the remaining noncombatants in the event they fall in the line of duty. I assembled the personnel under my charge and put the issue to them. I found there weren't any noncombatants in the US Marines, and that none would surrender. The chaplains said they would neither fight nor surrender, but would stand with us, to give encouragement and aid. The mess crew in particular was adamant about not surrendering. I had to leave them to compose myself as I couldn't stop from crying. In all of the time I've been here, I viewed the mess crew as simply kitchen help, a necessity to feed us and to wash dishes. Today I realized we were all marines, and if we die here, I count it as a privilege and an honor to make my last stand with these fine marines."

"Men, it has been an honor to serve with you. Semper Fi," said COL Cavender.

The Soviet commander interrupted his last words to his men. "This is COL Glaskov. We wish to discuss the terms of surrender."

"If you leave your equipment behind, and leave Luna forever, we will spare you," retorted Col Cavender.

"I take it you will not surrender, then? Good! Have it your way. Prepare to die!"

"CPT Lacey, we've gathered all of the paper records from all of the quarters and offices and my men are incinerating them now," reported post security Chief Higgins. The rest of my security team is putting bullets in the hard drives of all computers save the one for environmental controls as per your orders. The greenhouse is wired so we can blow the whole affair, but we will wait until the last moment."

"Very Good. Mess SGT Muldoon?"

"Yes, sir."

"It looks as if we're going out with a bang. Set up our best food and drink on the table in the officers' mess. Today everyone is an officer."

"Sir, yes sir."

"Just outside of guntower range, the Soviets set up their artillery. They systematically pounded all of the artillery, the armory, recycler, factory, and tactical operations center into rubble. One by one, all buildings were destroyed. Only the post HQ and greenhouse remained. Once their artillery destroyed the guntowers and turrets, the Soviets sent in the first wave of twenty tanks. The Americans fought valiantly and destroyed ten enemy tanks, but the sheer force of numbers overwhelmed them. None of the pilots who ejected would surrender. In one last act of defiance, COL Cavender, CPT Smith and 2LT Baker pulled their service revolvers out and fired on the advancing tanks. They died with honor doing their proud duty as US Marines. I, CPT Lacey, bear witness to this. Our satellite tower has been destroyed, and I'm uploading this account to our satellite by shortwave radio. This will no doubt be my last transmission, as I doubt I'll be able to recount our end. We remain steadfast. Semper Fi! Remember Eagle 1!"

COL Red Fangs listened to the account with a mixture of anguish and pride. The men who were awake had been huddled close to the radio to hear the details. The men were silently pondering the reality of the final holdouts defending their post to the death. COL Red Fangs cleared his throat. Tears were starting to form in the corners of his eyes, and he knew he had to change the mood, lest his men regard his emotional state. COL Red Fangs shouted. "The Texans had their Alamo—we have Eagle 1!"

"Remember Eagle 1!" echoed through the ship.

"Captain America, take us to our new post."

"Aye sir, full speed ahead."

July 14, 1970—Zero Five Hundred Zulu

"COL Red Fangs, satellite optical and thermal scans show no signs of life on Eagle 1," reported CPT America. They were on radio silence to make sure the Soviets couldn't hear them. He pulled up the satellite rendering of Eagle 1. COL Red Fangs silently surveyed the rubble that was once Eagle 1. Where the greenhouse complex had been, was a gaping, ugly hole in the lunar surface. It would have been the last thing the Americans destroyed, to make sure the Soviets didn't get any of their food or processing equipment. The colonel made no show of emotion, as he hadn't expected any survivors. He entered the bridge of the transport freighter and addressed the captain.

Looking at the video display of Luna before him, he asked, "Captain, where's Landau Crater?"

"Sir, just on the light side of the terminator line, right—down—there," he said as he pointed to the spot.

"Could you give me a ballpark estimate of how many hours of daylight we have until darkness if we landed now?"

"I can give you a very close estimate, but it will take a minute." COL Red Fangs studied the globe before him patiently while the captain did the math.

"Sir, the terminator line will cross Landau Crater zero at nine thirty Zulu, July 18th. Sir, in relation to the terminator, I can put you down with roughly over four days of light just after the Soviet satellite passes over. The Soviet satellite passes over Landau once every two hours, has a good visual and can take instrument readings for ten minutes. You have a little less than two hours from landing until the Russkies leave their post to pay you a visit."

"Affirmative. Take us down, and try to avoid their satellite for the longest period of time you can."

"Aye, sir. I'll send for you when we're ready to land."

"I want all the build time we can get in daylight, but dark when the Soviet tanks arrive. One more thing Captain, I want all of the high-resolution pictures of the landing area I can get, along with laser imagery. I need a very clear 3D topographical map of the landing zone."

"Aye, sir." They were still on radio silence. He opened up a laser digital pulse line-of-sight communication in Morse code to the other ships, advising them to fall in formation behind him in orbit. They would be sending their landing zone coordinates and time when ready. The captain completed the topographical survey for the colonel and sent it by way of his first officer twenty minutes later. COL Red Fangs thanked the young officer and sat down to a cup of coffee to study the proposed landing zone where he would build his post. He took a sip of coffee and opened the file…

Landau Crater
Coordinates-41.6 °N, 118.1 °W
Diameter-214 km or 132.97 mi
Depth-3.25 km or 2.02 mi
Colongitude-121° at sunrise

Frost Crater is overlaid on the center of the southern rim, seventy-five km in diameter. The inner wall is wider and heavier along the northern side where it has been reinforced by the former rim of Landau. Wood Crater is inside of Landau on the northeast side, seventy-eight km in diameter.

The colonel considered the size of the crater, his mind exploring the possibilities for the best post construction. Given it was a hole approximately two miles deep and 133 miles wide, it was unlikely the Soviet hovertanks could scale the walls if they were steep enough. He quickly thumbed over to the topographical pictures CPT America had given him. The captain combined topographical laser imagery with other known satellite images, constructing a remarkably accurate 3D model of the crater.

COL Red Fangs studied the walls until he found what he was looking for. The walls of the west side of the crater were extremely steep, with the exception of a pile of rock slabs. The rocks were overlapping one upon another from the bottom of the crater floor, winding up at a sixty degree angle overall from north to south, changing angles to as steep as seventy degrees in some spots and dropping downward to twenty degrees in others. This could make a natural staircase up the side, wide enough for the Soviet tanks to ascend to the rim in single file. He thought for a moment. That crater edge would be a great place to position the back of the post, effectively cutting off half a circle to defend. There was only one weak spot, the natural staircase. It would be easy enough to put a few gun turrets, and a guntower or two close to the place where the Soviets would ascend, but he genuinely didn't want to deploy much defensive hardware there. If the Soviets saw the rim's edge heavily fortified they wouldn't come up that way, and the investment of their defenses, which were badly needed at the front, would be wasted. Unless…

LTC Judgment Day was reading a scientific report on Luna over a cup of coffee when COL Red Fangs found him. After the customary salute, COL Red Fangs sat down, opening the file of maps and technical data of the Landau Crater.

"I found something of interest to us." The colonel slid the topographic map of the Landau Crater to his XO. "This natural staircase here," he said, tapping his finger on the spot, "is a way the Soviets can come at us from the back side if we center the back of the post to the crater's rim. Right above the top of the natural staircase it is an overhanging ledge probably weighing about fifty tons, Earth weight—about eight tons, lunar weight."

"I take it we're not trying to avoid the natural staircase, but exploit it?"

"Yes, it will cut the line of attack down fifty percent to have our back to the crater, which the Soviets will use for the main thrust of their attack. They will split their forces and try to sneak up through the crater to attack what they think is our unprotected flank."

"So we show them we're not exactly as unprotected as they think."

"Yes, I want you to oversee it personally before they get there. The preparations need to be done during the satellite blackout window. Just make sure the bait is very enticing." His XO grinned.

"I'll arrange a surprise for our guests. Sir, this maneuver will also cut off our escape should things go wrong."

"We have no escape route. We're committed to staying with our oxygen, fuel, food, water and shelter. That will all be at our post. Concerning the appearance of cutting off our own escape route, this will make the men fight desperately if they think it is a fight to the death. It is our best hope for survival, but it will appear we're in desperate straits." His executive officer pondered for a moment.

"Sir, this is going to be a *bad bear*, isn't it?"

"It will be very tight. We came to win the right to stay here, not to retreat. When I was young, I learned a valuable lesson. If you bloody the nose of the school bully, you earn certain rights. I intend to make the siege of our post so painful that it will never be attempted again."

"We'll give 'em hell, sir."

July 14, 1970—Zero Eight Hundred Zulu

The captain had just started a cup of coffee, cream, no sugar, just how he liked it. It was time to call the colonel. His first mate chose the alias Bucky as a joke to complement his captain's call sign.

"LT Bucky!"

"Sir, yes sir!"

"Find COL Red Fangs. Inform him we're ready to break orbit and land within the hour."

"He was getting a cup of joe and preparing to come here when I last saw him."

"Very well." He should have known he wouldn't have to summon the colonel. He would have planned on being ready and waiting when they approached their landing zone to build and defend their new post. The captain took note that COL Red Fangs was more relaxed than the last time he saw him. COL Red Fangs approached the bridge with a cup of hot coffee in his hand. *Apparently he does much better in a crisis than in waiting for something to happen*, he thought.

"Is it time to land, Captain?"

"Soon, Colonel, we should be on the lunar surface by zero nine hundred. We've been listening to all radio transmissions the Soviets are sending back to Earth. It looks like they don't know we're here."

"Excellent! I want to catch them with their pants down. We need every break we can get."

"Aye, sir." With that, CPT America signaled the rest of the vessels trailing him to prepare to follow him down.

An oxygen extraction and metal refining plant would be constructed to ensure his men's survival and give them building materials. Ilmenite, a lunar mineral rich in oxygen, also contained iron and titanium. Rich in oxygen was an understatement. Ilmenite consisted of forty-three percent oxygen. The computer banks of the alien vessel recovered from the Navajo crash site revealed a treasure trove of technological wealth. The most important one for building a self-sufficient post was the formula for processing Ilmenite into iron, titanium and oxygen.

The process essentially took a rock crusher, a solar furnace and a little chemical manipulation to turn $FeTiO_3$ into the pure elements that allowed them to survive. Once the buildings had their air in them, a very efficient carbon dioxide filtration system would keep it clean. The iron and titanium would be used to construct lunar steel in the mill they would construct.

Luna has sunlight for only half of each month, so the passive solar electric plant could be used for the half-month long days. After the darkness descended upon them, they would have to rely on conventional fuel for all of their energy needs until the light returned for two weeks. The Americans had little room for error in their construction plans. Within forty-one hours of landing, the Soviets would have a full tank regiment knocking at their door. They had to have their defensive grid up and enough of their artillery line up to stop the Soviet tanks from starting the charge right away. The colonel had to manage four things: men, equipment, time, and alloy-x. They also had to get some scavengers salvaging alloy-x on the Frost crater as soon as possible before the Soviets shut the operation down. They would be sending some of the ships back as soon as they unloaded to get more men, equipment and supplies. Other ships they would recycle as soon as the recycler was operational. The men still needed to be able to eat and sleep somewhere until the main building was built, so some ships would remain as barracks for a while. Timing was critical for everything.

July 14, 1970—Zero Seven Thirty Zulu

The captain would be breaking orbit soon. The descent would be a bit bumpy, so the men were all awakened and fed breakfast before they descended to their landing zone. COL Red Fangs had joined CPT America on the bridge, coffee cup in hand.

July 14, 1970—Zero Eight Thirty Zulu

"Breaking orbit and descending now," reported the captain.

"Colonel, I'd get rid of that coffee cup and strap in if I were you. The descent may get a bit bumpy."

"Thank you Captain." The colonel drained the last of the cup and placed his empty cup in a secure locker.

The Soviets' highest priority would be to stamp out Eagle 2 before it was established, ending America's plans for colonizing the solar system. Captain America wondered if the post would still be standing when he returned with more supplies.

Vietnam had taught the colonel one thing, if nothing else. Superior numbers didn't always win battles. Air support was the deciding factor in many battles won in Vietnam, but here he would have to rely on artillery.

Mines were also useful, and he would utilize all they brought with them. The order of the day upon landing was to get the defensive grid up—complete with minefields, build their environmental support system and produce as many artillery pieces and tanks as they could muster, with the emphasis on the artillery.

Tanks alone couldn't take their post, and artillery pieces were slow and lumbering in transport. The colonel knew if the Soviets brought their artillery, the whole siege force wouldn't be here for almost four days. The choice location was somewhere on the far side of the moon because that was where the alloy-x was, not to mention for security. The Americans didn't want some college student at an observatory somewhere viewing a developed military post with a telescope. The "dark side" or far side is the side of the moon never visible from Earth because the moon's rotation and orbit are synchronized in such a way that only one side ever faces the Earth. It would be more correct to call it the far side as it gets the same amount of light from the sun, and the bright side would best be referred to as the near side. The best radio transmissions to Earth were from the near side. To keep their post from detection, they would build it on the far side, and use satellite relays for radio transmissions.

At precisely zero nine hundred, fifteen minutes into the one hour fifty-minute Soviet satellite blackout window over Landau Crater, the Americans landed.

LTC Judgment Day was in charge of the nuts and bolts of coordinating the different construction projects while COL Red Fangs ran the overall operation. The post would be constructed with its back to the west side of the Landau Crater and the natural staircase, terminating dead center of the post, as COL Red Fangs had instructed.

Tactical operations would be run from the bridge until the post HQ building was built and technical functions could be transferred to their own room. Then the medical supplies, food and rest of the perishable cargo would be moved into post HQ and CPT America could return to Earth. The doctor and nurse set up a temporary sick bay, and coffee and mess were set up on three different freighters.

The men rolled out of the transport freighters and started unloading the recycler. Part of the construction crew was assigned to set up the recycler as quickly as possible. Two heavy mining trucks, a crawler excavator and an excavator backhoe built for the harsh lunar environment were unloaded next along with a furnace pot and rock crusher. The Americans now had four empty freighters ready for recycling. Six other vessels were refueled and sent back to Earth to get more men, equipment and supplies.

COL Red Fangs set up his command center and tactical operations on the bridge of CPT America's ship. This would give him nearly instant status updates from his tech boys as well as communications with the construction crew. COL Red Fangs approached the bridge, and his two technicians saluted.

"Captain, is everything set up?"

"Right over here, Colonel. This workstation was set up so you can communicate with all of the work teams at all times. I'll be available at your call if you need any assistance. These three switches are your comm. links to LTC Judgment Day, CSM Rainmaker, and the mess sergeant to have him send food over. The light next to them will light up when you have an incoming call. Just flip the switch if you wish to answer or call out. If you flip two switches at once, you'll be able to conference both. Closing one switch will allow you to terminate that call and still remain connected to the other. The switch on the far left will open a link to them all at once for a general message to all. Anything else?"

"No, thank you. That will be all, Captain."

"Good, my last cup of coffee has summoned me to the head. I will be right back." The colonel looked at his two technicians keeping an eye on the Soviets with the satellite uplink. They had access to areas of interest when the satellite did a flyby.

"CPT Watchful Eye?"

"Sir. Yes sir?"

"I want a report of what the Soviets are doing every time the satellite passes over, even if it's not interesting." CPT Watchful Eye was the Chief of tactical operations and acting as the lead technician while they were operating with a skeleton crew during setup.

"Sir, yes sir. We're also monitoring all channels for any Soviet radio messages. If we hear any activity, we'll try to break their encryption."

"Very good, son. By the way, where can I view the construction activity outside?" The young officer walked over to the colonel's workstation and typed some commands into the keyboard. The computer monitor showed several pictures of the construction team doing various tasks.

"There are eight cameras, sir. You can access the menu here and view them all at once in small screens, or type in the number of the camera, and it will become full screen. To return to the main view of them all, just hit escape."

"Very good." Just then CPT America returned with a cup of coffee for the colonel.

"Thank you, Captain. Maybe we need to put a coffee pot on the bridge," he joked.

"I thought about that, Colonel but going for coffee and to the head is half my exercise." The room settled down, and the tech boys watched their screens for something interesting in an otherwise boring *stakeout* while the colonel kept an eye on the building progress. His executive officer stayed with the group setting up the recycler. It was clear that he would be staying with the highest priority job unless he was needed elsewhere. CSM Rainmaker was the artillery battery's noncommissioned officer in charge, and the "walking boss" of the construction battalion.

The colonel dropped by his quarters and grabbed his file on the Soviets and another cup of coffee. Coffee cup in hand, the colonel carried the file back to his workstation. He wanted to read the profiles of the Soviet commander and his executive officer, and the officer most likely to assume command if both of them were dead. He sat down, opened the file and started reading.

COL Boris Nikitich Glaskov
Birthplace...Moscow, Russia
Age forty-two

Career Soviet Army, with good political connections. He's thought to have relatives in the Soviet government, but none on the Central Committee. Considered to be one of their best Soviet commanders. Rumored to have political aspirations, and will retire from the military soon to take a government job in the politburo. Considered a good pilot, but a better military strategist.

COL Red Fangs considered thoughtfully what the report said. His friend's death would no doubt bring this man the promotion he sought. Perhaps he could do something to tarnish the afterglow of his victory over Eagle 1. He sipped his coffee, and read the file on the Soviet executive officer.

LTC Rurik Alievich Averbukh
Age thirty
Birthplace... Leningrad, Russia

He was a former first officer in Spetsnaz, Soviet Special Forces and is a superb pilot and sniper. Leadership and tactical abilities are his strongest points. It is estimated he's a stronger leader and strategist than COL Glaskov. It is assumed he'll take over the lunar post if COL Glaskov gets promoted to the politburo.

COL Red Fangs mentally noted LTC Averbukh as a high priority target, took a sip of coffee and opened the last file. He scrolled down the bottom line summary as he had the first two...

MAJ Feliks Aleksandrovich Cherenkov
Age twenty-eight
Birthplace... Smolensk, Russia

He's the best combat pilot the Soviets have. His administrative skills are rated only average, but as a combat officer in the field, he's unequalled. The colonel closed his file, mentally noting how to use all three pieces of information to their advantage. The gears in his mind were turning, and a plan was formulating…

July 14, 1970—Ten Forty Zulu

"Sir. Colonel, I have something on the satellite feed."

"What is it?"

"The Soviets are leaving with forty-five tanks headed our way. I'm also watching their artillery pieces leave, too."

"How many artillery pieces?"

"Sir, I see twenty, with an escort of ten more tanks. Satellite zoom photographs of the artillery estimates the barrel length of forty-five calibers."

"Keep an eye on them."

"Sir, yes sir."

"Command Sergeant Major?" asked the first officer.

"Sir, yes sir."

"When the freighters are as unloaded as they can be, send a detail to start drilling the mine holes around the post perimeter, two clicks past guntower range. Have them open a link to our tech boys. When the Soviet satellite passes over, make sure the mess isn't visible from the air and equipment is cleared. Everyone else is to join the rest of the construction effort. Place them where they will do the most good."

"Sir, yes sir."

The construction crew had to dig the mine holes in the solid rock around the perimeter of the post before the Soviet satellite blackout window closed. To place a mine, the rocky ground had to be chiseled eighteen inches deep. Once the holes were dug, the demolition teams would set and ready the mines, then re-fill the holes with crushed rock chips, sand and dust. Then they would tamp it down until it settled, fill it again and cover the hole and surrounding area with a smooth covering of fine moon dust to wipe out any footprints. The mines had electronic safeties that could only be armed remotely.

COL Red Fangs had anticipated that mines would be a key element in their defense and brought more than enough with him from Earth. After mining the camp's perimeter, there would be plenty to use elsewhere, if needed. One mine could take out one tank. He knew he had one chance to use them effectively before the enemy was wary of their presence.

The Soviets would most likely set their artillery pieces and tanks initially outside of guntower range, but close enough for artillery. Hopefully, between the mines, artillery and his defensive grid, he could do enough damage to make the Soviets go home. That would give them a chance to both complete a proper post, and harvest any alloy-x scrap left behind by the Soviets.

COL Red Fangs entertained the thought of the Soviet commander positioning his tank over a mine. He decided he had another fate for his enemy and smiled for the first time since he arrived.

The Soviet satellite orbited at an altitude of one hundred kilometers and had an orbital period of two hours. This limited the Soviets' ability to spy on them to ten minutes every two hours. If the job took over one hour and fifty minutes, work could pause and then resume until the satellite passed by the next time. They had to clean up the area and hide the equipment just before each fly-by. The mine construction project had to work carefully around the Soviet satellite's monitoring.

By eleven hundred hours, the construction crew had finished setting up and dialing in the recycler, and the hungry beast was ready to transform scrap and structural alloy-x into a processed product ready to build other vital structures and equipment. Four empty freighters were recycled, and the bulk of the construction crew concentrated on building the factory while part of the crew started assembling the oxygen extraction plant and steel mill.

July 14, 1970—Sixteen Hundred Zulu

The factory was now complete. The equipment based on the alien designs was ready to produce artillery, combat and utility ships. The factory building was also sharing space with the armory and hangar crews. The armory was already equipped to make the weapons modules to arm the offensive hovertanks. The hangar crew was on standby to repair any equipment breakdowns if necessary. Until then, they assisted with building construction. All hands of the construction crew stopped to get ten scavengers built to begin immediate alloy-x salvaging on Frost Crater. The second and third shift tactical operations technicians were lending their technical skills to the building of the scavengers or working on the oxygen extraction plant and steel mill. The tac ops techs were on sixteen hour days: one shift on the bridge, two hours off, then another eight hours helping other crews, then six hours of sleep. The colonel couldn't afford to have any of them falling asleep on the bridge. The post was going up at an unbelievable rate. From a distance, the post looked like a beehive, swarming with busy bees.

July 14, 1970—Eighteen Hundred Zulu

When ten scavengers rolled out of the factory bay, the scavenger crew headed out to the Frost Crater to start the salvage operation. They had just been fed and would bring more food and water with them. Their operation would be non-stop until the Soviets arrived and forcibly shut them down. Knowing they would be utterly exhausted by then, the crew programmed each vehicle to retrace its path back to the post; autopilot would allow them to sleep. There would be no other rack time for this crew until the Soviets put an end to their salvaging.

The construction crew finished building a mobile construction unit. By twenty-one hundred it was up and running, starting to build the guntowers. The factory was beginning to build artillery pieces. The mess crew had cycled all of the workers through supper, and all hands were back at it again. Thankfully none of the equipment had broken down, and so far there were no accidents. COL Red Fangs found that his walks to the coffee pot and the head weren't enough to keep the kinks out of his muscles. He suited up and made a quick inspection on the ground, mostly to stretch his legs.

COL Red Fangs left the ship wearing an impassive expression, but inwardly he was worried. It was going to be difficult to deal with twenty artillery pieces and fifty-five tanks. It would be calling it very close. When the Soviets arrived, he needed enough artillery to destroy their artillery battery, and a strong enough defensive grid and tanks to defend their post during the post siege. Salvaging of alloy-x from the battlefield would favor the Americans because it was very close to their post. But—they had to survive first. *If we win, we can recycle the Soviets' scrap and some of their hardware to build the proper post,* he thought. *If we lose, there will be nothing to worry about.* He found his executive officer overseeing the construction of the guntowers.

"LTC Judgment Day, a word with you."

"Sir, yes sir."

"I fully expect COL Glaskov to call when he arrives to offer terms of surrender or meet with us to do so." COL Red Fangs pondered the timing for a moment. "What would you do if you were the Soviet commander arriving with forty-five tanks and no artillery for three days, with the enemies' post so heavily fortified that you couldn't conduct a successful siege?"

His executive officer considered the question. "I'd offer terms of surrender, note that pending doom awaits, and play mind games with you for three days until my artillery arrives. Then I'd destroy your artillery and defensive grid, and charge in with an impressive number of tanks. I certainly would harass you so that it would be difficult for you to sleep."

The colonel frowned, "Yes, that's what I'd do. What are the chances we can entice some of their men to defect?"

"In a cheap American b-movie, perhaps. In reality, it isn't likely. They're the best of the best, and they've been carefully trained politically. It would take time to capture and *re-educate* them, and time is a commodity in short supply."

"I'll trust your assessment since you've spent a lot of time in Soviet studies. At twenty-two thirty give the entire crew six hours of rack time, with the exception of the tac ops boys on duty on the bridge."

"Sir, yes sir." The colonel left his first officer to his work and returned to the command vessel's bridge.

July 14, 1970—Twenty-Two Thirty Zulu

COL Red Fangs headed to his quarters, private but very small, consisting of only a table and chair, a bed and a small locker. The three command officers and the freighter captains were the only ones with private rooms.

After taking a sailor's shower and getting dressed for bed, he inserted a Chuck Berry cassette into his tape player and pressed play. The music played in the background. He usually read from *The Art of War* before retiring, but he was too beat. He fell into a deep sleep. The strong, loud sound of his snoring competed with the music.

"Deep down Louisiana close to New Orleans
Way back up in the woods among the evergreens
There stood a log cabin made of earth and wood
Where lived a country boy named Johnny B. Goode
Who never ever learned to read or write so well
But he could play the guitar just like a ringing a bell
Go, go Johnny go, go…"

LTC Judgment Day retired to his quarters. He readied himself for bed and put in one of his favorite cassettes, one by Credence Clearwater Revival. He opened the first of his Old Milwaukees and tried to relax. Their weight limit was tight for personal possessions, but he made it a priority to get a six-pack in his baggage, which afforded him one beer per night. They should last until after the encounter with the Soviets. Wondering if he had overlooked any preparation for the Soviets' arrival tomorrow, he changed for bed. The words of the song caught his attention.

"I see the bad moon arising.
I see trouble on the way.
I see earthquakes and lightnin'.
I see bad times today.
Don't go around tonight,

Well, it's bound to take your life,
There's a bad moon on the rise."

That's all I need, he thought. After changing the tape with another one
from Neil Diamond, he felt a little better as the music began to play…

"Where it began, I can't begin to know when
But then I know it's growing strong
Oh, wasn't the spring, whooo
And spring became the summer
Who'd believe you'd come along
Hands, touching hands, reaching out
Touching me, touching you Oh, sweet Caroline…"

After finishing his beer, the post's first officer called it a night and hit the
rack.

July 15, 1970—Zero Five Hundred Zulu

SGT P-38 had the post ahead in his sights. He screwed the lid back on his
thermos after pouring a cup. He shook the sleep out of his eyes, blinked and
nearly pinched himself. It wasn't a dream, he decided. Taking a sip, he
wondered again for the hundredth time if he would see his mother and
Billings, MT ever again. He pulled into the recycler bay, unloaded the
precious cargo, and turned right back around to the scrap field again. COL
Red Fangs viewed the whole scene with pleasure, beginning to see some
encouraging signs in this tight setup.

"1LT Boolean? What's the estimated time the Soviet tank regiment will
arrive?"

"Sir, if you mean at this post, they're due west of our position, and
estimated arrival is twenty-four and one-half hours. Twenty-three hours, if
they stop just outside of artillery range."

July 15, 1970—Zero Seven Hundred Zulu

The colonel opened up a link to his first officer. "What's our artillery
piece count?"

"Colonel, I'll have our first artillery ready to deploy in one-half hour. We
should have enough ready by the time the Soviets arrive to make them think
twice about an early charge."

"Very good! We will also need two tanks."

"Sir, yes sir."

"What does the alloy-x inventory look like?"

"Sir, the scavengers just did their first offload, and are just about to leave for the Frost Crater. With what we have now, we can build two tanks, a total of five artillery pieces, one forward observer vehicle, about a half-dozen spy drones. When they return from their next offload, there will be alloy-x to build more tanks."

"Very good." The first officer called up the command sergeant major.

"Sir, yes sir."

"First priority... I need more artillery pieces ASAP. After that, I need two tanks built."

"Sir, yes sir."

The command sergeant major had their tanks ready by zero eight hundred.

July 16, 1970—Zero hundred Thirty Zulu

"1LT Boolean?" asked CPT Watchful Eye.

"Sir, yes sir."

"We've completed wiring the radar array. Once you run the software you should be up and running."

"Very good, sir."

"Roger that Watchful Eye, Boolean out." The captain set up the software on his end and all diagnostics passed. They now had "eyes on the ground" and didn't have to wait for the satellite. True, it wasn't long range enough to see the advancing artillery, but it could keep track of the Soviets. COL Red Fangs would be very pleased.

The first five artillery pieces set up under the shadow of the guntowers. The men didn't have coordinates for a firing solution, but armed with high explosive shells, they loaded the barrel's breech in readiness for the Soviet attack. They didn't remain in the big gun, but went back to work in the factory. They would be ready at a minute's notice for a "scramble" if needed.

July 16, 1970—Zero Two Thirty Zulu

COL Red Fangs joined his first officer at breakfast. At present, the only way to keep command discussions private on Luna at present was to meet in the cargo hold on the command vessel and close the door. The colonel pulled up a box, laid his tray on it and sat on another sturdy looking box that looked as if it would support his weight. Looking through the file again, he considered what he would be discussing with his XO in their pre-battle strategy meeting.

"Good morning, sir."

"Good morning." He took a sip of hot coffee, a fork full of reconstituted scrambled eggs, then a bite out of a biscuit, and opened his file. He gave his XO time to pray and make the catholic sign of the cross before disturbing him. The colonel was respectful of his men's beliefs. When he saw he was through, he continued.

"Let's get down to business. Status report?"

"Sir, forty-five Soviet tanks will arrive due west of our position at approximately zero four hundred. Ten more of their tanks are flying escort for their artillery. Our two tanks have been built and armed and are ready to meet the Soviet delegation. The defensive grid was completed while we slept, and the radar array is fully operational. We have five artillery pieces deployed on the line. It is enough to keep them at bay for now. The steel mill and oxygen extraction plant are both expected to be fully operational by zero six hundred. We can't recycle any of the freighters until the post HQ is built. Our scavenger crew is expected to unload and leave back for the Frost crater by zero four hundred."

"Very good! As soon as the steel mill is online, have them start constructing a post HQ/barracks as soon as possible. Make it submarine-tight, Colonel; don't waste an inch of space. When are the freighters with the fittings and fixtures for the new building due?"

"On our next fleet of six ships. ETA July 17, seventeen hundred."

"Very good."

"Colonel, I dropped by tactical operations before getting breakfast. Software has been installed on both of our tanks, and we will be able to control the minefield detonation. We will have discriminator circuits on all of our tanks and equipment so we can't set them off. The technician I spoke with said that the mines could be set to exclude a specific target, and I wondered why we would want to do that."

"Good, depending on how the battle goes, we may have to prioritize whom we want to live or die among the Soviet command staff."

LTC Judgment Day served in Vietnam with COL Red Fangs and knew when something was a little off-kilter. As his first officer and devil's advocate, he knew it was his duty to get to the bottom of this.

"Sir, exactly whom should we mark among the Soviet command staff as a high or low-priority target, sir?"

"First of all, COL Glaskov's total victory over Eagle 1 has given him a tentative promotion to the politburo. Secondly, LTC Averbukh is deemed to be an even more difficult adversary should we kill COL Glaskov, or he gets promoted to post commander after COL Glaskov leaves. Thirdly, in a tank charge, MAJ Cherenkov is the highest-priority target. He's a hard charger, and in a post siege, the men will follow him to the death without hesitation."

LTC Judgment Day digested the facts, but had a nagging feeling something was left out.

"Sir, with all due respect, we've served together for a long time. What are you not telling me?"

COL RED Fangs face flushed red, and the vein on the side of his head was swollen, resembling an angry red worm. He'd seen that look before, back in Vietnam when they found some of their men's mutilated bodies the VC had tortured.

"COL Cavender was my friend. He was a fine marine. The men of the Black Dogs Battalion were all fine marines. I'll be damned if I let COL Glaskov get promoted for killing them!" he growled. The mask was off now, and the deep emotions he was hiding over the fall of Eagle 1 were now laid open like a festering wound.

"So, you want to kill him?"

"No! I want to let him live!" Suddenly it occurred to the first officer that his boss had been plotting this out in intricate detail.

"I'm your first officer, and I can't help you if I don't know your mind."

"Very well. Yes, I'll kill him someday, but not now. I fully intend to make him suffer. I want to kill his first and second officers, repel his siege of our post, and recover most of the alloy-x. If I'm right, we will have enough alloy-x to supply the landing team at Mars. In short, I want him to suffer the humiliation of failure, and have his politburo appointment withdrawn. I want him to live for a time with the bitter taste of failure in his mouth. Then when he's suffered enough…"

"And then you'll kill him?" The tension drained out of the colonel's face. He smiled for the first time.

"And then I'll kill him!"

His first officer knew that this had become personal. In truth, he too had been changed by the unfolding events of the end of Eagle 1. Even with the personal motives, they could achieve all of their objectives with this plan. Their orders were to dig in, establish a post and survive the assault on their new post.

"Understood. Sir, if I think your motivations are counterproductive at some point?"

"Then it would be your duty to point that out. Now, do you have any counsel to make this happen?"

"Yes, sir. I'd keep the scavengers gathering scrap on the Frost Crater until the Soviet tanks are dispatched to the intercept them. I'd then pull them in and refit them as minelayers loaded with proximity mines and redfield generators. This will remove the radar signature from the minelayers so that they can do their work undetected. It will be dark this afternoon for the next two weeks. Wait until the next Soviet satellite blackout window. Have the minelayers swing wide north and behind the Soviet lines and mine several of the small craters in the direct path of their artillery. With any luck, we should be able to take out a couple artillery pieces and a tank or two. When they return, refit them again as scavengers for scrap recovery on the battlefield.

Then finally, when all other vital projects are complete, prepare the *backdoor surprise*."

The colonel thought about it for a moment. "Good, I like it. Be ready to implement that plan when we can't salvage any more alloy-x. Concerning the mines—set the mines in the mine holes to ignore COL Glaskov. Only take him out if he breaches our post defenses personally. If he makes it within range of our guntowers, he's fair game for snipers, tanks or anything else."

"We'll need his heat signature."

"I know. If we knew one another, COL Glaskov would call to offer terms of surrender over the radio. I suspect since he doesn't know anything about us, he'll press for a meeting instead, to size us up. We will get his heat signature during the meeting. Even more, I want to hold off his attacking our scavengers as long as I can. Every piece of alloy-x scrap is vital. Bob, what do you think COL Glaskov will want to say at the meeting?"

"Probably offer us mercy if we surrender, noting what happened to the first American post."

"What would you respond to that?" asked COL Red Fangs.

"I'd refuse, of course."

"I agree. Think of something original and have it ready."

"I'll have something ready for the meeting."

"Glaskov will be calling me when he arrives at zero four hundred. I'll purposely be busy and unable to take his call. That should show disrespect and get him a little upset. No sense in looking too eager to meet."

"I agree, sir."

July 16, 1970—Zero Four Hundred Zulu

The Soviet commander arrived, positioning his tank regiment to the west, just outside of the American artillery range, and hailed the Americans.

"This is COL Glaskov. I wish to speak with the American commander."

"COL Red Fangs isn't on the bridge. I'll have him paged to call you," informed 1LT Boolean.

Red Fangs? He has got to be joking! "Very well." He then abruptly terminated the call.

July 16, 1970—Zero Four Thirty Zulu

COL Red Fangs sat his third cup of coffee on his workstation on the bridge. He'd already spoken with CPT Watchful Eye and was aware of the Soviet colonel's call, and the fact that he sounded about as hostile as his ex-wife.

"Captain, get COL Glaskov on the horn."

"Sir, yes sir." The captain transferred the call to the colonel's workstation. "COL Glaskov, this is COL Red Fangs, returning your call. What can I do for you?"

"I would like to meet with you and your first officer to discuss the terms of your surrender."

"Very well, I'll have a bioshelter constructed outside of our guntower range. I estimate you can make it here in one and one-half hours. It is now zero four thirty Zulu. We can meet at zero six thirty."

"Very good."

July 16, 1970—Zero Five Ten Zulu

PVT Badger scooped up another shovel of rocky lunar dirt with his backhoe bucket, swung it around and deposited its load into the bed of the mining truck. He scraped the ground with the teeth of the bucket on the retractable arm of his rig to loosen some more dirt, and then stopped to check a chip light. It indicated trouble with the cooling system that protected the computer and battery from the extreme lunar heat. He radioed his walking boss.

"CSM Rainmaker, I have a chip light on the cooling system."

"Take your backhoe into the factory's mechanic bay. I'll get a crew to meet you to repair it."

"Yes, sir." Getting the oxygen extraction plant and steel mill up was to no avail, if the earth moving equipment was not operational. He turned the rig around and drove his tracked excavator back to the repair bay. The heavy equipment repair crew was already there when he arrived. PVT Badger shut the machine down and the lead technician, SGT Journeyman was quick to start work diagnosing the problem. He took his meter out and started troubleshooting sections of the cooling system to isolate where the trouble was. Within five minutes, he had the answer. CSM Rainmaker was nearby to get the earliest status.

"What's the verdict, Sergeant?"

"Sir, the compressor failed, sir." The command sergeant major was irritated that he had a breakdown on brand new equipment. They'd paid a premium to have them manufactured and tested to the highest military specifications.

"You have a spare compressor; get it back up and digging."

"Sir, right away, sir." The repair team had the old compressor out and the new one installed in record time. PVT Badger was back digging again. They were only down for twenty minutes.

COMPANY CALLS

July 16—Zero Six Thirty Zulu

COL Boris Glaskov knew he didn't have the resources yet to take the American post. The American commander would see that and would no doubt refuse terms of surrender. He had arranged the meeting so he could study the man and get a sense of whom he was fighting, above anything else. Usually he would be studying the man's files, but he didn't even have his picture, much less a file on him. He was alone in his tank, flying to meet with the American. Glaskov put some water into a metal cup, stuck the "stinger" into it and listened to the water hiss as he boiled water for a cup of tea. The stinger made a hiss as he dropped it in the teacup, the water made bubbling noises while it heated the water. After steeping his tea, he pondered what kind of man he had for an adversary. *Well*, he thought, *I will know soon enough.*

MEETING THE SOVIET COMMANDERS

COL Red Fangs, his aide PVT Ancillary and his executive officer flew to the bioshelter, entered the airlock, and took off their helmets. Their Soviet counterparts weren't there yet, but radar confirmed their ETA was four minutes. The post commander addressed his first officer.

"Well Bob, have you figured out our response to the Soviets?"

"Yes sir, I thought we should say no, politely of course.

"What kind of answer is that? You know the meeting is recorded and sent to ASDC Command. I wanted a more memorable quote."

"I wouldn't eat more than one slice of chocolate cake." His eyes twinkled, revealing that he was withholding the punch line, but wanting the colonel to ask for it.

"What's special about this cake?"

"I was telling the mess sergeant it was a pity we couldn't poison them, and he offered a solution which allows us to keep our honor as officers and gentlemen."

"Which was?"

"He sweetened the cake with applesauce, pureed prunes and figs, and added a very strong chocolate to mask the other flavors." LTC Judgment Day retrieved a bottle of Pepto-Bismol from his pants pocket and began the shake it vigorously.

"You rascal! Since it's untainted food, it isn't a violation to feed it to them, especially when we're eating it, too."

"Yes, sir. The best way to poison your enemy is to drink out of the same cup they do. Providing, of course, you have the antidote."

"How much does the mess sergeant say we need?"

"A triple dose, just don't eat a second slice." The colonel laughed at the thought. "I'll bet that messes up their astronaut diapers."

"Yes, sir. The mess sergeant assures me it works in about one-half hour, very suddenly with very little warning."

"I wonder where he learned that trick?"

"The mess sergeant said he learned that from one of his drinking buddies in 'Nam, another marine cook. It just so turns out his commander was a surly character who mistreated his men and the cook afflicted him thusly from time to time. The poor colonel thought he was suffering from bad water or bacteria." COL Red Fangs search his memory to see if he suffered from the runs while in Vietnam and decided it must have been another commander.

"We'd better be nice to him," he said, smiling.

"But seriously, I'd like it better if we could poison both of them with something that caused unbearably agonizing torment that lasted at least three days."

His first officer thought about Eagle 1. He considered such an act, and though tempting, knew it was not honorable. "Yes sir, me too."

Both men dosed themselves up for the dessert at the meeting, hid the medicine bottle and waited for the Soviets.

July 16, 1970—Zero Six Thirty Zulu

The Soviets arrived at precisely zero six thirty. The colonel's aide was finishing the final preparations. A coffee pot was busy percolating next to the chocolate cake on a table to the side of the conference table. The Soviets killed the jets to their hovertanks, and a cloud of fine lunar dust filled the "air" over them. The Soviet commander and his first officer entered the meeting room after the outside door of the foyer was closed. As the Americans rose to their feet, COL Red Fangs greeted their guests.

"Good evening, Colonel, please remove your helmets and make yourself comfortable." He motioned to the second spare table as the place where they could lay their helmets.

"Thank you," replied COL Glaskov. With that the two Soviets removed their helmets and placed them on the offered table.

"Coffee?" the American commander offered.

"Yes please," he answered, eyeing the cake on the table. The server poured both Soviets a hot cup of coffee, placing cream and sugar on the table. COL Glaskov put a spoonful of sugar in his cup, but his first officer added a little cream, no sugar. They were both tea drinkers, but COL Glaskov had developed an appreciation for coffee when he was posted in Georgia close to the Turkish border by the Black Sea. COL Glaskov sipped his coffee, entering into an awkward silence. He didn't have much in the way of small talk to say to the Americans. Elevator talk was being quickly exhausted. Both of them knew the whole purpose was to offer the Americans the terms of surrender and let them make their decision. The Soviets believed that if this American post failed, they wouldn't have any alloy-x to send another landing force. The Soviet satellite on Luna had closely estimated the amount of material the Americans had shipped back to Earth for the Mars post construction.

The Soviet commander began, "I do not have pleasant words to say to you. I thank you for the coffee, but I am here on business. I am offering you the terms of your surrender. We will spare your lives if you surrender unconditionally. We will take possession of your post and all of your equipment and resources. If you cooperate fully, you will be transported home to a neutral country where you will all be free to go, provided you swear never to return."

COL Red Fangs glanced at his executive officer. "With all due respect, we cannot accept your offer."

71

"Then you will all die, just like the first Americans."

"Perhaps, but we will keep our honor and fight you with all of the resources we possess. We believe we have a strong enough defense to hold off your attack."

"We have artillery and more tanks coming."

"The answer is still no," he replied calmly.

The Soviet rose to his feet and slammed his palm on the table. "Then you will all die!"

LTC Judgment Day lifted an eyebrow and looked at his commander. To his credit, COL Red Fangs seemed calm, most likely enjoying the idea of the Soviets changing their astronaut diapers. The American commander calmly nodded.

"We may be enemies, but I respect you. Since we now know where we all stand, then this meeting is concluded. Would you like some more coffee? I had my mess sergeant bake us a cake, which would be a shame to waste just because we can't come to terms."

"Are you attempting to poison me?"

"No, if I'd wanted to do that, I'd have put it in the sugar and cream while we took our coffee black. I have four slices cut. You can choose your pieces; we will eat the slices you don't choose." The Soviet delegation relaxed a little and decided that a freshly baked dessert would be okay, a diplomatic courtesy. They chose two of the slices and had another cup of coffee. The server had cut the small cake into six slices, so there were two left over when the four men were served.

"This is very good, I have never tasted cake so moist," commented the Soviet commander. His executive officer agreed, in between bites, and sips of coffee. Finally, they were all through eating and drinking.

"We only get one chance to act toward one another in a civilized manner," said COL Red Fangs. "Why don't you finish off the last of the cake? The next time we meet we will be trying to kill each other."

The Soviets had the last two pieces with another cup of coffee, put on their helmets and departed back to their line. The American construction crew broke down the meeting room unmolested and returned back to the post. COL Red Fangs smiled trying to imagine the two Soviet command officers changing their diapers on the way back. Maybe there was nothing memorable to quote for the historical record, but they would laugh about this for years.

On the trip back to the Soviet front line, suddenly and without warning, COL Glaskov lost control of his bowels. COL Glaskov fumed as he cleaned himself up, wondering if it were a deliberate act of the Americans. He radioed his first officer. "LTC Averbukh?"

"Comrade Colonel, I cannot talk. I seemed to have eaten something that disagreed with me."

"Did you have to change your underwear?"

"Yes, Comrade Colonel."

"It seems we have been tricked! We have obviously not been poisoned, but the Americans have made sport of us!" With that, he terminated the radio call.

It was zero seven fifteen and the first shift was on duty. COL Red Fangs arrived at the bridge, and his technicians rose and saluted. "Captain, did you isolate and log the heat signatures of the two Soviet officers' tanks?"

"Yes, sir," CPT Watchful Eye said, cracking a smile. "Got 'em dead to rights, sir."

"Excellent! As you were, then. Make the information accessible to all artillery teams, defensive positions, forward observers and spy drones. I want to know where these three are at all times on the battlefield."

2LT Surveillance addressed the commander. "Colonel, I have the Soviet commander on the horn, and he is quite upset."

"Patch him through to my station."

"Sir, yes sir." COL Red Fangs answered the call. "Good afternoon, COL Glaskov. Have you reconsidered and are calling to surrender?"

"I will take much pleasure in killing you." This was followed by a sharp click, announcing the call was terminated abruptly.

The post commander called his first officer. "I thought I should let you know. The cake kicked in, and he's upset," laughed COL Red Fangs. "It isn't botulism, but it will have to do. Well done, Bob."

"Sir, thank you, sir."

CPT Watchful Eye addressed his commander. "COL Red Fangs, sir?"

"Yes, Captain?"

"Sir, two squads of Soviet tanks have just left the Soviet line headed in the direction of the Frost Crater."

"Are they within artillery range?"

"Sir, no sir. Their path appears to be following an arc staying just five kilometers outside of artillery range. They appear to want to stop our scrap salvaging and are careful to stay out of artillery range."

"Where's the scavenger crew now?"

"Sir, they've been salvaging at the east rim of the Frost Crater for about thirty minutes. They should leave for Eagle 2 in about ten minutes."

"Scramble the artillery and call the scavenger team back in, now! Put the post on yellow alert status. Scramble the two tanks. Send them to meet the Scavengers."

"Sir, yes sir." He opened a radio link. "Yellow alert, I repeat, Yellow alert! Artillery scramble! This is not a drill! LTC Judgment Day, report to the bridge." He called the Scavenger crew on the radio. "All scavenger units return to post now at full speed. MAJ Loki and CPT Ares—scramble to escort the scavengers home." All teams had been on alert and were waiting on the call.

"On my way," replied LTC Judgment Day.

"Roger that, Eagle 2," replied SGT P-38.

"Roger wilco," responded MAJ Loki. Within two minutes, MAJ Loki and CPT Ares were travelling at top speed to rendezvous with the scavenger crew.

All six artillery crews scrambled quickly to man the big guns. They'd been warned this might happen and had already set four of them up in the direction of the Soviet line; the rest were aimed at their squads. Only one forward observer vessel had been built. SGT Monitor was flying out immediately to get a target fix on the Soviets. If their squads decided to change their mind about attacking the American scavengers, he had to get a firing solution ready.

SGT P-38's crew started back to the post with his precious cargo. He knew that the scrap they carried would make a difference in the post's survival.

July 16, 1970—Zero Seven Thirty Zulu

LTC Judgment Day was on the bridge taking over the artillery battery with the assistance of CPT Watchful Eye and 2LT Surveillance. COL Red Fangs busied himself watching the progress of the post construction. 1LT Boolean was summoned to the bridge to take up a work station to assist COL Red Fangs, and to keep an eye on the Soviet front line. The light on COL Red Fang's workstation announced that he had an incoming call from MAJ Termination, the construction foreman replacing CSM Rainmaker.

"Yes, Major."

"Sir, the oxygen extraction plant is complete and producing. The steel plant is likewise up and rolling."

"Very good, get the steel mill rolling out the parts to construct a proper post barracks/HQ. Once that's up, build a fire direction center building. It's time to build stuff out of something other than alloy-x."

"Sir, yes sir." SGT Monitor was within range of the Soviet tanks and completed laser sightings, and measured speed and direction of travel of several of the tanks in the Soviet squad. The Soviets were still holding their course, just out of range of the American big guns. He radioed the readings back to the bridge.

"Sir, the Soviets are staying out of range, no firing solution."

"Very well."

July 16, 1970—Zero Eight thirty Zulu

"Sir, LTC Judgment Day, the Soviet squads have reached the Frost Crater and are holding their position. Our scavengers will be back to the post by ten hundred hours."

"Very good. Cancel the yellow alert. Get the artillery crew back to work, but keep an eye on the Soviets."

"Sir, yes sir." The captain sounded the orders on all channels. "Yellow alert is canceled, all hands return to their workstations."

July 16, 1970—Zero Nine Hundred Zulu

LTC Judgment Day's demolition team was rigging the natural staircase to blow fissures wide enough that the Soviet hovertanks couldn't span across them. These wouldn't be blown unless the Soviets retreated before getting stuck on the MTS mines. The preferred plan was to have the Soviet tanks trapped by the powerfully magnetic MTS mines and take the tanks intact and the pilots alive. The mines would be remote controlled to ensure all of the enemy ships would get into position before they were locked down. If that didn't work, though, he would blow the ledge and drop it on top of them, as the mines had been strategically placed just below the heavy rock ledge. If the pilots started popping out of their tanks to use a tool to try to dislodge and destroy the mines, snipers from above would get them.

July 16, 1970—Fourteen Ten Zulu

MAJ Termination hailed the first officer. "Sir, The scavengers have finished their refit, and have just left to go place the mines."

"Excellent! How much scrap do we have?"

"Sir, if we build nothing but artillery pieces, we will run out of scrap by seventeen hundred today. By then the temporary post HQ structure will be finished, and our fittings, fixtures and equipment to finish the permanent HQ should be arriving by freighter. Once we have the environmental systems and lighting up at post HQ, we can unload the four ships we're living out of and recycle them to make the last few artillery pieces and a couple of tanks."

"Very good, as you were."

"Sir, yes sir."

July 16, 1970—Seventeen Hundred Zulu

Morale was an element of management just as well as food, equipment and weapons. The fact that the Americans had held all of the Soviets outside of artillery range was a victory of sorts. It bought them time to get ready for the attack that would surely come when the Soviet big guns arrived. COL Red Fangs decided that he wouldn't take his supper on the bridge, but with the men in one of the freighters serving food. For the first time since being there, he was feeling optimistic about the siege to come. He hailed his first officer. "Bob, join me for supper."

"Sir, yes sir. Be there in ten." The mess crew was serving spaghetti and meatballs, hard biscuits, fruit cocktail, and hot coffee. The redeeming quality of the spaghetti was that if you dumped enough hot sauce on it, it was edible. COL Red Fangs decided that if they lived through this experience, he would press for better grub. His first officer grabbed a tray and sat down, prayed and made the sign of the cross. "Here, try some good old Louisiana hot sauce. It makes the spaghetti bearable," he said.

"No, thank you, sir, I never developed a taste for it."

"That's right, I forgot. Yankees don't eat the stuff. In Texas, they just put a baby nipple on the hot sauce bottle and hand it to the kids when they run out of milk." The post's first officer was glad to see his commander joking again. Having the men see him laugh was good for morale.

"Status report?"

"Sir, the minelayers left to mine the path of the advancing Soviet artillery at fourteen hundred fifteen this afternoon. We now have nine artillery pieces on the line. We started building steel for the main post HQ building at ten hundred. The oxygen extraction plant is operational and is able to produce the oxygen we need for the main post HQ building and anything else."

"Any indication that the Soviets are sending anyone around to our back door?"

"Sir, no sir. So far our satellite has accounted for all of the enemies' tanks either escorting the artillery, at the Frost Crater, or on the Soviet front line."

"Keep an eye on them. We need some of the tanks to split off and make a run for our back door. It won't be good for us if they don't take the bait." The colonel finished his meal, excused himself and went back to the bridge until it was time for bed.

July 16, 1970—Eighteen Thirty Zulu

COL Red Fangs retired to his quarters and read for a while from *The Art of War*. He came to a passage of interest. "The siege of a city is only done as a last resort." Master Sun.

Red Fangs consider the maxim by Master Sun and considered his situation. The last resort? For the Soviets, there was only one choice. Soon the Soviets siege on the American post would settle once and for all if the Americans could stay here. He placed a cassette tape in his player, took off his shoes and lay down on the bed. The Credence Clearwater Revival version of *The Midnight Special* played while he thought about the meeting.

"Well, you wake up in the mornin'
you hear the work bell ring.
And they march you to the table
to see the same old thing.
Ain't no food upon the table
and no pork up in the pan.
But you better not complain, boy
you get in trouble with the man.

Let the Midnight Special shine 'er light on me,
Let the Midnight Special shine 'er light on me,
Let the Midnight Special shine 'er light on me,
Let the Midnight Special shine 'er everlovin' light on me."

As the music continued to play, he fell into a deep sleep. His cassette played until the tape ran out.

LTC Judgment Day had gotten the Tigers–Cubs baseball game from last Sunday downloaded from the satellite and was enjoying the game in his quarters over a cold beer. The only thing better would be to watch it with his little brother. The game was a much needed distraction to help him unwind so he could focus later on the unfolding events ahead. His hometown team the Detroit Tigers, won 3–2, and he hit the rack.

July 16, 1970—Twenty hundred Zulu

The Lunar steel plant had completed building the structural steel for the shell of post HQ. The construction team moved quickly to put up the structure right next to the water and fuel tankers. The barracks were Chiefly constructed of tungsten steel, a by-product of the oxygen extraction plant. Once the shell was put up, the construction crew would weld the seams and stress test the welds. All of the outside fittings would be welded into place, and finally the structure would be sprayed with fireproof insulating foam two feet thick, then when it set would be sprayed again with a heat reflective finish. The building wouldn't be complete until the final environmental equipment and interior fittings would arrive on July 17, seventeen hundred.

July 17, 1970—Zero Hundred Thirty Zulu

COL Red Fangs washed the sleep out of his eyes, shaved, brushed his teeth, got dressed, and headed for the bridge. Now, that the brief but tense moment over the scavengers had passed, the calm before the storm continued. 1LT Boolean didn't have anything unusual to report. His first officer joined him on the bridge for their daily meeting and to share breakfast in private. Both men grabbed their cups of coffee and breakfast trays, made their way back to the cargo hold and took a seat. COL Red Fangs held his peace in quietness as LTC Judgment Day prayed silently. His first officer finished by making the sign of the cross, and looked up.

COL Red Fangs took the lid off of his coffee cup, blew on it and had a sip of the dark, bitter liquid. "Status report?"

"We now have ten artillery pieces on the line. Our next fleet of six ships is to arrive at zero four hundred today with our last one hundred and twenty men, equipment and supplies. The minelayers are still out. In that regard, no news is good news since they're on radio silence running in redfield mode and haven't radioed a distress call. In any case, everything is running on or ahead of schedule, with two days until the artillery battle."

The post commander was silent. He knew full well he would lose most if not all of the sixty-four men of the artillery counter-battery during the Soviet attack. These men were cross-trained and highly skilled in other areas and not easy to replace, not to mention the values of their lives. He could see no other way to defend this post, but knowing that wasn't making him feel any better. Regret hung thick in the air like cigarette smoke in a Subic Bay bar, and his first officer sensed what he was thinking.

"I don't want to lose any of the men either. We will go to any lengths to minimize the losses," injected LTC Judgment Day. COL Red Fangs smiled as he remembered a quote by GEN Patton. "Yes, let's see what we can do about getting the Soviets to die for their country, rather than our men."

"That will remain my priority, but even so, I expect the losses to be extreme."

"Make sure all of the men have the opportunity to go to church services the morning the Soviet artillery battery arrives if they wish."

"Yes, sir."

July 17, 1970—Fourteen Hundred Zulu

The two squads of minelayers had returned and were in the process of being refitted back to scavengers. COL Red Fangs was watching the activity over his monitor with keen interest. The refitted scavengers would recover scrap from the artillery pieces lost during the artillery barrage. His second crew of men was eating breakfast now, and when done, all three hundred sixty men would be on duty at once, at least for a couple more hours. The pieces were all falling into place, and destiny was calling in two more days.

The Soviets had broken off into four units of hovertanks and were doing routine patrols just outside of the perimeter of the American artillery range. The action had two purposes. The Soviets didn't want any alloy-x salvaging going on, or anyone leaving the post to attack the artillery escort arriving on the 18th. It also gave the men something to do; COL Glaskov didn't want them getting lazy from inactivity. The Soviets tanks swarmed like bees just outside of the American artillery range. Watching them day after day would take its toll on the men inside the post; the psychological warfare was every bit a weapon as his artillery or tanks.

He looked up from the report he was reading and smiled. He remembered as a boy the day he cornered a fox in his hole and how a few smoking leaves brought him out of that hole and into his bag. He hoped that the American would not surrender—he would take much pleasure in killing him.

The Soviet commander opened a communiqué from Moscow confirming his appointment to the politburo after the end of the campaign against the Americans. This called for a cup of tea, which he brewed while listening to the song "Zhenshchina, Kotoraya Poyot," by his favorite Russian artist Alla Pugacheva.

July 17, 1970—Fifteen Hundred Zulu

The Americans had the shell of their post HQ up. They were waiting for the transports to deliver the fixtures to finish the inside, as well as the environmental equipment to regulate the temperature and air pressure. The next fleet of ships would have all the fixtures they needed and most of the post's men would be working to finish the interior construction.

The Soviet patrols had missed the minelayers, but the Soviet artillery escort didn't know that. MAJ Ilya Tarasov of the artillery battery escort was keeping a close watch on his detail to make sure the Americans hadn't planned any surprises for them. To lose even one artillery piece would end in a demotion for him. He'd been here since the Soviet post was constructed and had participated in obliterating the first American post. With care, they should repeat their success, and the Americans would be through on Luna forever. They weren't restricted to radio silence but were using an encrypted channel. By zero five hundred hours on the nineteenth he should have his detail safely to the front lines to start destroying the hated Americans. The landscape was boringly the same on this side of Luna, flat terrain with a thin brown layer of moon dust that kicked up in a small dust cloud when they passed by, and pock-marked with trillions of craters, some very wide and deep and others very small and shallow.

The Soviet detail was flying with tanks in front, back and sides of the artillery, ever watchful of possible attack from the Americans. MAJ Tarasov's last communiqué from the Soviet commander assured him that the Americans were cowering behind their defensive grid and were no threat. But, the major was sure the Americans weren't cowards. He'd seen that in the siege of Eagle 1. A cook had shot three of his best men with a handgun before going down. The notion that they were just cowering behind their defensive grid and doing nothing made him uneasy.

The proximity mine's triggers were set so that the ones in front couldn't be triggered by the smaller mass of a hovertank. This was done so that the lead tanks would drive over the front mines without triggering them. The artillery pieces with more mass would trigger the front mines, while the lead tanks would trigger the more sensitive mines further up. The moon shook violently under them when two tanks and an artillery piece were blown apart. No noise was made, but men seasoned in lunar warfare were accustomed to it. The officer in charge of the detail, MAJ Tarasov, was killed instantly, along with his wingman.

The next in charge was CPT Yakov Dvorkin, who called a complete halt to the detail. "Back up and leave the exact way that we came in. Once we are five kilometers due east, we will halt, and I will lead you to the front line."

The Soviet detail carefully reversed their paths, and their new unit leader took them an hour north, to plot a new course to the front line. His best friend and unit leader had paid the price for carelessness with his life. COL Glaskov would be angry that an artillery piece was lost. Still, with no other losses of the big guns or their tanks, they should be able to beat the Americans.

"Sir, our satellite just passed over the Soviet artillery battery."

"Well?"

"I'm sorry sir. The Soviet artillery count is now nineteen pieces led by eight tanks." He turned around and grinned. "It looks as though they lost a big gun and two tanks at the minefield, sir. The Soviets have deployed twenty tanks from their line to rendezvous with them. The artillery will be an extra hour and a half delayed to the line. They took a detour after being hit."

"Very good, inform my first officer."

"Sir, yes sir."

July 18, 1970—Zero Eight Hundred Zulu

The factory had finished building the artillery pieces. The count was seventeen armored *M110L (Lunar) hovercraft powered self-propelled howitzers*, with a barrel length of forty-five calibers, firing 155mm HE shells. COL Red Fangs hoped this counter artillery battery would do the job of neutralizing the Soviet artillery barrage, when it came. He knew such a battle of two nearly equal artillery forces would result in extreme losses of men and equipment on both sides. Since there was no cover or high ground for either side, it would be an artillery slugfest until most of the men on both sides were dead. He would wrestle with his conscience later. There was no other way to play this hand.

The factory was now busy building tanks with whatever scrap was found and the estimate was that only three more could be made. COL Red Fangs knew this was cutting it very close. The earlier comparison of Eagle 1 and the Alamo was made to raise the men's fighting spirit. With all of the alloy-x scrap the Soviets harvested from Eagle 1, this was beginning to look like the Alamo. The only hope for survival rested on being able to destroy the Soviet artillery and whittle the Soviet tank regiment down to a number small enough to repel, with five American tanks and their defensive grid. The colonel sighed. They had a big job before them, and timing was everything.

The post HQ building was complete. Within thirty minutes, the terminator would cross their post and plunge them into darkness, dropping the temperature down to -170 °F. The solar array would be out for another two weeks, leaving the fuel-driven generators to provide power for the post HQ until then. The power grid was ready to power the environmental control systems to make the dwelling livable. The electrical and environmental control teams had finished the inside. The new tactical operations room was complete, with all equipment moved in and installed. Some teams were still working on setting up the mess hall and finishing some of the interior. The last four freighters to be recycled were being unloaded. When finished, all construction hands awake and not building tanks or working on the post HQ's interior would be moving in. The command officers had their personal effects moved to their new quarters.

CPT Watchful Eye and 2LT Surveillance stayed on the bridge while 2LT Codecracker and 2LT Algorithm set up and tested the new tactical operations equipment. After equipment testing, and installing software on all workstations, it was time to test all systems. They ran quality tests to the satellite uplink, radar array, surveillance cameras, and the two radios in the working tanks. After proving their workstation computers performed as needed, they routed all surveillance, tactical and command functions to the new tac ops room.

The men quickly unloaded the food, medicine and other supplies from CPT America's command vessel into the post HQ building. CPT America bid his goodbyes, and within minutes the fire and smoke from the freighter *America's* exhausts disappeared into the night sky. Only the barest and most essential things were built until after the Soviet siege could be beaten back. The main focus was on post defense, and meager but livable quarters; the rest would be on beans, bullets and bandages.

July 18, 1970—Fourteen Hundred Zulu

The demolition team used lasers to measure from a "witness line" in the center of the post to each mine hole. The tactical team loaded the coordinates to their computer. Whenever a Soviet tank rested over or crossed it, they would be ready to blow it manually if they wished, or set it to go off if passed over by a target. For now, the mines were armed but had electronic safeties preventing them from going off prematurely. COL Red Fangs would send the electronic command to remove the safeties on them all just before the battle, and decide if he wanted them set to manual or automatic activation. Burying them in solid rock was akin to loading a charge into a cannon: the rock walls being the barrel. The minefield was just outside of guntower range and would help reduce the number of enemy tanks that could threaten the post. Anything that survived the counter artillery battery and the minefields would face the American defensive grid and whatever tanks the Americans could muster. The defensive grid was comprised of artillery, mines, guntowers and gun turrets essential for their survival. Fifty-three tanks had to be reduced to a number the American tanks could handle.

The post's first officer joined his commander in the cargo hold for supper before turning in. LTC Judgment day was carrying his last two beers. "Thank you, Bob. Sit down." He gratefully accepted the beer and pointed to the food cart. His first officer filled his plate and popped the cap off of his beer bottle, found a crate to sit on, prayed and started to eat. COL Red Fangs took a swig of beer, and considered the battle to come. "We should come out with an artillery piece or two left when the Soviets have lost all of theirs. Once the artillery is done with, they will most likely charge us. We will use any remaining artillery to fire upon the invading force. Combined with the heat sensors on the spy drones, we should be able to keep track of all three of their command officers. Status on the back door plan?"

"Done, I have all of the MTS mines deployed on the trail under the ledge. The mines aren't heat-sensitive, but the ledge explosives are. We've done all of the drilling, but since our explosives don't like temperatures above 265 degrees, we've had to wait for the ground to cool. The terminator has now crossed, the temperature has dropped and we've finished placing the ledge charges. When the time comes, I'll have snipers on the ledge in case we need to deal with anyone popping out of the tanks."

"I'd like some prisoners if we can pull it off, but I want all of the tanks intact. Only blow the ledge and drop the rock on them if and only if you can't stop them from getting up the ledge. I repeat; I want those tanks."

"Understood."

"I understand that the Soviets use transponders to keep track of the location of all of their units. If you can capture the tanks, have a crane haul them up, but not until after you remove the transponders. Make sure you don't destroy the transponders. Remove them from the tanks and keep them transmitting from below the ledge."

"Yes sir, I can have the Soviet tank's computer hard drives removed and replaced with one of ours in about thirty-five minutes. We can have multiple teams working simultaneously on several tanks at once. We can have all of the software installed and the controls relabeled in English."

"Very good.

July 18, 1970—Fourteen Thirty Zulu

COL Glaskov had sent twenty tanks to rendezvous with the artillery detail five hundred kilometers east of the front line. Twenty-five tanks stayed at the line, making sure the Americans didn't leave their post. MAJ Maksim Speshiloff relieved CPT Dvorkin of his detail while two of his tanks joined the captain on his mission to flank the Americans. The mission called for ten tanks, and the replacement tanks had been similarly equipped with redfield generators. The redfields could remove their radar signatures from the tanks but couldn't fool the American satellite. The Soviets knew exactly when the American satellite would fly over, and how long it could view them. They used the same technique the American minelayers used, drop into deep craters and pull black heat shield tarps over them until they flew over. It would take approximately eleven hours for the slower artillery detail to arrive at the front lines. Even after stopping for the enemy satellite, the unit flanking the rear should arrive at the American back door at about the same time.

COL Red Fangs had been up for eighteen hours and was about to grab some rack time in his new quarters. This was the last rack time for the first crew before the battle, and all of the construction and preparations for the Soviet attack were complete. He'd given orders to give all personnel eight hours of rack time on their last sleep schedule. He did a neck roll to relieve the stress of sitting in one position staring at a computer all day, yawned, stretched some more and moved toward the door. The private from the mess crew retrieved his tray and dishes.

"Lieutenant?"

"Yes, sir?"

"Keep an eye on the Soviets. I'm going to bed. If they do anything interesting, wake me up."

"Yes, sir."

The colonel hadn't had time to unpack his personal effects, which only amounted to what would fit in his seabag. Personal effects were limited to one seabag, no more than sixty pounds in weight. The colonel's bag contained a King James Bible, a shaving kit, three uniforms, socks, underwear, a small cassette player, and a collection of music tapes, mostly golden oldies from the fifties.

He was not a devout Christian but regarded the Bible's authority with respect. The chaplains brought courage to the men when they prayed before a battle, and comfort to them when they were wounded or dying. He had a Protestant, a Catholic, and a Jewish chaplain on this post, who were also cross-trained to serve as medics.

He had room for only one other book, so he chose *The Art of War*, by Sun Tzu. He wanted the best book of military strategy he could find, and this was it. Sun Tzu stressed adaptability and flexibility in changing battlefield conditions Written in 6 B.C., this was the oldest book on military tactics and strategy to be found, and greatly influenced eastern and western military thinking. He certainly would need to be adaptive and flexible in the events to come.

Tomorrow was going to be the big day. The Soviet artillery should be arriving in just under eleven hours. Getting a good night's sleep would be the key to his clear-headed thinking tomorrow, and he was going to make the most of it. All of the men were being rotated out to get a good night's sleep before the big battle. All the chaplains had reported that they were getting a lot of visits, especially from the artillery battery. The colonel unpacked his personal effects and arranged them in perfect marine precision. The rest of his personal effects would arrive on a later transport once the permanent post HQ was constructed, and there was more room for the men's possessions. He popped an Elvis tape in his cassette recorder and Love Me Tender played in the background.

He opened his book *The Art of War* and read a passage of interest. "Without deception you cannot carry out strategy, without strategy you cannot control your opponent." He turned out the light and resolved to discuss strategy with his XO in the morning. He put away his book, then fell into a deep sleep while Elvis serenaded him.

2LT Codecracker had just returned from the head and picked up two cups of coffee on the way back to the bridge.

2LT Algorithm was staring at the monitor. "Look at this!" He showed the recording of the last satellite flyby, which showed twenty Soviet tanks flying to meet eight tanks flying escort for the nineteen Soviet big guns. Then he brought up the live satellite feed to show eighteen Soviet tanks escorting nineteen artillery pieces. The other ten tanks were nowhere on the radar and the telescoping camera view couldn't find them. "I hate to wake the colonel up, but if he finds out later, they'll be hell to pay."

"Agreed." 2LT Codecracker grinned. "You discovered it; you do the honors."

"I know." 2LT Algorithm's call woke the colonel out of a dead sleep.

"Yes?"

"Colonel, we have something on the satellite."

"What is it?"

"The twenty Soviet tanks that were rendezvousing with the artillery battery?"

"Yes?"

"Sir. Eighteen tanks are leading the artillery to the line, ETA zero five hundred tomorrow."

"Where are the other tens tanks?"

"That's why I called you, sir. They were not on radar on the last pass. They could be hiding in craters, or employing redfields."

"Very good. I'll be on the bridge in five mikes."

"Sir, yes sir."

Col Red Fangs washed the sleep out of his eyes. He was waking up very quickly, and his excitement level was climbing. He was beginning to believe that they would win. He quickly threw on his uniform and headed to the bridge. Both technicians rose to salute as he entered the bridge. "As you were. Let's see what you have, son." He walked over to the young officer's workstation and 2LT Algorithm showed him both replays. COL Red Fangs grunted his approval and ran his finger along the printed map posted nearby. "They're most likely going to the north of Landau through the Wood Crater, then down through landau to the back of our post. I want you to analyze all flyby data, and keep looking for them with the radar, to the east of us, and later tonight toward the north side of Landau. If they don't pop up anywhere, I need you to calculate their probable location at all times. Can you do that?"

"Sir, yes sir. We know what their top speed is, where they're going, and how often and how long they have to drop out of sight when the satellite flies over. Right now they're right about there, he said, tapping the map on his computer screen."

"Very good work, son. Keep me informed of anything interesting."

"Sir, yes sir."

The colonel called his first officer. His call roused his XO out of a deep sleep. "Sir?"

"Bob, twenty Soviet tanks met their artillery escort ten minutes ago about eleven hours east of us, then ten of the twenty-eight tanks dropped off of the radar. Only eighteen tanks are bringing the artillery to the front line."

"Good! So, they're taking the bait, and there are ten of them."

"Get back to bed. I need you sharp for tomorrow's battle."

LTC Judgment Day yawned. "Sir, no problem, sir."

The younger man fell right back into a deep sleep. The post commander terminated the call and left the bridge. He was too excited to sleep, but it was vital that his wits were sharp for the big battle. He suited up and went to the Sick Bay on the next freighter. The medic gave him some sleeping pills that were potent but reputed not to cause groggy aftereffects in the morning. He took the recommended dose and turned on a Dolly Parton music tape. The childlike quaver and soulful delivery of Dolly's voice and the sleeping pills put him back to sleep in twenty minutes.

THE SIEGE OF EAGLE 2

The alarm woke the post's first officer at zero three hundred. It was estimated that the Soviet tank regiment would be knocking on their back door by zero four thirty, and he wanted to be awake for it. He rubbed his eyes and willed his body to comply. He was glad that he was accustomed to six hours of sleep; the pace had been grueling since they arrived. Last night was a luxury, getting eight hours of sleep was helping his body recharge for the day's critical events. After cleaning up and getting dressed, he suited up, save for his helmet and gloves, and headed for the mess hall. Their post's main building wasn't large enough to have a separate mess hall for officers and enlisted men, but there were officers' and enlisted men's tables.

SGT Marches On Stomach already had his crew up making breakfast. The mess hall was already serving some of the men whose jobs required early preparation for the battle ahead. Sniper Det Alpha had been ordered up early to accompany him to the rear of the post to greet their visitors, along with the crew who'd operate the crane, one of whom was a master Russian linguist. LTC Judgment Day found COL Red Fangs picking up a breakfast tray and a cup of coffee, and he followed suit.

"Sleep well?" asked the post commander.

"Yes sir, ready for the day." Sitting down his tray of hash, eggs, hot biscuits and gravy, he carefully placed the strong cup of coffee on the table. The breakfast was the best they had in their stores, for many it would be their last meal.

"I want church services started for all artillery gunners starting zero five hundred. Make sure all of the men who want to go have the opportunity. They need to be concluded with all services by zero seven hundred. By then, the entire artillery line must be ready to engage the enemies' artillery battery."

His first officer nodded. The artillery gunners would be taking breakfast at zero four hundred and the post chaplains, Captains Father Mike, Reverend Joe and Rabbi Aaron were holding their respective services. The chaplains were advised that the casualties on the artillery line were expected to be extreme, and to prepare their services accordingly. All three had served in the US Marines for over twenty years, and always assumed that today might be each man's last day. They took their ministries seriously and were heavy of heart for the men who'd soon die.

LTC Judgment Day, Sniper Det Alpha and the rest of the back door detail went to the first Catholic Mass. LTC Judgment Day asked CPT Father Mike to hear his men's confessions and bless them in an early service so his team could be on their way.

After services, they took their position above the ledge at zero five forty. He knew the Soviet ships wouldn't have a radar signature, so they set up a concealed camera looking down the ledge. There they were just below the MTS mines, with their engines off. They probably had orders not to attack the rear of their post until the artillery battle was over. The trap couldn't be sprung until the enemies' ships were all over the MTS mines. LTC Judgment Day left 1LT Relentless in charge of the detail, with orders to inform him if the Soviets moved into position. The first officer headed to join CSM Rainmaker at the fire direction center.

The men who didn't go to any services reported to the line. After the early service, the artillery gunners had climbed into their self-propelled howitzers—the big guns, and double-checked all systems one last time. Each team had a vehicle commander, a gunner, and two gunner's mates. The vehicle commander analyzed all the data fed to him from the control center, and in turn gave the firing solution to the gunner. The control center gathered their info from the radar array; the spy drones and forward observer posts using both radar and lasers to identify targets. The forward observers and spy drones were constantly moving to keep the artillery from hitting them, avoiding the Soviet tank patrols looking for them. Both targets were high priority, so they made their measurements on the run, stopping no longer than necessary.

Each self-propelled unit had enough HE shells inside the big gun to fire without having to be resupplied for one hour, firing four shells a minute. The big guns that survived the battle would be given special shells disbursing anti-tank mines for the charge that would follow.

The men knew that it was safer inside the howitzer than operating a towed vehicle—at least it was armored. This way they could only be killed if the big gun itself was destroyed. They also knew it was likely that most of them would be destroyed.

SGT Rolling Thunder and the crew of gun number six of bravo platoon were already loaded, and the vehicle commander was waiting for the first firing solution. The two gunners were responsible for handling and loading the 155mm shells weighing 7.1 kg., or 15.8 lbs., Lunar-weight. The gunner's mates were by regulation supposed to wear their spacesuits, with their helmets nearby, in case of a hull breach. They also wore hearing protection. The gun may not make any noise outside, but it sure was loud inside. The men didn't attempt to talk while firing, but pulled their muffs off during reload. The calm before the storm bore its own level of tension. SGT Rolling Thunder decided to find something positive to say about their present situation.

"You know, I find this assignment a bit better than Vietnam. Here, we don't have to sort out civilians and enemies, and there isn't one politician interfering with what we're doing here. Hell, we aren't even fighting second-hand communists. These are the original dyed-in-the-wool communists, Marxist-Leninist who started this whole mess: in China, Vietnam, Cuba and everywhere else. Yes, sir boys, we get to strike a blow for freedom today. Ooh rah!"

ARTILLERY BATTLE

Like the Supreme Court of the USSR, the Soviet artillery battery approached the line, ready to deliver socialist justice to the American dogs. Their forward observers already had the first coordinates to fire for effect and the guns were already loaded with the first round. It would take the big guns just under forty-five seconds after reaching their spot on the line to be fully operational. SGT Anton Magnitovsky of gun six of The Lunar Soviet 3rd Artillery Platoon was ready. His crew had been travelling for over four days—now the wait was over. His crew had won honors for being able to deploy their gun in under thirty-five seconds. It was critical to get his gun ready quickly to return fire. Losing an artillery piece en route was demoralizing, as the Americans would no doubt take some of their pieces before they could deploy them. After losing one piece, they only had two more guns than the Americans, which could change as rapidly as the Russian weather. Of Soviet superiority in battle, he had no doubts, but he'd been warned by his platoon commander not to underestimate the Americans. Now over their firing position, they cut power to their hover-drive and started their deployment.

The Americans now had the Soviet targets within range. The radio squawked the first firing solution into the vehicle commander's radio piece on his headset. SGT Rolling Thunder relayed the coordinates to his gunner CPL Long Reach, who in turn entered them into the computer and fired. The gun jerked back in recoil and shook the moon beneath it, but the stab hooks and recoil spade held the piece firm. Self-ejecting shell casings could have injured the men inside of the long gun, so the design was modified so that the men had to remove each casing manually. The first gunner's mate opened the breech, removed the old casing, and handed it to the second gunner's mate. The second gunner's mate accepted the casing, dropped it behind him, manually took the next HE shell off of the rack, armed the fuse, and handed it to the first gunner's mate. The first gunner's mate manually loaded the armed shell into the big gun's ramming device, loaded into the breech and locked it down, giving a thumbs up sign to the vehicle commander and stood to the side to avoid the big gun's recoil. While the shell was being fired, PVT Powder Monkey shoved the spent casing out the back of the Howitzer through a hole affectionately referred to by the gunners as the *bung hole.*

It was a good thing that these shells, weighing ninety-five pounds on Earth, only weighed roughly sixteen pounds here, thought first gunner's mate Powder Monkey. It would make it easier to handle the shells if their battle lasted over two hours, with no breaks. No difference. The Soviet and American artillery were so evenly matched that he doubted if any of the cannon cockers on either side would live to see tomorrow.

The first Soviet self-propelled, armor-plated howitzer made contact with the lunar surface and spread out its side stabilizers and recoil spade in nearly record time. Even so, a shell landed right next to them—the shock of the ground beneath them taxed the ability of the recoil spades to absorb the shock, and the vehicle shook as if an earthquake had rocked it.

The sergeant's gunner already had the firing solution loaded into his computer for the first round, and quickly fired it as soon as his gun was operational. Within two minutes, the Americans had managed to destroy four of the Soviets guns, losing only one. The Americans were ahead by one artillery piece, but the advantage was fragile at best. The explosions on both sides were like some silent picture, but the men knew they were real. The impact of each HE shell created a ground tremor and a brilliant flash of light, contrasted by the fact that night had provided only starlight to see by.

By the end of the first hour of the artillery battle, the Soviets were down to six artillery pieces, the Americans seven. Both sides reorganized their units into one last platoon. The Americans lost two of the three platoon command officers, MAJ Blowout and CPT Concussion, besides the loss of 1SGT Stovepipe and 1SGT Percussion, the NCO commanders of Alpha and Charlie Platoons. The only officers and NCO's left were LTC Judgment Day, CPT Salvo, CSM Rainmaker, 1SGT Backfire and SGT Rolling Thunder.

SGT Rolling Thunder and his crew had also survived the fighting and signaled the resupply vehicle to back up to them for a reload. The resupply vehicle loaded the shells through the four loading tubes in the rear of the vehicle. They were designed to allow reloading from the outside without letting out their heat and breathable air. Each shell was injected into a tube, a door sealed behind it, and compressed air shot the shell to the inside crew which manually loaded them onto the racks. The sergeant thought the whole process reminded him of doing business from a bank drive-in window. SGT Rolling Thunder grabbed the first shell and armed the fuse and used the ramming device to load the breech of the big gun. The resupply vehicle paused, and the crew stopped stacking shells in the racks while the big gun shook the ground when fired. The sergeant removed the shell casing and grabbed another while the resupply vehicle continued reloading. After getting the next firing solution from the fire direction center, he signaled to stop resupply and fired, then repeating the process until the vehicle was fully rearmed. The crew resumed their rhythm, and all hands were working together firing the big gun.

With a hot rearm and firing at the same time, they still set a new marine record for time. CPL Long Reach was having a serious nicotine fit. He wished he'd taken the advice of his commander and either quit or started dipping smokeless tobacco. A cigarette break right now would seal their doom and maybe that of the post.

SGT Anton Magnovska had survived the early fighting and was getting his howitzer reloaded with high-explosive shells from their resupply vehicle. They reloaded their racks, firing at the Americans in the same way they were fired upon. His leave was postponed because of this battle. Alina, his wife, had given birth after he left to come here, and he hadn't seen his daughter Natalia yet. She was already two years old, blond haired, blue-eyed and very beautiful. He had to shake the feelings of homesickness and concentrate on the task at hand. Reload was complete and they were back to shooting four shells a minute. The ground shook violently with a flash of bright light announcing a near miss. The Soviets renewed their attack with grim determination.

CSM Rainmaker was stationed along with LTC Judgment Day in the fire direction center, observing the battle and directing orders. The fire direction center came under a heavy barrage, and they had to abandon it with their staff. A crater was all that was left of CSM Rainmaker when the shell exploded. His death was reported to COL Red Fangs, who radioed the sole surviving ranking first sergeant from Bravo Platoon.

"Command Sergeant Major Backfire?" The battlefield promotion was noticed.

"Sir, yes sir."

"Take charge, CPT Salvo is still alive and your commander. Neutralize the enemy ASAP."

"Sir, yes, sir!" LTC Judgment Day had the forethought of having the fire direction center's communication links routed to his tank's computer and had taken over the "big picture" decisions while the target information from the last forward observer post and the last spy drone were being fed directly to the artillery crew's computers. The post's radar array was operable but not as good as the laser targeting from the forward observer and the spy drone. Soon it may be all they had.

COL Red Fangs sipped a final cup of coffee while keeping track of the counter artillery battery's progress. Soon it would come down to this. Have we moved the odds enough to our favor to survive? The maxim of Sun Tzu came to mind. "All warfare is based on deception. Hence, when able to attack, we must seem unable; when using our forces, we must seem inactive... Hold out baits to entice the enemy. Feign disorder, and crush him." He'd shored up their every weakness, prepared a good defense, held out his post as enticing bait and had deceived the enemy. Nothing was left but to execute the plan, and trust that the best trained fighting force America had ever produced would bring them to victory.

The Soviet's artillery line had redirected fire from shelling the American big guns long enough to destroy the American's fire direction center. This didn't achieve the desired result. The Americans rerouted their command and communication functions quickly. The redirected fire hurt the Soviets. The American line kept right on firing at their artillery. CPT Salvo was pleased with the gain. True, the fire direction center was the eyes and brain of the operation, but the function was quickly rerouted. The artillery line was the fangs of this tiger. Ignoring them for even a minute was a costly mistake. The Soviets were now down to one big gun, the Americans two.

LTC Averbukh advised SGT Anton Magnovska that they were the last unit on the line. He held his peace, knowing that his brother Yan was probably dead. He would have to grieve later, or he would never return home. The Soviet crew fervently loaded the big gun as fast as possible, expending whatever strength they had left. The end was soon, one way or another.

The Soviets took down one of the last two American artillery pieces— bringing the count down to one big gun apiece for both sides.

SGT Rolling Thunder and his crew had gotten a good laser sighting from the last spy drone before it was destroyed. He entered the firing solution into the computer and fired. The howitzer rocked in its report, sending the high-explosive shell toward the target. The shell struck the right stabilizer arm of the Soviet artillery piece and blew it completely off, turning the unit to the left and firing off-target. The American forward observer noted where the shell hit and called in a slight adjustment. The Americans adjusted their aim and fired. The shell landed squarely in the middle of the howitzer and exploded. It rocked the unit and the explosion boomed inside for half a second until the vacuum outside sucked the air out through the gaping hole left by the explosion.

The Soviets had already put on their helmets, but it was too late. The next shell went through the open hatch and blew the artillery piece apart, killing all of the crewmembers.

The American forward observer, SGT Monitor, reported the destruction of the last of the Soviet artillery line. LTC Judgment Day ordered him to hold his position and start to locate the heat signatures of the Soviet command officers. He was able to locate all three of them and withdraw ahead of their charge, keeping them in his instrumentation as he returned to the post.

COL Glaskov would have liked to have won the artillery exchange and destroy some of their post before the tank charge. If he failed to take the American post, his appointment to the Politburo would be withdrawn, he was certain. He'd already lost the men of his artillery line. He had forty-three tanks to lead the charge, with ten more at the Americans' rear, ready to strike at their unprotected flank. The Soviet charge would meet with the American guntowers, turrets, one artillery piece, and the feeble tank regiment. If they charged now, they could destroy the American post before they could recycle the scrap from the artillery line and build more tanks. He had a sense of foreboding, but if the charge succeeded, the Americans wouldn't be able to launch another expedition. If he returned to his post, he would be abandoning all of the alloy-x scrap gained by the destruction of the first American post, and the Americans would be dug in here forever.

"LTC Averbukh?"

"Yes, Comrade Colonel."

"Spread out, attack from all directions to take away their artillery advantage. The Americans have one gun left."

"Yes, Comrade Colonel."

The Russian artillery line had been set up ninety-six miles, or one hundred fifty-five kilometers from the American post. The Lunar gravity made the big gun's effective range longer. COL Red Fangs estimated that the Soviet charge would arrive in approximately fifty-four minutes, travelling at about forty-eight meters per second, which roughly figured as one hundred six miles per hour.

LTC Judgment Day moved to the back of the post where the Soviets soon would be attempting to climb to their back door. "1LT Relentless!"

"Sir, the enemies are moving into position now."

"Good. Hold steady until they're all over the MTS mines."

One by one the Soviets moved forward until they were over the mines, from the lead vehicle to the last.

"Let's collect our prize!"

"Yes, sir!"

The post's first officer ordered the MTS mines activated. 1LT Relentless was in charge of Sniper Det Alpha, and had his men line up over the ridge. There was no doubt when a ship was under the magnetic field of a MTS mine. The mines emitted a hum, the ship's instrumentation went crazy, and the pull on the ship made the gravity appear stronger. The Soviets knew that they were caught, like flies on flypaper.

CPT Yakov Dvorkin cursed under his breath. It was obvious the Americans expected them, and that they were snared by MTS mines. He grabbed his bang stick and popped the hatch open. The bang stick fired shells with a titanium alloy projectile having an explosive charge, which pierced the MTS mine casing and blew up the works inside, rendering it useless and releasing the tank. The other pilots followed suit, with the exception of two of the pilots who popped out with sniper rifles and trained their sights on the ledge above them. It was too late—both snipers fell to the ground dead. Two of the other pilots dropped their bang sticks and picked up their sniper rifles but were also killed before they could shoulder a round. The snipers above had been shooting everything that was standing, and stopped when only two men were left alive. The Soviet pilots looked at the carnage around them. They dropped their bang sticks and lifted their hands in the air. The Americans on the cliff above held up a sign written in Russian that said "do not move."

LTC Judgment Day ordered the team to go collect their prisoners. The Americans bound the Soviet pilots and lifted them to the top with the crane that was standing ready to bring up the Soviet tanks. The American technicians removed the Soviet ship's transponders and kept them powered up with external power supplies. They would continue to send a signal to the Soviets from below the ledge until the artillery battle was over. The Americans now had an enticing bait and an illusion of weakness. *Master Sun would have approved,* thought the first officer.

The Americans hoisted the ten ships up over the ledge, and towed them to the hangar deck. There the computer drives would be replaced so the American pilots could operate them. Now that the back door was secure, and the enemies' vessels were acquired, it was all up to the hangar deck crew to do the conversions expeditiously.

Four scrap-collecting scavengers were gathering up scrap from the destroyed artillery pieces and had been doing so since the first one went down over two hours ago. Like ants gathering food for the winter in their determination, they brought the alloy-x scrap to the factory building to build new tanks. The effort was paying off. It was estimated that four new tanks would be ready by the time the Soviets arrived, and pilots were standing by at the factory ready to take possession of them. The collections of scrap by the scavenger team under fire cost them three scavengers and their pilots.

The hangar deck was abuzz with activity as Chief Monkey Wrench was overseeing the changing out of the Soviet computers to replace them with American ones. It was not a new process. Every hangar deck mechanic had to learn how to convert a Soviet tank into an American one in their basic training, and they were working with marine precision and efficiency.

The only team that wasn't working on the conversion was the one repairing CPT Viking's tank, which was damaged by an HE artillery shell. The pilot was eagerly anticipating its repair so he could join the others. The shop was filled with the noise of air-powered tools, arc welders, grinders and men shouting back and forth to each other. It was a stark contrast to his usual noise level inside of his suit, where the only thing he could hear was the radio and his own heartbeat. Chief Monkey Wrench gave him the thumbs up signal.

"Thirty minutes Captain—we'll have you shoving off at the same time as the ten new tanks." The pilot smiled and nodded, grateful that he wouldn't be sitting out the charge of the Soviet tanks on their post. He didn't want to say he was on the sidelines when someone asked him, "Where were you during the Soviet assault on Eagle 2?"

Chief of Security SGT Casper was busy interrogating the two Soviet prisoners. To their credit, Lieutenants Gavrikov and Ivasheva weren't giving up anything. They were the best-trained and disciplined soldiers the Soviet Union had. The Chief decided they wouldn't get anything without torture, and he wasn't authorized to do that. He doubted they were even telling their real names. After an exhausting interrogation, he reported back to COL Red Fangs. "Colonel, the prisoners are alive and well, but not being cooperative."

"It's okay. The trap is set, and we don't need them as bait."

95

"Yes, sir." It would have been good to get something from the captives, but he was holding their post out as the bait and that hadn't changed. Concealing their capture helped with the deception. To reveal their capture to the Soviets would tip his hand that he'd acquired the Soviet tanks. COL Red Fangs raised his first officer on a not-so-secure radio channel.

"Status report?"

"We lost one tank in the artillery battle, leaving us with four. We may have four more built by the time the Soviets arrive."

"We'll have to depend on our last artillery piece to whittle them down before they get here or we're done."

COL Red Fangs switched over to a secure channel. "Now, what's the real status?" he asked.

"If we have enough time, we will have nineteen tanks by the time the Soviet tank regiment assaults our post."

"Then make sure that last big gun slows them down," COL Red Fangs said.

"Yes, sir. I'm already working on it."

The Soviet first officer was considered the highest priority target outside of guntower range, and MAJ Cherenkov was the next priority, especially if he got close to the Americans' post. SGT Monitor had located LTC Averbukh's heat signature and relayed the coordinates, direction and speed of travel back to LTC Judgment Day. The Soviets were twenty-five minutes into their charge. SGT Rolling Thunder had been broadcasting shells which dispersed anti-tank mines in the line of attack forty kilometers from the post in all directions, with the exception of the Soviet first officer's location. They specifically laid two heavy minefields on each side of his direct path, forcing him to hold a tight course. The artillery crew waited for him like a cobra with its hood spread and eyes fixed with their racks loaded with high explosive shells.

SGT Monitor fell back to the American side of the broadcasted minefields and started back toward the post in reverse, keeping a fix on the Soviet first officer's position as long as possible. His vehicle in reverse was slower than the advancing Soviet tanks, and had orders to return to post at full speed when the Soviets came too close. The Soviets pressed a circle around the last spy drone and destroyed it. SGT Monitor held his position, knowing that he was barely out of reach of the enemies he was spying on, much like a cat teasing a dog just a foot off the end of his chain. He knew it was dangerous. At any moment, the status quo could change, and the dog might break free of its chain.

The first four Soviet tanks hit the minefields placed by the artillery shells and blew up within thirty seconds of one another. The explosions sent chunks of metal and body parts mixed with smoke and fire flying outward in all directions. It was reported to COL Glaskov, who ordered them to reduce their speed by forty percent and be on the lookout for mines. Even at this speed, six more tanks were lost in the minefields. The Soviets reduced to half speed. The American forward observer noted the speed reduction and reported the change. COL Red Fangs was delighted with the news. The extra time would give them some more tanks from the factory—maybe only one or two, but that was enough. The American satellite has just flown over and the Soviet tank count was confirmed at thirty-three. The Soviets still thought they had forty-three, with their back door crew.

SGT Rolling Thunder and his crew got his last laser sighting of LTC Averbukh's position, direction and speed of travel. The artillery crew loaded HE shells into the big gun, and fired every fifteen seconds for two minutes where the Soviet should be, where he was going, and where he had just been. The Soviet saw the first shell strike the ground in front of him, making the ground tremble, and felt the shockwave rock the nose of his hovercraft up and back. He righted his craft, came to a full stop, and put it in reverse. The second shell struck his tank and made a breach in the hull large enough to drive a truck through. The second shell took his life and scattered the smoldering pieces of his tank and body along the lunar surface. His wingman, who had been moving westerly toward the American post and five kilometers north of the first officer, reported LTC Averbukh's death to COL Glaskov.

The Soviet commander cursed and informed MAJ Cherenkov that he was now second-in-command. *It was still all right*, he thought. *MAJ Cherenkov is a fearless and skilled pilot and the men will follow him in the charge. After all, that's what we're doing, attacking their post. All of the strategy has been worked out, and attacking is all that's left. Yes*, he decided, *he's a good man for this.*

SGT Monitor began moving as close as possible to the Soviet charge, moving back and forth, looking for MAJ Cherenkov's heat signature. He was getting dangerously close. All of the spy drones had been destroyed. SGT Lookout had to fall back to the post when he got too close to the Soviet line and suffered severe damage to his ship. Finally, SGT Monitor locked in the Soviet Major's heat signature and started toward the post, keeping track of the major and relaying his coordinates to the last American big gun.

SGT Rolling Thunder's crew got the coordinates for MAJ Cherenkov and started to fire using the same technique they'd used on the Soviet first officer. The Major flew as close to the minefields on each side as the big gun tried to direct his path with high explosive fire. They hoped to be able to nail him before he ever got near the post. The Major was bolder and flew in a snaking pattern, making it harder to obtain a firing solution. The hardest chargers of the Soviet tank regiment were two minutes from the minefield surrounding the American post.

A mine blast violently ripped through MAJ Cherenkov's tank and blew his gun turret off, sailing it twenty feet into the air. The mines continued to slow the first wave of Soviet attackers—five more Soviet officers who had followed the major had lost their lives; their tanks having been savaged by the American welcoming party. American radar confirmed the Soviet tank count at twenty-eight. The death of MAJ Cherenkov was noted by the rest of the regiment and it took the fire out of the Soviet charge. COL Glaskov was informed and none too happy about it.

Right on cue, the Americans started bringing the Soviet transponders up the cliff and into the post, mimicking the enemies' assault to their flank. The reconditioned tanks and their new tanks, nineteen in all arrived at the line with COL Red Fangs in front of the guntowers. The Americans now stood to defend this post behind their defensive grid with twenty-one tanks to the Soviets' twenty-eight. In COL Glaskov's mind, he still had ten more.

SGT Monitor was still on the job and had identified the Soviet commander's heat signature. His laser target designator pinpointed the colonel's tank and sent the coordinates to LTC Judgment Day. The American first officer relayed the coordinates to the artillery crew, with orders to stand-down, but stand-ready until further orders were given.

The remainder of the Soviet regiment was within ten kilometers of the post now, soon to be within American guntower range. COL Glaskov checked his onboard radar. Something was wrong; he was reading over twenty tanks in a line. He saw no evidence of damage to the post. There was no way the Americans could have that many tanks this quickly, unless... There was no reason for his tank unit inside the American post to be on radio silence now. They should be attacking by now. COL Glaskov keyed the mike and radioed his team leader.

"CPT Dvorkin?" There was no answer. He got no answer from any of the other tanks. But the transponders were still transmitting from all ten tanks... One thousand more meters and they would be within guntower range and in fierce fighting. He quickly did the math. Without his ten tanks attacking the American post from the inside, this was now an entirely different battle. If the Americans found a way to convert those tanks they would have a strong edge behind their defensive grid. At best, there would be a draw and what was left of his fleet would be in shreds. With any luck, a few of his ships would survive and be left to limp back to their post, leaving most of the alloy-x on the battlefield for the Americans to recover. In such a weakened condition, the Americans might well attempt a siege on their post. He cursed his misfortune under his breath as he saw his political aspirations evaporate like dew on the Russian grass.

"This is COL Glaskov. To all boards, break off the attack and regroup where we started." The Soviet tanks were within one hundred meters of American guntower range when the order came.

LTC Judgment Day noticed the Soviet retreat and didn't give the order to fire on COL Glaskov. SGT Rolling Thunder received a message that the Soviets had called off the attack, but stood ready in any case. He still had the firing solution for COL Glaskov's tank in his computer and was keeping it updated.

The Soviet commander opened a channel to the Americans. "COL Red Fangs."

"Yes, COL Glaskov."

"Well done, you are a worthy adversary. We will meet again. Next time, I will not underestimate your ability to use deception. I will win next time."

"You're a worthy adversary, as well. I have two of your pilots to return if you wish to honor the accord."

Glaskov was silent for a few seconds as he considered this news. "I would like them back."

"In exchange, I want a favor from you."

"Yes?"

"I want to send a delegation to the D'Alembert Crater under truce to place a memorial for the men of Eagle 1."

"Agreed. We can meet then to renew the accord. We will serve dessert this time."

Col Red Fangs suppressed a snicker at that remark. "Very good, until next time."

The Soviets sent a single craft to the American post to pick up their pilots. COL Red Fangs was relieved that he wouldn't lose more men in the final assault. The factory kept building more tanks, just in case the Soviets changed their minds. He was sure that the Soviets wouldn't be able to carry back more than a fraction of the alloy-x on the battlefield, which was good news for them. They had the materials to finish building a post. With the alloy-x field they found on the southern rim of the crater, they should have enough to finish a proper post here and export the materials to build a proper post on Mars.

The Soviets returned back to their starting point, slowly and carefully this time, avoiding any mines. COL Glaskov had fifteen scavengers load up and head for home. They were only able to recover one-eighth of the alloy-x that they brought with them. The deaths of his first and second officers had been a great loss for him. His first officer had been offered a command here once he was promoted to the politburo. He'd turned it down in favor of accepting the command of the new post the Soviets were soon to establish on Mars. He knew he would lose him soon, but not like this. He was a brilliant, fine young officer and now he was dead. MAJ Cherenkov's death was costly in another way. He inspired the men like a legendary hero of old. His death would be hard on morale.

CPT America returned back to Luna with more men, equipment, food and supplies two days later. He also carried the granite memorial monument with the names of the members of Eagle 1, and a second one for the artillery crew who died in the failed assault on Eagle 2. The Soviets and Americans met at D'Alembert crater and signed an accord over tea and gozinaki, this time provided by the Soviets. The Americans were careful to eat and drink modestly. The Americans placed the first memorial stone there; the second one was placed at Eagle 2. Another memorial for Eagle 1 was erected in front of the post HQ of Eagle 2. A bronze statue of a marine facing down a Soviet tank with his sidearm served as a reminder of the steadfast courage of the men of Eagle 1.

GEN Colson was pleased with the reports that more alloy-x metal was harvested than they needed to build a proper post on Luna. The icing on the cake was that COL Glaskov's politburo appointment was withdrawn. There was more than enough alloy-x to build a post on Mars. The next step was to choose the personnel and commander for the new post. He poured another cup of coffee, two sugars and one cream, and sat back down at his desk. He looked again through the two files of men to whom he'd considered for the post on Mars, deciding on the naval lieutenant commander. He would have full control over his team selection. It was time to take the war with the Soviets to the next world...

VIETNAM

July 8, 1970—Zero Three Hundred Zulu

LTJG Eugene J. Bordelon, Jr. US Navy HA(L)-3
Solid Anchor Naval Base, Song Cua Lon
Republic of Vietnam

We'd had a busy shift. Early last night we had to give aid to a local Ruff Puff outpost which had come under attack, and rescued some South Vietnamese sailors in the Cua Lon when their boat was sinking due to mortar damage. The VC welcomed us back to the base with small arms fire from behind the triple-thick canopy of the mangrove swamps surrounding Solid Anchor. We responded appropriately to the threat, and when all the muzzle flashes had stopped, we set our bird down on the helo pad. The thick, moist air covered our base like a warm blanket; my shirt was soaked with sweat and plastered to my skin. I was glad I could grab a shower and get a beer in our air-conditioned hootch.

Solid Anchor was home to a Navy SEAL Team One, a Seawolf detachment (det One), and a support base including its own miniature Navy, consisting of all the Brown Water Navy oddities that were born out of riverine warfare.

A fire team consisted of two Huey gunships. The crew of each bird consisted of a pilot, co-pilot, and two mechanics, who served as the door gunners. The pilot of the lead bird was the FTL (*Fire Team Leader*) and the Trail AHAC (*Attack Helicopter Aircraft Commander*) piloted the trail bird. Each det had two crews. Each crew was on alert for twenty-four hours, and stood-down for twenty-four hours. There was no drinking while you were on your shift (on alert). Whenever we were not in our helos, we grabbed some sack time. This was our schedule year-round. There were no holidays or days off, not even Tet (*Vietnamese New Year*), when the VC usually agreed to a truce. During Tet cease-fires, we flew weapons-tight, not firing unless fired upon. The VC used Tet cease-fires to move troops, supplies and weapons into position. It took some creative, borderline harassment to get them to fire at us so we could fire back.

I was the FTL on my shift, and my counterpart from the other shift LCDR "Wild Bill" Jernigan, FTL of the first shift and OIC met us at the pad. I turned my bird over to him. His crew rearmed and refueled, tied down the rotor blades and started with their preflight inspection and safety check.

I still hadn't gotten a letter from my fiancée Beth in the past two weeks. No matter, my mail must have been rerouted to Binh Thuy as I was about to return stateside. My DEROS (*Date of Estimated Return from Overseas to*

Stateside) was now one more off-duty shift, and one last shift in-country. After my last shift, off to Binh Thuy—then to Saigon—then San Francisco. From there I'll catch an Air Force flight to England Air Force Base, which was five miles from my brother's house. Beth, my brother and his family should meet my plane at England AFB when I get home. My fiancé had gotten me an interview with the Baptist Hospital in Alexandria, LA., to fly an air rescue helicopter. I had a couple of postwar plans. First, marry Beth, and then take the job offer. We'd save our money and eventually buy a bird of my own to start a helicopter transport service. Yes, indeed, my future looked bright, even if the prospects for Vietnam didn't. The United States had lost its heart for this war. We were engaged in withdrawals and were turning the war over to the Vietnamese government, a process called *Vietnamization.*

The war in the delta was pretty much subdued, and things were quiet in late 1970. However, in the mangrove swamps, in the heart of the U Minh forest, Charlie was imbedded in the last VC sanctuary. Solid Anchor was a bold move to challenge the VC in their sanctuary. The Navy's Riverine forces, SEALs, Seawolves and Black Ponies continued to bring the war to the NVA and VC, even as the US Army regulars were pulling out. Solid Anchor was in the southernmost tip of the delta, on the Song Cua Lon (Cua Lon River). Since Charlie couldn't move around freely in the delta anymore, he laid specific claim to the dense triple canopy cover of the U Minh's mangrove swamps. This was no man's land. Young men who served here found their faces age twenty years in a year. Previously in the war effort, the government didn't care much if Charlie owned the mangrove swamps. There were only a few charcoal makers and woodcutters who even lived there. Everybody else was either Viet Cong or North Vietnamese Army Regulars (VC and NVA). The pacification part of Army insurgency doctrine that promoted getting the populace to accept the government and the United States didn't apply here. In the mangrove swamps of the U Minh, Charlie didn't seem to want to be pacified. He owned the U Minh. Solid Anchor was here to challenge Charlie's deed and title.

It was time to head to the mess hall and pick up some grub. One thing the Navy could do in this God-forsaken hellhole was to feed us well. Huge steaks that covered your whole platter and lobster were common items at the mess. Showers with clean water, on the other hand, weren't common. All clean drinking water was barged in. We bathed and washed our clothes in the river. My skivvies had taken on the color of brown river mud over time. As soon as I got home, I wanted nothing more than to get into a hot bathtub and soak the remainder of Vietnam off of my body.

After finishing off a huge steak, I stopped by my barracks to remove my skivvies. Next stop was the SEAL barracks to share a beer and find out where they were planning their op tonight, and then hit the rack for some much needed sleep. The off-duty SEALs would be there this morning, and it didn't pay to wear skivvies when drinking with SEALs. SEALs had their own dress code. They seemed to think that skivvies were for civilians and other lesser mortals. The real reason they didn't wear skivvies was because it kept their crotch drier and prevented various forms of jungle rot. Without warning, they would shout, "Skivvie Check!" to make sure that everyone who was drinking with them would drop their pants to prove that they weren't violating their underwear dress code. Anyone caught wearing skivvies while drinking with them would suffer the fate of having them ripped off. That quirk aside, it was very good to drink with SEALs when the opportunity presented itself. They were a crazy, overachieving lot of push-it-to-the-limit warriors who lived hard, and played hard. SEALs loved Seawolves. We had their back when they were in trouble, and they didn't forget that. Any time a Seawolf was being molested by Army pukes or anyone else, SEALs would defend us like body guards.

On the way to the SEAL barracks, I found my Trail AHAC, LTJG William "Prophet" Forrest, walking toward one of the two spare helo pads. A SEALORD was making its descent. Rumor had it he was bringing in my replacement. Prophet motioned me to join him. My Trail AHAC and I liked to haze the newbies a bit. There wasn't much entertainment here, so we made do. It was too far for any radio station or TV, and there were no American women here. Finally, the chopper rotors stopped the whomp, whomp, whomp sound and the occupants climbed out. That would be him, I thought. He bore the marks of a newbie: new clean uniform, a seabag in his hand and a look of relief that he hadn't already been shot down on the descent or killed by a sniper. Prophet immediately greeted him.

"Are you the new Seawolf pilot?"

"Yes sir, LTJG Donald James, Cherry Hill, NY."

"Welcome to Solid Anchor. Your shift isn't on alert. Relax, Charlie doesn't start trying to kill us until after dark. I'll show you your bunk, and we'll go over to the SEAL barracks and get a beer and introduce you. By the way, we don't drink when on alert," finished Prophet.

We took the new pilot to the barracks, got him settled in his new bunk and advised him to see the quartermaster later to get squared away with the personal flight gear he needed. Prophet would have a ball hazing this young Yankee. I kept silent and let him take the ball and run with it. We introduced our newbie to the SEALs and accepted a cold beer. Prophet put his crosshairs on the newbie, who started relaxing a bit, happy he wasn't already shot dead, bitten by a snake, or blown up.

"Newbie, what's your DEROS?!" Prophet demanded loudly.

"Sir, 360 and a sunrise, sir!" Prophet looked at him as an object to be pitied and removed his Colt forty-five auto from his shoulder holster. He chambered a round and checked it to make sure it was loaded, then put the safety on and laid it on the card table.

"Son, if you shot yourself in the head right now, no one will think the less of you. But do not, I repeat, do not throw yourself out of *my helicopter*. You'll irritate the hell out of me if I have to fill out an incident report on you falling out of my bird," he growled. Prophet hated unnecessary paperwork worse than the VC and had no use for a newbie inconveniencing him. The newbie swallowed hard and shook his head.

"No, sir. I'm here to be a Seawolf and to grease commies."

"You sure?"

"Yes, sir."

"All right, then, I guess I'll put this back up." He retrieved his pistol and removed the round from the chamber, placing it back in his holster. The newbie had endured phase one of our hazing ritual. There were some amused looks from the SEALs, but by and large, no one gets very attached to anyone new until they'd proved that they weren't going to get killed right way.

My tour of duty afforded me a couple of medals, thankfully none of which was a purple heart. A point of pride for me was that none of the men in my bird got one. Staying alive for a Seawolf pilot was an accomplishment indeed. The NVA had a five thousand dollar reward and a month's leave back home for anyone shooting down one of our birds. Our crews were especially hated. We expected to be tortured and killed if captured. It seemed that every VC took risks to bring us down. We were hated and feared almost as much as the *green faces* (SEALs). We flew close air support for the RPB, the Riverine Patrol Boats that made the backbone of the Mekong Delta's Brown Water Navy. We also worked very closely with Navy SEALs, offering air support, and sometimes insertions and extractions if it was dangerous and needed a gunship to do the transport. The SEALs were quite loyal to us, and we were loyal to them. They liked to see us show up in a timely manner when they were in trouble.

I settled down to the card table with a beer and my thoughts while the SEALs introduced themselves to our newest arrival. Prophet grabbed a beer and began his usual endless drone of the causes for us being here. Prophet, my trail AHAC, always tried to vocalize some rational cause and effect for why we're here.

"The way I see it, it is the fault of the French. If they hadn't colonized Indonesia eighty years ago, there would have been no struggle for national sovereignty. Once the Japs left it would have been business as usual. There would be no emotional fuel for communism, no Ho Chi Minh, and no Americans dying." He paused for effect, looking to see if anyone would argue the point. None did. We'd heard it all before. Prophet wasn't actually a prophet; he was just a student of history looking for an audience. He was a tall, dark-haired country-boy from South Carolina who seemed to hold various philosophical viewpoints, mixed with a smattering of religious references now and then. He was not unlike the plantation owners and aristocrats of the old South in his convoluted mix of politics, philosophy and religion. But, he was the closest thing we had to a sage who bothered to find some rational cause for the war. After nearly a year of being in-country, we needed someone to make this all make sense.

I contemplated surviving one more twenty-four hour shift and going home. Prophet wasn't through trying to get some conversation and headed to the card table.

"Hey, Cowboy. How does it feel to be going home to a target-rich environment of round-eyed women?"

I laughed. "Just cover my six one more shift and I'll write you back all about it."

"One more shift," he snorted. "You're due for a sick call. Don't tempt fate. Nobody wants the get killed on his last day in-country, especially during a withdrawal. I've already passed my fit rep, done my FTL flight check and have a green light to take over as FTL when you leave. Your replacement is already here to start as co-pilot of the trail bird." The SEALs listened intently to see if I agreed with his proposal.

"Not my style, you know that. Honor first day—honor last day—and all the days in between. Besides, if one American serviceman or friendly died the day that I faked being sick, you know I would take that to my grave. Tomorrow I start the last shift of my tour. When I'm through, I leave with no regrets." SEAL faces broke out with approving smiles.

But I did have regrets. We killed NVA and VC guerillas by the thousands, but the late Ho Chi Minh's DRV continued to wage war against the South. Though the kill rate was one of ours to ten of theirs, they never quit coming. Something ate at me about how we never seemed to get to the cause of communism. It seemed like we were perpetually trying to overcome an enemy who never seemed to want to quit.

I wasn't one to make speeches, but I rose, lifted my beer and called for a toast, "To Ho Chi Minh and Mao Tse Tung." You could have heard a pin drop. "May they rot in hell!"

"Here, here," several voices echoed while the tension left the room and the conversations returned to normal. They were all relieved that I was leaving Vietnam with the same conviction and loyalty to my country that I had on the first day here. I hunkered down at the card table to carry on my conversation with my Trail AHAC.

"Prophet, President Nixon has assured us that the *war of northern aggression* is almost over. I fully expect when I get home to Louisiana that the Yankees will have all gone home."

Prophet loved that one. He laughed until the tears streaked down his face like raindrops down a windowpane. I made the promotion to FTL two months earlier, still a jaygee (lieutenant, junior grade) but having the most combat hours in the seat on our shift. Ironically, my co-pilot LT Robertson outranked me but didn't have enough hours to be Trail AHAC or FTL. The FTL would take the lead and the Trail AHAC would follow behind and above and to the lead bird's starboard side, so he could see ahead and to keep out of my rotor tail wash. Hueys worked best in pairs. They weren't the fastest birds in the sky, and the fully fueled and armed Bravo model does not hover! It's a good thing that Solid Anchor has an airstrip, versus the old LST of Sea Float, so we can get a full fuel tank and rocket load and still lift-off. A pair of Hueys with two seasoned door gunners was a force to reckon with.

The SEALs were getting our newbie a little drunk, and it was nearly time for phase two of his hazing. Chief Butler screamed out loudly, "Skivvie check!" to which everyone in the bar dropped his pants. Well, almost everyone. Our newbie pilot looked dazed and confused. He had a few beers in him, and I'm sure this ritual made no sense at all to him. Chief Butler approached him with a growl.

"Skivvie Check!" Our newbie looked dumfounded. The Chief pulled his pants down, and finding brand-new, clean, white, skivvie-shorts, he ripped them straight up and off of our newbie.

"Plumb forgot to warn that young Yankee pilot about wearing skivvies in here with the SEALs and all," said Prophet, his face set with a Machiavellian grin.

"I wonder if it still hurts to have new skivvies ripped off of you," I laughed. I had first-hand knowledge of that myself, having once been *the* newbie. With a full belly and a few beers in me, I started getting drowsy and headed for my barracks. I needed a long, deep sleep. I wanted to be sharp for my shift and not slip up on my last day. My personal effects were already packed. I just needed to survive another shift, get some sleep, and stateside here I come. My fiancée Beth would be waiting for me when I got home. I took Beth's picture out of my pocket and looked intently at the vision of the woman I was going to marry. She was the most beautiful woman at Louisiana College: long, thick chestnut-brown hair, warm brown eyes and the figure of a swimsuit model. Beth's major in college was business, always the practical one. She would run the business end of my helicopter-transport service when we could scrape up enough money to start up.

I breathed deeply of Vietnam. Vietnam had its own smells: the spicy scent of tropical flowers, sweat, river mud, aircraft fuel, fish and rotting jungle vegetation, and a touch of salt on the breeze from the Gulf of Thailand nearby. Vietnam was hotter than back home, and more humid. Having been raised in Louisiana, I was acclimated to it, somewhat. We were just about sea level here, though it rained more here than back home.

I surveyed my bunk. All my gear was packed and at the foot of my bunk, and the only things out were my zoom bag, flight helmet, flight boots and my holster with two Colt revolvers. I'd thrown my dress whites and dress-shoes away after they'd succumbed to some sort of mold that seemed to afflict everything here. I had slightly altered my zoom bag by sewing my canvas holsters and gun belt onto it. I didn't want to fumble around trying to put it on during a scramble. I only had to jump in my zoom bag, zip it up, buckle my gun holster, and zip up my flight boots.

I wondered again if any of my letters from Beth were being held up in some kind of APO screw-up. I couldn't sleep, so I afforded myself another beer from the fridge in the barracks. The excitement level was making my mind race, and I felt restless. After another beer, I was able to slow my mind down enough to fall deeply asleep. I woke up about eight hours later, to the sound of a poker game in progress. I played poker with Prophet, our copilots, our newbie and our gunners until we broke for breakfast. Afterward we resumed our game until after lunch, when it was time for my last pre-shift nap. I awoke feeling ready to finish my final tour.

It was time. Our shift was soon to start. The men started to suit up and make it to the helo pads to greet the crew coming in from the end of their shift, refuel, reload, do a quick preflight check, and get ready for the call if it came.

LCDR Jernigan, FTL of the first shift and OIC was putting his/my bird down on the helo pad for the shift change. They hadn't scrambled during his shift and pretty much ran routine patrol patterns and stayed on alert. The natives were unusually quiet on his shift. I was beginning to hope that my last day in-country would be as boring and uneventful. The shift change occurred one hour before dusk, so we had a chance to do a preflight inspection in the daylight before starting our shift. Most of the enemies' activities were at night, when Charlie could use the cover of darkness. Navy pilots were instrument trained, so we were up to the task of night flying. As soon as we relieved the first shift crew, my gunners refueled my bird. My copilot checked the rocket tubes to make sure they were still loaded and armed while I started my preflight inspection. The Huey was not quite designed for being a gunship. It was an afterthought born from necessity for Vietnam. I never knew what the designers were thinking when they set up all of the circuitry. Each weapon system had its own switches, with one master breaker. We kept all of the systems hot when ready to scramble to some hotspot in a hurry. We did this by leaving all of the system breakers hot and just throwing the main breaker when we wanted all systems up. My inspection revealed that Wild Bill hadn't added any new gun holes, cracks, breaks or other damage to *our* bird. Preflight check complete, we were ready for a scramble or a patrol.

We weren't called to scramble. We'd take the fire team out on patrol. Scrambles were called when someone was in trouble, with us humping it on double time. The klaxon sound of oogah, oogah, and the dispatcher calling "Seawolves Scramble!" precluded the mad dash to jump into your zoom bag, zip up your flight boots, and strap on your personal close protection. (For me was a pair of Colt forty-five revolvers which my grandfather gave me, hence the name "Cowboy" I was given by the other pilots). A scramble could bring you out of your bunk fast asleep to wide-wake and in the air in less than two minutes. (My personal best time to lift-off was one minute, forty-two seconds.) Scrambles could catch you at the mess hall eating, playing cards, in the head, wherever, but one thing was sure. Life as you knew it ceased to exist at the urgency of the scramble call. A scramble call was heart pumping, adrenaline rushing, with nerves on edge propelling us into the unknown—which was already identified as dangerous for somebody. Scrambles could be called for the support of PBR's (Patrol River Boats), defense of a Ruff-Puff outpost at the canal crossings where we refueled and rearmed, the defense of ARVN friendly troops or American troops in the field.

For the Navy SEALs, we offered insertions, extractions, and fire support when needed. Last but not least and the most urgent was the defense of our own base from where we operate. The scramble on the latter was extremely urgent because our choppers were the enemies' number one priority targets in a base attack. Our birds on the helo pad were at their most vulnerable state. The best defense of both them and the base was to get them in the air, and hunting. Charlie launched an attack of some kind on Solid Anchor every night.

On my last shift I didn't want to get in some hairy firefight that could get me killed, but I still wanted to see some action.

My senior mechanic and right door gunner, ADJ1 (mechanic, first class) Chief "Crazy Mike" Thornton had the kind of pinpoint accuracy that made our crew quite effective. When he needed practice with the M-60, he would shoot seagulls in the air. I never saw him miss—he always got the bird by the second tracer.

There was no urgency to get airborne quickly. LT Robertson and I snapped on our flotation LPU's, put on our helmets, strapped on our seat harnesses and sat on our chicken plates. The chicken plates were bullet-proof vests. Since we were usually shot at from below, it made more sense to sit on them than wear them.

My senior gunner grabbed the fire bottle and got seated and gave me a thumbs up. My second gunner untied the rotor blade that held the tail boom and held onto the rotor blade while I hit the starter. He maintained his hold against building engine pressure until there was enough for acceleration without the danger of the rotor blades striking the tail boom or the deck, then he released it. He took his place in his seat. When we got about six inches off the ground, I checked power and gave a thumbs up to my Trail AHAC. We took off down the runway until we could get enough rpms up for transitional lift. Previously when we had to take off from an LST (our floating base), we had to be real careful how we lifted off. Bravo model Hueys didn't have any real hover capabilities, and lift-off from an LST was a little hairy at times.

The U Minh was unusually quiet tonight, and our patrol was uneventful. *Too quiet* to me was as unnerving as *too hostile*. We put our birds back down at the helo pads, refueled, ran though the safety checklist, tied down the rotor to the tail boom, and headed back to the mess hall. SEAL Chief Butler had advised us earlier that they were doing a snatch-and-grab operation tonight and were being inserted by one of our mike boats. He gave me his radio frequency for the op and his call sign, code name Sour Mash, just in case. If all went well, the mike boat should pick them up just before dawn with their prisoner, a notable VC tax collector. This was a very bad man, who worked his way across the delta and extracted taxes of rice, fish, and money from the scared peasants.

We ate with the SEALs, and they shoved off. Then we retired to our barracks and got a couple hours of shut-eye in anticipation that we may have to scramble later. The stars were out at about twenty-three hundred when I awoke. My det mates had a poker game going on, so I joined them. This was my last shift on alert in-country. I invited each of my brother Seawolves to come see me in Louisiana when they were stateside.

About zero three hundred the klaxon sounded, oogah, oogah, and the 1-MC announced, "Now scramble, Seawolves!" My adrenaline started pumping and transformed me from a care-free poker player into a Seawolf pilot. I put on my zoom bag and boots in record time and got the details from the dispatcher. The mike boat that was to extract the SEALs was under mortar fire and couldn't make the pick-up. Det Five was being scrambled to assist the mike boat, and we were to extract the SEALs, who were now reporting they were under intense fire.

The SEALs were only fifteen minutes away, and one of our birds would have to do the extraction. My engine was brand-new and had more lift potential than Seawolf One-Two. We needed to have our max gross weight down to pick up a six-man SEAL team and hostage, so we pumped some of the fuel out of my bird until we were down to seven hundred pounds. However, I needed to clear a landing zone in the triple-thick Mangrove forest, so we loaded all fourteen rocket tubes with fourteen-pound HE rockets. This made us a bit heavy, but I'd be expending all of the rockets before the pick-up. The SEALs had informed the dispatcher that they didn't have enough C-4 and det cord to finish clearing a proper landing zone. We needed a clear runway so we could overcome our dead-man zone fully loaded down and lift-off. My Trail AHAC would leave his fuel tank full and "loaded for bear," in case more time was needed to cover the team or us. I estimated we needed to be about thirty minutes from flameout with our rocket tubes empty and jettisoned, and most of our ammo expended to get our gross weight down enough for the pick-up.

Arriving at the SEALs' extraction point, I raised them on the radio. "Sour Mash, this is Seawolf One-One. What's your status?"

"Cowboy, I hope you got your spurs on. We got the package. Doc Peavey's been wounded, but can walk with assistance. Charlie has a regiment so close to us that we can smell the fish on their breath. We need out now!"

"Roger that, Sour Mash. Pop some smoke so we can see you." The SEALs hand-held M-79 mortar gun delivered a smoke grenade just above the mangrove canopy about one click due northeast of our position. "Sour Mash, I see your smoke. Where's Charlie?"

"Charlie is about one hundred meters due northeast of where we popped smoke. Hurry! There's a whole NVA regiment on our six!"

"Hold on, Sour Mash, we're going to lay down some suppressive fire on Charlie while you back up southwest. We need you as far back as you can get before we blast a landing zone."

"Roger that, One-One."

We started a run on the VC position with guns only, no rockets. I wanted to back the VC up a little while the SEALs were backing up so we could get a safety margin before clearing a landing zone. The visibility on the ground was zero because of the triple-thick mangrove canopy, but we opened fire with the minigun in front, and both door gunners giving it all they had. We had the capability of firing a combined total of five thousand rounds per minute, but the minigun only had fifteen hundred rounds loaded in the tray, and the door gunners had about the same amount. We moved over the deck above the VC, and the door gunners fired continuously through the trees while my copilot fired three second bursts through the thinnest part of the foliage.

A three-second burst could deliver six hundred rounds. We moved around behind my Trail AHAC, and he delivered the same to the area. We lined up for our rocket run as soon as Prophet broke right and moved to our aft while my copilot reloaded his minigun tray.

"Sour Mash, we're ready for our approach."

"One-One, we're clear and still moving. Hurry every chance you get!"

"Roger, coming in."

We came in for our rocket run at the highest altitude we could manage, keeping us high enough for safety and the rocket spread right. The gunners retreated inside the bird to keep from getting hurt by the molten slag and sparks from the rockets. I ripple-fired the entire load of fourteen HE warhead rockets at the mangrove forest below, and sat back to watch the show. I'd never seen an explosion of this magnitude, except for a couple times we'd destroyed enemy ammo bunkers and a fuel depot. I broke off the rocket run and rolled right into a two hundred and seventy degree turn, and exposed my right door gunner to hose the area down with fire while my trail bird began his rocket run. Prophet unloaded all of his rockets save his two fleshettes (nails). This significantly expanded the clearing and providing a larger landing zone. Once my Trail AHAC was through with his run and had ascended out of the dead-man zone to one thousand feet, we broke off our gun circle and ascended to a safe altitude.

Having expended all of the HE rockets of both birds, we made one more pass, this time with our minigun and two door guns blazing away into the north edge of the clearing. It sounded like mayhem with the engine noise and all three guns firing. I broke off the attack and rolled left and maintained a gun circle with my left door gunner spraying the forest down. We were just above the mangrove canopy while our trail bird repeated our run.

The plan was now to get into formation again, with the trail bird in front. Prophet would go low and keep the area hosed down while I dropped down and attempted to pick up all seven SEALs and one prisoner. My gunners ejected the rocket tubes and deep-sixed anything loose we could part with into the Song Cua Lon. We needed to get our gross weight down, so lift-off was possible when we picked up the SEALs. The only thing we hadn't thrown overboard was our ammo, med kits, spare gun barrels and wrenches to change the gunner's barrels. Prophet started the last run and flew dangerously low in the north opening of the landing zone site, just above treetop level. They sprayed into the mangrove forest with all three guns, jinking the bird up and down to *theoretically* make a harder target to hit. I hated that he was in that position. This was too much like a fair fight.

I set my bird down, and the SEAL team started climbing aboard, with their prisoner held securely with his hands tied and mouth gagged. Getting the thumbs up from my co-pilot, I pulled back the collective to lift-off. The bird simply wouldn't lift-off! My co-pilot signaled to the SEALs to drop off three of their men, us keeping the prisoner and three of the heaviest of them. My Trail AHAC would have to make the pick-up. This would call for more time for us in the hot LZ, and I was not happy about it. Chief Butler stepped off first with two of his men, making sure his Stoner man was on the ground with him. We lifted off and were about ten feet off of the ground, moving toward the enemy and beginning to climb.

"Prophet, I left three SEALs behind. Lift-off, we're coming in." We'd just enough runway, but we were in danger because the runway led to the NVA regiment. My trail bird lifted off, rolled left, and made a one hundred and eighty degree turn to go back to pick up the remaining three SEALs. We moved forward, with all three guns blazing while my trail bird descended behind us on the southwest side of the man-made opening in the forest. The noise was so loud that even if I wanted to talk on the radio or speak with my co-pilot, it would have been futile. We couldn't hover in the dead-man zone, so we took turns pulling up starboard and port and circling around, one gun circle after another.

This was not my idea of a good last day in-country. We were in the middle of a hairy firefight, and a fair fight to boot! My mind protested. No! Not on my last day! I jinked the bird up and down, but didn't rock us side-to-side. I didn't want to screw up the gunners' stable platform. The minigun had used up its tray of ammo, and my co-pilot was reloading it. Both my gunners were hammering away with no regard to their own safety, riding the skids and firing at any available target. My co-pilot started firing the minigun again in three-second burst until it jammed. My personal pucker factor gauge had reached redline and was climbing. I'd never been so scared in my life, but kept steady hands on the controls. We heard a loud whack numerous times reporting to us we'd been hit by small arms fire. The smell of burnt gunpowder and human sweat filled the helo.

Crazy Mike's barrel was so hot that he was now cooking off rounds. My co-pilot motioned me to turn and show my left side to the enemy with my gunner and his fifty caliber while my left door gunner changed barrels. Now we're down to one gun and offering the enemy a bigger target to boot! Red at the right door fired continuously until his barrel overheated. Crazy Mike was though changing his barrel and ready to rock and roll, so I rolled to the left and gave him all the access he needed for a one-man show. Red had his asbestos gloves on, changing out his barrel, which seemed to take forever. Finally, he gave a thumbs up, and I faced the nose of the helo back toward the enemy and both gunners renewed their firing. I had to be careful to keep the bird level without dropping the nose down, or my own gunners would be shooting into our rotor blades. Time seemed to be irrelevant. Our world was moving in slow motion, but I knew the whole process wasn't long at all. Adrenaline in the heat of battle can cause a sense of time distortion. The radio interrupted my thoughts.

"Cowboy, pull up and roll left. I got my package and one last surprise for Charlie."

"Roger that, up and left." With that, I pushed my bird upward while Prophet moved toward the north end of the landing zone. The minigun was blazing away, and I saw two last rockets clear his tubes before he pulled up and rolled left behind me. He'd saved two fleshette warheads to spray nails into the forest where the enemy was as he pulled up and out. Each warhead had twenty-four-hundred 1 1/2 inch darts which struck with devastating force. True, most of the VC were hiding behind trees, but anything out in the open was going to be killed instantly. We both stayed above the deck of the mangrove canopy, to diffuse the sound of our helos so the enemy couldn't figure out which direction we went. The others had lived to fight another day, and I was going home. The SEALs motioned the gunners, who motioned to my co-pilot, who tapped me on the shoulder.

"We've got a chip light! We took a bullet through the transmission case and we're bleeding transmission fluid like a stuck pig," informed LT Robertson urgently. Bell Helicopter had stated in their spec sheet that a transmission would run dry for twenty minutes. Whether I believed that or not, didn't matter. We were running on fumes and were close to flameout with a hole in our transmission. We had no option but to return to base. It was a close call. I made it to the helo pad as I was running out of fuel, having to auto rotate to a landing. Now that the adrenaline rush was over, my neck, shoulders and thighs were terribly stiff. We all stunk of old sweat and burnt gunpowder. This was one day I longed for a long soak in a hot bathtub. We all got slaps on the back from the SEALs and an invitation to drink with them when we weren't on alert. It didn't matter much. With a hole in my transmission case, my bird was grounded until it could be repaired. My zoom bag reeked to high heaven. Since I'd be grounded, I could clean up if you could call it that, in the muddy waters of the Song Cua Lon and get into a clean set of fatigues. My OIC, LCDR Jernigan met us at the pad.

"You would have to get my bird shot all to hell on your last shift. Seriously, Cowboy, well done. I'm putting you and Prophet in for Distinguished Flying Crosses. Since our bird is grounded, you're officially off-duty. Det five is a bird short too, so they're flying one of their birds down here to fill out the fire team until we get ours fixed. When they arrive, I'll take your trail bird and start the next shift. This was too close a call. I don't want one of my men to get killed on the last day of his tour. You guys have earned it. Go get drunk with the SEALs—that's an order."

"Aye, sir. It has been a pleasure serving with you, sir." With that I saluted my commander for what may be the last time. He returned the salute.

"Same here. I understand you're going back home to be a civilian, good luck!" he said as he shook my hand.

"Thank you, sir." We counted the holes in the bird. We'd been hit fourteen times, including a hole in the tail rotor. Other than Doc Peavey who was wounded before pick-up, our prisoner was the only one wounded when he took a bullet through the shoulder. I asked the SEALs if he gained an extra hole because he wouldn't cooperate and Chief Walker said that he was a much better shot than that close-up. Talk about a charmed flight! We'd no idea of how many KBA the enemy lost in the firefight. No one was going to risk his life to go back in the swamps to count bodies.

I got cleaned up as well as one can here, and headed to the mess hall for a nice lobster dinner. My stomach had grown accustomed to steak and lobster in this hell-hole, but I'd gladly go back to regular rats, if I could take a real shower with clean water. I've been dreaming of a long, hot, soaking bath in a tub since my last leave. Soon dreams would yield to reality. When I got home I'd take my '65 Mustang off of the blocks and go for a ride, with the radio blaring. I'd get to listen to an honest-to-God American radio station and ride down the road without worrying about someone shooting at me.

In all of this, I felt our service here was only delaying the inevitable. What would happen when the Americans and all other foreign troops were all gone? The NVA would move to invade the South again, again, and again, until they eventually united Vietnam under communism. Sadness covered me

113

like a veil as I recalled a verse from a poem about military futility caused by making a failed command decision.

'Forward, the Light Brigade!'
Was there a man dismay'd ?
Not tho' the soldier knew
Someone had blunder'd:
Theirs not to make reply,
Theirs not to reason why,
Theirs but to do & die,
Into the valley of Death
Rode the six hundred.

We had waged a highly successful campaign here, but what did it matter? The end was going to be the same. Even so, I had no regrets for the part I played, for I was one of the six hundred. I shook off the sadness and made sure I wasn't wearing any skivvies in case the SEALs dropped by for a beer. They did. The entire SEAL team came to the Seawolf officers' hooch to say goodbye. I drank with the SEALs, my crew mates, and any other sailor that showed up. After telling the story about fifty times, (it seemed to get better with each beer and retelling), I was ready to hit the rack. Chief Butler blocked my path to my bunk.

"You're sleeping with us. We will be damned if you get yourself killed while off-duty waiting for a ride home, after last night. Our fridge is loaded with beer, and we have one empty bunk. If you're not in the rack, they will accompany you. Any objections?" He motioned to Seamen Tucker and Walters, who were armed to the teeth and reputed to be the toughest SEALs in the team. Tucker, holding an Ithaca pump twelve-gauge, asked me if I was ready to go. Actually, I did have objections. I wanted to spend my last off-duty hours playing poker with my crew mates.

Chief Butler sensed that and announced, "We're having a poker game until Cowboy leaves, in the SEAL barracks. All Seawolves are invited." That settled that. I wasn't about to insult them by turning down the protection they offered. It was their way of saying thank you for saving their bacon. I nodded to my two bodyguards that I was ready, and most of the Seawolf barracks cleared out to go with us. Poker and beer with my fellow warriors was a fitting end to my tour. I never did get any sleep. Since I didn't want fly home with a hangover, I drank slowly and kept some food in my stomach to slow the rate of alcohol absorption. We played poker until I was informed that the SEALORD had arrived.

I was told that they would be leaving as soon as they dropped the mailbag off and picked up the other passengers back to Binh Thuy. I begged them to wait until the mailbag was sorted. I had until the SLC was refueled and safety-checked. Mail call was also called "sugar call" in navy slang, and I was looking for sugar today.

With my bodyguard in tow, I followed the SEALORD co-pilot to the mail room. The post office clerk signed for the locked bag, and laid it on his desk. Once the pilot left, I looked over the counter and cleared my throat.

"Waiting for a letter?" petty officer Jackson inquired.

"I am. I have only about fifteen minutes until I hop aboard that SLC for home.'

"Congratulations, sir. Let me sort that bag real quick." He grinned. Looking for the letter that smells like you brother's barn or the feminine script that smells like roses?"

"The latter, but a letter from my brother would be nice, too."

The clerk unlocked the bag, and pulled out two bundles of letters, and placed the three packages over to the side. "LTJG Eugene J. Bordelon," he said as he handed me my brother's letter. He removed the rubber band off of the second stack and started looking through it. The suspense was killing me. I stood and waited, being one letter away from everything that now mattered to me in life.

"Here you are, one letter with that girly script. Hmm, doesn't smell like roses today. Well, anyway, have a nice trip home."

"Thanks, petty officer."

"Sir, it's time," said Seaman Walters.

Stuffing the letters into my pocket, I double-timed it with my two bodyguards to the Seawolf barracks and picked up my seabag and pistols. I had thrown away my old zoom bag and was wearing my tiger-striped camos I'd bought on the black market. My bodyguards delivered me to the SEALORD transport in time, and we lifted off to begin the first leg of my journey home. Several Seawolves and SEALs fired smoke grenades from M79's in different colors as a salute when we lifted off. Now settled in, I had the opportunity to read Beth's letter.

Dear Gene, I didn't want to send you this letter, and I didn't mean for this to happen. I fell in love with another man, and by the time you get back to the states I'll be married. I'm sorry to do this to you.

Beth

The "sugar" in my mouth turned as bitter as gall. I couldn't believe this! I was on the way home and dumped like yesterday's garbage. I read Roger's letter and was informed the culprit was a young doctor from the same hospital where I was to fly air rescue. My Beth, the practical one, it looks as if she got a better offer. I looked up from my letter through wet eyes and noticed for the first time who the other passengers were. Three body bags of River Rats, (Brown Water Navy Sailors) were in the back, being transported home for burial. This should have been the best day of my life. I was near exhaustion, needing sleep badly. The noise of the helo engine and rotor blades would hide my weakness from the pilots. I turned my back to the SEALORD crew; lay down and hot tears ran down my face like two candles dripping wax until troubled sleep claimed me.

SEAWOLF HQ/BINH THUY

The SEALORD pilot awoke me when we arrived at Binh Thuy. I awoke feeling better physically, but depression was a predator, patiently stalking me and waiting for me to surrender to apathy so that it could devour me. Every time I'd been here before to go back stateside, Binh Thuy was a welcome sight. The Seawolf HQ was every bit the same as when I was last here, but seeing it didn't generate any excitement in me. It was funny; one letter changed the world for me. Binh Thuy hadn't changed; I'd changed. Always before I had a plan, now I was just another soon-to-be ex-sailor with nowhere to go.

First stop, after grabbing my seabag, was to the o-club for a beer. Popping the top off of my beer, I slowly sipped it, contemplating the hand I'd been dealt. Yesterday I was a hero. Now I'm returning home to a place that didn't appreciate heroes after a civilian stole my girl. I suddenly realized I had no plan, no purpose. My parents died and left the farm to my brother, my girlfriend was gone, and the job offer seemed pointless.

I needed a clear head to think this through, and booze wasn't helping. I needed to stop drinking. My old buddy "Mad Dog" wrote back that there was no respect or honor from the public for the returning vets. He hadn't handled it well. The last I heard was that he crawled into a bottle and was trying to drink himself into a stupor. I didn't want to share Mad Dog's fate. I was at the crossroads of the rest of my life, and being a drunk didn't seem to be the right path. Pushing the beer aside, I looked around. SEAL Team Two's corpsman, Doc Steuben was in the bar.

"Hey Doc, can you do a Seawolf a favor."

"You bet, name your poison."

"Don't need poison, just a bunk for a couple more hours sleep."

"We have an extra bunk." He set me up, and I hit the rack for three more hours. I awoke feeling better physically, but still troubled.

I thanked the corpsman and went to see the chaplain. I hadn't particularly been a religious man while serving here, but there was nowhere else to turn but booze or God. LT Caffrey was a Catholic priest. I was raised Baptist, but today was not the day for doctrinal prejudices. Clearing my throat, I knocked on his office door.

"Come in," called the deep, bass voice from inside. I opened the door and beheld the man. At the sight of him, my jaw dropped, and my eyes grew as big as saucers. I had expected to see a scholarly type, soft from years of catechisms and prayers and hearing confessions. He looked to be about thirty years old, red-haired, and a towering giant built like a brick outhouse. I didn't expect to see such a rugged-looking man in such a gentle profession. He sensed my surprise. "I was taking a break from working on my sermon while I put on a new pot of coffee. Join me for a cup?"

"Yes, thank you, Padre." He poured us both a cup and motioned to the cream and sugar. I added cream to my coffee and sipped the hot liquid slowly. He noticed me eyeing him over.

"Is something wrong, Lieutenant?"

"Um, you're kind of big for a priest."

He chuckled softly. His eyes twinkled, recalling a time long ago before the war, when he was happy just being a college student. "I got a scholarship at Notre Dame to play football, but my real calling was the priesthood. I'm Father Michael Caffrey. How may I help you, Lieutenant Bordelon?"

"Gene will work. I'm nearly a civilian anyway."

"Call me Michael. You didn't call me father, since you're not Catholic. Since you're not here to confess anything, I suppose you have something to talk about."

I thought it over a moment and decided that calling him Michael wouldn't do. I was here to seek spiritual advice, Catholic or not. "Padre, I'm not Catholic, but I do have to speak with someone. I guess you've heard it before. I planned to marry my college sweetheart, but she sent me a Dear John letter just before I was to ship stateside. I feel lost, like a ship adrift. I've dreamed of going home to her. It was so real I could taste it. It was what kept me going in dangerous situations: bad weather, loneliness, and the feelings of hopelessness following the start of the United States' withdrawal."

He lit his pipe and puffed it a bit and gave it some thought. "Do you recognize God as the creator of the world?"

"Yes."

"Do you believe He has a purpose for the world he created?"

"Of course."

"Do you know that God is interested in you personally?"

"I hadn't thought about His caring much about the specific details of my life. But, ok... I might believe he cares what I do and where I go."

"Have you considered that God could be closing one door and opening another one?"

"No, I hadn't thought past my pain."

"I want you to do this. Keep an open mind and forgive everyone involved. Keep your eyes prayerfully open and expectant of what God may do next. Faith is the key. When the door opens, you'll know it." The words of the chaplain penetrated my heart as surely as a surgeon's knife. He prayed with me, and we had a second cup of coffee. A load was lifted off my shoulders and I felt I could be free. With no plans, the possibilities were endless, not just purposeless. I had my lifeline, and I would take it. I visited with the chaplain, and he told me stories of his glory days at Notre Dame until it was time to go.

I took an uneventful flight to Saigon, and then hit the military transport to San Francisco. When we reached Travis AFB, I picked up my baggage and checked for a flight that would be going to England AFB. I was to report stateside to San Francisco to a MAJ Callahan for debriefing, which I thought was unusual because I was a naval officer, and major was not a naval rank.

GOING STATESIDE AND THE OFFER

I assumed I was to be processed out. MAJ Callahan met me at the airport personally. As I looked at the other servicemen, I realized that no official military officers were greeting them, and I was curious. I followed the major out to his car and threw my seabag into his trunk. The major directed me to sit in the front passenger's seat. As the car moved down the interstate, I drank in all of the sights and sounds of my country like a child discovering it for the first time.

MAJ Callahan saw me looking at the radio, which was turned off. Seeing my interest, he motioned an invitation for me to turn it on. I was all over it like a fat kid given a cake. In no time, I had a rock-and-roll station tuned in and was listening to Simon and Garfunkel singing "Cecelia." "Cecelia, you're breaking my heart..." *That will not do*, I thought. I changed it to another station, and Santana was playing. "You've got to change your evil ways, baby." I wasn't in the mood for heartbreak or evil woman songs. I turned it off and looked out the window as the government sedan traveled down the interstate.

"Dear John letter, Lieutenant?"

"Sir, yes, sir."

"Lieutenant, what are your plans?"

"Sir, I haven't any, sir. My girlfriend dumped me, my parents are dead, and my little brother is running the family farm." Vietnam's future and my own uncertain future was a dark storm brewing over my mind.

"You're a fine pilot. Ever consider continuing to serve?"

"The war is winding down for the US, and it looks as though all Charlie is waiting for is for us to leave."

"What if I were to tell you that I can get you into a unit that takes fighting communists to the next front? There will be no cowardly politicians or antiwar protestors to worry about. And, what's more, you will make a difference. Be warned, there will be no glory for battles won, no public recognition."

Suddenly I saw the open door that the padre told me about, and I wasn't about to let it close. "I'm not in it for the glory; sign me up."

As we pulled up to his office, I had a sense that the offer was genuine. MAJ Callahan bade me to follow him to his office. "Lieutenant, have a seat." He took a seat at his desk, and I sat down across from him. "Lieutenant, were you serious about starting a new chapter in your service to America?"

"Absolutely."

"Do you have any business stateside?"

My parent's farm was willed to my brother and the only property I had was a red convertible '65 Mustang on blocks at the farm. My ex-fiancée married someone else while I was in 'Nam. "I have no unfinished business."

"Okay then. I want all of your property including clothes that have any military identification." MAJ Callahan threw me some civilian clothes just my size. "Lieutenant, please change your clothes."

I handed him my seabag with all of my personal effects in it, and quickly changed into the civilian clothes he gave me. He opened my seabag and revealed the walnut carrying case containing my two pearl-handled Colt forty-fives.

"Very nice. Do you have any shells with it?"

"Yes."

"I'll take the shells; the pistols you can keep."

I surrendered three boxes of .45 shells. He checked the cylinders in my pistols to make sure they weren't loaded and handed the box with my pistols back. After changing into the civilian clothes that he gave me, the major took all of my personal identification and the pictures of my grandparents and parents.

An uneasy feeling was settling upon me, replacing the sadness that was dominating my mind the previous minute. The major had seen that look before. "Relax, you'll get these back when you arrive at your post." The major was busy filling out paperwork, in a file that was marked LTJG Eugene J. Bordelon, Jr. After he finished writing, he pulled out an inkpad and stamp and firmly stamped it on one of the papers, pressing it evenly so the mark was clear. I caught a glimpse just in time to see the word "DECEASED" in red letters on the page. Instantly my mind thought of stories I'd heard of some kind of covert CIA ops where the agent is officially "dead." *What was I getting into*? I thought. My internal klaxon inside was sounding off, as real as any all-stations alert, causing tight knots to form in my stomach.

He chuckled as if he was party to an inside joke. "Don't worry. Where you're going, son, there are no newspapers or protesters following you—just Soviets to fight."

"I noticed you are a major and I am in the Navy. How did you get access to my discharge papers?"

"Someone very important decided to pull some strings to invite you to join an elite force."

I was beginning to feel like Tom Sawyer at his own funeral. I pointed at the paperwork. "How did I die?"

"Officially, you were part of a helo crash from Bin Thuy to Saigon. Bodies burned beyond recognition, that sort of thing. All of the paperwork of your getting to Saigon and coming home will be shredded. Your family will be notified. I am sorry for the loss they will feel, but it can't be helped. Your "body" will be flown back and buried with full military honors in a closed casket ceremony."

"What if the offer doesn't work out? I mean, if you find me unsuitable for the task?"

"Then we'll discover that we were mistaken about your death, and apologize to your kin for upsetting them."

I was given three days' liberty in San Francisco, but I was ordered not to discuss any of this with anyone. For my liberty, I was given civilian ID, some money, a phone number and an address to report to at zero eight hundred on the third day. Spending the next three days seeing San Francisco, I tasted the food, went to Chinatown, rode the trolley cars, and talked confidently to women I'd never met before and hoped to make some memories. Soaking in a real bathtub every night for an hour was a luxury I had sorely missed. The three days were over way too soon. I sucked it up and reported to the address I was given.

I checked the address on the paper one more time and knocked on the door. 1LT Wilson gave me a new flight bag with what seemed to be all the gear and personal things needed. He motioned me to follow him. As we got close to the door, I noticed two other young men dressed just as I was, standing at the door. We all piled into his van and were driven toward New Mexico—into the desert. The fact that I was officially "dead" and being taken for a ride into the desert set off my internal claxon to the color of blood.

WELCOME TO HELL

Our driver, Corporal Heily gave us our travel rules. "You are not to ask or reveal your real names to anyone in this van. We will be eating in the van when we do eat. I'll go into the establishment and order our food "to go." You will not get out. Stretch breaks will be done on desert highways when there's no traffic. We will have bathroom breaks at small gas stations along the way. When we stop, do your business and get back in the van. You are not allowed to wander around or talk with civilians. I'll do all of the talking. If you can't avoid a civilian, keep the conversation short and respectful." Our driver was not very talkative; he only spoke when he had to, and nothing more. I got to know the men that rode with me in the van, as much as you can without real names, that is. We were all either marines or sailors. We all had one thing in common. We were not ready to quit fighting communists. You might say we all had some unfinished business.

Twenty-two hours later we arrived at an undisclosed location somewhere in the New Mexico desert. We'd passed barbed wire and private property signs about fifty miles back. We pulled up to a group of barracks and stopped. The driver left us alone in the bus without saying a word. About a minute later, a door opened and a very large black man in a uniform I didn't recognize stuck his head into the bus. He started screaming at the top of his lungs in the most intimidating way imaginable. "You sorry excuse for human beings, get out of my bus! No! You are not human beings, you are whale crap, and it is my duty to my country to make sure each and every one of you fails this training! MOVE IT! MOVE IT! MOVE IT!" Everyone was trying to get out at once. There were four exits: two front doors, side sliding door and a rear door. We looked like a bunch of cockroaches surprised by someone turning the light on at night. When we finally got out, we were made to fall into formation.

The man that startled us out of the van was even more intimidating as he stalked up and down our line, sizing us up and eyeing us with contempt. "My name is Master Sergeant Darkside. You are training for a nameless elite force of the United States of America which has no affiliation with the five military branches, to fight communists. You are never to speak of this unit in public. As far as the American public knows, you are all dead, and as such, I can do anything I want with you. I'm your Senior Drill Instructor! You will refer to me as Senior Drill Instructor or Sir! Each time you address me you will start with sir and end with sir! I am not your friend! My last class had a seventy percent dropout rate, but I'm on a learning curve right now." He smiled for a moment as his eyes shone with appreciation for his own accomplishment. "This time I expect to wash out more of you, maybe all of you, as you are much more pitiful than the last class. This class is twelve weeks long. If there is any defect or weakness in you, I will find it. I will exploit it with every mean and evil trick I have at my disposal." His eyes bored holes into me with that last remark. "If I wash out all of you, I get to spend the rest of the training session chasing women and drinking beer in southern California... and working on my suntan."

He paused to see if anyone cracked a smile thinking of a man so black talking about getting a tan. I was fairly petrified and his joke didn't faze me one bit. "Anyone who is unusually stubborn that tries to deprive me of my liberty will suffer. There are two other instructors, Sergeant First Class Ironsides and Staff Sergeant Iron Fist. We are to be obeyed without question. You will not talk back, make excuses, or let down your teammates. We turn the lights out at twenty-two hundred each night. Before we turn the lights on at zero four hundred each morning, you will hit the floor and begin dressing. You will eat your meals without talking, keep your sleeping area clean and orderly and make your bed each morning after dressing. You will be taught how to make a proper bed, and I better never see a wrinkle or crease in the sheets or blankets. You are not to tell any of the other trainees your real name, or ask theirs. You will be identified in the following manner." He pointed to each man in turn and said, "Jones, Smith, Williams, Carter, Holmes, Lewis, White, Black, Green, and Brown." (I was now Smith) "You are to join the rest of the trainees that arrived yesterday. Line up, single file and report to the quartermaster to receive your gear and uniforms."

I was issued a seabag and two new khaki uniforms. They marched us to the barracks, ordered us to put on one of the uniforms and instructed us to pack the contents of our seabag in the footlocker at the foot our beds. Once we were in uniform, MSG Darkside spoke once more. "You are to report to the armory to receive your training rifle. The armory is the last building on the left. MOVE IT! MOVE IT! MOVE IT!"

We all lined up and marched in quick time to the armory. We met SSG Iron Fist there, who handed each of us a cadet's training rifle that weighed about the same as a sniper rifle, with a rifle strap and a fake sniper scope. "Okay ladies, this is my sniper rifle. I had better never see you without it. You will carry it during all of your training. You will keep one hand on it while you eat, and it will be placed next to your bed while you sleep. DO NOT lose my rifle! There will be hell to pay if you do! The reason that this isn't a real rifle is that we don't give a real rifle to little sissy girls. You have to prove that you are a man before that will ever happen. I seriously doubt any of you will ever get a real rifle."

He stopped speaking, and suddenly a look of unbelief emerged on his face, as though he was in charge of the worst bunch of idiots alive. "What're you looking at? Fall in, in front of the building!" he screamed.

After we fell out, he eyed us like an eagle looking at a mouse. "That rifle is your companion. The day that I catch you without hand on it or its sling, you are through. You will even do push-ups with one hand on the rifle. The only exceptions are when you are asleep or in the shower. When showering, it had better be just outside the shower, but don't let it get wet! The proper placement of your rifle when you sleep, and until you are dressed is against the wall, within three feet of you at all times. You will find my favorite form of character building, or in most of your cases, washing you out, is to run. Run, run, run." For the first time he smiled and I knew we were in trouble. "There are twenty trainees that arrived yesterday, nearly as sorry as you are. We will now join them. Fall in, single file, double time."

We followed him to the end of the compound where a class of twenty men was still doing pushups from when he walked away and left them. He ordered them to fall in with us, and we started running. Considering this was a desert, he seemed to be holding back from what he would have done in a milder climate. Even so, it was brutal. I was acclimated to jungle humidity, and this was a stark contrast. We ran, then we walked and then we ran some more. We stopped to get some shade every once in a while, but the instructors made good use of the time by lecturing us on communism and freedom. When they decided we were up to it again, there was more running and walking, running and walking.

On the second day, we were joined by another sixteen trainees. By the end of the second week, they adding rock climbing and repelling with a sixty-pound backpack to the routine, with ropes and climbing gear. I began to notice a pattern. They ran us very hard early in the morning and just before dark, when it was cooler. During the heat of the day, we did physical training or PT inside of the main training building, or on the shaded side of a mountain.

We had a weird setup with the instructors. Two of them were *pushers*, who seemed to delight in torturing us in any way imaginable, but SFC Ironsides was the *encourager*. The encourager's job was to try to get the trainees to keep going, appealing to their sense of teamwork and honor. He said, "If you quit, you'll let your teammates down. You don't want to be a quitter, do you?" The idea was for the pushers to push us past what we thought we were capable of, and the encourager would help us draw on anything else we had left. Even with the encouragement, by week four we were down to thirty trainees.

Normally, at least you would have the personal satisfaction of knowing you were training for the Marine Corps Force Recon, Navy SEALs, or Army Rangers. In those elite units, while the instructors were tearing your pride down, you were developing another sense of pride in what you were training to become. It was not so in this case. The ones who washed out were never to know what they washed out of. This way they couldn't reveal anything about the organization. I knew nothing other than I was training to fight communists.

If I left, I would be resurrected "from the dead" and discharged. I was sure there were a bumper crop of ex-military pilots competing for jobs with the major airlines, with the war in 'Nam winding down. Besides, even if I didn't know where we were going, the idea of continuing the unfinished business with the communists had hooked me. I was here to stay. I was determined that they couldn't kill me and anything short of that couldn't stop me.

Then it happened. During week six of the training, one of the trainees known as Green, collapsed. The instructors sent us on a light duty drill with SFC Ironsides, our encourager, while they took him to a medic. It was later learned that he'd died from a congenital heart defect that he had from birth that no one had caught in the physicals. The stakes had now been raised. SFC Ironsides gave us the news about Green. He said it was a tragedy, but it couldn't have been foreseen. He told us to take heart. Our class would be getting a strenuous physical examination before we resumed training. All of us were examined again from head to toe by a new doctor and pronounced fit to resume. I'd convinced myself that they would have to run me off or kill me to make me quit. Now I was unsure about whether or not I could die in training.

By the end of the week, we were down to twenty-two trainees. The death of Green was disheartening to some. Each man knew he could die in training, and the washout rate increased.

Once the pushers were convinced we were fit and that we weren't going to die on them, they turned up the pressure. Now we were able to run all of the time, except for the hottest part of the day. The order of each morning was to perform a circus, which was doing PT until you collapsed, which we despised. There didn't seem to be a minimum standard for us; we just had to give one hundred percent. It was their job to push us to the limit and beyond. At first I thought they were trying to transform us into supermen. It became clear to me that the goal was to keep the ones who couldn't accept failure as an option, who would see the possibilities and not the obstacles. In short, they wanted men who were physically and mentally tough, who could get the job done.

By week ten, it became apparent that if I were going to finish, I had to be able to ignore my body's protest for lack of proper food, sleep, and water. I had to force it to function on autopilot. Every part of my physical being cried out for rest, and it seemed I functioned at times asleep on my feet. Like the myth about earwigs that bored into a man's ear and then into his brain, the desire for a big, fat, greasy cheeseburger had burrowed itself into my mind and would not leave. I had to push thoughts of pleasant food out of my mind, or I feared I'd go insane.

Early one morning I was doing pushups. I noticed a scorpion crawling in a direct line toward me. By now, though, I was more scared of MSG

Darkside than that scorpion. Even so, I believed that if I were stung I might end up back home, or at least set back to another class. Not willing to repeat the last ten weeks if I could help it, I stopped at the top of the upstroke of a push up.

"Sir, Senior Drill Instructor, there's a scorpion crawling toward my hand, sir."

MSG Darkside walked briskly toward the scorpion scarcely four inches from my left hand and crushed it with his boot. He looked at me, still frozen in the upstroke of a push up and screamed at the top of his lungs.

"You worthless piece of whale crap, did anyone tell you to quit doing pushups? On your feet!" SSG Iron Fist took over his class while MSG Darkside took me on my very own circus. He pushed me outside until it was too hot, and then pushed me in the shade and indoors. When the sun grew low in the sky, he pushed me outside some more. When I was about to collapse on my feet, MSG Darkside ordered me to attention. He got right in my face. "Why are you here!" his scream held the force of cannon fire aimed at my resolve and splitting my ears. "You are taking up valuable space in this class that could be used to train someone that's a real man. You will never make it. Why are you torturing yourself? Go ahead and quit. You and I both know you want to."

"Sir, Senior Drill Instructor, no sir!" He spent a good ten minutes trying to convince me I was worthless, and that all of my pain was going to be for naught because he was going to wash me out anyway. I dug in and tried to ignore every word, but my body was almost to the point of breaking. Finally, he dismissed me.

I was too tired to eat that night, so I skipped supper, showered and fell into bed. Zero four hundred came very early, and I nearly didn't get out of bed before the light switch clicked on. Now my error of not forcing myself to eat was catching up with me. I almost couldn't make it through my morning PT before breakfast. Breakfast was too little, too late, and I devoured it like a ravening wolf. "Brown" was watching me and knew what was happening. We'd become very tight during training, and even though he was very hungry, he slipped some extra toast under the table to me. My eyes searched his, imploring if he was sure and he nodded. Giving him an appreciative look, I stuffed the toast into my mouth. I was determined that I'd pay him back. He was now more than a trainee. He was my brother. It took determination to overcome the setback of not eating anything the night before.

Within two days, I seemed to be back to normal, if normal is being exhausted, starving and running on reserves. We started doing daily drills carrying a man across our shoulders. We carried him until we were unable to carry him any longer, then we switched. The idea of not leaving a man behind was drilled into us. Individuals were washed out. They were training teams. By the end of week ten, we were down to twelve trainees.

We saw changes to the morning run on week eleven. The instructors put belts with metal clips on them on each of us and tied us all together with a rope on each side of the belt during our runs. We were already accustomed to it during rock climbing exercises, but this seemed to make it apparent that we had to all stay at the same pace. By midweek, they broke us into three groups of four. Each of us had to strap our sniper rifle over our back and placed an eight-foot pine log on each shoulder about five inches in diameter to do our runs. It was actually more of a quickstep than a run. The logs were fresh cut and oozing pinesap. Our t-shirts were examined periodically to determine if we were shouldering our load or ducking under it. Each group of four was grouped by height, to keep the shorter ones from being under the load. The sticky pinesap was nasty in the hot sun, but we knew better than to avoid letting some of it get on us.

By the end of week eleven, we were down to ten trainees. The most stubborn of us still remained. I couldn't say we were the strongest. A bodybuilder left the first day and some of the more physically imposing specimens left, as well. I'd say the only thing those of us who remained had in common was that we refused to quit. I was beginning to feel as though I would make it to the end. I was dying to know what the unit's name was and where we'd serve. Ten trainees were left: Brown, Carter, Alvarez, Graham, Jones, Garrett, Wilson, Clark, Hunter and me (Smith). We were forbidden to ask anyone their real name. In truth, I'd never met any of these men before here. I thought it odd that a tour in Vietnam didn't acquaint me with any of these men. It was only later that I found out that we'd been screened to keep from having men in the same camp with anyone they knew. I'm sure they couldn't be absolutely certain. The way Carter and Jones regarded each other when they got here indicated they might have slipped up, though neither man said anything.

Week twelve started with ten trainees. We were to take our end-of-training test at the end of the week. The instructors were driving us harder than ever, and each step was a challenge to make it. Some of the other trainees and I took hot sauce from the breakfast table and rubbed it into our eyes to keep them open. Now we trained on teamwork courses. Each drill was designed so that if we didn't work together, we could not complete them. On the day before graduation of this evolution, we were put through our qualifying test. It was a combination of strength, endurance and sheer stubbornness, combined with a need to show strong teamwork skills. If we graduated, there would be a banquet prepared for us. Afterward we'd be transported to the next evolution of training. The encourager hinted this phase of training would be more technical.

The qualifying test for graduation started at zero five hundred. We started running with a full pack and rifle, a log on each shoulder and tied to four other men. When it seemed it couldn't get any worse, they made us run across loose, rocky terrain. Each man was tied to the others, and it took a maximum level of teamwork to keep from stumbling. We had to be careful to stop and allow a teammate to recover when he stumbled. Finally, after we ran for what seemed forever, we were able to cast off the accursed logs. Next we were to climb Diablo Point, a sheer rock face and the hardest climb we'd seen yet. We all made it up to the top alive and repelled down the other side. It was now noon. Usually we trained in the shade or inside, but not today. We were informed that the end of our course was twenty klicks across the desert. We had exactly four hours to make it, and we couldn't leave anyone behind. SFC Ironsides issued us each a full canteen. With a full pack, sniper rifle and canteen in the hot sun, we started our quest. If anyone fell behind, the only way to finish the course was to drag or carry him with you. I was determined that if I had to drag all nine of them, I was going to finish. We made it just less than four hours. Thankfully I didn't have to carry anyone.

At the finish of the course, SDI MSG Darkside begrudgingly admitted that we'd completed this phase of the course and didn't make any disparaging remarks about us failing the next course. Then he gave us our first clue. "You men have completed the first phase of training for the ASDC, American Space Defense Corps. You'll be briefed on the nature of your service in your next phase of training. A graduation banquet has been prepared for you inside. Lights out tonight will be at nineteen hundred. You may sleep in until zero six hundred tomorrow. After breakfast in the morning, you'll pack your gear and the bus will take you to the ASDC Academy. Enjoy your meal."

The first thing that I mentally calculated was that we were being offered eleven hours of sleep! My bunk's siren call beckoned, but not before I ate my fill. We went inside to find a spread that would make any restaurant proud: roast beef, chicken, potatoes, rice, gravy, hot fresh baked bread laden with butter, vegetables of all sorts and fruit tarts, pies and cakes. And then I saw it—a pan with greasy cheeseburgers and grilled onions. The cheeseburgers called my name and my stomach rumbled a reply. My body obeyed the call with no conscious effort of my own. Like an animal snare, the cheeseburgers were set to take me prisoner. Inwardly a ravening wolf, I knew I'd be very sick if I didn't eat slowly and stop when I got full. I shared that with the others, and some listened, some didn't. It took all of my discipline to quit. Near starvation had given me a hoarding mentality. Taking an extra helping of roast beef, I made sandwiches out of some rolls. Wrapping them up in a napkin, I took them back to the barracks for later. No one seemed to notice, and the instructors seemed not to care. At least three men ate until they puked their guts out. I couldn't wait until bedtime for the luxury of five precious hours of extra sleep.

I hit the sack at nineteen hundred and slept until midnight, woke up to use the head and finished off my stash of roast beef sandwiches. Afterward I slept like a dead man until zero six hundred. The mood was upbeat as we packed to leave. After a breakfast of eggs and sausage, biscuits, gravy and pancakes, with real maple syrup, we met the bus. I must confess that most of us shoved extra biscuits and sausages into our pockets. We'd all developed a concentration camp mentality about food.

Our driver was SGT Foster this time, but I was too tired to care. We loaded into a white panel truck with no passenger windows and were driven back into the desert. I dozed off as soon as we left the training center. How long I slept, I didn't know. Since there were no side windows on the panel truck my only clue of the time of day was seeing the stages of the sun and night through the driver's front windshield, and our breaking for meals. None of us had any watches. It didn't matter. Most of us slept part, if not the whole trip. I awoke and rubbed the sleep out of my eyes. I was hungry again and wolfed down the sausage and biscuits I'd hidden in my pockets earlier. Real strength was beginning to seep back into my body, not the reserve autopilot strength loaned to my sheer will, but real physical strength. I was beginning to feel like the worst was over, and I could handle whatever they threw at me. Even so, I was apprehensive about where we were going.

ASDC PILOT'S SCHOOL

How long we traveled into the desert or which direction, I didn't know. We finally arrived at the mouth of a box canyon. The panel truck didn't allow us any side view, but we could see through the front windshield. We passed two guard towers as we entered its mouth. I straightened up and looked over the dash to see a sign pass by that read, PRIVATE PROPERTY, NO TRESPASSING. As our van entered by a checkpoint, the guard examined our driver's credentials and let him pass. Finally, we arrived at a large building and the van rolled to a stop. "Get out of the van, and wait here," SGT Foster commanded as he walked off.

Ten minutes later we were greeted by Sergeant Major Lionheart. "Fall in," he commanded.

After what seemed to be forever, an officer with a uniform I didn't recognize arrived and addressed us. "My name is General Edwards. You're all here because you're the best, you love your country, and you don't think the war should be over until the enemy is defeated. I'm giving you all a chance to finish some unfinished business. You're now cadets in the ASDC and will be trained as pilots. When your training is complete, you'll be given an officer's rank and new orders. May God be with you."

SGM Lionheart addressed us. "Follow me." We were taken to our barracks and given a classroom schedule. It was more like officers training than the hell we'd just experienced.

The next six weeks were very similar to Naval Aviator School, but the ships were more like hovercraft with awesome weapons I didn't think existed. The physical training here was different. The training facility had twelve floors. Every morning and afternoon we stretched and spent an hour climbing up and down stairs. Each session was followed up with a half an hour of aerobic training. We were allowed a full seven hours of sleep a night and fed better. Slowly I was beginning to regain my strength.

Each of us was issued an honest-to-God sniper rifle, which we practiced with an hour a day on the range. The rifle I was issued was a Winchester .308 caliber, bolt-action with a very expensive Leopold scope. We were warned to be very careful with that weapon and not to drop it. In class, we were taught to compensate for differences in atmospheric pressure, temperature, windage and gravity. Some of the atmospheric pressure readings and temperatures were off the charts.

We also had classes in both Russian language and Soviet tactics. Training also included maintaining and caring for a flight suit that was more like a space suit. Finally, in the last two weeks we were taught the terrain and particulars of Luna and Mars. We were informed we'd engage the enemy as an elite fighting unit, which was highly classified.

I couldn't sleep for a while after hitting the rack the night before graduation. "Brown," I whispered.

"Yeah, Smith."

"Are you apprehensive about tomorrow?"

"Yeah." He was on the top bunk; I was on the bottom. He peeked over the side the bunk to see my face.

"Graduation is tomorrow. We get our orders after the ceremony."

"It doesn't seem real. All this talk about fighting on other Luna and Mars…"

"From what I hear, if you're former Navy, you get assigned to Mars. The commander there is a former SEAL and seems to prefer sailors working for him."

"Mars! This still seems like a dream. But it has to be real. Nobody would go through all this effort and trouble, to play a joke on us. Still, it's hard to take it all in. By the way," I whispered, "my name is LTJG Eugene J. Bordelon from Rapides Station, LA. If I die, I want somebody to know who I was."

"Same here. LTJG Tobias R. Jackson, McComb, MS."

"Joseph."

"What?"

"My middle name is Joseph, what's yours?"

"Romeo. If you tell anyone, you won't have to worry about the Russians." He paused for effect. "I'll kill you, myself."

The following day, dressed in our new class A uniforms, we graduated in a solemn ceremony and were presented with a sword. The MC of the graduation ceremony, BG Edwards informed us we were shoving off at zero nine hundred the next morning for our new duty station.

We were then stripped of our personal identity. BG Edwards instructed us that we were to drop our regular names and use call signs only. He explained that early in the solar conflicts the Soviets had learned of some of their names. The Soviets traced them back to the pilot's families, and they suffered retribution. "For this purpose you're officially dead. You'll choose a name to be referred to from now on. If you select a name you later grow to dislike, you may change it with your CO's permission, or at promotion time." My fellow officers chose their names. My good friend from the Academy "Brown" became Ricochet. Other names like Phantom, Stone Cold, Hitchhiker, Joker, Rain Cloud and Grim Reaper were chosen. When the colonel got to me I just replied "Cowboy, sir."

"Your tour is four years. For Luna, you get two weeks leave a year. For Mars, you get one month's leave on Earth every two years. You'll be sent home at the end of your enlistment, depending on the distance from the Earth at the time. You don't ship off when Earth's orbit makes for a long trip home. If your service is over and you're not re-enlisting, then you have the option of working as a noncombatant until the next transport leaves. Food is a precious commodity and all of us do something to earn their keep, even if they're waiting on a transport home."

Tobias and I packed our seabags that night and celebrated at the o-club with our graduating class with a few beers. The next morning after breakfast we were ushered to the transport freighter *Odyssey*. It looked different from anything I'd seen before. There were twelve graduates, young lieutenants that boarded the vessel. We were instructed to put on our spacesuits. I began to get an uneasy and at the same time exhilarated feeling. Just then the transport freighter pilot interrupted my thoughts. He was at least thirty-five years old. He seemed to have a confidence born from being past the new stage and settled into the familiar routine. His name was CPT Ripsnort, which I thought was unusual.

"Boys and girls, you're about to embark upon the final frontier. I hope you all have your wills prepared." We all looked up with questions in our eyes, but were cut off before anyone could speak. "You boys remember San Francisco? You know, pretty girls, fine food, music and culture? Where we're going, there isn't any of the aforementioned," he said, laughing at his own cleverness and our uneasiness. "Fasten your seatbelts; we're going to your new home." We stowed our gear onto the transport freighter and buckled up. The freighter lifted off in a plume of fire and a cloud of hot gases—we were past the point of no return and I was committed. Part of me thought, *well, you've gone and done it now*; the other part of me said, *bring it on.*

Once we broke orbit on the way to our new post, CPT Ripsnort gathered us together. "Okay, we should arrive on Luna in sixteen hours. Those getting off on Luna will need to stay in a space suit for the trip. Your suit is pressurized to four hundred millibars, which is our standard for all posts. Since you've recently undergone high-altitude training, you're already adapted to it. The gravity onboard is artificial and matches Luna for the benefit of you boys going there, but will be adjusted to Martian gravity for the rest of the trip for you other men. The cabin pressure for the rest of you is seven hundred fifty millibars to start, and will be tapered down to four hundred gradually over the course of the trip to Mars. For those going to Mars, we're going to be together for a little over two months so don't irritate me. We have a few ways to help you pass the time during our trip. The ship has a gerbil gym, and you're expected to exercise regularly and keep fit during the trip.

There are a lot of old movies in the library, and we have lots of games. Your new commanders want you to play some flight and combat sims, based on past encounters with Soviets. Also, there's an orientation video I know you all will enjoy. After you have seen it, sign off on the training sheet.

You'll also continue your Russian language studies. I'm a qualified instructor."

The orientation video piqued my interest. I had a lot of questions, and I felt I'd find most of my answers in the video. The other pilots were curious, too. The video viewing room was big enough for three people, and it was finally my turn. We were looking for some answers, to change the uncertainties of the unknown into the certainties of the known. The screen flickered, announcing the beginning and the narrator began to speak.

"The struggle between the Soviets and Americans isn't new. While the Americans have a public war going on in Southeast Asia and a very public space race, we're conducting a secret war on other worlds in our solar system with the Soviets.

The ASDC uses technology and materials from an alien race called the Ktahrthians. The technology we have extracted is either from crashed spaceships we've recovered on Earth, or from archaeological digs for relics on Luna and Mars. From the relics we've deciphered, we've determined that the alloy-x we do have comes from a vessel about the size of Earth's moon, which served as their space station, home world and ship. The relics cipher told the story of a race who had to abandon their home world because their star went into nova stage. The Ktahrthians built the great vessel to transport their colonists, ships and technology to look for a suitable home world. The disc that crashed on Earth in 1959 was part of an exploratory expedition. They'd hoped to colonize Earth. They'd built a base and started an aqueduct system on Mars, only to have their colonial ship blow up from some kind of mechanical failure, killing all of the colonists and sending the material from the station flying into space.

According to the archaeological digs historical account, only a few ships that were away from their space station survived. That included only a handful of discs along with the technicians and support staff on a couple of bases. From what we read, the ships and their crews left our solar system. The technology from the archaeological digs on Luna and Mars is the basis for much of the technology we use in our ships and buildings.

We also have other advanced technology in medicine, computers, communications and mechanical engineering that we've gleaned from the relic ciphers from different archaeological digs. We use the controlled-release strategy to market some of the technology, using the cash to finance our war efforts. The ASDC mission focuses on both the fight to obtain any alien technology left in archaeological digs and the possession of alloy-x. Alloy-x still falls in meteor showers, and we still fight battles over it.

Luna has no atmosphere and the atmosphere on Mars is nearly one hundred percent carbon dioxide. Fortunately alloy-x can also be used for constructing ships and weapons based on alien designs. We're limited to hovercraft physics, because of the weight of the fighting vessels and weapons. The hovercraft we use have antigravity drives to hover and conventional carbon-based fuels for propulsion. The original alien discs as well as the transport freighters we use for space travel are completely antigravity driven. Our brass use a faster antigravity transport freighter with hyperdrive, but it actually consumes the alloy-x antigravity drive after a time. It may cause the transport freighter to fly twice as fast, but it wastes the very valuable alloy-x. We use heavy transports to move everything from troops, machine parts, water, food, medicine, tools, and everything from toothpaste to live fish and plants. Luna is far from self-sufficient. Mars is as close to being self-sufficient as it gets.

An expedition will soon establish the newest post on Ganymede, one of Jupiter's moons. Eventually all of the Galilean moons of Jupiter will have posts, as well as Saturn's moon Titan."

The rest of the video was technical in nature. It covered how we maintained and built life-support systems and other operational details. I was particularly interested in the Rules of Engagement, negotiated by accords struck with the Soviets on Luna and Mars.

Sixteen hours later we arrived on our first stop, Earth's moon, and I was utterly amazed. I'd no idea we could travel that fast. On the lunar post, we met some other pilots who manned the post there. None of them used real names. Names like 2LT Joystick, CPT No Name, and SGT Slingshot were some of the names we encountered. Afterward we were all given our bunks, and told to report to mess at eighteen hundred. I grabbed a tray and looked around. I had the sense of awkwardness a kid has in a new school on his first day. Finally, my eyes met up with someone, who looked as if he'd give me the time of day. I wanted to know what I'd gotten myself into. *A post on the moon*, I thought. *The American public had no idea. What else didn't they know about?* I sat my tray next to the lieutenant. "2LT Cowboy," I announced.

"Good name. I'm known as 2LT Undertaker. I guess you've got a lot of questions. What did they tell you?"

"They said that I'd be fighting Soviets, and I wouldn't have any politicians or antiwar activists to worry about. They showed us an orientation video that answered some questions. My duty post is Mars." I took a bite of scrambled eggs and washed it down with a sip of coffee.

"US Navy, I'll bet," he stated, as though it should be have been obvious.

"Sure, I am or was a sailor."

"The first Commander of Luna was COL Cavender, a marine. Luna is a *Marine-only* post by tradition. Mars is a *Navy-only* post. They are a little more relaxed. You'll hear an occasional *aye* instead of *yes,* and it usually regarded as a correct military courtesy there." He paused to let it sink in, and attacked his eggs and biscuits. "How was your first spaceflight?"

"I'm still thinking if I pinch myself that I'll wake up and learn it was just all a dream. It is hard to believe that space travel on short notice already exists. I feel like I left Vietnam and woke up in a science fiction movie. As far as the ride over, re-entry was pretty rough."

His eyes twinkled like firelight, and a knowing smile played across his lips. "Only VIP transport freighters that carry the brass are exact replicas of the original alien discs. Our tanks use a combination of antigravity technology and hydrogen gas combustion propulsion. Troops are moved with hybrids of conventional and alien supply transports unless the need is particularly urgent. The real differences in flying alloy-x ships using strictly alien technology are in the amount of weight they can carry and how smooth the landing and takeoff are. ASDC command isn't worried about soldiers having a smooth ride. To be sure, antigravity technology makes re-entry and launch as smooth as silk. Rocket technology is a real rough ride by comparison. Everything hinges upon the economics of alloy-x, and we can't waste any."

"I can't believe I'm actually on the Moon. Tell me about the post here."

"The space race was not what it seemed. ASDC's first commander, GEN Colson took the picture of the Ranger 6 Lunar Lander in '64 with a camera. The first American post, Eagle 1 was later destroyed by the Soviets and this post is Eagle 2. The first battalion on Luna was called the Black Dogs, with all marines under COL Cavender. The marines of Eagle 1 died rather than surrender. Marines here are very proud of them. You'll hear of the Black Dogs from time to time. There is a Bronze statue of CPT Smith facing down a Soviet tank with his service pistol in front of this post." His eyes shown with pride, and it was clear that because CPT Smith was a marine, my new friend shared in his historic and courageous stand. "To keep our secrecy from lunar probes and Landers, we have people working inside NASA, providing the codes for the transmission feeds. This way whenever a probe or Lander tries to take live pictures, our computer actually takes the equipment over and gives them archive feeds of old pictures before we got here. Luna was the first world the ASDC colonized, and the most important."

"Tell me about Mars."

"The commander on Mars is COL Squid, a former Navy SEAL. He prefers to have naval personnel working for him. He's a tough one, a fourth-degree black belt in Okinawan Karate, and makes his men work out three times a week. If you're going to serve there, it is because he chose you, not the other way around."

"I understand I'm officially dead and have a new identity. How did they do that?"

The young marine flashed a knowing smile as if he were about to reveal a club password or secret handshake. He stabbed some scrambled eggs with his fork and pointed it at me. "One of the big shots on the Central Command is LTG Amidio Mondragon. He job is information and influence. Think CIA, only without government controls. If you need records created or destroyed anywhere, he's your man. The ASDC has secured a large amount of social security numbers over the years and has built identities when needed around them, complete with work and tax records, driver's licenses, high school diplomas and the like."

"What happens if I'm ever fingerprinted back on Earth? My fingerprints are in the Navy's database as belonging to a certain dead junior-grade lieutenant."

"Not to worry—we have people in the Navy and other branches of government that take care of that. The real magic starts with one of several coroners whom we have in our employ. Every time a dead body shows up, they scan the fingerprints and send them to our spook group. The spooks run them through all known databases. If they have no previous military, government service, or arrest record, the prints are proclaimed "clean." Those fingerprints are then swapped with the ones in your own file. Then they attach your real fingerprints to your cover as an active duty naval officer, in your case—alive and kicking."

"Amazing."

"LTG Mondragon is one good friend to have—definitely not someone you want as an enemy."

"I'll keep that in mind. When my tour of duty is up, then what?"

"Eagle 2 has been here since July, so we haven't been here long enough so that any of us has finished a tour yet. However, Eagle I was here since November of 1963, so we have a little history to go on. If you are ready to retire, they will magically resurrect you as though you'd never died. If not, you'll go back to the Academy as an instructor, or accept a promotion and another duty assignment. Some of them retired to some civilian or government job, with a selective type of amnesia if you get my drift. Believe me, if you still alive after four years, you'll be instructor material."

I held my fork up to indicate I was about to bring up an important point. "I haven't seen any women here."

"Yeah, that's a serious drawback. This is a hardship post, no women or children. The next time I'm on leave I intend to spend a lot of time in their company."

"If my understanding of planetary science is right, sometimes Mars is a very long way from Earth. What about my leave time or discharge?"

"Well, with Luna being only sixteen hours away we've been promised two weeks every year. Mars is a different story. You're a minimum of two months away from Earth, and it can be up to four. Mars is a very new post, but I've been told Mars will only get leaves every two years, one month plus travel time. So far no one has been there long enough to go on leave. On Mars, they only intend to launch transport freighters when the orbital alignments make for a shorter flight. There's been talk that we are soon to start a new post on Ganymede, one of Jupiter's moons, which is even further away for travel time. It's twice the size of Luna. There is enough water ice on the surface to melt for water, and an oxygen atmosphere, though it is very thin. The reason they're going there first is the geological survey team sent out reported that there is more alloy-x there than in the other moons combined. I was offered a transfer there with a three year enlistment and a six-month leave in between if I re-enlist and a large cash bonus."

"You didn't volunteer?"

"No, I'm a marine, and marines serve here."

"The new commander setting up the post on Ganymede is not a marine or a sailor?"

"No one knows yet."

"Hey, I'm not shipping out for a couple days. Any chance of my flying patrol while here on the moon?"

"Not a chance, if we lose one of you boys before you get to your post, there will be hell to pay. Besides, COL Red Fangs is a former marine, and we're all former marines. He doesn't like squids in his tanks, sorry."

The next three days were spent in Russian language class. We were informed we weren't tourists, and we had to get prepared for our service ahead. On the third day, CPT Ripsnort said, "Okay, children, we're going to your new home. Pack your gear."

I got to know the other young officers fairly well. 2LT Ricochet, who was my friend "Brown" in basic training, became my best friend. It was a long trip. We arrived sixty-six days, sixteen hours and eight minutes after we shoved off. CPT Ripsnort announced, "Okay children, we're home, and may God help you." As the transport freighter made its rough descent, we saw an ever-growing image of a post similar to the one we left on the moon. There were differences. The terrain around Eagle 2 on Luna was tan, and the surface was pockmarked with craters. As we approached Mars, the globe resembled Arizona, albeit without any plant or animal life, and with fewer craters than Luna. I looked out of the ship's porthole, and the sight the Martian Grand Canyon left me breathless. It made Earth's Grand Canyon look very small indeed. I couldn't take my eyes off of the terrain. As we made our descent, I ventured to look out of the window, and saw flames reflecting off of our heat shields. As we neared our landing, I noticed that the ground color was that of whitish sand. I didn't know what else lie in store, but to me it was beautiful and knowing where I was settled my spirit somewhat. It reminded me of the Sahara desert, but with a red sky and some mountains to the distance. I was told that Mars usually had a blue sky. It was only later that I learned that the red sky color was caused by the presence of dust particles that were suspended into the thin Martian atmosphere by a recent dust storm, effectively diffusing the blue spectrums and creating the *red sky* effect.

CPT Ripsnort skillfully landed our vessel, and the aircraft conveyer moved our freighter through the transitional airlocks, and then into the freighter hangar. After unloading, we were met by LTC Exit Wound. Immediately his wingman, 1LT Night Hawk announced, "Attention!" We all snapped to attention. The post's first officer looked like a bull, but my internal klaxon alerted me that this man was as dangerous as a tiger stalking his prey. In boot camp, MSG Darkside was intimidating but was a pussycat compared to this man. I controlled myself and remained stiff as a board, eyes forward.

"Men, this theater of war isn't cold, and the battle lines aren't confused. Cowardly politicians haven't compromised our mission. Protestors won't harass you. Here, there are no innocent civilians that you have to keep an eye on to see if they're in reality the enemy. Everyone on Mars is either your friend or your enemy. Our turnover rate is high. We're in a desperate struggle with the Soviets. Keep alert and fight as a team alongside your fellow pilots. 1LT Night Hawk will show you to your quarters, schedule and duties. Each one of you will be called to meet COL Squid personally after you're settled in. The colonel is currently out on maneuvers. You'll find this unit is the best in the solar system and we all stick together. Dismissed."

1LT Night Hawk led us to our quarters. "LTC Exit Wound is as tough as boot leather. You'll all do well to remember that. The same is true for COL Squid, though he's more of a thinker than LTC Exit Wound. We're a brotherhood here, and we're all family. We live together, eat together, drink together, fight together and sometimes die together." He dropped me by my quarters. "It's all about loyalty. You watch your brother's back, and he watches yours. Understand?"

I nodded as he handed me a printed copy of my schedule and a map of the post. "The buildings on this post are all underground and constructed of concrete, bricks and Martian steel. The cement for concrete we import from Earth, but we make the bricks and steel here. Martian steel is high in magnesium which we mine from regolith. It's light and very strong. We get basaltic sand from here to add to the cement to make concrete. The main building you're in now is our post HQ. It contains the command officers' offices, barracks, mess hall, sick bay, exercise and rec rooms.

This post is built like a wheel underground, with spoke-like corridors from each building to the post HQ in the center, and a corridor around the outside circle of the wheel. There are only two structures outside of the wheel. One is the above-ground satellite tower, though there is an underground corridor from the wheel to get there for the technicians who have business there. The other structure, or structures, rather, is the green house complex, where we grow and process food. It also has a corridor from the main wheel to get there."

Once his speech was over, I thanked him and entered my new quarters. It appeared as though one other pilot was already living here. The room had a TV and two PCs, two bunks and some sparse furnishings. I saw some pictures of a tall, blond man holding up a big fish and another of him kneeling before a Virginia whitetail deer that he'd killed. A placard next to one of the computer desks said CPT Chainsaw. I didn't know it then, but there was a reason for this. I was going to be his wingman and he would be teaching me. I unpacked my bags and opened my pistol carrying case, taking pleasure in the dark glow of the polished walnut. *No shells*, I thought. I guessed I'd have to hang them on the wall as ornamental. I'd spent the short time in Vietnam flying and wearing them on my hips as Seawolf pilots weren't armed. If an enemy got past the door gunners, they were already in the helo. For a pilot, the only sensible weapon for a pilot was a pistol. I had given up my share of the family farm to my brother. The pistols my grandfather had given me were now my only inheritance, and as such—my most prized possessions. My familiarity with them gave me confidence and were a symbolic bridge to my family.

CAPTAIN CHAINSAW

Earth date: March 6, 1971—Martian year 192, Sol Mercurii, sol 3 of the Martian Month Taurus—sol of the Martian year 303

I settled my clothes in the empty dresser and mounted my pistols on the wall next to my new bunk. I heard the door open and the man in the fishing picture greeted me. He was about six-feet tall with sandy-brown hair and brown eyes. He opened his mouth in a deep southern accent and said, "How ya doin'? I'm CPT Chainsaw." I went to attention and saluted. He laughed. "This will get old real quick if you think that's necessary in our quarters. At ease. You're excused from saluting in here from now on, and never salute me in the field. Saluting in the field is called a *sniper check*. Understand?"

"Yes sir."

"Good," he said, extending his hand.

"By the way, what's your first name?"

"Captain," he replied with a gleam in his eye. "I believe my mamma named me Captain."

"So it isn't encouraged to reveal much about your identity, I take it."

"Affirmative. That way if you're captured by the Soviets, you can't tell them anything. It will be my job to teach you everything I know and your job is to guard my six. I want to finish my four years, go home, get married, get fat, have a couple of kids and hunt or fish every weekend. Allowing me to get killed is a violation of a direct order. Got that?" I nodded an affirmative. "Good, we'll be sticking closer than any family you've ever had. For you to keep me alive, I must keep you alive." He spotted my pistols on the wall. "Nice colts."

"My grandfather's, I wore them in Vietnam when I flew." I took the box down, removed one of the pistols from the display case, and flipped open the cylinder out of habit. Finding it not loaded, I handed it to him.

He inspected its nickel-plated finish, scrollwork and pearl handles admiringly and then handed the pistol back to me.

"Any questions?"

"What can you tell me about this place?"

"Mars," he began, "is a subject of many legends and myths. These are the facts. Mars has two moons, Deimos and Phobos, but they're smaller than most cities, 12.6 and 22.2 kilometers, respectively. They're so small you can't see them as they pass overhead. I wouldn't call them moons, they're more like asteroids from the asteroid belt between here and Jupiter trapped in Mars' gravity. They have no alloy-x as we have long picked them clean and they're too small for posts.

A Martian solar day or sol is 24 hours, 39 minutes and 35.244 seconds. They keep us on schedule by resetting the clock back to midnight thirty-nine minutes and thirty-five seconds after midnight. We go by the Darian calendar. A Darian month is twenty-eight days: every sixth month it is twenty-seven. The twenty-fourth month of the year, Vrishika, is twenty-eight days, except leap year. Days are referred to as sols here, but don't get hung up on trying to change the whole English language. We still say yesterday, today and tomorrow. The sols of the week are Sol Solis, Sol Lunae, Sol Martius, Sol Mercurii, Sol Jovis, Sol Veneris, and Sol Saturni. A Martian year is 668.6 Martian solar days."

He stopped and smiled. "I hope you know if you signed up for a four-year tour it is 7.53 Earth years. Leaves are 3.57 years apart, Earth time." He grinned at my shocked expression.

"Just kidding. We go on the Martian calendar and day here, but your papers were signed on Earth, so your service is in Earth years."

"One question?"

"Shoot."

"How do we keep track of that extra thirty-nine minutes and some odd seconds added to a day? I mean, we have to be able to keep time properly for mathematical calculations."

"Okay, the best way to explain it is this. Let's say it's twelve minutes after midnight. On Earth it would be referred to in military time as zero hundred twelve. Here is said to be twenty-four hundred twelve. Zero hundred doesn't occur until after the extra 39 minutes, 35.244 seconds are added into the previous day. This keeps our time square with the Martian sol. Our computer programs adjust and keep accurate track of the time. However, if you get an Earth standard clock in your quarters, you must set it back 39 minutes, 35 seconds each night when you go to bed to keep it on time."

"So adding them after midnight gives us more time in the rack, or a longer work day?"

"This is a hardship post and in the short time we've been here we've seen a high mortality rate. You might've noticed that there are no women here. They give us more rack time when they can to improve morale.

Let me see, where was I? Oh yes, Martian gravity is only thirty-eight percent of Earth's. You'll need to exercise regularly in the exercise room that has corrected gravity to keep your heart strong. Mars is a cold place and a desert. You wouldn't guess it by the pictures. The surface temperature can get down to -200 °F at the poles in winter and up to 68 °F at the equator during summer days but it isn't typical. However, the air temperature rarely gets above 30 °F. There's surface water that's liquid in briny pools and ice patches, mostly where the Martian crust is broken by meteors making craters. The crust is broken and the underground water rushes out, only to have half of it quickly sublime away while the rest freezes. In almost all temperatures, the sublimation rate will cause the water to evaporate to salts and minerals. The two icecap-covered poles have a mixture of frozen water and carbon dioxide sandwiched between layers of dust, although the South Pole has more water ice than the North Pole. The water that sublimes around the globe winds up as snow over the poles.

There are shallow pools of water underground close to the equator. This is one of the reasons we built our post here. The second reason is a more moderate climate than elsewhere. Last of all is position. Valles Marineris is to our back and a fracture system north of us which makes the enemy go through narrow canyons to get to us.

Our main buildings are underground and heated. We have five wells on the post, which are under part of the complex to keep the water from freezing. The good part about the water here is it has no pollution or harmful microbial life in it, but we have to run it through a desalinization process to remove the peroxides and salts. The atmosphere is composed of ninety-seven percent carbon dioxide. The atmospheric pressure here is about what it is on Earth at twenty-two miles above the surface. For all practical purposes, it is a soft vacuum. We produce breathable air from peroxides that we extract and refine from Martian regolith. Our suits and the main buildings have carbon dioxide filtration systems, but we lose a little air when we open an air lock or take off a suit. Our production facilities make enough oxygen to make up for the loss."

"What's our commander like?"

"COL Squid was a green face on SEAL Team Two, as were LTC Exit Wound and MAJ SEAL. This is a Navy-only post. COL Squid teaches Okinawan karate classes to all pilots three times a week and it is mandatory that you train. He likes competitive games: running, boxing, karate and chess. He expects your best. If he challenges you to some contest, beat him if you can. If you throw a match to try sucking up, he'll put you on crap detail for a month. Oh, by the way, COL Squid is back from maneuvers. He wants to see you in his office," he said, grinning. "I'll notify your next of kin. If and when you make it back, I'll take you on a tour of the hangar deck and show you around."

"I'm not asking you your real name, but where did you serve?"

He thought for a second. "I'm not going to be able to hide this from you, being my roommate and all." Pulling his shirtsleeve up, he revealed a Seawolf tattoo from Det Four on his upper right bicep. I responded in kind by showing off my Seawolf tattoo. He smiled like a kid in a candy shop. "We're going to get along just fine. In case you wondered why you got the invite to this party here, this place is run by SEALs, and they love the hell out of Seawolves."

I asked for directions and followed them to the post commander's office. The outside door to the commander's office led to COL Squid's aide's office, which served to keep anyone from bothering the commander unless the business was specifically with him.

"COL Squid is expecting you," informed PVT Gray Eagle. The young private looked as though he may come into puberty any day now and ask someone to teach him how to shave. He had high cheekbones, dark eyes and hair: Choctaw or maybe Cherokee, I surmised.

The inner door to the commander's office was an oddity here, real polished oak with nice grain. I knocked on the door to hear, "Just a moment." I heard a thunk sound hit the door.

"Come on in," beckoned the deep, resonant voice from within. I wasn't entirely prepared for what I saw. The man before me was holding a four-foot long blowgun. He looked beyond me and pointed to the door. "Not bad, huh?" I turned toward the door and saw six blowgun darts stuck into a cork dartboard. All six darts were either in the center or very close.

"Not bad," I agreed.

He motioned for me to retrieve the darts and try it. I did so and came nearly close to equaling his, to which he appeared pleased. CPT Chainsaw's description of a man who likes to compete in games was accurate. Good to know my intel so far was straight. Before me was a very muscular man in his mid-thirties, about six-foot tall. From his accent, I suspected he was from the northeastern US, probably Maine. Dark brown eyes and short brown hair accented his square face and Greek nose. He met my gaze evenly, and then dropped his eyes to read something else.

"Son, do you know why you're here?"

"I've heard some of what's going on here."

He pointed to the picture on the wall showing a field of alloy-x scrap being gathered by some utility vehicles, guarded by tanks. "This is the reason we stay here. This resource is extremely precious and neither side is willing to let the other side have any of it. The rest of the space race is soon to be carried to other worlds, but we remain here. Just the alloy-x scrap that falls on Mars alone could cause the rise of the next superpower. We patriotically defend this planet and fight for every piece of scrap. We call it scrap because it is either pieces of the original Ktahrthian's colonization vessel that exploded in space, or scraps of exploded tanks or other structures here. Any questions?"

"Just when do I start?"

"That's the spirit." He smiled at me as though I was his new best friend. I would learn later that though he was tough, he inspired men to follow him because he cared for them as if they were his sons. He looked down at the report in my file and looked up. "I personally handpicked you for this post from the recruiter's list. As a Seawolf pilot, you had a good record, kept your nose clean, did your job and never let the other sailors down. I see your detachment flew support for SEAL Team One. In addition to the ribbons and medals you were previously awarded, you have also been "posthumously" awarded the Distinguished Flying Cross," he said, with an easy smile and glint in his eye. "That was one hell of an engagement. It takes a lot to impress me. That's what brought you here." He handed me the medal. "I think we'll get along fine. The inventory of your personal stuff has listed a pair of Colt forty-five pistols. Do they have sentimental value or are they tools only?"

"Both, I used to wear them over my zoom bag and they were my grandfather's."

"Can you shoot?"

"I'm not as good as my grandfather, but I like to think I'm okay," I said, frowning a bit.

"What's wrong?"

"MAJ Callahan let me have my pistols but wouldn't let me bring any shells."

He smiled at the mention of the major. "MAJ Carnage made a name for himself on Luna. He is the one who "killed you" with a rubber stamp." But shells are not a problem." He opened his desk and handed me the three boxes of shells I had to give up to MAJ Callahan. "I want to see you shoot. If you're any good, I'll order you all the shells you can shoot. Oh, and I suppose you'll want this," he said as he handed me my parents' and grandparents' pictures. Then he presented me with a box and bade me open it. It was leather-bound King James Bible. "Church services are Sol Mercurii at nineteen hundred, Sol Solis at zero nine hundred and nineteen hundred. karate classes are at eighteen hundred on Sols Lunae, Mercurii and Saturni."

"Sir, is that an order, sir?"

"The karate classes, yes. But you shouldn't have any trouble with that. You are listed as being a first-degree black belt in Keichu-Ryu Karate. I've heard of that style. You will be expected to share your style with us. We follow Bruce Lee's philosophy of adapting what is useful, rejecting what is useless and adding what is specifically our own, so that our style is continually evolving. SGT Samurai shares Aikido techniques with us.

As for the church services… no, it is not mandatory. But, I'd be disappointed if you died not knowing God. Everyone here has the freedom of religion. But true courage and wisdom comes from God above."

I nodded. "I'll be attending both."

"Excellent! Now, I suppose you would like to know what's expected of you. You're to be CPT Chainsaw's shadow from now on. As wingman your primary responsibility is protecting him and performing any mission duties that you're assigned. Keeping him alive is a direct order. Do not disobey this order! I have lost eight pilots in the two months we've been here. If you survive until the end of your four-year tour, you will no doubt be on my senior staff, or offered a job as an instructor back home."

After being dismissed I found CPT Chainsaw back at our quarters.

"Okay, it's time for the tour. Do you intend to wear those pistols outside of your space suit?"

"If it's practical, and doesn't cause me any issues, yes."

"I see you got some shells. Well, load your pistols and bring them with you."

After I loaded my colts, he took me to the hangar deck, where he gave me a tour of our equipment and gear.

"You have three weapons once you're outside of your ship, the sniper rifle, your service revolver, and your combat knife. The sniper rifle is a scoped, bolt-action Winchester .308. We'll be spending a lot of time making sure you are proficient in that. Your standard issue revolver is a .357 Colt, but you can use any revolver you like. Semiautomatics jam too easy because of all of Mars' ever present dust, so we don't use them. Finally, this is your combat knife."

I was unimpressed as he showed it to me. It was just a double-edged knife with a five-inch blade. "I've seem bigger knives in 'Nam." He unsheathed it, walked over to an old flight suit that had failed safety inspection and sliced the oxygen hose off of the helmet, then cut a slash in the suit. He tapped his head with his finger, indicating I should use my head.

"You don't have to stab anyone here."

"Understood."

"The Martian environment is harsh and unforgiving. Mars demands respect and will try real hard to kill you. Always keep that in mind. This is your flight suit. It is designed just like a spacesuit as it has to keep you warm, provide air and maintain the proper pressure inside. It will take a while to get accustomed to walking in it. The center of gravity is on the outside of your body now instead of your body-center. This suit is very resistant to rips and punctures, but it isn't perfect. Don't let your flight suit get ripped. Your flight suit has hot patch kits in your left sleeve pocket, and it is imperative you fix a leak quickly. If you get shot, the wound isn't your first concern, patching the hole is. You have to get a hot patch from your utility pocket or your suit will start the decompression process. You will suffer great pain in a matter of seconds. Getting a case of the bends isn't pleasant, I assure you. With complete decompression of your suit, your mucous membranes and surface fluids in your eyes, nose and lungs will boil, and you'll experience severe abdominal pain from trapped gas pockets in your intestines.

Being gunshot is another story. Your suit has packets next to your skin. If punctured, these packets release medicine that kills pain, stops bleeding, and fights infection. Nothing can stop an alloy-x sniper bullet, though. A surgeon will have to get the bullet out if the wound isn't fatal."

"Will I die if my suit decompresses and I can't patch it?"

"Yes. Your suit decompresses in about fifteen seconds. Then you develop the bends, fall into unconsciousness and suffocate, long before you freeze to death. Did they teach you how to use a hot patch in basic training?"

"Sure."

"Suit up." After I was fully suited up, he helped me strap my pistols on over my flight suit. He retrieved a stopwatch from around the neck of a mannequin that was wearing an old flight suit. Before I knew what was happening, he unsheathed one of my pistols, and fired three shots into the mannequin. BLAM, BLAM, BLAM! I was a bit stunned that he took such liberties with my piece. But as I was to learn later, the captain felt that important lessons needed to be visual and action oriented.

"Now, show me. Our lives depend upon it. You must be able to apply the patch quickly. Here, grab this bag full of patches, and we'll practice on this old suit until I'm satisfied that you can do it right and quickly." He motioned for me to demonstrate how to apply the patch. I pulled out a number three hot patch. It had a clear backing that I had to peel off to activate the chemicals heating up the adhesive on the side. The peel-off backing protruded an inch past the patch to make it easier for a pilot with bulky spacesuit gloves to handle it. I had the patch securely applied in eighteen seconds.

"I regret to inform you that your son was killed in the line of duty for being too slow! Now we will be here all day if we have to, until you get it down to ten seconds or less."

It didn't take all day. I got my speed down to nine seconds within fifteen minutes. He continued with my orientation.

"After you patch the hole you must send an encrypted distress signal before you lose consciousness. This helps your rescuers get to you before the Soviets do, and to get you medical attention. There's very little atmosphere here. When ejecting away from the battlefield if your tank starts to blow, you have retrorocket boots that have just enough fuel to let you drift to the ground.

The helmet and suit maintain air pressure and help heat or cool you. We use a closed-circuit rebreather to breathe. The parts of the unit are a sealed facemask, a counterlung, a breathing bag and a carbon dioxide scrubber. You breathe through a sealed face mask inside of the helmet. When you exhale, the carbon dioxide is redirected to a carbon dioxide scrubber tank. If we didn't have this setup, your only hope would to be rescued by the Americans or captured by the Soviets before your air runs out. If your suit is torn and you can't patch it, your partner can help you before your suit decompresses. If no American is present and the Soviets are, it is preferable to be captured than to die from the bends. This isn't a good idea, but it beats death. All prisoners are examined thoroughly. They may not know your real name, but they will fingerprint you, record your voice, x-ray your teeth, take a DNA sample and weigh and measure you. You'll be catalogued to the last detail. It is good not to let that happen. It is best not to get captured, but it is better than death. Don't give up any information about us. We will have a few bits of disinformation to give them in case you're captured.

We have an accord with the Soviets for prisoner exchanges, but sometimes they kill pilots instead. Sometimes it is a judgment call as to whether a pilot is killed in a battlefield situation or captured. Oh, and you're going to love this piece of equipment." He grinned like a jackass eating saw briers and held up what looked like an adult diaper. We hadn't had to wear them on the flight over because there was a proper head on the shuttle. When he saw that the idea of wearing my own excrement disgusted me, the captain gave me an amused look. It brought to mind the hazing we'd given new Seawolf pilots, and I realized the shoe was on the other foot, now. "It's an astronaut diaper worn under your flight suit. You may get accustomed to it, but trust me, you'll never like it." I rolled my eyes and wondered if there was a way to avoid getting caught on missions taking a dump in my astronaut *skivvies*.

"Oh, and another thing, you'll probably collect sand and fine dust in the joints of your suit if you get out of your ship. It is mandatory to vacuum all of dust off of you when you enter an airlock and come into the buildings. The dust here is ultra-fine and gets into the bloodstream if inhaled, which isn't healthy.

A radio inside your helmet allows you to communicate with your fellow Americans. The speakers are in your helmet and the microphone is inside your rebreather mask and both are wireless. While you are flying, if you don't receive a transmission or speak, you can listen to music from your ship's music program."

"What if I decide to sing along?"

"The music shuts off."

"Okay, I guess communication is the most important thing."

"Correct. To continue... There's a voice-activated feature to switch to a common channel to talk with the Soviets if you need to. We'll have to tweak the adjustments when you get suited up or you'll get echo and feedback. Your helmet is very abrasive resistant and will withstand sand blasting from blowing dust and sand. Dust devils will kill you if one hits you while you're outside of your ship. They're often as tall as fifty kilometers and your space suit isn't able to stand up to the abrasive effect of basaltic sand at high velocities. We've lost scientists and pilots to dust devils. They usually occur when Mars reaches perihelion, which starts dust storm season. The dust storms can be global sometimes and reach two hundred miles per hour and we're unable to predict them. If it gets bad enough we'll all get grounded until the storm is over.

The sector we're in is referred to the Tharsis Plain, which has four very large inactive volcanoes and the Martian Grand Canyon, Valles Marineris.

The area where we're located is mostly a "young" basaltic lava surface covered with sand and dust from a few centimeters to a hundred meters thick. We have some sand dunes here. The wind seems to be constantly changing the surface of the planet."

"Do we ever get a break from the fighting?"

"Our treaty with the Soviets gives us a cease-fire on Christmas, May Day, Thanksgiving, October Revolution Day, USSR Constitution Day, the Fourth of July and New Year's Day. The first two cease fires we've had were this month, USSR Constitution Day was October 7th, and October Revolution Day was October 25th. Wouldn't you know it that the Soviets would get the honor of the first two cease fire days?"

"What did you do with your cease fire time?"

"I went sightseeing with 2LT Kestrel to the four main shield volcanoes, including Olympus Mons, the tallest mountain in our solar system."

"2LT Kestrel died this month?"

"Last week," he said quietly. I saw he wasn't in the mood to talk about his old wing man's death, so I changed the subject.

"What other duties do we have besides fighting the Soviets?"

"We have scientists in teams at various locations around the globe, but they're not armed or escorted, as the treaty puts geological and scientific studies as nonmilitary. However, archaeological digs aren't protected. Should one of our geological surveys unearth what would be classified as an archaeological dig for alien technology, the gloves are off. We aggressively fight for any alien technology we can find. Once in a while you may get called to help defend an archaeological dig or act as a military escort for some scientists coming back from regions around the globe.

The backbone of the Soviet fighting force here is the Stalin, a tank like the American Grizzly you flew at the Academy. Its forward speed is 27.94 meters per second, slightly one-half mile an hour faster than ours. However, the Grizzly is slightly more maneuverable than the Stalin. In short, we're built to fight, not to run. However, having said that, the ever-present dust on Mars can be your friend if you're being pursued. Your exhaust jets kick up a dust cloud behind you similar to running a car over a dusty road and it gets difficult to pursue you closely. Your dust trail also marks your trail from a distance. If their satellites pick up your dust trail and enemy ships are ahead of you, they can send a dispatch to cut you off. We fly as a group in a *flying v* formation, to keep the dust out of your fellow pilots visual and radar." He opened one of the lockers and handed me a sniper rifle. "This will be yours; it belonged to my old wingman, 2LT Kestrel. His plaque is in the memorial room. I'll do my best to make sure you don't receive that same honor."

"How did he die?"

"Defending me." He became thoughtful and added, "He gave his life for mine, and I'd have done the same for him."

He took me down to the quartermaster and got me fitted out with all the gear I needed. Afterward he took me out on a short run in our tanks close to the post and started teaching me how to do coordinated moves with him in order for us to work together on the battlefield. He worked with me every day for a month. I was not allowed on patrol until I was familiar with how the units worked together and in particular, how I was to work with him. He taught me how to use the exhaust jets of my engine to kick up the sand and dust behind me to my advantage. Dust and sand were everywhere. Our hovertanks reminded me of my dad's old '54 Chevy pickup driving down a dusty road, leaving a trail of dust behind as it went along. I was just young enough to enjoy kicking up clouds of dust and became quite good at using this to my advantage on the battlefield. I also had to spend three hours each day for a month learning how to use a sniper rifle on Mars. True to his word, COL Squid got me some forty-five shells for my colts and I spend a lot of time target-practicing with them.

The old-timers of this station had only been here three months. Even so, they were the experienced ones. I became CPT Chainsaw's shadow. I learned to fight side-by-side, back-to-back and never wander off or let the enemy draw me away from his side. He spent every waking hour teaching me the ways of an ASDC pilot. He instructed me at meals, after hours in our quarters and every opportunity in between. I studied his every move and came to predict even when he would turn left or right. I knew what he would do next in battle just by observing the situation. This enabled me to be just where he needed me. When my presence was beginning to irritate CPT Chainsaw, he would tell me to go play. I'd go shoot basketball, watch TV or play cards with 2LT Ricochet and the other junior pilots.

The first six months were hard on the junior pilots. Lieutenants Phantom, Joker, Hitchhiker and Rain Cloud were all killed in skirmishes, followed by solemn services and plaques on the memorial room wall. A sniper bullet shattered 1LT Night Hawk's hip socket. After a hip replacement, he still wasn't able to pass his fitness exam for a pilot, so he rejoined us as legal counsel. Only half of the pilots I came to Mars with survived the first six months.

Combat provided more opportunities for promotion for the survivors, and the colonel was pleased to promote both Ricochet and me to first lieutenant. Ricochet became LTC Exit Wound's wingman to replace 1LT Night Hawk.

It was Earth year 1973, March 12. Being a "greenhorn" doesn't last long here. I had survived two years of combat missions (twice as long as I was an active duty Seawolf pilot) and went home on leave. 2LT Stone Cold had died two months before his first leave. Of the eight pilots that I had arrived with, only Lieutenants Ricochet, Grim Reaper and I were still alive to go on our first leave. Grim Reaper had plans of his own. He wanted to stay the entire time at Miami Beach, lie in the sun and chase women. Ricochet and were both Vietnam combat pilots, and had spent two more years fighting the Soviets on Mars. We desired to see some symbols of American freedom. We visited several symbols of American liberty: Mount Rushmore, the Statue of Liberty, the Lincoln Memorial, the Tomb of the Unknown Soldier, Arlington National Cemetery, and Congress and Senate in session. Last but not least— we went to a Yankees–Red Sox game.

Finally, it was time to call my brother Roger. At first he thought the call was a cruel hoax from someone who opposed the war. He had attended my closed casket funeral. I had to tell him the story about how he got the scar on his right shoulder before he believed me. Then I apologized again about that one; honestly, it was an accident.

Understanding that I was not permitted to meet him in Alexandria, he agreed to meet us in New Orleans for three days of deep-sea fishing. Ricochet and I spent time with Roger and his two sons, which we promised to do every time we came back. It was understood that Roger and the boys couldn't ask what I'd been doing. I let them know that it was honorable service to our country, and that I could say no more.

Soke Marx met us in New Orleans at a friend's dojo for a week of Keichu-Ryu training. This would become my practice on every leave home. He was impressed with my cross-training in Aikido and Okinawan Karate and by the end of the week promoted me to second degree black belt in Keichu-Ryu.

We still had enough time left to meet Grim Reaper at Miami Beach for a week of girl chasing. I didn't take the same girl out twice in a row. Beth had taught me a lesson about long-distance relationships. I had some laughs but didn't keep any phone numbers or addresses. I had nothing to offer since I was going back to Mars.

On November 19, 1973; in a joint effort, both Ricochet and I got a battlefield promotion to captain for saving COL Squid from a sniper. Tobias couldn't resist the joke, so he changed his call sign to "Kangaroo."

I followed my orders to the letter, and in the Earth year 1975 I saw MAJ Chainsaw to the transport freighter home. I became MAJ SEAL's wingman when 2LT Dust-off bought it.

It was November of 1975 and leave time again. Kangaroo, Grim Reaper and I had survived thus far. It was also decision time. We would have to declare at the end of our leave if we were returning or processing out. The three of us would make that decision later. We all decided to take our leave together. First we trained with Soke Marx for three days and then we fished with my brother and his sons for another three days. Kangaroo had sold us on going to Alabama to turkey hunt. ASDC's planners helped us to book a hunt which included a lodge, equipment, licenses, and a guide. All three of us tagged out with nice, fat gobblers. I had my bird deep-fried, southern-style, packed on dry ice and ready to take back with me. Time was short, but we made it to Miami and chased girls for a few days before driving non-stop back to Utah. We all re-enlisted.

The fourteenth day of the month of Kumbha in the Martian spring, Earth year 1976 became a turning point in my career. When a sniper killed MAJ Headache, I was promoted to major and got my own wingman, CPT Grim Reaper. Later that year I lost my first wingman and friend to a sniper. This weighed heavily on my heart. During my whole tour in Vietnam, not one of my crew so much as received a purple heart. Of the pilots that I arrived on Mars with, only Kangaroo and I were still alive.

I got my new wingman, 1LT Dutchman, straight out of Naval Aviation Top Gun School. I was now accustomed to the routine. Other than the high mortality rate, this felt like home. My wingman and I tuned into each other and were in sync almost from the start. We had Vietnam service in common. He had flown an F-14 Tomcat off of the USS Constellation providing air support for Operation Frequent Wind, the evacuation of Saigon. He sported a tattoo on his upper right arm of a tomcat with a holster and pistol, one of the patches of the VF-2 Bounty Hunters. We had several shared interests: martial arts, chess, fencing, and baseball. To my relief, I was able to keep this wingman alive.

In the Martian spring during the month of Makara, Earth year 1978, it was time for my third leave. Usually MAJ SEAL did not take leave at the same time that I did. He had been unable to go on leave for the last three months because of orbital alignment issues, so he was going on leave with Kangaroo and me. We headed for New Orleans to meet Soke Marx for advanced keichu-ryu karate training and then a little fishing with my brother in the Gulf.

We had an open invitation to stay at my pen pal, Warren Hard's farm in Lebanon, MO., and we stayed with them overnight on the way to New Orleans. The three of us were more than welcome, and his wife Gladys cooked up country heaven. Considering all of the soy and fish we'd been eating for two years: roast beef, mashed potatoes, Dutch apple pie and cold goat's milk was going to be the talk of our return trip home. The next day we said our goodbyes and headed south.

We spent the second week of our leave with Soke Marx and the third week with my brother fishing in the Gulf of Mexico. MAJ SEAL left us after the fishing trip to go visit his family in the Chuska Mountains on Navajo Nations land. His mother still lived in a hogan next to his Grandmother Mary, Uncle George and Aunt Elsie Mae.

We didn't want to go to Miami Beach to chase girls, so we stayed in New Orleans. Grim Reaper's death was still on our minds, and we didn't want to think about it. New Orleans was a great place to meet beautiful and interesting women. Even so, I still elected not to keep any addresses or phone numbers. We spent the rest of our leave in New Orleans, enjoyed the music, the food, and the ladies until we had to go back. As usual, it was over all too soon, and we reported back to the Academy to fly back to Mars.

Once home, I settled back into the familiar. I thanked God that my wingman was still alive, which was how I aimed to keep him. On the sixth day of the Martian month Sagittarius, Earth year 1979, LTC Exit Wound was offered his own command on Europa when a sniper killed COL El Tigre. He accepted, and MAJ SEAL was promoted to lieutenant colonel.

The Martian summer, Earth year 1979 brought more changes. COL Squid was shot out of his tank in a fierce battle and was finished off by a sniper before we could come to his aid. LTC SEAL was promoted to full-bird colonel and made post commander. I was called into his office and promoted to light colonel. COL SEAL's wingman, CPT Kangaroo was promoted to major and decided the joke was over and reverted back to Ricochet.

I became COL SEAL's friend and right-hand man. He was a Navajo and proud of his uncle, who'd been a Marine Corps Code Talker. He didn't approve of ragging on marines. He was a tall, muscular man, with thick dark black hair, high cheekbones and dark eyes—a man of action, but also a deep thinker. I resolved that I would remain his executive officer and serve here as long as COL SEAL remained post commander.

BLAZE

LTC Cowboy sat down at his computer desk with a cup of tea, steam rising from the cup, filling his senses with the pleasing aroma. Being a command officer now allowed him more bulk shipping of luxury items, like his special blend of tea: black pekoe and black currant, with a touch of cinnamon. Loneliness can affect men differently. Cowboy needed the company or correspondence of country folk to help him set his anchor. He accessed his digital writing stylus and pad, and began to write a letter. The apparatus converted his script to digital format as he wrote. When completed, he would hit *send*, transmitting the letter to ASDC HQ on Earth, where a machine would recreate the letter using a pen, adjusting pressure to match the original, giving the illusion that it had been written here and not 225 million kilometers across space. He carefully finished his letter to Warren and Gladys Hard of Lebanon, MO. Officially, LTJG Eugene J. Bordelon was long dead. At any rate, in correspondence and on leave back on Earth, he was now CMDR Eugene J. Martin, complete with military papers and a driver's license that could pass scrutiny should he ever be challenged. He used the cover story of serving abroad in the U.S. Navy, thanking them for their hospitality on his previous trip through on his last leave. Once he had ended all of the "safe" small talk that he was allowed to share with outsiders, he addressed the envelope and hit the *send* button. The ASDC mail clerk would print his hand-written letter and envelope, put the proper APO stamp on the envelope and mail it.

The man in bibbed overalls and a flannel shirt surveyed the sky for signs of rain. He needed a little, or that last hay crop before winter wouldn't amount to much. This would drive up the cost of feed, and cause the local farmers to sell off more of their cattle than they would like. Farming was sometimes called *gambler's ruin*, meaning that if you stayed at it long enough you would eventually lose. A wise farmer managed his finances to cover bad times, and prayed that the bad times didn't last very long. Warren Hard had already seen a couple of his neighbors lose the gamble, borrowing too much against what they owned, and not having anything in reserve against a rainy day. His father had so drilled into him the laws of sound financial management that he had survived where others had failed. He had been to too many bank auctions lately. There was no pleasure in these auctions; they were the bones of his friend's dreams. He bought from them what he needed, but felt guilty about it.

One of his friend's wild dreams was to raise wolves for sale. There was an emerging market he said, for wolf-hybrids. He had kept the pure male wolf in a pen to breed his malamute bitch when she came *in season*. Before he could get the prescribed permit to keep the animal, the wolf dug out of the pen and escaped into the woods. The neighbors were nervous about a wolf near their stock and kept their rifles close. It wasn't winter yet, and the wolf apparently was getting enough rabbits and small game. So far no one had reported any livestock killed. Today Warren was attending his bank auction: like the man's other dreams, vanished like a vapor in the wind under the auctioneer's oaken gavel. He picked up a hay rake for three hundred and fifty dollars. One more family farm ruined from poor management.

Warren removed the ball hitch on his pickup truck, slid the rake hitch over the hole, aligned the three holes, and dropped the pin through it. He finished it up by fixing the clip through the bottom pin hole to keep it from popping out if he hit a bump somewhere. Next, he took the rake out of gear so that the rake wouldn't turn when the wheels did as he drove it down the road. He reached in the back of his pickup bed and grabbed a triangle sign and affixed it to the rear of his new purchase. Finally, he climbed into the truck and took it slow going home, driving with the rake partially off the road and to the right to make sure he gave enough room for vehicles to pass him if needed.

Farmer Hard had given up raising goats and now had only cattle, horses, a chicken house and two hundred acres of hay. However, there was one last cash asset from the goat business: Princess, his great pyrenees bitch which he intended to breed to sell puppies to goat herders. She was in season now— the intended suitor would be brought in the day after tomorrow, and she was safely penned up.

Warren turned on the radio to his favorite station. "It's partly cloudy with a twenty percent chance of rain today, high of fifty-nine degrees with a low tonight of forty-two. Tomorrow is going to be a little warmer with a high of seventy degrees, and a low in the night of forty-six. You are listening to "The Coyote," 107.9 FM in Lebanon, MO." Warren listened to the radio and sang along with Waylon Jennings and Willie Nelson.

"She's a good hearted woman
in love with a good timin' man.
And she loves him in spite of his ways
that she don't understand.

And through teardrops and laughter
they'll pass though this world hand in hand.

155

Now this good hearted woman
in love with her good timin' man."

He turned onto the dirt road to his farm and drove past his mailbox. His two working dogs, Cocoa and Missy greeted him with excited barks. Farmer Hard backed his newly acquired purchase up to the fence and unhooked it from the truck. Finally, he hopped out and removed the triangle sign from the back and placed it behind his truck seat.

His wife Gladys was walking out of the front door of the farmhouse with a hot casserole dish in a cloth carrier. She placed the dish in the back seat of her car and waved at her husband. He waved back and smiled.

"I'm taking this casserole dish over to Cheryl's. I haven't seen the baby yet, so I expect I will be a while. I'll be back in time to make supper."

"Have a good visit. I'm going to take the dogs and move the herd into the back pasture."

Gladys waved goodbye and climbed into the driver's seat, strapped on her seatbelt and drove down the dirt road to the paved highway, leaving a cloud of dust behind her.

Warren finished up with the cattle, put both dogs in the back of the pickup and drove back to the house. As he drove up, he saw a gray-haired canine moving away from Princess' pen toward the woods. The dogs clamored to give chase, but he held them back, fearing the wolf might kill them both. He walked to the pen and saw a hole dug under the fence. He felt his face flushed red with anger, cursed under his breath, and after he calmed down, realized that there was nothing he could do about it. *What's done is done,* he thought. *There goes the profit from breeding and selling pure-bred herd dogs.* He called a man that he knew of in the next county who raised wolf-hybrids.

"Hello, Albert Smucker speaking."

"Hi, my name is Warren Hard over in Lebanon. I understand you sell wolf-dogs."

"I do. I have a permit for full-bred wolves which I use as breeding stock for malamute, husky and German shepherd crosses. Are you interested in a pup?"

"Well, not exactly. My great pyrenees bitch has gotten herself pregnant by a wolf that got loose from a neighbor's farm. I was wondering if such a cross would be worth anything to anyone."

"Not really. The desirable breeds to cross with a wolf were those that looked somewhat wolf-like already, pointed ears, wolf shaped body, that sort of thing. You will probably have to give them away."

"Would you be interested in the pups yourself?"

"I would not."

"Well, I thank you for your time. Have a nice day."

"You, too."

That evening Warren wrote a letter to his navy pen pal, with all of the usual talk of needing rain, and how much hay he expected to buy this winter if he didn't have enough. He shared about the accidental breeding of his Princess with the wolf, and how it would cost him a pretty penny.

LTC Cowboy returned his letter, advising that he was sorry about the turn of events, but told him he would buy a pup at the pure-bred price. He only wanted to make sure that the pup was of the color of the mother, and if it had yellow eyes, so much the better. When the time came he would have someone from the Navy pick the pup up and pay him.

When the pups were weaned, the farmer chose a girl from the litter for his pen pal, being the only one who was both white and had yellow eyes. An ASDC officer posing as a navy officer came to the farm, paid Warren and put the little white ball of fur in a pet carrier for her trip to the Academy and ASDC spaceport in Utah. He relinquished his charge to CPT Ripsnort, shuttle commander of the *Odyssey*. The captain took to the pup immediately, placing her bed on the bridge. When he was through with one of his stacks of newspapers, he rolled it out on the floor to train the young pup. It was a bit ironic. The stack of newspapers that he had was supposed to be delivered to LTC Cowboy: The Boston Globe, The Times Picayune, the New York Times, The Los Angeles Times and The Chicago Tribune. Mars' executive officer liked to read the print, even though it was three months old by the time he got it. He looked at the stack. *Yup*, he thought. *By the time he got to Mars, he would be out of newspaper and the dog would be housebroken.*

The captain doted over the pup, feeding her, grooming her, training her and cuddling her on the three month trip to Mars. As the shuttle got closer to Mars, the captain began to prepare himself for the inevitable separation from his new pup to her rightful owner. He couldn't help but regard her as his own and she adored him. She had been in his care longer than in her own mother's.

The pup read the body language of her transitional master. She had no way to know that their relationship was to be short-lived. He was regarded by this "pack" as the alpha male. His relationship with her was different than it was with other members of the pack. The captain didn't hug, play with, pet or feed the other members of the pack. His tone when talking to her was that of endearment, but with the others is was different. She had no language in which to frame her thoughts of their relationship. She knew that the alpha male favored her as special, and in the world of wolves and men favor was understood and felt.

The trip was coming to an end. As Mars grew closer in his viewer, the captain rationalized that a shuttle was no place for a dog, wolf or whatever she was anyway. *The post would have a lot more room, and a dog needed some open space,* he told himself.

The *Odyssey* acquired an orbit around the planet named for the god of war, and the captain keyed his mike. "Camp Freedom, this is CPT Ripsnort of the shuttle *Odyssey* requesting permission to land."

"We read you, *Odyssey*. Permission granted."

"Roger that, bringing her down."

The *Odyssey* broke orbit and descended amidst a shower of sparks on the vessel's heat shield. The captain kept an eye on his external and internal heat sensors, and watched his angle of descent very carefully. The post at first was a small dot, and then grew in size, looming larger as the shuttle grew nearer. The captain lowered his landing gear and slowly cut the power to his engines to manage the "fall" of his vessel to the ground. The shuttle landed, and the aircraft conveyer moved the freighter through the transitional airlocks, and then into the freighter hangar.

LTC Cowboy had been informed of the shuttle's arrival and was waiting at the shuttle dock. Several pilots made their way down the loading ramp carrying duffle bags. For some of the pilots this was their final destination; others would layover here until the shuttle was finished with routine maintenance and refueled, and then continue to their posts. Finally, CPT Ripsnort descended down the loading ramp with his duffle bag over one shoulder and a white ball of fur cradled against his chest. The post's executive officer greeted him.

"She any trouble on the trip?" Cowboy queried him.

"Only trouble is giving her up. We've become quite close. You'll find she's house-trained, good-natured and probably the smartest animal I've ever met. Hadn't gotten her to heel yet—but she does sit and lay down when I tell her to. I had to eject your newspapers out of the airlock with the rest of the garbage." Cowboy nodded that this was an acceptable price for her care, studied the captain and thought about asking for his pup, then reconsidered. The captain was still holding the pup, hoping perhaps that Cowboy would tell him to go ahead and keep her.

"Thank you, captain." Cowboy could see that parting with her was hard on the man. "Tell you what. You don't leave until morning for Titan, and I have afternoon patrol to go on in five minutes. Keep her with you and bring her to my quarters for supper. I'll feed her well and when she goes to sleep you can slip off. That way the anxiety of changing masters will be lessened. She'll simply wake up and you'll be gone."

The captain was relieved that he had the rest of afternoon to say goodbye. "What time?"

"Nineteen hundred."

"Very good, we'll be there."

At nineteen hundred sharp, man and dog arrived at Cowboy's quarters, with her bed, food and water dishes, and her chew toys. Cowboy loved to cook; when he wanted to show favor or gratitude, he always cooked his guest the finest meal that he could. Tonight he was cooking the last three steaks in his freezer. Meat was a precious commodity; it had to be imported from Earth. He also added some not so rare, but hard to get baked potatoes and some salad greens that were plentiful from the greenhouse. Captain Ripsnort's affinity for apple pie and a good cup of coffee was well-known, so some favors from the mess sergeant were called in to round out the meal.

"Here, let me have those," Cowboy said, taking the pup's items, placed the food and water dishes on the kitchenette floor, and the bed and toys in the small living room. He took his t-shirt off and placed it in her bed to help get them acquainted. Cowboy disappeared into his bedroom and grabbed another shirt. Returning, he motioned to the man to let the dog down to wander. The pup walked around, sniffing each item in the small living room. Satisfied by her inspection and soothed by soft music from the stereo, she settled down with one of her rubber chew toys.

Cowboy placed two salads on the table and motioned the captain to have a seat while he checked the oven to see if the baked potatoes were done. Not quite, he decided, and closed the oven door.

"How do you like your steak?"

"Medium rare."

"Well, then, this one is done. I like mine to stop breathing first," he chuckled. "Does the pup have a name?"

"I've been calling her Blaze."

"Why?"

"My daddy owns a horse ranch. When there is a streak of white on the head of a horse, it's called a *blaze*. With her being white all over, it suited her."

"I see. Then Blaze she shall remain."

Finally the last steak was grilled to suit Cowboy. He arranged the steak and potatoes on the two plates, cut the third steak into pieces and placed it in Blaze's food dish. He brought the bowl into the living room, and held it up for her inspection. She took an immediate interest.

"Come, Blaze." She followed him to the kitchen, and submitted to being petted and talked to while she ate. Cowboy took it as a good sign, washed his hands in the sink and joined the captain. Dinner was a time of sharing news of both Mars and other posts, and sure enough—Blaze curled up on Cowboy's shirt and fell asleep.

Captain Ripsnort finally arose to leave and looked evenly into Cowboy's eyes. "Take care of "my dog"."

"I certainly will. You are welcome to spend time with her every time you come through."

"Thank you." He took one last look at the sleeping bundle and went back to his guest quarters.

MAJOR NORSEMUN

The alarm clock gave its irritating report—its buzzing sound designed to rouse even the most resistant from slumber. Its horrible noise could be used to interrogate victims into revealing state secrets. Cowboy hit the snooze button, rolled over onto his left side and buried his face into the pillow. His consciousness was slowing climbing the stairway from deep REM sleep to fully awake. He had purposely set his alarm clock to go off ten minutes earlier than he wished to get up, preferring a slow journey from the world of dreams to the world of reality. The second alarm intruded into his dream world. He hit the snooze again and quickened his pace up the staircase to consciousness. His eyelids opened to survey the clock's time and gauge how much sack time he had left. Three more minutes, he told himself, closed his eyes and rolled over. The sleek and quiet figure climbed up into his bed and crawled to the head beside him. The white wolf-dog pup nuzzled and licked the man's sleepy face, and he opened his eyes in wide-awake surprise. Recognition dawned upon him. He cradled Blaze into his arms, attempting to keep his wake-up routine. The alarm clock signaled its obnoxious sound for the third and final time.

Cowboy opened his eyes fully, and the pup licked his face again.

"Well good morning, Miss Blaze." The pup wagged her tail and washed his face some more with her wet, pink tongue. "We definitely have to do something about your morning breath." He picked her up in his arms, regarded the taste in his mouth, and realized he was the one with "doggy breath." The man put the dog down, used the head, washed his face and brushed his teeth. *Ah, more like it*, he thought.

The pup followed her new master to the kitchen, where Cowboy was pleased to learn that she had hit the newspaper target he had laid out for her. He was going to have to find a solution for her *necessary breaks* before he ran out of newspapers, since he was now a stack shorter than he expected.

He made them both a breakfast of fish and soy from his small fridge. A dog wasn't allowed in the officer's mess, and he hadn't quite made arrangements for her yet.

He shaved, put on his uniform and picked the dog up to carry her first to Col SEAL's office on the way to his own.

The pup was now in a different world, in a different pack, with a different master. She studied the others in the new pack and concluded that she was as special to this new master as she had been to CPT Ripsnort. The body language of the others showed both submission and deference to her new master. She carefully studied the sights and sounds about her new

161

environment and the body language of every member of her new pack. Not only was this hunting area much larger than the one she had just left, but the pack was much larger.

PFC Gray Eagle rose and greeted the first officer with a salute. "The colonel is in."

"Thank you, Private, as you were."

Cowboy shifted his dog under his left arm and knocked on the oak door with his right hand.

"Come on in," the smooth baritone voice from within called.

"Good morning, Colonel."

"Good morning." He smiled. "I see we have a VIP among us. I have never seen you carry anyone around the post before."

Cowboy grinned ear-to-ear. "Yes, sir—and thank you for the time to get her adjusted."

"She's a beautiful pup. I guess now that you have a companion I won't expect to see you desert us to go home and get married."

"That was the idea. I am a career officer, and this is my post."

"Good. She reminds me of one of my dogs back home, Betty." The colonel looked thoughtful. "Do you remember the orientation film on the shuttle over here?"

"Sure."

"Do you remember the way this whole secret arms race started?"

"Yes, the alien ship crashed on the Navajo Reservation, some kid found it." Light dawned in Cowboy's eyes. "Did you know that kid?"

"I *was* that kid."

Cowboy straightened up abruptly and Blaze squirmed in his lap, and he tightened his grip. "You?"

"Yes, me. What was not known was that I found one of the aliens still alive, and he spoke to me, presumably telepathically before he died."

"Incredible! What did he say?"

"Something about failing to do his duty and crying for his dead wife—as a military man, I understand the first part. I've had dreams about space ever since that day."

"Do you find it curious that your journey came full circle and that you joined the service that your discovery helped to start?"

"I find it too coincidental to be by chance. When I was in Vietnam, COL Squid and I were approached by ASDC recruiters. I don't know if they knew I had prior knowledge of the aliens, and then again, maybe they did. I learned just enough to know it had something to do with that spaceship that I had found. I was hooked, and talked COL Squid into taking the position." His face displayed a shadow of sadness and regret as if it were a floating object that he had held under water until he lost his grip on it, causing it to rise to the surface and bob atop the troubled waters tellingly. "I am the one responsible for him being here."

"We're warriors. Death could claim us anywhere: in the jungles of Vietnam, the barren Martian landscape, or on the plane back home."

"You're right, and his was a good death."

The colonel's aide brought the two men a cup of hot tea. Blaze calmed down a bit, and Cowboy was able to manage his cup. The wolf cub studied the body language of the two men. She learned that though her new master was important, he was the beta wolf of this new pack, not the alpha. Never mind, he was important to the pack, and she was important to him. Though she had no words to articulate these thoughts, she knew and felt them as all animals know their place in the world.

Cowboy carried her to his office, which was between tactical operations and the hangar deck. His role on the post was to be the point man for his commander for all the departments, but especially these two. His usual job when he was not on maneuvers in the field was to be available for all heads of the other departments, do inspections, and keep up detailed reports to submit to his commander.

He arrived at his office and put the pup down beside his desk, so she could explore a bit. COL SEAL had granted Cowboy three days of exemption from patrol duty, to get the pup settled. He could have started as soon as the pup arrived, but he didn't have the heart to tear her away from CPT Ripsnort. Normally being confined to post was akin to punishment, but this was a very kind gesture on his part. It was something Cowboy hadn't expected from the colonel, and he appreciated it.

After catching up with all of the routine paperwork, Cowboy put his teapot on to boil for a cup of tea, and took the time to contemplate how he was going to have his dog cared for when he was on maneuvers. The hangar deck and tac ops did have some personnel who worked the night shift. Maybe one of them could care for Blaze in their off-duty time. It wouldn't be a good permanent solution as off-duty personnel mainly just wanted to sleep. The teapot whistled its invitation to take a break. Setting the cup to steep, he pondered what to do. When his tea had finished steeping, he picked up the cup, inhaling the pleasing aroma of black currant, black pekoe and cinnamon. He sipped the hot liquid, slowly at first while he considered any and all possible answers. Still no good solution came to mind. If he had an aide it would be easy, but no executive officer in the ASDC had one.

It was not yet lunchtime, so he decided to take the pup on rounds with him. He skipped the hangar deck, as it was loud and noisy and may spook the pup. Tactical operations was a different story. Geeks liked quiet, and tac ops was geek territory. They were the brainy types that were more comfortable with cerebral endeavors, like literature and music while his pilots were more likely to pursue sports and more physical things in their off-time. He knew it was a generalization. CPT Cipher loved basketball and boxing while Cowboy painted and played the Navajo flute for enjoyment, when he wasn't playing basketball or one of the other physical pursuits.

Of all of the tactical operations personnel, none fit the geek stereotype quite like MAJ Norsemun. When the major, then known as Erik, was seven years old, his mother told his father that their brilliantly gifted son could not seem to make connections with people. With an IQ over two hundred, his math skills astounded his teachers, even then. His mother pressed his father to buy him a dog, and he complied. The boy immediately fell in love with the border collie pup and named him Pi. He seemed to endure all the social awkwardness of his gift/disorder as long as Pi was waiting at home with his wagging tail. The unfairness of dogs aging seven years to the boy's one caused him to succumb to old age by the time Erik was ready for college. His gifts caused him to excel, and he became the youngest cryptanalyst the CIA ever had. But Washington was too busy with people, so when the offer to go to Mars came up, he gladly accepted. His life became ordered around numbers and facts, and he felt safe. His gift and disability was known by the company shrinks as Asperger's Syndrome. He was the indispensable master of numbers at the post that kept all things statistical and mathematical in order and running smoothly.

Cowboy carried Blaze in his arms to tactical operations. The foot traffic in the corridors on the outside ring of the complex was too heavy to let her down. MAJ Norsemun was debugging a computer program, with his eyes fixed on the monitor. CPT Cipher was checking satellite data from a recent flyby, and two junior technicians were doing routine number crunching on Soviet fleet and arms strength.

MAJ Norsemun looked up and acknowledged the first officer's presence, businesslike as usual. He and his staff rose and gave the customary salute, and when Cowboy returned the salute with an "as you were," all but the major went back to what they were doing. The major wasn't much for socializing. His unusual interests in puzzles and obscure literature and his inability to share the interests of others kept him from connecting with people. In social situations that weren't work related he often got anxiety attacks. It was not that he lacked the desire to interact with people. He did. He just lacked the ability to "read' people in regards to their needs and perspectives, mostly because his narrow focus did not include being interested in them on a personal level. His inability to connect with people caused him frustration and sometimes anxiety attacks.

But here in tac ops, he was in charge, and in the structured work environment of the TOC, he adapted well and was high functioning. Being in charge of tac ops, he developed a coping mechanism of being a stickler for process and strict adherence to the smallest detail. His team all knew of his issues, and though they found him a bit odd, the discipline of military life made it easier to keep business and interactions at the major's comfort level.

The major's eyes caught sight of the wriggling white bundle under the first officer's arm. His eyes softened at the sight of her, opening a door to his heart that had been closed since Pi died.

"And who is this?" the major queried.

"Blaze, my dog, or wolf-dog, as it were. She will be staying here with me. My duties are confined to the post for a few days while I get her settled in and figure out what to do with her when I have field maneuvers."

The major interests didn't include people, but this dog was a different story. "May I?" he asked. Cowboy handed Blaze over to the major, who took her into his arms. His awkwardness of touching another being melted against her warm, furry body.

Until now, her new master had not allowed anyone to touch her, not even the alpha male of his pack. She had been sure that he regarded her as special, and now he had handed her to one of the subordinate members of his pack. Realization dawned on her that this pack member was very important to her master. She trusted her new master completely; she trusted his subordinate pack member not just because her master did, but because she knew his heart to be guileless toward her. She licked his face, and the major immediately sought to establish a joint-custody arrangement.

"Colonel?"

"Yes, Major?"

"I think I can help you with your problem."

"Go on."

"Well, you go on routine patrols six days a week, twice a day, and sometimes unscheduled field maneuvers, which are unpredictable, both in their timing and duration. I think Blaze could stay here in tac ops with me. I am a former dog owner, you see. I am quite familiar with the care and feeding of a dog." The major's pleading eyes revealed that this was more than just an offer; it was an earnest request.

Cowboy had never seen this side of the major before. He had made an emotional connection with something right before his eyes. He studied the man and the revelation came to him that this would benefit the man more than the dog.

"Major, that is quite generous of you, and I accept. Where would she stay?"

"I would put her bed, food and water bowl next to the desk in my office, and she could stay out here unless she has to eat or take a nap."

"Very good. I have been working on the potty angle. I am short on newspapers."

"No problem, sir. I have paper reports I shred every month. The ones that are not sensitive, I can turn over to you for "target practice.""

"Very good. We can start a trial this afternoon. I will bring her stuff and leave her here two hours a day for the next three days."

"You can leave her now if you like."

Cowboy looked at the major, still holding his pup, and decided that it might cause the man some emotional distress to pry her loose from him at the moment. "Okay, two hours."

"Thank you, sir."

Blaze fit in perfectly in tac ops, and by the end of three days it was clear she could stay with the major when needed. Cowboy noticed that the major was calmer and more content than he was before the visits began. Blaze grew in size and Cowboy taught her to heel and to walk beside him, now undaunted by the foot traffic of the outer ring of the complex. Cowboy had a spacesuit made for her for walks outside of the building complex. He felt like he was no longer alone. True, she was not a wife, but a sweet companion who took the edge off of his loneliness nonetheless. The major wasn't the only one calmed by her presence—Cowboy had fewer bad dreams.

WYATT EARP'S SYNDROME

Commander's Log: COL SEAL—Earth date: June 27, 1979—Martian year 196, Sol Veneris, sol 23 of the Martian Month Libra—sol of the Martian year 583

We have been hard on the Soviets over the last six months since COL Squid's death. The tide is beginning to turn in our favor. If we continue to enjoy success on the battlefield, it is conceivable that a siege on the Soviet post may be possible in the future, perhaps by year's end. Morale among the men is good, and our fleet strength is strong and improving with each engagement.

COL SEAL,
Camp Freedom, Mars

The dark-haired haired commander closed his computer log, opened his desk and retrieved his Navajo flute. He cleared his mind and played a tune passed down to him by his father. A white man may have characterized the tune as mournful and lonely, but to a Navajo, it was spiritual.

A sharp knock on the door interrupted his song. "Come in, Cowboy."

"Don't stop playing on my account. I haven't heard that one before."

"It's called the "Warrior's Song"."

"Would you teach it to me?"

"Sure." COL SEAL played the piece through twice and looked up. "Got it?"

"I think so."

Cowboy's mentor handed him the flute, and he played the piece through twice, looking to his teacher and friend to see if he had made any mistakes.

"Very, very good," his teacher said, his voice brimming with pleasure.

"Ready to go shooting?"

"Just wrapped up the last bit of business."

"Good."

"I have a riddle for you," said COL SEAL, grinning mischievously.

"Is it a SEAL or Soviet joke this time?" his first officer deadpanned.

"Why can't it be both?"

"No reason. Okay then—shoot."

"What's the difference between a Navy SEAL and a Soviet politician?"

"Other than the obvious?"

"Yes, other than the obvious..."

"Dunno."

"SEALs earn their medals."

"I'll have to remember that one the next time I do some pre-battle trash talking to the Soviets. I got one for you. When we go out on a recreational outing, like today, shouldn't we be called playing 'Cowboy and Indian?' "

"It might, if Cowboy was the boss. I prefer to call it playing 'Indian and Cowboy,' " he said, an easy smile playing on his lips.

"Roger that. Well, we're burning daylight. Ready?"

"Ready."

The white-haired man with bushy eyebrows and a glowering expression read the report of the last failure in a series of failures on Mars. He removed his reading glasses and placed them back in his pocket. His anger rose like the mercury in a thermometer placed in boiling water. GEN Kuznetsov slammed his fist on the desk. "Svetlana, connect me to COL Tkachenko on Ganymede!" he demanded.

"Yes, Comrade General," hurrying to her task in an attempt to *manage* the general before his anger boiled over into her office.

It was zero two hundred on the Soviet post on Ganymede when Svetlana made the conference link. The fairly petrified young officer that received the video conference request rushed to get COL Tkachenko to take the call.

The general knew what time it was here, and wouldn't be calling at this time of night unless someone was in trouble.

"Yes?" answered a sleepy COL Tkachenko.

"Comrade Colonel, GEN Kuznetsov is requesting video conference immediately."

"Advise comrade general that I will take the call in my quarters in five — no, make that two minutes." Tkachenko knew that the general would not be calling at this hour unless he was angry, and it was not good to make an angry general wait.

"Yes, Comrade Colonel."

COL Tkachenko washed his face and quickly got dressed and made it to his workstation desk in time to take the call as promised. GEN Kuznetsov's face was bright red, like a boiling tea kettle soon to whistle to let off steam: angry at someone, hopefully not Tkachenko. When generals weren't happy, colonels weren't happy.

"Greetings, General... And to what do I owe the honor of your call?"

"You and your first officer pack your things. You are being transferred to Mars. That fool Kiknadze is losing us Mars!" he spat. "You will relieve Kiknadze. LTC Matulevich will return on your shuttle to Ganymede and take your post there."

"With the present orbital alignments, the trip will take eight months." Tkachenko knew better than to ask the fate of COL Kiknadze in the general's present frame of mind.

The general's eyes widened, lifting his white, bushy eyebrows from his angry blue eyes. "Then you had better leave right away."

"Of course, Comrade General. Is there anything else?"

"Yes, make it your highest priority to kill both the American commander and his first officer. Then destroy all of the Americans."

"Of course, Comrade General."

"Colonel, what pistol did you bring from your collection?" I asked.

"German Luger, I like to try them all. You need to try something new."

"I think I'll stick to my colts."

"Spoken like a true cowboy."

I spotted a familiar rock formation, placing us about ten clicks from Valles.

COL SEAL and I weren't only karate enthusiasts; we shared a passion for collecting, shooting and throwing pistols and knives. He made me his confidante and friend. Whenever we could, we would hop into our tanks and go to Valles Marineris, the Martian Grand Canyon, to shoot pistols and practice throwing knives. Valles is just over three thousand kilometers long with a big collection of canyons, and four times as deep as Arizona's Grand Canyon, and is just south of our post. We liked to practice at a favorite canyon which was reasonably safe from ambush. Of course, we always made sure the area was clear according to satellite and radar before we went in. It was during those times that he shared with me the secrets of command that he never revealed to others: like how much to let your men know, how much to keep to yourself, and various philosophies of war and peace.

Nearing the canyon, I glanced at my radar, surprised to see five blips materialize on my screen. Only stealth devices could have concealed the enemies' radar signature until we were right near them. It was the only explanation why we hadn't detected the enemies' radar signatures until we were right near them. The only thing that could hide them from radar was the redfield generator, which had been outlawed by treaty nearly four years earlier.

"Redfields," I shouted as Soviet tanks surrounded us. They must have been hidden here all night after slipping in during our satellite blackout window. We assumed a back-to-back defensive position like we'd done many times before, but this time I knew there were too many. Two tanks decided to converge on me while the other three attacked the colonel. The thought flashed through my mind that they knew who we were, and they knew that COL SEAL was in the other tank. The adrenaline started pumping and my heart pounded in my chest like a double-action steam locomotive driving up the Rocky Mountains. Quickly I strafed left and did a vertical lift hop. Two bright orange pairs of particle beam cannon blasts fired right under me, missing me cleanly while I scored a direct hit off-center with both barrels to the tank facing me on the right. This caused it to turn slightly to the right so it couldn't shoot me back.

I fired again, severely damaging the ship, but couldn't finish it off. The other tank scored a direct hit on my ship. The impact force thrust me back. It shook me so hard that I bite my tongue. With the taste of blood in my mouth, I hammered his tank with a couple of cannon blasts of my own. I kept the enemy tank I was fighting between me and his partner, using the first one as a shield so the second tank couldn't shoot at me. I took another grazing hit the port skin of my tank. Firing a volley, I struck the first tank slightly off-center, turning his whole tank to my starboard side and moving his cannon barrel, so it pointed away from me. One more quick blast and the first tank exploded into flames. The second tank was too close to the blast and the explosion damaged it further, the sound reverberating across the Martian plane.

"Warning, your hull integrity is forty percent," reported the familiar voice. Quickly I dropped a splinter mortar in front of the tank, fired both of my particle beam cannons, and then backed up. Between the mortar and two more blasts with my particle beam cannon, his ship exploded, too. Being dangerously close to the explosion, the concussion wave rocked my tank, but it sustained no further damage. I knew the dogfight with the two tanks couldn't have lasted more than a minute, but with the adrenaline pumping, everything seemed in slow motion.

I hard banked to port and did a one eighty to aid my commander and friend. During the two dogfights, we had been separated and were no longer back-to-back and close. COL SEAL had destroyed one ship and was trading punches with the other two. All three ships were smoking. I sped there as fast as my damaged tank would allow. My instruments indicated I was down to only three double blasts of my particle beam cannon, while my hull integrity was about thirty percent. My smoking tank was now in range where I felt my shots wouldn't be wasted. Two Soviet tanks were hammering the colonel's ship, and I saw it explode. As he ejected I saw one of the enemy ship's cannon blasts tearing right through his body, vaporizing him. With a shout, I pressed my attack with what little particle beam energy and hull I had left. My angle of contact was about forty-five degrees off the two Soviet tank's port sides. Neither of the tanks had a good shot at me, and both were smoking badly. Taking careful aim, I emptied two rounds into the first tank, knowing I only had one shot left for the second tank. The tank must have been ready to explode on its own because it blew. The explosion caused some damage to the other ship. I quickly placed my last shot where I saw the smoke pouring out near his engine, and held my breath. Suddenly, the last ship's hull ripped apart like peeling the skin of an orange, followed by the pilot ejecting and then a loud explosion. There were five pilots that ejected from the enemy tanks. Although I was mad, I was still no fool. Vengeance would have to come another way. I couldn't snipe them all, and my particle beam cannons were completely discharged. Logging my GPS coordinates, I called the post. CPL Disaster patched me through to MAJ Ricochet.

"Sir, Ricochet here. Colonel, what can I do for you?"

"I need a sweeper team to these coordinates south of our post approximately seventy-five kilometers. There are five snipers on the mountain there. Bring back their heads! I want no prisoners!"

"Sir, what's going on?" answered the taut voice. The gruesome image of decapitating our enemies and bringing their heads back as trophies was appalling to the major.

"COL SEAL and I were ambushed. He is dead and I want vengeance. I have a practical use for the heads. I will dip my sword in Soviet blood until it is fully satisfied! Any questions?!"

"No, sir!"

I knew he felt like I did about COL SEAL and wouldn't come back without all five heads, now more angry than appalled. COL SEAL was our leader and friend. We held him almost in awe because of his knowledge and abilities. In my mind, I thought he couldn't be killed. I was in shock, grieving and felt pains of guilt about letting my commander get killed.

Now that the fight-or-flight situation was over, I slowed my breathing and purposely attempted to relax to come off the adrenaline state-of-alert. I was still upset about losing the colonel, but I had to get my body and emotions under control. My computer announced that my engine was on fire. Reality intruded into my thoughts and I realized the immediate need of putting out the fire in my engine before it reached critical stage and blew.

Once clear of sniper range, I stopped my tank, grabbed an emergency fire extinguisher and put out the fire in my engine.

An examination of the back of my tank found no obvious electrical damage. My engine was undamaged, but my ship was leaking fuel from the forward thrust, jump jets and slow forward fuel flow lines. After I shut down the flow valves ahead of the leaks, it was safe to start my engine again without worrying about whether it would catch on fire. The only seals intact were on my reverse thrusters. I restarted my engine and put it in reverse. After swinging my tank into a circle and aligning my ship's rear with the post, I started back to post flying backwards. The high from the adrenaline rush was over. I was soaking wet with sweat and all of my muscles ached. My travel back to the post in reverse had the feel of retreating, but retreating was the furthest thing on my mind. Soon—very soon—I'd even the score with the Soviets, with interest. My mentor and best friend was dead. I felt darkness cover me like a mist.

The original accord signed by COL Squid and COL Kiknadze banned the use of stealth weapons. The ban on stealth weapons included *the phantom* which makes the craft invisible to cameras and the naked eye, by "reading" the light images from one side of the craft and broadcasting them from the other side. It worked the same way from underneath the vessel, so it also fooled satellite cameras. That little bit of technological "sleight of hand" was the work of a master illusionist, to be sure, but it did not fool the radar. The redfield generator was a different story. It absorbed the radar waves and did not return them back to the sender. However, it did not make the object invisible. Both devices had certain inherent flaws. They could not remove shadows on the ground, hide dust trails of moving vessels, or remove a vessel's heat signature.

The down side to these stealth weapons is that they can't be used at the same time. We tried once. The cloak worked briefly, and then burned out both units. One makes the ship invisible to the eye; the other stops radar from picking it up. For years, we've pursued the *Holy Grail* of stealth, to marry them both together, but without success. The traitor Dr. Eichmann deciphered a Ktahrthian relic while on an archaeological dig on Luna, which revealed the secret of the ultimate stealth device. The Chinese had just established their presence on Luna, aided by alloy-x cleanup on some of the fifty-nine smaller of Jupiter's moons that hadn't been mined by the Soviets or Americans. Dr. Eichmann stole the secret, and the Chinese picked him up at the site, after killing everyone else there, including the squadron assigned to defend it. Before the Chinese left, they destroyed the entire dig site, including the relic. The Chinese call it Youling Doupeng, translated as "Ghost Cloak." It was the successful "marriage" of the two stealth devices. They were devastating if used right. As with any stealth device, heat signatures, engine exhausts, dust trails and shadows were still a problem.

The Chinese are actually making inroads on planets and moons where it was previously just the Soviets and the Americans. In any case, all agreements of civilized engagement were done. It was just as well. I was not feeling very civilized. It caused no little stir to see me arrive at the post flying my tank in reverse without COL SEAL. I parked my tank in the hangar and told the Chief to have her fixed and equipped with a redfield generator and two mag cannons.

"Is it an all-out war?"

"Affirmative," I quipped and took leave of him with no further comments. Then I went straight to my office and accessed the 1MC. "Attention, this is LTC Cowboy. We're on the highest state of alert. This morning COL SEAL was killed in an ambush. We will be waging a full-scale war. GEN Spears will be informed and a post commander will be chosen. In the interim, I'm your commanding officer. Cowboy out."

MY PROMOTION

I established a secure link to ASDC Command priority one. GEN Spears, the ranking officer of Central Command answered.

"What can I do for you, LTC Cowboy," he said in a polite voice. He had an idea what this was about as protocol wouldn't have me calling in.

"I regret to inform you COL SEAL was killed in an ambush today about two hours ago. I'll send in a report and you may download the satellite account at any time." For a brief moment I saw a fleeting expression on his face that made him look very old.

"Very well, let me access some records. After a long pause, he spoke again. Let's see, I don't have a senior officer I can spare. Your last fitness report by COL SEAL showed that he recommended you for a command on Callisto, but you refused. Why did you refuse?"

"I was loyal to my commander and didn't want to leave."

"Excellent, I like loyalty in a soldier. I'll review the satellite account of the incident and your report. For now, you're the commander of this post. What do you intend to do?"

"I expect the Soviets to test my mettle by swiftly launching an aggressive campaign to take our post. I intend to keep their hands so full dealing with our field forces that they won't have the opportunity."

"The colonel was right about you. Will be in touch, Spears out." The screen faded to the ASDC symbol.

I suspected GEN Spears knew what I intended to do. COL SEAL was a favorite of his, almost like a son. I purposely didn't tell him of my plans. I planned to wage war with all the brutality I could muster. I was not waiting for the Soviets to test my mettle. As long as Kiknadze and Matulevich were alive, there could be no new accord.

I stopped by my quarters and retrieved an obsidian knife from my collection. Holding up my hand, I cut into it until the blood droplets splashed to the floor and I swore an oath. "I swear by my blood that I will kill COL Kiknadze and LTC Matulevich or die trying." This was not a practice I learned in Sunday school; revenge was not a Christian teaching. I felt lost and outside of God's shadow. Retrieving a bandanna from my dresser, I wrapped my hand.

In my mind, a plan was taking root. I called the hangar deck. Chief Wolverine answered, "Yes sir, Colonel."

"Chief, I need ten more ships equipped with two mag cannons and redfield generators, and I need them yesterday," I ordered. He didn't question me or act surprised. This was indeed a violation of the accords, but he knew me well enough by now and probably guessed this was coming.

"Yes, sir. I'll get all hands on it now." It was already arranged by COL SEAL that MAJ Intercessor would conduct his memorial service. I called him and advised the memorial services for COL SEAL should be soon, which would include my giving a eulogy honoring our fallen commander. It was important to have our memorial service before the next confrontation with the enemy. Something to make his death seem real would help these men to focus. Something like, "let's win one for the Gipper." But, time to make the first strike was running out. I knew that if we didn't strike first, they would. I wanted the psychological advantage of the first strike. MAJ Intercessor was willing to have a service this evening as I convinced him that we'd soon be at war.

The service was set for nineteen hundred, and I transmitted the announcement on all channels. Afterward I went to the colonel's quarters for a couple of his personal items to include in the memorial room. I chose his black belt, some pictures, and his favorite knife he used as a Navy SEAL. I could feel the colonel's presence in his room, almost as though he was looking over my shoulder. Yesterday I was good humored, and life held promise. Today my reality had shifted, and like quicksand, grief was trying to plunge me into the depths of despair. Shaking it off, I left his quarters and focused on the service tonight and the battle ahead. I could grieve later. Right now I had to get through the service and then exact retribution for this cowardly attack.

MAJ Ricochet hailed me over the link from his tank in the hangar deck with his report. "Mission accomplished, sir. What do you want me to do with the five objects?"

"We are not barbarians. Just pack them in cold storage and don't show them about to anyone who hasn't seen them. I personally don't want the post personnel thinking that I'm worse than the Soviets. I have a practical use for them, which I'll explain later. Thank you for the faithful execution of your orders." I didn't want MAJ Ricochet thinking I was losing my mind. He was my best friend, and now my right-hand man here.

I went to my quarters to write the eulogy, which I completed in twenty-five minutes. COL SEAL wasn't hard to write about. I tried to focus on his life as a commander and as a friend. I purposely tried not to inflame the men out of respect for MAJ Intercessor. I realized how easily we could become a bunch of animals and that we may not be able to transform back into men. An instant message arrived, advising me that I had a video letter from COL SEAL. I accessed the link where it was stored and played it on my computer.

"LTC Cowboy, greetings. If you're viewing this, then I must be dead. I never told you my real name, though you were my best friend. My name is Benjamin Begay, of the Coyote Pass People, born for the Bitter Water People. My maternal grandfather was of the Towering House Clan, and my paternal grandmother was of the Water Flows Together Clan. I hereby bequeath to you my knife and gun collection; all my other property I leave to my mother and my two sisters, Jannalee and Victoria. Please do me this one last honor. When you visit Earth again, go see them and tell them I died with honor as a warrior.

I have the utmost confidence that you will command our men with strength and honor. I've recommended you for post commander to GEN Spears. Thank you for being my friend. SEAL out."

COL SEAL's family thought that he was still a Navy SEAL on SEAL Team Two and that he was still doing work on Earth that he couldn't talk about. They lived in Taos, New Mexico. His mother, both sisters and their husbands had a business together that sold authentic Navajo turquoise and silver jewelry, baskets, paintings, blankets and rugs. Jannalee and her mother were weavers and Victoria painted Navajo life in oil and pastels. Other items, like pottery and baskets were made by other Navajos and sold on consignment. Their husbands, Joseph Tso and Jimmy Bluehorse worked as silversmiths, making all the silver and turquoise jewelry.

I'd have to collect all of his unclassified personal belongings to transport them home. An ASDC officer would take the things to one of our lawyers to execute his will. All pictures of him on Mars would be excluded, of course. There were plenty of old unclassified navy photos which we could send to his family for keepsakes. I'd have to clean out his quarters and box up his personal possessions. I couldn't put it off for long, but his quarters haunted me with an eerie, surrealistic presence. It was like opening a grave that my mentor would never have. I felt like a ten year-old boy, with eyes wide as saucers, hands in his pocket, whistling as he walked past a graveyard and telling himself that everything was all right. But everything was not all right. I knew that I would not ask someone else to do something so personal. Uneasily I rushed through the chore of packing up his belongings, and then quickly vacated the room and returned to my office.

I wrote a letter of condolence to his mother and sisters and added them to the personal effects to be shipped. My mood needed to be lightened; an inspection was just the distraction I needed. Maybe I had just lost my best friend, but I hadn't lost my *only* friend. Chief Wolverine had befriended me as a junior pilot and was one of my closest friends. I walked down to the hangar deck to check on progress. The Chief was in his usual position, his lanky frame crawling under the console of a tank, with an adjustment tool in his hand.

"Hey Chief, how's progress?"

"Sir, be ready in a couple hours, sir." The sadness in his eyes was not just empathetic—he felt the loss, too.

"Then your men will have time to clean up before the service."

"Yes sir, we'll all be there." It was important that the spirit of heaviness that shrouded the post be dispelled.

"Very well, carry on," I said as I departed.

COL SEAL'S MEMORIAL SERVICE

NINETEEN HUNDRED HOURS

The chapel was packed out at nineteen hundred as MAJ Intercessor brought words of comfort to the men. He delivered a message on a man's legacy. It touched each of us deeply as the chaplain expounded on how every man leaves something of himself behind in the good he imparts to other men.

Following the chaplain's message, I told stories of how COL SEAL had impacted my life and that it truly had been an honor to serve under him. I also expounded on the theme of COL SEAL's life: duty, honor, discipline and courage. I concluded my eulogy and nodded to the bugler and honor guard. The bugler, in his dress uniform and white gloves, was cradling the bugle against himself as though it was a sacred object. He solemnly stepped forward and blew taps. The sound of it was as mournful as a mother bereft of her child. The honor guard of eight men led by Chief Wolverine, fired three volleys of blanks outside of the chapel. There was perfect silence while the shots were being fired and I knew that tomorrow they would be ready. The service was concluded with a prayer. MAJ Intercessor sought a word with me afterward, but I avoided him. What I intended to do had no room for the voice of reason or a conscience.

I stopped MAJ Ricochet in the hall after the service was over. "Major?"

"Sir?"

"In the morning after breakfast, send the usual two squads on patrol. Here is a list of pilots that I want to remain behind to form up two squads. Have the men on that list in my ready room at zero nine hundred."

"Sir, yes sir."

I ate breakfast alone in my quarters and lingered over a second cup of tea, contemplating the merits of the plan I had concocted. It was risky, but I believed it would work, I finally decided. I arrived exactly at zero nine hundred to find all the men I had requested were already there.

"Attention!" ordered MAJ Ricochet.

I returned their salutes. "At ease, gentlemen. Please have a seat."

MAJ Ricochet was now my right-hand man and second-in-command, even though neither of us had yet been officially promoted. There were two long tables in my ready room, one for senior officers and one for junior ones. Since I only had two squads in attendance, only one table was needed, each man seated according to rank. COL SEAL's death had moved me from the first officer's place on the camp commander's right, to my new place at the head of the table. MAJ Ricochet was now occupying my old seat.

"First I want to thank the sweeper team for quick completion of the task assigned. I also hope to convince you that I am still in command of all my faculties." There were some smiles over that remark, but they were fleeting as the mood soon became serious again. "I have a practical purpose for taking the enemies' heads. So here is what we're going to do…"

I dismissed the meeting with orders to deploy in one hour. Following the briefing, MAJ Ricochet requested a meeting with me. Since my ready room was cleared, I closed the door to hear him out. As my acting first officer and oldest friend, he had my ear in a way no one else did.

"Colonel, may I speak freely?"

"You may."

"This plan is madness."

"The plan is to feign madness, which is quite sane." He was not quite sure.

"You quote often from *The Art of War*. May I offer you a passage to consider?"

"Go on."

"I quote, 'If you want to feign weakness to induce haughtiness in opponents, first you must be extremely strong, for only then can you pretend to be weak'. Du Mu, *The Art Of War*. Weakness is both physical and mental, so building on that thought, let me expound further."

"I'm listening."

"Following that line of reasoning, you have to be extremely sane to feign madness. Are you extremely sane?" MAJ Ricochet was my closest friend and right-hand man. His job was to view any risky plan with skepticism, and he played that part faithfully. I was mindful of the scripture that said; "faithful are the wounds of a friend." Proverbs 27:6

"I'm quite sane, and the plan is good, but I appreciate your concern. Will that be all?" Seeing that I would not be swayed from my course, he relented.

"No sir, but I want to go on record that I opposed this plan as unnecessarily dangerous. I strenuously disagree with your plan to play "staked goat."

"The record will show that you have disagreed, quite strenuously. And Tobias?"

"Sir?"

"If you had not voiced your opinion, I would have been disappointed. Is that all?"

"Sir, yes sir."

"Then you're dismissed."

At the appointed time, I met the men at the hangar deck. "You all know what to do, let's do it." We all passed through the last transitional airlock of the hangar deck and proceeded north. At a fork in the trail, my wingman CPT Dutchman and I proceeded farther north and the rest of the patrol split and continued north by northeast. We observed radio silence as we traveled northward. We planned to intercept the Soviet patrol where they swung the furthest point from their post and the closest to ours. I was to go forward while the others went to the predetermined destination.

It was time for my wingman to leave me and go meet the others. He hesitated, and then flew ahead. We had a discussion earlier where he tried to allow me to have him stay with me throughout the next part of the plan, and I told him no. I said it wouldn't work any other way, and I needed everyone else at this point off enemy radar. I wouldn't have a wingman that wouldn't have protested this plan. If there were any slip-ups, I could be killed. Now was the time to find out if I was *sane enough* to feign madness.

I proceeded to the intersection point. My radar showed eight ships coming directly at me from due west. I estimated that I would be outside weapons range for about ninety seconds. My heartbeat quickened, and I got my breathing under control and focused on the task ahead. Quickly I hopped out of my tank with the box I'd packed and emptied it on the ground. All five heads of the dead Soviet pilots rolled out. I'd seen bodies on the battlefield and in the morgue, but the sight of the severed heads was obscene and disturbing. I broke off my gaze and remembered that I didn't have the time to study our handiwork. After hastily jumping back into my tank, I took off at full speed. After firing several quick sprays at the group of ships with my mag cannons, I took off like a scalded dog due east.

LTC Matulevich couldn't believe his good fortune. The American dog was alone, and he looked as if he were crazy, drunk or stupid—or maybe even all three. Matulevich was already on a fast track for promotion after personally killing COL Squid, having made the very short list of Soviet officers who had killed an American command officer. At first he had thought it a bad thing that the American first officer survived the assassination attempt, but today he had the opportunity to kill his second American commander. With the war effort going against them since COL SEAL took over, it was easy to play on that fool Kiknadze's fears and manipulate him to launch an assassination squad against the American commander and his first officer. Kiknadze alone bore the decision for breaking the accord: he faced the backlash of the Americans and the political fallout from the Soviet central command alone. He had moved Kiknadze like a pawn on a chessboard and soon he would be in command. Now he could either kill or capture alive the new American commander. Never before had they taken an American commander prisoner. This would further enhance his reputation but would also be credited to his own commander. As much as he wanted to capture him alive and torture him for intelligence, he would not share the credit with Kiknadze. He would kill the American. For Matulevich was loyal to Matulevich.

"This is Sub Colonel Matulevich. We will overtake the American. Do not attack him. I want to kill him myself."

1LT Daniil Ryzhkov sighed. The honor of killing the American would go to the first officer—again.

My radar showed the enemy ships stopped where I dropped the heads. They hesitated briefly before resuming course at increased speed, attempting to overcome me. I started flying slightly erratically to give the illusion of being either drunk or insane. My instruments showed that they were flying at maximum speed and were probably mad as hornets. This wouldn't be a good time for engine failure. I was thankful Chief Wolverine was good and thorough. They followed me about thirty-eight kilometers to a place of my own choosing.

We neared an opening that was a narrow defile about sixty meters across with shadows heavy against the rock walls. I neared the preplanned location and begin to slow down, turning completely around and engaged my reverse thrusters. Finally arriving at my prearranged spot, I threw out a splinter mortar in front of the lead tank, continuing at full speed in reverse. The mortar caused all of them to stop while it spun in front of the group, throwing fifty caliber projectiles in all directions. The payload of the splinter mortar was constructed of alloy-x shrapnel, propelled outwardly by four small successive mag bomb explosions as the mortar bounced and spun off of the ground like a whirling dervish. Suddenly out of the shadows, all ten of our tanks threw out splinter mortars, surrounding the Soviet tanks' group with the spinning *death wheels*. The mortars surrounded the enemy tanks, inflicting damage while effectively cutting off their escape. My men and I were charging up our mag cannons while the Soviets were dealing with the mortars. Just as the splinter mortars stopped throwing projectiles; all ten American ships discharged their deadly purple balls of energy toward their targets. The ground shook as all eight tanks exploded in a deafening roar. The mag charge that hit the tank closest to me ripped off its hull like peeling an orange. It took a minute for the smoke and fire to subside so we could count the enemy survivors.

The combined force of all the mag charges killed six of the eight pilots as they were trying to eject. As if right on cue, all the tanks started tracking the last two pilots. I was the first one to find LTC Matulevich. He had broken a leg when his retrorocket boots malfunctioned. I drew my colts and made my way to him before my wingman or any of my pilots arrived. He had his service revolver pointed at me, but dropped it when I put a bullet through his right wrist. My enemy's eyes were as cold and hard as onyx stones, and he offered me one last defiant one-fingered salute. I stood over him for a few seconds, and then shot him through the helmet in the forehead. His helmet had a star in it as if in need of glass repair—his head bearing a neat hole dripping blood. *One down, one to go...* I accessed my radio link in my suit. "I want that other pilot alive!"

The one surviving Soviet pilot was 1LT Daniil Ryzhkov. I had a couple of men restrain him while we pulled the tooth with the embedded tracking device. I called the scavenger crew to reclaim the precious alloy-x and called up the satellite.

Our satellite showed a well-defended Soviet post with nine guntowers and ten turrets, well-placed for maximum defense. The Soviet factory was spitting out tanks and bombers as fast as possible. An attack didn't look advisable at this time. We'd lose too many ships and men and all the scrap would be recovered by the Soviets. I assigned an escort to deliver the prisoner back to our post for questioning. The loss of LTC Matulevich was going to hurt COL Kiknadze. We sat and waited while the scavengers picked the area clean, then returned to our post.

I had my Chief interrogator, CPT Black Ice, work on our prisoner. To his credit, the young officer didn't seem to be giving up anything, so I gave the captain the approval to turn up the interview a notch. We didn't officially exist as far as the Geneva Convention was concerned. After yesterday, we assumed there was no agreement about the handling of prisoners. We'd also had an agreement about using redfield generators. Since both sides had now used them, I assumed that no previous agreement would be honored. Since there were no Rules of Engagement, we'd torture our guest. Had I not been in a state of grief and suffering from guilt, I'd have seen there was no honor in this. CPT Black Ice put the Soviet in a room with a brightly flashing strobe light while playing rock music very loudly. Then he left the room to go to supper. He would leave him there all night and check on him in the morning. We would be celebrating the most successful complete victory in my recollection.

I ordered the best food and drink served to our men. We all ate and drank together and the story was told and retold. The only thing missing was COL SEAL. I asked CPT Black Ice how our prisoner was doing, and he said he would be most cooperative by morning. When the men had finished eating and drinking and had told the story about a hundred times, I bid them all goodnight.

We got some very good information out of the young pilot in the morning. We learned some things about the hierarchy there and their routines that we previously didn't know. Even more valuable was the information about their commander. COL Kiknadze had ordered COL SEAL killed because he feared him. It was an act of a desperate man. We also learned some information about his own personal habits, especially a place he liked to go alone when he wanted to think. He was an avid mountain climber and usually did this alone, with only two wingmen for security. All of this could be misinformation, so I asked CPT Black Ice to give him sodium pentothal to confirm our prisoner was telling the truth. The young pilot wasn't lying. I submitted the report to GEN Spears, but omitted the details of the pilot's interrogation. CPT Black Ice had left the details of the interrogation except for the sodium pentothal out of his report at my request.

GEN Spears called to inform me that he'd read the report. Effective immediately, I was promoted to full colonel and assigned the permanent position of post commander. MAJ Ricochet was promoted to lieutenant colonel. I requested a name change from Cowboy to Kahless, named after the unforgettable warrior icon of the Klingon race from Star Trek. He chuckled a bit and granted my request. He also granted my request to rename the post to Camp SEAL and change our unit's logo to a pair of crossed Colt forty-fives. I went down to the hangar deck and painted a picture of a Klingon warrior on both sides of my tank.

That evening we assembled in our dress uniforms for a post christening ceremony. I kept a case of champagne in my office, which was reserved to celebrate the complete removal of the Soviets here. Today I'd use a bottle of that champagne to perform the ceremony of changing the name of the post to Camp SEAL. The entire post was present in front of the main building complex for the ceremony. MAJ Norsemun, the head of the TOC, in his dress uniform and white gloves, carried the bottle to the front as though he were carrying a ceremonial saber. After a stiff walk to the front of the procession, he handed me the bottle and saluted.

I addressed the men. "GEN Spears has granted my request to rename this post Camp SEAL in honor of our fallen commander." I smashed the bottle on the inside front of the building. "I christen this post Camp SEAL, may her voyage be long." The men took notice of the references to "her" and "voyage." I'd always felt this post had the soul of a ship. It made no difference that there was no sea, sails, wind, or quarterdeck under my feet. I felt her soul, and it was the soul of a ship as much as any that sailed the seven seas.

Normally such an occasion should be followed with celebration, but I dismissed the men; who quietly returned to their duties. I made a mental note to have that bottle of champagne replaced soon. It simply wouldn't do to be short on champagne if I succeeded in killing every Soviet on Mars.

A silent war raged within my soul. Any of the chaplains would try to talk me out of what I was planning. My Chief surgeon could put a stop to it altogether with an *unfit for duty* assessment. I avoided making eye contact with any of them whenever possible

FORGING A SWORD

I couldn't stop thinking about killing Kiknadze; it ate at my soul like corrosive acid. I wanted to do it at close quarters with my hands and look into his eyes as I took his life, knowing who killed him and why. My recent choice of call signs, the fictional Klingon Kahless, would have no doubt just impaled him with the blade of his bat'letH. I had no idea how I'd get him close enough to use a blade, but I decided to make one nonetheless.

The *Star Trek* story of Kahless was indeed interesting. The Klingon dipped a lock of his hair into a volcano, pulled it out and hammered forged a bat'letH. He quenched the fantasy blade in a lake. I laughed to myself as I contemplated what winds up in science fiction.

First I went to the machine shop and requisitioned Chief Wolverine to release about twenty pounds of alloy-x to experiment with making edged weapons. One thing we knew, this stuff was amazing, and I often wondered if it made a good blade. I'd made my Arkansas toothpick out of some scrap tool steel, but never thought to use alloy-x.

The machine shop had a facility for making and heat-treating tools. Then I went to my locker and pulled out my welding leathers, leather gloves and torch glasses. Growing up on a farm where we did a lot of our own repairs and fabrications, I'd made some knives in our shop back home. We had a bench vice, bench grinder, belt sander, buffer, an anvil and a drill stand close to the forge and heat-treating kiln. I adjusted the anvil's height to suit me. Since alloy-x had an element in it that was previously not on any elemental chart, I'd have to do some experimenting. Oh, we had data from over twenty years of building ships and weapons with it and the Chief had used some to make tool steel. We weren't completely ignorant of its properties. Alloy-x was dubbed that because of it amazing qualities. Alloy-x was comprised of iron, carbon, a little nickel, and an element we referred to as element x. If it didn't contain element x, it would only be medium carbon-nickel steel with nothing to brag about. But this element constituted fifteen percent of the alloy-x. Although we'd made tools with it, heat-treating it like steel, I felt this metal had a secret to unlock. There were quite a few different temperatures to quench steel at and different quenching mediums, as well as different tempering temperatures.

After three months of experimenting, I had a boot knife that passed all my tests beyond my wildest dreams. Heating the alloy-x and hammer forging it into shape, I then reheated it to a dark cherry red and quenched it to a subzero temperature and repeated the process again. Finally, I reheated it to dark cherry red and quenched it in brine and tempered the blade to a peacock color. What I was looking at was a metal that didn't follow conventional metalworking rules. The knife bent ninety degrees in both directions without breaking. I hammered it into a barrel and then hammered the back of it, causing it to shear a cut a foot long through a steel barrel. After all of this abuse, it still shaved hair off of my arm and afterward easily cut through a free hanging one-inch Manila hemp rope. But I'd also seen earthly steels do all this. So I decided to find out if I could break it. Pulling out a half-inch piece of plate steel, I proceeded to hammer the knife into it, point down with a five-pound sledgehammer. To my amazement, it cut right through, but it stuck. Flipping it over, I pounded the point of it back out with the hammer. I was dumbfounded. The knife dropped out without as much as a chip or crack on the point. Excitedly I called the Chief and repeated the test. He was as impressed as I was. After polishing the blade on the muslin wheel of the buffer-grinder, I drilled some rivet holes in the tang and fixed a red linen Micarta handle to it and gave it to Chief Wolverine.

The next step was to make a fearsome weapon out of this amazing metal. I hammered out a double-handled sword, forty inches long from tip to tip, with four blade edges which would have given even the most discriminating Klingon eyes filled with blood lust and fangs showing an appreciative smile. The two outside blade edges were fifteen inches long apiece, and the two inside blades, twelve inches long in front, acted as blade catchers. It had two handle cutouts in the back of the blade to grip it with both hands.

I tempered it the same as I did the boot knife. It took two assistants to handle the bellows so I could get all of the blade edges hot enough to hammer out. Using the inside cutouts of the weapon to achieve the balance I wanted, I wrapped the handle cutouts in strips of leather soaked in resin. The end product looked like a cross between a sword and a flying bat.

We had an old scout that was going to be recycled soon. My attempt to cut through the walls of the craft with my blade and was successful. It was important to me that my new sword to be fearsome in appearance, as well. I gave the back of the blade a flat-black anodized finish, but the inside of the cutouts and blade edges I made blood-red. It gave it the look of a bat in flight with bloody wing tips and evil eyes. Its amazing functionality and fearsome look made me smile as I imagined myself impaling or beheading COL Kiknadze.

I completely quit doing katas in my karate class with any other weapon, save my sword. I wrote six katas for my sword, and when I needed to think, I went to the practice room and practiced katas. Real practice was impossible with the blade as it was too deadly, so I had a pair of hard wood replicas made with a heavy layer of rubber on the outside for practice with a partner. Even so, CPT Dutchman and I had to put on helmets and padded gear after we cracked a couple ribs and busted some knuckles.

A technician, whose specialty was upholstering vehicles, made me a sheath out of Cordura nylon and metal snaps to hold it in place beside me in my tank when I flew. I'd purposely disabled the automatic leveling flight controls on my ship so that I could do nose up and down maneuvers.

However, this could get hairy at times because sometimes the ship would attempt to roll on its side and need to be manually controlled to keep it upright. The idea of being gutted by my own blade was not very appealing, to say the least. I snapped it firmly in place, and unsnapped and re-snapped it a few times to get a feel for how fast I could retrieve it if needed.

The next six months were very hard fought. I lost six more pilots: Lieutenants Magnum Force, Hard Core, Jolly Roger, Perdition, Crazy Horse and Skywalker. We also lost a lot of ships. I had a close call and was shot out of my tank, but my wingman picked me up before the enemy could take advantage of the situation. Each new transport freighter arrived with new pilots to replace the ones we were losing, and I greeted them with a guilty conscience. The next new crop of pilots, Lieutenants Death Before Dishonor, Scourge, Pool Shark, Cross Swords, Pac Man and Janus Dread arrived with a nervous sense of expectation. I promoted CPT Dutchman to major, and he changed his call sign to Killer Instinct. I assigned 1LT Cross Swords as his wingman, and I chose 1LT Janus Dread as mine.

THE KILLING OF COL KIKNADZE

The parameters for our satellite were set to inform me immediately if COL Kiknadze left his post with only two other tanks. It was early zero five hundred when I heard my comm. buzzer. Blaze barked an alert that I had to attend to business. Accessing my computer, I got an alert, "COL Kiknadze is traveling with two other tanks directly north northeast, at twenty meters per second, approximately ten kilometers from his post." The intricacies of this plan had been hatched months before. I entered the access code for the security system for the whole post: satellite, security, radar, and communications—to disable everything by forcing it into a self-diagnostic routine in fifteen minutes. MAJ Norsemun ran these once a month when the area was secure, and we had no patrols out, but I triggered it now on purpose. Locking out a security override was out of the question—we may need it back up. Erasing the computer log of my activity would ensure that the technicians would think the diagnostic was triggered by a glitch in the system. It was imperative to get my tank out of the last airlock before the diagnostic started.

Quickly I threw on some clothes and headed straight for the hangar deck. Entering the hangar, I encountered only night security and dismissed them without explaining anything. Hurriedly I donned my flight suit and helmet, and pulled my ghillie suit over it and climbed into my tank. Then I booted my onboard computer up, ran the startup diagnostics and found all systems up. Most importantly, the redfield generator was operational, and all weapons systems were hot. Now I was prepared to shove off, with one minute, twenty seconds left to spare before the security self-diagnostic routine locked all the hangar doors.

I had previously gotten my hacker team to get an open door to the Soviet satellite that covered the time of the day that COL Kiknadze usually went mountain climbing. They had a particularly mean virus, ready to infect it at my command, which would format the entire satellite's hard drive. The program was already loaded to our comm. tower, and I had the authorization codes in my tank's computer. A simple password would initiate the attack. It's funny—rank can allow you to be stupid sometimes, and only a few people will challenge you.

If my second-in-command, LTC Ricochet or my wingman 1LT Janus Dread had been up, I could not have stopped either from coming along. If they had to, they would shadow me from a distance. The same was true for my former wingman, MAJ Killer Instinct. Accessing the hangar deck controls from my tank's computer, I unlocked the three transitional airlocks and checked my watch. This was cutting it close—only forty seconds left to clear the third airlock. Just before clearing the last airlock, I erased the computer log of the transaction. Ten seconds later the security self-diagnostic routine started and locked down the whole post. Unwilling to be tracked later, I pulled out a pair of wire cutters and disabled my ship's transponder. All American combat officers had transmitters imbedded in their legs for search and rescue attempts. I had wrapped my leg with aluminum foil to stop the transmission—certainly less painful than cutting the transmitter out of my leg.

Leaving my post behind, I headed straight north by northeast, adjusting my course to match where our satellite said the colonel was heading. I kept an eye on my radar, constantly getting updated reports from my satellite.

CAMP SEAL—TACTICAL OPERATIONS
ZERO FIVE TWENTY HOURS

MAJ Norsemun awoke to a page. *No problem, my alarm will be going off in ten minutes anyway,* he thought. He called the TOC. "CPT Black Ice here, Major. We responded to an unscheduled communications array and security system self-diagnostic."

"Anything unusual?"

"Nothing so far, but I'm doing a scan log to see if anyone hacked into our system."

"Be there in five mikes, Norsemun out."

Despite all of the major's quirks, he was high functioning in his professional life, and known for precision and running a tight ship in the TOC. It was probably nothing, he knew, but this could be a brilliant cyberattack on the post if it were hacked from outside. That gave him an idea for his people to try for a new assault on the Soviet system. He did not want to wake COL Kahless if it was a false alarm. He was dressed and on the way to the TOC in record time. Arriving in exactly five minutes, he found CPT Black Ice and the night technicians trying to isolate the *system glitch*.

"Any luck finding the cause?" queried the major.

"No sir, dangdest thing, too. There was no outside access to our system, and no one inside accessed the system. The diagnostic just started to run by itself."

"Very good, put us on yellow alert and stop the diagnostic. I want a log of all computer activity on this post, one—no, make it two hours prior to the shutdown."

"Sir, yes sir."

It was now time to tell the colonel the reason for the yellow alert. He should have already been calling him demanding an explanation.

Communications were now restored. MAJ Norsemun rang the colonel on the comm., and failing to get a response, paged him—still no answer.

"Computer, locate COL Kahless."

"COL Kahless' location is unknown," the sweet voice replied.

"Computer, access COL Kahless' transmitter chip and compute his location."

"We are not receiving a signal from COL Kahless' transmitter chip."

The major was beginning to hate playing Simon says with this idiot computer. Being the resident geek, he'd never betrayed to anyone that he, too, had a love-hate relationship with computers at times. "Computer, compute probable location of COL Kahless."

"Unknown, not enough data." MAJ Norsemun quickly contacted LTC Ricochet.

"What is it, Major?"

"COL Kahless is missing, and there was a security breach this morning."

After the major finished explaining, the post's first officer called Chief Wolverine, who was grabbing a hot cup of coffee in the hangar deck's break room.

"Good morning sir, what can I do for you?" responded the Chief.

"Is the colonel's ship in the hangar?" He glanced over to the bay where he'd been doing some routine maintenance on it himself at the close of business yesterday.

"No, sir."

"Check the airlock logs, now!"

"Sir, yes sir."

The Chief accessed the hangar deck's security logs of the airlocks and found nothing, but that didn't surprise him. He'd watched his friend become consumed with grief over the death of COL SEAL, and he feared something like this might happen.

"Nothing sir. According to the airlock logs, they haven't opened today."

"Then where's the colonel's ship?" he demanded.

"I suppose if you find the colonel, he'll be in it."

LTC Ricochet was sore tempted to take out his frustrations on the Chief for that last remark, but he appeared worried, too.

"MAJ Norsemun, I have the computer activity logs. COL Kahless got an alert from us that COL Kiknadze had left his post with two wingmen just after zero five hundred," reported CPT Black Ice.

"I didn't authorize that alert."

"No sir, he did. In any case, our department notified him and he's gone."

The major contacted LTC Ricochet. "Sir, COL Kahless got an alert that COL Kiknadze was flying with two wingmen outside of his post."

"My God, he's gone after him alone."

"Yes, sir, it appears he has."

LTC Ricochet decided against launching an all-out search. If he sent every tank he had looking for the colonel, the Soviets would know something was up and scramble every tank they had and start looking, too. Odds were that COL Kahless was now deep in Soviet territory and starting an all-out search could sign his death warrant. He would send only the usual routine patrols and wait. His next task was an unpleasant one. By now, CPT Black Ice had already reported the security breach and the colonel's absence. He had to file his own report to GEN Spears.

THARSIS PLAIN (COL Kahless)

I knew very well that it might be a trap, similar to what we first laid for the Soviets just over six months ago. But from the information we *extracted* from our captive, COL Kiknadze had to have times of solitude, going mountain climbing with only two wingmen. I was betting everything this was what he was doing.

It wasn't time to disable the Soviet communication system yet. To do so would be inviting the Soviets to send more tanks to protect their commander. However, I had to be concerned with the Soviet satellites when they flew by. My ship's computer had a map of all of the craters deep enough to hide in when the satellites went by, and was well aware of when they would be watching. I hit my first crater just about five minutes before the next Soviet satellite would do a flyby. The crater was thirty meters deep and sixty meters wide. Leaving my antigravity hover device engaged, I shut down my propulsion jets and nosed down into the crater. It simply wouldn't do to stir up a dust cloud in the crater's bottom for the satellite to see. Then I covered my ship with a dark-colored heat-shield tarp. When it was safe to proceed, I pulled off the tarp, fired my engine up and continued my quest. By the next satellite flyby, the dust will have settled. I had to repeat this four times before getting into Soviet territory. Flipping the toggle switch, I engaged the redfield generator. Being discovered before reaching Kiknadze would be disastrous.

I traveled for four hours north-northeast. I was within radar range now and picked up the three Soviet ships. The mountain the Soviet was climbing was part of a ridge that ran north to south. Parking my ship on the south side of the ridge in the shadows and out of sight, I placed a camouflaged heat shield tarp over it.

Walking over to the south edge of the ridge, my boots crunched the salt-hardened sand, making radial fractures around my boot prints. The crust was called caliche, made up of calcium carbonate deposits from surface water sublimation. I had to crawl a hundred meters to get into position to see what they were doing. That took time. The ground was littered with stones, and I had to rake them aside before belly-crawling forward. The caliche in the surface of the sand held the stones like weak cement and cracked when I broke them from the ground. The ground crunched as I crawled along the surface, moving stones and crunching the calcified caliche surface. The whole process took over thirty minutes. Finally, I had the three tanks in view. Kiknadze's two men were outside of their tanks facing the mountain. COL Kiknadze was descending from the cliff face. I figured he would be down in about fifteen minutes. It was time. Returning back to my tank, I initiated the virus attack on the Soviet satellite, grabbed my sniper rifle and crawled back to my spot. This trip only took five minutes because the rocks had been cleared on my first trip.

The Soviet commander was another five minutes from being on the ground. I used my spotting scope and judged from the lack of dust that there was almost no wind today. My rangefinder indicated the shot would be about two thousand meters—not too bad, considering the air density and gravity here. Even with less gravitational pull on the bullet and less bullet drag because of the thin atmosphere, I still had two more calculations to make. At this distance, the curvature of the planet and Mar's orbital rotation had to be calculated. This was not a problem—I'd been practicing shots like this for years. After finishing my calculations, I put my flash suppressor/silencer on the end of my rifle, set up my tripod and watched the two wingmen with a razor-sharp focus. Three times they almost gave me the shots that I wanted and COL Kiknadze was now about two minutes from getting his feet on the ground. Patience, move over, just a little more… The two Soviet wingmen were both facing Kiknadze, one about a meter forward of the other and on his right. It would take about three seconds for the first shot to arrive, so I had to make this good. Bringing my scope into focus, I selected the pilot to the rear and on the left, and after making all of the compensating adjustments, I aimed for his gut and spine. After carefully squeezing off a round between my heartbeats, I quickly chambered another round. The second pilot had two kill areas exposed, his lower spine below his oxygen tanks and his head. My finger squeezed off the shot at his spine one second after firing the first shot. Three seconds after I fired the first shot the first pilot fell. The second pilot turned his head to see his partner drop to the ground just as the bullet caught him in the lower back.

Both men were now lying on the ground. A cursory check with my spotting scope revealed that they weren't moving. The Soviet commander was now on the ground and was running as fast as a man in full flight gear could manage to get into his tank. I fired again and caught him on the run, shattering his right ankle. He fell face-first onto the ground, and I followed up with another shot to his left ankle. Kiknadze dragged himself to one of his wingmen and grabbed his rifle. My third shot went through his right shoulder and he dropped the rifle.

Removing the camouflaged tarp from my tank, I hopped in and fired it up. Then I flew over to the wounded Soviet, unsnapped my sword and hopped out of my tank. One of the Soviet wingmen's arms was still twitching, so I beheaded them both. Time was of the essence; Kiknadze had lost a lot of blood from his shoulder wound and soon he would be in shock. He'd had the presence of mind to patch his suit in three places before his suit depressurized. The strength spent on the suit repair left him too weak to resist when I arrived.

With the Soviet satellite down and their commander away from his post, the Soviets would be on high alert and scramble their entire fleet. I wanted him to know who was doing this and why. He hadn't lost consciousness yet. He was sitting up, so I put my boot hard into his wounded shoulder to force him to the ground. His eyes met mine. Despite his pain, he knew who I was. He knew it was over and he was making a show of being brave. The lust for revenge that welled up within me didn't want to end this yet. Laying my sniper rifle down, I plunged the left end of my two-handled sword into his belly above his navel. Cutting in a circle, I continued to cut with the blade now moving toward his ribcage until I had finished disemboweling him. He would die a hideous death before the effects of decompression or suffocation took over. His bowels had spilled out of the slash in his spacesuit while his suit started decompressing. COL Kiknadze was now in excruciating pain, his face a grotesque death mask, his eyes revealing only madness. Something about the madness in his eyes awoke me from the madness driving me. Suddenly I realized that no man should die this kind of death. I lifted my sword and beheaded him right there. His head and helmet rolled three feet away and came to a stop against a rock. His headless body spurted blood, while his low-pressure air hose created ripples in the blood spray. I surveyed the macabre scene. One thing remained. Taking my utility knife from my suit pocket, I cut his blood-soaked name patch off of his suit and stuffed it into my pocket.

Next, I checked his tank and typed in the security codes that the young Soviet pilot we'd captured had given us. Everything looked good to go, so I started it up. Walking over to my tank, I removed the flight recorder, transponder, and the pictures of my parents and grandparents from the dash. Taking my ship out of redfield mode, I accessed the partitioned part of my ship's computer that controlled the actions of scuttling my ship. Next I released the quarantined virus and executed it so it would start eating all my ship's data with the exception of the separate partition. From that partition, I activated the self-destruct sequence, specifying to blow the ship the next time the hatch was opened or being towed. Writing on a piece of paper in Russian, I stuck the note with some tape to the inside of the transparent hatch. I was hoping their curiosity would get them to open the hatch. Using the security codes we extracted from our prisoner, I fired up Kiknadze's tank and was on my way. Radar showed four squads of Soviet tanks three minutes and closing.

My reason was beginning to return to me, so I decided to get the hell out of there. I flew south by southwest at maximum speed. Since I knew Russian, I accessed the proper console buttons and switches to get all the features I needed up, including their own redfield. I remembered the arduous task of learning to read and write Russian and how badly I wanted to skip those classes, but today I was glad I hadn't. I needed to keep the redfield going until I was clear of Soviet territory and at least had a strong enough lead on them so they couldn't catch me. Leaving the radio on the Soviet frequency, I kept my ears open. The radio reports that they have my disabled tank on their radar. I kept an eye on my radar, searching for what I thought was the first opportunity to call my post. I heard the Soviets saying they'd arrived at my tank. There was some real agitated conversation.

"They have killed our colonel!"

"It is the American colonel's tank, but where is he now?"

"Where the tank of our colonel?"

"The American has it!"

"He is probably long-gone now in our colonel's tank. Let us open his."

"What is this? There is something is written in Russian."

"Nyet, you fool!"

I wondered who'd win the argument. I'd now achieved a comfortable lead and heard a very loud explosion over the radio. I guess they all lost. I heard some more talk that some of them were dead and that some of the remaining tanks had been damaged.

My head finally cleared of my obsession. It dawned on me that if there was a town called Stupidville; I could get elected mayor. However, the scales were coming back into balance. LTC Matulevich killed COL Squid; Col Kiknadze had COL SEAL killed. Since I had become commander, I had killed them both and stolen a Soviet tank for our tech boys to pick apart. I still had to face the music when I got back. As commander, I had given standing orders that none of my men leave the post alone. I had issued those orders to my men, not to myself. Specifically targeting the opposing command officer was part of planning that usually included the chain of command. I had disobeyed no direct order. I had not consulted the chain of command on this decision, but that was a gray area. My standing order as a post commander was "to maintain the post and its integrity." This was my only written and recorded order. The details of how I was to do so was verbally given to me by the protocol officer when I was promoted, but wasn't part of any record. I was unsure of what legal trouble I would face when I got back, but I was sure I was in trouble.

I was deep into American territory, and I realized the error of flying into American territory unannounced in a Soviet tank. Putting my tank on autopilot, I stripped my suit down and removed the aluminum foil covering my transmitter chip, hotwired my transponder to the Soviet tank and turned it on.

"LTC Ricochet, I have transmission signals from both COL Kahless' ship transponder and transmitter chip on a heading of mark zero two zero from your position, on a course heading of one niner five. But get this—satellite feed shows it's coming from a Soviet tank. Approach with extreme caution. You should have him on your radar in five mikes," reported MAJ Norsemun.

"Roger that, moving to intercept," responded a hopeful but suspicious first officer. He keyed his mike. "Soviet vessel, identify yourself."

"American patrol, this is COL Kahless. I'm in a Soviet tank, headed your way. Please don't shoot me."

"Please confirm your identity."

"Mr. Brown, I appreciated the toast."

"This is LTC Ricochet, we see you on radar," responded the relieved but peeved first officer.

The squadron escorted me back to the post, but on radio silence—not so ordered but a clear message, nonetheless. Once inside of the hangar deck, LTC Ricochet, MAJ Killer Instinct, and 1LT Janus Dread were the first to greet me. My wingman looked like a teenager who hadn't been invited to the senior prom. LTC Ricochet spoke first. "Colonel, why didn't you get some help?"

I looked around at their concerned faces. "Colonel, I expect if we live long enough, we will all eventually do something real stupid. Have Chief Wolverine's crew take Kiknadze's tank apart and extract any information and resources that they can. LTC Ricochet?"

"Sir?"

"Tobias, I would like a word with you, privately."

"Yes, sir."

"Did you report my absence to GEN Spears?"

"Yes, sir. It was a regrettable duty I had to perform."

"You did the right thing. I guess it is time to face the music." I had some time to reflect on what I'd just done on the last leg home. Somehow even with the success I'd just enjoyed, it occurred to me I'd acted foolishly and could very well have been killed or captured. Now I'd have to address damage control for my own unit, brought on by my own foolishness and take full responsibility for my actions.

"Are you quite through, sir?!" The last part was said in a condescending tone. I had betrayed his trust and would feel the same way if our roles were reversed. My whole career here I owed to Cadet "Brown," who treated me like a brother and wouldn't let me fail boot camp.

"I'm quite through taking matters into my own hands. From now on you'll know where I am at all times."

"Yes, sir. I assure you I will know where you are at all times."

I had a feeling he knew more than I did about that right now.

"1LT Janus Dread, walk with me." I looked at him as we got out of earshot of the others. "Lieutenant, I noticed that you seem to be upset by my actions. I owe you my life many times over. If you have anything to say, say it."

"Sir, my job is to protect you, and you didn't let me do it. How would you feel if when you were COL SEAL's wingman, and he had left you behind the day that he died?"

"I suppose I would feel as you do now. I swore a blood oath the day COL SEAL died that I'd personally kill COL Kiknadze and as I said before, that was probably stupid. Going maverick may have cost me my career, but COL Kiknadze was hated by ASDC Central Command for the assassination of COL Seal. I may be forgiven."

"Sir, I take it you're now through being reckless and will allow me to do my job?"

"Lieutenant, I assure you that I'm through with taking things into my own hands and I won't go anywhere without you in the future." I glanced at CPT Black Ice heading his my way, his expression set hard as flint. "You shouldn't worry; I may not be going anywhere for a while."

"CPT Black Ice?"

"Sir, it is my duty to inform you that you are under arrest for failing to maintain this post and its integrity, and abandoning your post. You are hereby relieved of your command and confined to your quarters. All communications to Earth are hereby subject to my approval. Do you need me to read you your article thirty-two rights?"

The gravity of the situation hit me full force. "No, Captain, I fully understand my rights."

"Then these two men will escort you to your quarters. CPT Defender has been appointed as your legal counsel."

"Understood."

Kahless was brewing a cup of tea when he heard the knock on the door.

"Come."

CPT Defender entered, with a briefcase and a tape recorder in hand— wearing an expression more like that of a funeral director. His lawyer was handsome, dark-haired; dark eyed, in his mid-thirties, and looked fit for a man in this profession, but walked with a pronounced limp. There was something about his bearing that spoke of a different past.

"Colonel, I have been appointed to represent you."

The teakettle whistled, and Kahless turned the burner under the teapot off. "Captain, please have a seat at the table. Would you like a cup of tea?"

"No thank you. I just had a cup of coffee." The attorney laid his briefcase and recorder on the table and took a seat. Kahless poured himself a cup of tea and took a chair at the table.

"Colonel, I am here to take your official statement and discuss the nature of the charges against you."

"Understood."

"I have to advise you that even though I am assigned to defend you, I represent the interests of the ASDC. Please do not lie to me. I will defend and represent your interests strenuously as long as they do not come into conflict with the interests of the ASDC. In short, you know how this works. This is not a civilian matter. Understand that in these proceedings, you are not afforded attorney-client confidentiality as in civilian cases. If I find out anything that the prosecution needs to know, I must turn it over. Also let me advise you that as a decorated command officer, I shall strive to defend your reputation just as strenuously."

"Understood."

The captain turned the tape player on, held up one finger to cause his client to pause, then began to speak… "Before we begin, let the record so reflect that COL Kahless is a decorated command officer with an unblemished record. It is also not the purpose of this inquiry to malign or defame COL Kahless' character."

CPT Defender directed his gaze at his client. "Colonel, state your name for the record."

"My call sign is COL Kahless, my given name is Eugene J. Bordelon, Jr., or it was."

"Do you swear that the statements you are about to make are true?"

"I do."

"COL Kahless, do you understand the seriousness of the charges against you?"

"I do."

"COL Kahless, on the twenty-fourth day of the Martian month Kumbha, Earth date March 8, 1980; did you willfully override the post's security protocols?"

"I did."

"Did you leave the post in a tank alone?"

"I did."

"It is the position of the prosecution that in doing so that you jeopardized the integrity and security of the post. Do you have anything so say concerning this?"

"I did leave the post in a tank alone, but I believed I did so to preserve the security of the post."

"Please explain."

"The post itself was secure enough with or without me. My men do a fine job of defending her. COL Kiknadze had already sent a team of assassins after my former commander. In light of that, I viewed COL Kiknadze as a direct threat to the integrity of my post."

"For the record, are you saying that you did so in defense of your own life?"

"Perhaps. In any case, as long as Kiknadze was alive, any American command officer was in jeopardy of an assassination attempt."

"I see. Did you have any assistance or aid from anyone else in this…" he hesitated, reconsidered, and continued. "…In this event?"

"I did not."

"COL Kahless, what happened on the twenty-fourth day of the Martian month Kumbha, Earth date March 8, 1980?"

"I overrode the security protocols on the post, took my tank and found COL Kiknadze and his two guards. I shot and beheaded them all. I wiped my tank's computer, set my tank to blow if tampered with, then took Kiknadze's tank and returned to my post."

The attorney paused and turned off the recorder. "Colonel, I find this quite amazing. You went into enemy territory alone, killed the Soviet commander and his two guards, stole the commander's tank and hardly have a story to tell. I've heard men come back from a deer hunt with longer tales."

"My providing more details doesn't change the truth as it relates to the charges, does it?"

"I suppose not." The captain turned the recorder on again. "Colonel, is there anything else you would like to say?"

"Only that I consider it an honor to have served my country up to this point and would like to continue to do so."

His lawyer turned off the tape, looked thoughtfully at his client. "Colonel, the prosecution's case concerning the failing to maintain the integrity and security of you post charge entirely rests on the fact that you jeopardized the post's most valuable asset—you. I believe I can win that argument. We may not be so fortunate with the abandoning your post charge. Normally no one would put their career on the line to order an unscheduled fitness exam for a decorated command officer, but you are due for a routine exam right now. If you do not pass your fitness examination, your detractors will win without going to trial."

"How strong are my enemies?"

"In any military order, there are some high-ranking officers who are results oriented hard-charges. They think the rules can be broken, from time to time—if you win. Then there are those that are so focused on the process that they take it as a personal affront to their authority if you break one of their rules."

"Who's going to be on the tribunal?"

"The Central Command staff, minus your distinct commander BG Moore: GEN Speers, LTG Mondragon, BG Edwards, MG MacNeil, MG Whitacre, and BG Buchanan."

"Are the sticklers or hard-chargers in power?"

"It's split down the middle. The two ranking officers, GEN Speers, and LTG Mondragon are solidly for you, along with BG Edwards. In the opposing camp, MG Whitacre, and MG MacNeil strongly oppose you. Even though they are not the two ranking officers, two major generals won't be ignored.

"Where does BG Buchanan stand?"

"He's MG Whitacre's nephew."

"I see."

"Understand this—the sticklers want you found unfit for duty and expelled from service. The hard-chargers admire what you have done, but feel that you've left them out of the loop by striking out on your own."

"How can I keep my command?"

"The act was obviously premeditated. That works against you. The fact that you appear to have planned it a long time ago speaks to possible emotional instability

Your first hurdle is to pass your fitness examination with MAJ Sawbones. If the doctor gives you a green light, we'll discuss the next step."

"Understood." Kahless launched and then aborted a smile. "I guess I'll have to study for my sanity test," he said, dryly.

CPT Defender rose, gathered up his tape player and briefcase. "Colonel, even if you pass your fitness exam, the sticklers will try to force some censure or demotion upon you."

"Why is it so important to them?"

"You've been locked up since you got back, so I guess it won't hurt to tell you. Our satellite was in position during the "event" and recorded it all. Your story has spread like wildfire from Earth to Titan. From what I've heard all ready, you are being referred to as some sort of superhero, ten feet tall and bulletproof. It is important to the sticklers that you are not venerated as being a law unto yourself. They must bring you down a notch."

"The hard-chargers?"

"They like superheroes. They rally the men and give them someone to emulate. They will not let you be destroyed, but they will compromise with the sticklers to appease them. The failing to maintain the integrity of your post charge is weak, but abandoning your post is the one we have to worry about."

"Where do we go from here?"

"Pass your fitness review first, and then... I'll fight for your career."

"What if I am crazy?"

"Then the fight is over before it starts."

"One more thing... May I have visitors?"

"Yes."

"May I be allowed in-house communications?"

"Only if you go through security, but you can relay verbal messages of course through your visitors."

"Thank you. Will you please contact my aide and ask him to come by for a visit?"

"Of course. One more thing—you may not be visited by anyone who is being investigated for your "event": LTC Ricochet, MAJ Norsemun, CPT Black Ice, Chief Wolverine, or any officers in security, or any technicians who maintenance the hangar door locks. They haven't been cleared yet, and they may yet be called as witnesses."

"Very well."

"You will get your examination with MAJ Sawbones in the morning. In the meantime, I have a lot of work to do." CPT Defender left the room, passing between the two guards outside Kahless' door.

CPT Defender promptly advised PFC Gray Eagle that the colonel wished to see him. The young man picked up Blaze from tac ops and walked her to the colonel's quarters. As the young private passed by, men stopped moving, stopped talking and stared after him, hoping to learn news of their commander. He arrived at the colonel's quarters—one guard on each side of the door, who were gravely quiet with expressionless faces. The ranking guard conceding that entrance was acceptable: PFC Gray Eagle was not on the restricted visitor list. Gray Eagle knocked on the door.

"Come."

The young man walked Blaze into the room. The colonel had been watching *Star Trek* on his TV. The colonel turned off the volume on the TV set.

"You know, Private, Kirk cheats death and sometimes defies authority, but at the end of the story, he always winds up on top."

"Yes sir." Gray Eagle looked awkward as the colonel looked intently into his eyes as if looking for an answer.

"You want to know what I think?"

"Sir, yes sir."

"William Shatner had control over the script. It's science fiction, not reality. Me—I don't get to write the script. I'm just a man in trouble and that's the truth of it."

"Sir, is there anything I can do for you?"

"Just stop by and pick up Blaze and drop her by tac ops in the morning. No doubt MAJ Norsemun is upset that I bypassed his system to take leave of the post. Blaze will help him adjust to his world being disturbed."

"Anything else, sir?"

"No, thank you, Private. Have a nice evening."

The young man sighed, saluted and left Kahless alone with his dog.

Blaze looked at Kahless, trying to interpret his mood. "You know Blaze, I should have negotiated for script control," he sighed and went to make them both supper, but was interrupted by a knock on his door.

"Come."

The door opened, and SGT Gutshot pushed in a food cart. He stopped, sharply saluted, and then rolled the cart to the table. "Good evening Colonel, Blaze."

"Good evening, Sergeant. You could have had someone else deliver that. You didn't have to bring it yourself."

"Sir, this is an honor. I have never felt so proud to be an American as I am today." He wiped a tear from his eye and pointed at the cart. "Enjoy." Embarrassed by his display of emotion, he quickly excused himself and left the colonel and his dog to their supper. The colonel took the stainless steel cover off of the food cart to reveal some of his favorite dishes, steak and chicken smothered in onions over rice, a spinach salad, and pecan pie for dessert. There were two cold long-necked beers in an ice bucket, and a sizzling-hot steak for Blaze.

"Well, girl, looks like we still have friends where it counts."

Kahless had finished feeding Blaze breakfast just in time. A sharp knock on the door announced that his aide was here to pick her up. The young private called her to heel and walked her to tac ops. Kahless heated some leftover rice and steak from last night and set the teapot to boil. After breakfast and two cups of tea, Kahless got dressed for his interview with MAJ Sawbones. Wearing his uniform jacket and with hat in hand, he walked with his "escort" to sick bay. At the sight of their highly respected but troubled commander, everyone that he passed became still and quiet, and snapped to attention and held the salute until he was no longer in sight.

MAJ Sawbones greeted Kahless when he arrived at sickbay. He directed the guards to wait outside of sick bay, and ushered Kahless into his office. Mounted on the wall behind his desk was a medical diploma from the

National Naval Medical Center, alongside a diploma declaring he had completed his Surgical Critical Care fellowship. He pointed at the couch.

"No thanks, Doc. I'd rather sit."

"Suit yourself." Both men took a seat.

"Colonel, this is a routine fitness exam that you are required to take every six months. It is not linked to the events of yesterday, but I would like to use those events to gauge your fitness. My duty is to be objective and determine one thing, and one thing only—to identify if you have a physical, emotional or mental problem that would prevent you from doing your job in a safe and effective manner, or jeopardize the men under your command. I will ask you several questions about the recent events, to determine if you have a firm grasp of reality regarding these events and if the thought processes driving your behavior were rational."

"Understood."

"Colonel, the report states that you did willfully, without consulting any of your superiors or even you own men; sneak out of here with the intent of killing COL Kiknadze. Is that about right?"

"That sums it up."

"Why did you do it?"

"COL Kiknadze was a clear threat to our post. His recent breaking of the accord and the assassination of COL SEAL showed that he was willing to set ambushes for command officers, even at the cost of violating the accord and plunging us into all-out war."

"Ah, COL SEAL... And exactly when did you decide upon this course of action."

"The day of the ambush near Valles Marineris."

"Did you feel responsible for COL SEAL's death?"

"I felt I had failed to protect him."

"Did you believe that your two tanks could defeat five or theirs?"

"No, but we did defeat them—though the cost was very high."

"Were you responsible for his death?"

"No, I did not order the attack."

"Did you feel responsible?"

"Yes."

"How could you have been responsible?"

"I was not, but knowledge and feelings are two different things. I felt as if I had failed to protect my commander." The doctor wrote some more in his notebook, then looked at Kahless, his eyes narrowing.

"What were the circumstances surrounding the death of LTC Matulevich?"

"We laid a trap for two squadrons of Soviet tanks. LTC Matulevich was among the enemy casualties."

"Did you kill him yourself?"

"I did."

"Was he trying to surrender?"

"He was not."

"I see…" MAJ Sawbones stroked his chin thoughtfully, jotted down some more notes, and studied his patient. Kahless felt uncomfortable under the doctor's scrutinizing gaze. "Colonel, I understand that you forged a rather impressive blade."

"I did."

"Was this to kill Col Kiknadze?"

"I was hopeful."

"You waited some time for the opportunity to act on this plan."

"I was patient, yes."

"Did you suffer from disturbing dreams or nightmares during the time between the death of your commander and the killing of the Soviet commander?"

Kahless hesitated, touched his nose, and then his mouth. "No."

The doctor took off his glasses, rubbed his eye absent-mindedly, placed his glasses back on and wrote in his journal: *Subject is lying, when he says he hasn't been having bad dreams or nightmares.*

"Let's move along, Colonel. Why did you feel the need to go it alone? You have a very good sniper team, headed up I believe by CPT OSOK?"

"Yes, my sniper team is top-notch. Frankly, I felt that ordering an assassination was an immoral order."

"Hmmm." The doctor chewed the end of his pen, obviously lost in thought. "You regularly deploy sniper teams to take out enemy targets on the battlefield. What makes this different?"

"He was not on any battlefield."

"Why was your dispatching of Col Kiknadze any different from an assassination?"

"I was one of the intended targets of the assassination attempt. He had a debt to pay. We had lost two post commanders in less than a year. The scales were unbalanced; our position here was threatened in both the posture of the enemy and also the morale of my men." The patient was sitting with both palms on the table, face up and relaxed.

The doctor wrote some more in his report: *the patient believes he had good reason for his actions, and possesses rational thought.*

"Colonel, do you feel that your quest to kill both Matulevich and Kiknadze was an obsession, clouding your judgment?"

"I have a question for you, Doctor, if I may be so bold."

"Okay."

"Let's say, in hindsight, I admit that this was probably a poor judgment call based on an obsession."

The doctor leaned back and rested his hand on his chin, eyes studying his patient with keen interest. "Okay, go on."

"Both objects of my obsession are dead. Doesn't that remove any motivation for clouded judgment in the future?"

"If in hindsight you realize that it was not the best action to take, yes."

Kahless paused, eyed the doctor, exhaled but said nothing.

"Colonel, consider this. Are you are a chess player?"

"You know I am."

"Yes—and a good one."

"Just this… The queen is the most powerful piece on the board, correct?"

"Yes."

"What do you think about a player who launches an attack his opponent with just the queen?"

"Foolish—high risk—sometimes wins, often times lose the queen and then the balance of power shift dramatically and he loses." Kahless exhaled, leaned over and pinched the bridge of his nose, then moved his hand to his cheek, looking thoughtful. "Me, right?"

"Yes, you. What happens when the chess player uses all of the resources of the board?"

"Less risk, more chance of victory."

"Colonel, this interview is over. I will submit my report to central command."

"How did I do?"

"From the perspective of emotional or mental defect, I find no issues that you can't solve with the help of the chaplain. Your blood work is still outstanding, but I expect to find nothing physical."

"Thanks, Doc. I guess my escorts are waiting."

"No hurry. They either stand by your door or mine. Anyone buy you a drink for killing Kiknadze?"

"SGT Gutshot dropped off a couple of beers and supper last night, but nobody's sat me down and bought me a drink."

The doctor pulled a key out of his desk drawer and unlocked a cabinet on the wall. He opened the cabinet door and pulled out a dusty bottle and blew off the dust. "Wild Turkey, eight years old, straight Kentucky bourbon… I've been saving this for such an occasion." He grabbed two glasses and poured each of them a drink of the amber liquid and slid the glass over to Kahless. "Colonel, I am a man just like you. You—you're a fighter; me—I'm a healer. But I'm here for the same reason you are." He lifted his glass. "Here's to a successful, though ill-advised mission," he paused and a slight smile formed at his lips, "and coming back alive."

"I'll drink to that." Both men took a sip, nursed their drinks and made them last as though they were trying to freeze this moment in time, a snapshot of calm within a storm. Finally it was over, and Kahless returned back to his quarters, and contemplated his fate being decided by lawyers.

CPT Litigator arrived to find CPT Defender already seated at the table, briefcase open, and papers on the table. The defense attorney rose. "Captain, care for a cup of coffee?"

"No, thanks. Have a seat. Let's get started."

"Very well."

The prosecutor opened his briefcase, took out some papers, took his glasses out of his coat pocket, and slid them onto the bridge of his hawkish nose. "You're client is facing two charges, failure to maintain the security and integrity of his post, and abandoning his post. I have read his statement—interesting read. Are you prepared to take your case to trial?"

"Sure. Let's talk about the charges."

"Ok… failure to maintain the security and integrity of his post. It is the position of the prosecution that your client did willfully place a valuable asset of the post in danger, namely himself, in a foolhardy venture. Had he been captured, especially without an accord, he may have been tortured to reveal sensitive information to compromise the integrity and security of the post."

"Seventy-two hours—anything sensitive can be changed in seventy-two hours. A missing commander would cause security changes to be initiated immediately, and in fact, they were… And, he wasn't captured."

"Still, it is bad for morale to have their commander captured. This weakens the integrity of the post."

"He was successful. You can't argue that. It is very good for morale that he killed their commander."

"You're client—"

"Dammit Pat, my *client* is a decorated colonel and a command officer, and he will be referred to as *colonel* in this meeting."

"Very well, John. At the very least, your client, COL Kahless showed very poor judgment."

"Maybe… but it was a judgment call, and his to make. His order to defend the integrity and security of the post is something left to interpretation."

"I saw the statement. So COL Kahless is maintaining that he acted in the interest of this post?"

"The results speak for themselves. That charge will not hold up. I will make you look very foolish at court-martial."

"Let's move along to the charge of abandoning his post. He left his post, alone, without being properly relieved."

"Every day COL Kahless goes on patrols and engagements in the field, and he remains commander, even though he is away from the post. It is our contention that he left his post, not to abandon it, but to engage the enemy."

"Hmmm, interesting…"

"Pat, you got nothing. If you bring this to court-martial, you will lose, and whoever started this witch hunt will find it ending his career."

"Off the record?"

"Off the record."

"The driving force behind this is MG Whitacre—two star general, district commander over Ganymede, Callisto, Io, and Europa. BG Moore, district commander over Luna and Mars, is said to be retiring soon. MG Whitacre has his eye on moving his command closer to home."

"Why is that a concern for COL Kahless?"

"June 1976—CPT Cowboy, now COL Kahless, spent time at Miami Beach on leave."

"Okay."

"Let's just say that he met a pretty girl on summer break from college, spent time with her: left her, never called, and never wrote. Let's say this girl went home and wept for three days, quit college and married some pothead. They had a couple of kids. Then he went to prison on drug charges, and now they're divorced."

"Tell me why this is an issue for Col Kahless."

"Her name was Wendy Whitacre—and that, my friend, is off the record."

"This is harassment and a personal grudge."

"Maybe so. I have been instructed to get my pound of flesh."

"You got nothing, and you know it."

"True, but the court-martial will be on Earth. Somehow shuttle schedules have been altered. There won't be another one leaving here for two months. By then the orbital alignments will be such as it will take four more months to get there. The court-martial will drag on until even if COL Kahless wins— and I have no doubt of your litigating prowess, then the colonel will be due to take his one month leave. By the time it's over, the orbital alignments will give you another four month trip. Oh, did I mention by that time BG Moore will be retired, and MG Whitacre will be his new district commander? I guarantee you that MG Whitacre has enough juice to survive a failed attempt to court-martial COL Kahless. In any case, if you fight it, the process will have COL Kahless out of action for over a year. He may then find that after he returns to duty that he is working for a new district commander who hates him. Satisfy the general now or satisfy him later."

"And if COL Kahless cooperates?"

"We'll drop the first charge and reduce the second one to being AWOL, *absent without leave*."

"What if he pleads guilty?"

"Demotion of rank to lieutenant colonel for six months but he keeps his command."

"Is that all?"

The prosecutor smiled. "You've heard the saying that all regulations are written in blood?"

"Yes, once the blood of our men has been spilled from some screw-up, the legal boys start writing regulations."

"Exactly. In this case, the regs are written in Kiknadze's blood. However, there was the potential of it having been your client's blood. Your colonel has made history. He is the first and last post commander ever to leave his post alone."

"Meaning?"

"The temptation to repeat the colonel's ill-conceived venture is being removed. Central Command is rewriting all post commanders' orders, and implementing security measures to ensure compliance." He made a clipping motion with his two fingers. "Your colonel is getting his wings clipped, one way or another. This alone goes a long way toward appeasing the general."

CPT Defender put his papers back in his briefcase and rose. "I will submit this to my client."

"The colonel?" A tight smile formed at the prosecutor mouth at being able to catch his opponent calling him *client* after making an issue out of it.

"Yes, the colonel."

"John, it was nothing personal. I've got a job to do. Ironic isn't it? If you hadn't had your hip socket destroyed by a sniper bullet, you might have been COL Night Hawk."

"The right man has the job."

"You genuinely admire him, don't you?" his voice laced with cynicism.

"Yes. You don't?"

"It's not my job to have my vision clouded with hero worship. My job is to uphold military justice. Well, if your client, the colonel, signs off on this, we can grab a beer later to conclude the deal."

"Sure—seventeen hundred, my quarters."

"You're on."

Kahless was alone in his quarters, dressed in a t-shirt, fatigues, and sneakers, doing push-ups on the living room floor. There was a sharp knock on the door.

"Come," he called. He got up, grabbed a towel and wiped off his sweaty brow.

The guards at the door granted his attorney access. Briefcase in hand, his demeanor was more relaxed this time. "Colonel, I've just spoken with the prosecutor."

"Have a seat," Kahless pointed to the table and threw his towel into the dirty clothes hamper. His advocate took a seat and placed his briefcase on the table, and Kahless joined him. "What do you have for me?"

"To start with, nobody is going to repeat your behavior. New orders are being cut for every post command officer, specifically spelling out that leaving alone is a violation. No command officer will have access codes to do the things you did. Quite frankly, no command officer will be able to open a hangar door without his first officer, tac ops and the hangar Chief's approval."

"Should have seen that coming. Oh, well."

"Colonel, I think I have a deal you might accept."

"Go on."

"I have a compromise that will let you keep your command."

"What's it going to cost me?"

"They are willing to drop the 'failing to maintain the integrity of you post' charge, and reduce the 'abandoning your post' charge to AWOL. In exchange, you plead guilty and get busted to lieutenant colonel for six months, but keep your command."

"It sounds like they didn't have much of a case. Why are we pleading guilty?"

"Off the record?"

"Sure."

"Your case is viewed as a mixture of success and failure all at the same time: successful foray against the enemy, failure to use common sense. I could probably have gotten you off on both charges."

"Why didn't you?"

"To summarize your position… GEN Spears is the highest ranking member of the central command staff, and he likes you, which means no one can destroy you without changing his mind. BG Moore, your present district commander, is retiring in the next year. Your chief opposition comes from MG Whitacre, district commander of Ganymede, Io, Europa, and Callisto. If we don't plead guilty to reduced charges, you will have to face court-martial on Earth. Wait time for the next shuttle, travel time to Earth, length of trial, your leave time, and then trip back will add up to your losing your command for over a year. By then MG Whitacre may be your new boss, and irritated as hell that he lost in his attempt to humble you."

"What's his beef?"

"Are we still off the record?"

"Sure."

"In 1976, a young captain named Cowboy spent some time on leave at Miami Beach. That same young officer met a young lady, home from college on summer break. Do you remember her?"

"Who could forget? Wendy was a gorgeous redhead with beautiful emerald-green eyes that pierced into your soul with a single glance, and a laugh that was infectious. I had a hard time leaving Miami that year. So what does that have to do with anything?"

"Well, you left and made it clear you could not call or write. She went home heartbroken, quit college, married a loser, had two kids and is now divorced from her loser husband."

"I am sorry to hear that. She deserves better."

"Do you remember her last name?"

"Wycliffe or Whitfield, I think."

"Whitacre."

Kahless looked down, then away, and then sighed. "To wait four years to get at me means that he's been planning this for some time."

"Apparently you're not the only one who can plot his revenge. He's been watching your career with interest and waiting for you to screw up. You've provided him that opportunity. He wants to humble you for what he feels that you did to his little girl. You can give him something now and save yourself the wear and tear of a long legal process. If he is satisfied, maybe you can work for him next year without losing your eagles over something else."

"What is your recommendation?"

"Take the deal. You know how high-ranking spots are like musical chairs. He may get the position he wants, he may not. In any case, six months from now you will be a full-bird colonel again."

Kahless absentmindedly stroked his chin. His eyes held the look of a man locked in a room and told there was only one door out and searching to see if it was true. "All right, we have a deal."

"Here's the paperwork." He laid the papers on the table and handed his client a pen. "Sign here, here, and here."

Kahless signed the papers. "When will I get back to work?"

"In the morning, I assume. I have to file this with the prosecutor. You'd better polish your old silver palms and put your eagles up for a while. Security will dismiss your guards as soon as I submit this paperwork to the prosecutor."

The attorney arose. "Off the record, Colonel—I'm glad you shot him."

Kahless arose and offered his hand. "I'm getting a lot of *off the record* appreciation lately." He gazed intently at his attorney. "Night Hawk, I thank you for defending me."

His lawyer warmly shook his hand. "My pleasure, Colonel." His attorney left with his briefcase in hand, and headed to return the post back to normal.

THE SIEGE OF THE SOVIET POST

As promised by my attorney, I was reinstated as post commander the next morning, with a lieutenant colonel as my first officer. This was highly unusual—my first officer now outranked me because he had more time in grade as a lieutenant colonel, but I still held the position of post commander. The court order had established a true military paradox. Two weeks later and with the full agreement of my first officer, I submitted a mission plan to lay siege to the Soviet post. Our intelligence reports showed that the enemy's alloy-x was at an all-time low. Their fleet strength and their defensive grid were weaker than ever. Never in the history of our struggle here had either side attempted a post siege. Central command approved the action, and tomorrow morning we would head out. I ordered the pilots on second shift to meet me in my ready room.

My ready room was filled with expectation, like a dam overflowing, ready to burst when I addressed the men. "Men, first I want to apologize for using poor judgment on my excursion three weeks ago. I let my personal feelings taint my judgment concerning COL Kiknadze. I didn't allow my wingman to do his duty and failed to file a flight plan so that anyone knew where I was. I promise you won't have to worry about me anymore. From now on, I'll do my soldier's duty and leave God's business to God." My decision to play it by the numbers was in line with what Central Command had so ordered. There was something about what MAJ Sawbones said made it easier for me to comply without *chomping at the bit*.

I looked around, and I saw relief on my men's faces. I knew that many commanders would never think of apologizing to their men, but I've always tried to show respect to the men that may have to die under me. I took a deep breath and continued.

"Men, we will be starting an offensive on the Soviet post in the morning. COL Kiknadze is dead, and we estimate the odds of taking their post are better than they've been in a long time. You men have done a great job waging war against the enemy, and we've determined that the enemies' strength and morale are low enough to start an offensive. We will position eighteen howitzers behind our line, and start pounding on their infrastructure. The enemy will respond and challenge our gun positions. That's where we come in. We will provide support for the howitzers while they're doing damage to the post. If all goes well, we will enter the post and destroy the rest of it. Any questions?" There were none. "Good, we depart at zero six hundred tomorrow."

They'd been anticipating this moment for months. All that was left was to finish the job. I arose at zero four thirty the next morning to pray and examine my motives for today's actions. Careers were made with successful post sieges and broken with failed ones. To win was everything, to lose usually meant the loss of enough men and alloy-x scrap to turn the tide of the war to the enemies' favor. I checked our latest intel once again and decided it was time. The enemies' post defenses and fleet strength was estimated as weak, but we'd bring every unit and artillery piece we had. I was able to field thirty-five tanks and an artillery battery of eighteen pieces.

After the post chaplain lead us in prayer for our success and safety, we left for the Soviet post at precisely zero six hundred. Morale was high among the men, and there was a feeling that today we'd make history. We moved through the Kennedy Pass into the Eisenhower Plain and into Soviet territory unopposed. Even with the slower artillery pieces, we arrived at the Soviet post by eleven hundred. CSM Hammer was the NCOIC over the artillery battery, and LTC Ricochet was the OIC over the line. I keyed the mike and radioed MAJ Norsemun.

"Major, are we still a go?"

"Sir, the last American satellite went over fifty minutes ago. It was still a green light but wait another five minutes for another look.

"Affirmative, Kahless out."

I decided it was time to contact the Soviet commander. I most likely would be talking to LTC Oleg Menshutkin. "This is LTC Kahless. I'd like to speak with the Soviet officer in charge."

"This is LTC Menshutkin. What do you want?" he asked, with the cold hostility of a Siberian blizzard.

"We will be laying siege to your post in five minutes. I'm sure that you've seen us coming and already know your answer. We're offering terms for your surrender."

"What are the terms?"

"Unconditional surrender, we will spare your lives, and take possession of your post and all of your equipment. You'll be transported back to Earth to a neutral country as soon as possible. You must also swear that you'll never return."

"This is unacceptable. We must decline your offer. We will stay and fight."

"Very well. I did warn you." It occurred to me that considering all of the savagery with which I'd fought the Soviets in recent months, they may not trust me to honor the terms. "One more thing."

"Yes?"

"Any survivors who surrender will be given medical attention and treated under the terms of the old accord."

The ice in his voice thawed slightly. "Thank you. You have our word that we will do the same." With that, the Soviet officer terminated the transmission.

We were now taking artillery fire just short of our position. It was estimated to be eight artillery pieces firing. This agreed with our previous intel. It would take us a little over a half minute to deploy each artillery piece. The Soviets apparently were inviting us to come and play. MAJ Norsemun called back.

"Still a green light, Colonel, but we have five more minutes we can observe before the flyby is over—I'll keep a watch. Confirmed eight enemy artillery pieces on their line with barrel lengths fifty calibers long." I waited out the five minutes. MAJ Norsemun confirmed that there were no other artillery pieces besides the eight.

"Very well, Kahless out." I gave the order to my XO. "LTC Ricochet, deploy the line."

"Aye, sir. CSM Hammer, deploy the line," echoed my XO.

"Aye sir." With that, the American artillery battery approached the line within range of the Soviet artillery battery. Satellite footage showed Soviet artillery barrel length was the same of ours, fifty calibers long. This meant that our ranges would be the same with a 155mm HE shell. We knew that the defender drew the opening advantage because they would be firing while the attacker would be setting up. This would cost us a couple pieces, it always did. We started setting up the line so we could dismantle the Soviet defenses prior to our tank charge.

Alpha Battery, gun four was the first to be destroyed, along with Charlie Battery, gun five. Two of the members of Charlie gun five were rescued, but the Chief gunner and the crew of Alpha gun four were all killed.

"LTC Kahless!" called MAJ Norsemun on the radio.

"Yes, Major."

"It's a trick! They have eight artillery pieces deployed and are bringing up more from three underground elevators, and we haven't seen the end of them yet. Get out of there! The first three that popped out of the elevators have a barrel length of fifty-five calibers."

The increased number of big gun volleys toward us confirmed the major's report. The first three out of the elevators had set up beyond our range and were firing upon our line. Their elevators were beyond our range so we couldn't stop the deployment of the longer firing Soviet artillery. We could move our line further up to reach all of their pieces, but we'd lose more pieces in the transition. Besides that, they could simply move their long guns further back, moving them out of our range again. Wasting no time waiting for the chain of command, I spoke to the radio so all could hear.

"Pack up the artillery line, return to post, Kahless out."

"Aye, sir," responded both my XO and NCOIC over the line.

The Martian terrain we occupied was pockmarked with new craters, this time the variety made by the Soviet shells. We'd lost an additional two pieces, with all hands dead. While packing up, our artillery was still being fired upon, and we lost two more pieces. LTC Ricochet flew over to gun six of the Bravo Battery to help pick up two survivors. He took artillery fire, and his tank was on fire and smoking badly. He elected not to try and eject for fear of being hit by artillery fire in the air. He popped his hatch, jumped to the ground, and quickly moved away from his tank. MAJ Killer Instinct took note of my XO's plight and flew over to pick the two survivors of gun six along with LTC Ricochet. The two gunners climbed into his tank as they awaited the post's XO to arrive. His tank exploded with a deafening roar, sending chunks of hull outward with violent force. A piece the size of a man's fist hit LTC Ricochet squarely on the lower spine, and he fell to the ground.

CPL Blast and PVT Swab of gun six bailed out of CPT Killer Instinct's tank and moved quickly to their XO's side. He was unmoving, lifeless. His suit was torn in the back, losing air and depressurizing. CPL Blast pulled a hot patch out of his utility pocket and quickly patched the tear. The two men carried him to the tank and out of further danger. I never saw my friend alive again. The autopsy later revealed that his lower lumbar spine was crushed by the piece of flying debris from his own ship.

They say that hindsight is twenty-twenty. During our after-operations review, tactical operations rehashed all of the details and concluded that the unaccounted alloy-x scrap used to build the extra artillery units must have been imported from Luna, carefully landing the scrap transports during our satellite blackout window. Since all of the artillery was built and stored underground, we never saw what they had until we laid siege to the post. Our satellites saw only what the Soviets wanted us to see. Our count was badly off.

We recycled all of our fifty caliber guns and built an all-new fifty-five caliber artillery battery. It looked as if we were deceived, but such is the art of war. Our losses overall were light for a failed post siege, but the personal loss of my executive officer and friend weighed heavily on my spirit. The Central Command review board concluded that I did nothing wrong, but my heart convicted me of the loss of my best friend. LTC Ricochet was the last of my teammates from ASDC Academy. "Brown" was my best friend, and now he was dead. I'd never felt so alone.

We held a memorial service and paid honor to our dead. After the service, I called MAJ Killer Instinct into my office. I didn't feel like talking, having lost COL SEAL six months earlier and my best friend very recently. I knew that my former wingman was the best choice for my executive officer. I was still officially a lieutenant colonel myself, so the promotion was green-lighted by ASDC command. I called him to my office and advised him of his promotion to lieutenant colonel. I tried my best to convey to him that I was pleased about his promotion, but my troubled heart got in the way, and I finally dismissed him. My new executive officer showed leadership skills and in time would prove to be invaluable to me, both as a comrade in arms and as my best friend. In time I would see and appreciate that.

THE GREENHOUSE

I had lied to MAJ Sawbones about having bad dreams, and I believe he knew it. He had no doubt cut me some slack on that last fitness report because the lawyers were trying to bury me. He would keep an eye on me and do his duty to protect the post and the men that served under me, now that the charges were no longer an issue. Killing Kiknadze didn't cleanse me of my feelings of guilt, or stop the conflict within me. In addition to the turmoil I felt over COL SEAL's death, my heart was heavy over the death of my executive officer. My inner struggles were taking a toll on me. I'd seen too much death. Guilt gnawed at my insides like a feeding lion every time I came back alive, and another man didn't. There was no avoiding my annual physical if I wanted to stay in command. The wear and tear of all the stress I was under was revealed during my physical: irritability, stomach problems, and insomnia. When I did sleep, I had nightmares of dead comrades and murderous Soviets. The good doctor looked as though he'd been waiting for an opportunity to get me alone and examine me. I'd been avoiding him since my fitness exam following my arrest. MAJ Sawbones poked and prodded me, drew blood and performed every test known to man. Returning to my office, I awaited the results. The next morning, I was summoned back to the doctor's office, and I promptly returned. He motioned me to sit on the table and he sat in the chair next to me, not saying a word, just thinking.

We were alone. It seemed that the major had dismissed his staff for my visit. I studied his face, trying to discern if I was in trouble or not. The doctor was as quiet as a librarian and seemed to be thinking of what to do next. "Well Doc, what's the verdict?"

"Colonel, you have what's referred to as Wyatt Earp's syndrome. The early symptoms were of course your rage and compulsion to kill the ones responsible for your pain. Now in the latter stages, you're suffering from depression, brought on by feelings of guilt and anger, battle fatigue and headed toward breakdown. Of course, you probably knew that, if you were being honest with yourself. Our tests revealed nothing more than a man who's carrying too heavy a load, and can't physically bear it. If you don't deal with what's eating on you, you will die. My experience with you has shown that you aren't the kind of guy to lie on a couch and bare your soul." He reached into a cabinet and retrieved a bottle of Kentucky bourbon and two glasses, set it on the counter and poured two doubles. After handing me a glass, he called my XO on the comm. and advised him that he was in charge for the rest of the day and that I was taking the rest of the day off sick.

"To your health," he offered as he raised his glass.

"Doc, you have an unusual way of practicing medicine."

He laughed. "That's why they call it practice. I haven't perfected my craft yet."

I was a bit apprehensive at his methods, but he refilled my glass a second time and I was starting becoming just a wee bit lit up. He must have been waiting for the walls I'd built over the years to fall before the power of his Kentucky elixir.

"Colonel, you came over here with eight other pilots from the Academy, right?"

"Seven."

"Where are they all now?"

"Dead, every last one."

"Your first wingman, what was his name?"

"2LT Grim Reaper."

"Yes, I remember. He's dead, too as I recall. Then there was COL SEAL and LTC Ricochet. You're suffering now from what I'd refer to as survivor's guilt. This usually follows Wyatt Earp when all of his enemies are dead. You see, Colonel, you've killed almost every last enemy you have that's caused you pain." He rose from his chair and opened a drawer and handed me a mirror. "Look in that mirror, son. He's the last one alive who's causing your pain, and you're trying to destroy him. You're eating yourself alive from the inside out with guilt. I'm going to write you a prescription. If you don't fill it, I will be forced to declare you unfit for duty and relieve you of your command. It isn't an option," he said gently but firmly. "Your welfare directly affects the welfare of all the men that serve under you."

I sighed. "And what does the good doctor order?"

"You'll report to the greenhouse at zero nine hundred each Sol Jovis and work under the authority of SGT Samurai until twelve hundred, where you'll eat lunch with him. I'll be making sure that you do. It's for your own good." I suppressed the urge to bristle up and try to buck his authority because I knew he was right.

"Yes, sir." I was the post commander and outranked the doctor, but still he could declare me unfit for duty. Such is the paradox of command. I set down my unfinished second drink and got permission to leave. Today was Sol Mercurii so it looked like I was in for my first *therapy session* tomorrow.

SERGEANT SAMURAI

After breakfast in the morning, I did paperwork until zero eight thirty and left for the greenhouse. I'd given my aide, CPL Gray Eagle, the half day off with no explanation.

The greenhouse complex was actually more than one building. It was seven buildings. There were five greenhouses, one soybean processing facility and one composting facility. I walked down the corridor from my office to the greenhouse complex, resigned that I would cooperate fully with the doctor's orders. At exactly zero nine hundred, I arrived at the main greenhouse of the complex. The greenhouse complex was all underground, to keep the temperature just right for the plants and fish. The walls of the buildings were all concrete, and topped off with a two foot thick layer of special glass designed to filter out radiation and cosmic rays on the top that was both very clear and insulated. We also used reflectors around the buildings to maximize the sunlight coming in through the roofs. Maintenance did cleaning sweeps twice daily to clear off the dust that accumulated on the glass roof. During dust storms, we used electric grow lights. We kept the whole complex pressurized at four hundred millibars, forty-five percent of Earth's atmospheric pressure at sea level, which worked for farming and people.

The greenhouse was more than just a place to grow plants. Two of the seven greenhouses have very large fish tanks in the middle of them, full of fish and aquatic plants, with its own filtration and aeration system. We have three water wells drilled underneath the greenhouse and food processing plant. When the post was established, there was a large gulley here with plenty of water under it. The Americans widened the gulley, drilled some wells, and built underground installations over the top of the wells. This became the greenhouse complex. Around the edges of the greenhouse were rows upon rows of plants of all varieties, mostly dwarf soybean, rice, and barley plants, along with some fruits and vegetables. The soybeans kept us from starving in case our supply lines ever got cut off. We weren't set up to raise grain to feed animals for meat. It simply wasn't efficient enough. We imported what products we couldn't make from soy: real meat, spices, dairy, hops, and yeast to brew our own beer. But we could make a great deal of soymilk, meat substitutes, cheeses, soy oil, and even soy flour. It is a matter of survival, and we intended to survive and flourish.

Martian regolith is unsuitable for farming because of the high levels of peroxides and salts, not to mention a complete lack of biomass. The same peroxides that guarantee our survival as a source of raw material for oxygen here are a bane to farming. Once the oxygen production facilities extract all of the peroxides and salts, we have a rough product to start constructing soil. To that base product we've had to add a couple of minerals that were lacking, and add composted human and plant wastes. We add imported worms to work the new soil to leave more castings and aerate it. We also remove the nitrogen from our urine to make fertilizer.

I found SGT Samurai alone, transplanting a young soybean seedling to a larger pot. He greeted me with a stiff salute, and I returned his salute and looked around. Of course, I'd inspected the building before, but not with the idea of working in it. The large fish tank in the middle was surrounded by thousands of plants. A pipe above them, running along the sides of the greenhouse, was spraying a mist of water through pinholes, operated by a timer. SGT Samurai spoke again, and I quit looking around to give him my full attention.

"Welcome, Colonel. That salute was the last one you'll receive in the greenhouse, during the hours of zero nine hundred to twelve hundred, on Sol Jovis. You don't need to salute me, but I'm in charge here. Doctor's orders. If you don't do as you're told, I'll simply fill out a report and send it to the good doctor. There will be no excuse for being absent, or late, unless the post is under attack, or a defensive action is needed in the field."

"Understood. I'll cooperate fully."

"Good, let's get started," he said, rubbing his hands together and smiling as if he'd waited all his life to order a colonel around.

"Where's your staff?"

"They're working in the other buildings today, but not here." I have all the help I need to clean fish tanks," he said, looking at me and grinning. Then suddenly it hit me. This was designed to have as few people present as possible, in case I needed to talk with someone, or confide something that didn't need to be repeated.

"Then do I understand that anything I say isn't to be repeated?"

"Absolutely, that was also doctor's orders, and I have a level six security clearance." I stared at him for a moment. His job title didn't require that kind of clearance.

He laughed. "You see, some time ago, a certain COL Squid got the same assignment and I was transferred here from ASDC security to work with him, too."

"And you've been running this greenhouse ever since in case I needed you?"

He laughed. "Not just for you, but any of the men. I also have to manage the greenhouse complex. Anyway, I love this kind of work and I love my country. I'm proud to serve it, even if it's just cleaning fish tanks."

"SGT Samurai?"

"Yes, Colonel."

"Call me Kahless. Since I can't be a colonel in here, I'll just be Kahless."

"Then you can call me Sammy."

The fish tanks had a filtration system, with collection tanks, which we used to fertilize the plants and an aeration pump. Today we'd be emptying the filter traps and applying the fish offal to the plants. We emptied all the filter traps, tested the tanks for ph balance, added chemicals to the water and checked the aeration pumps. Sammy showed me how much fertilizer to add to each plant and we spent the rest of the morning applying fish offal to them. I found the work real satisfying at a basic level. This work touched feelings inside of me, bringing up memories of working on my dad's farm. I worked silently, quietly, and let the memories of a more peaceful time play through on the screen of my life.

It was close to twelve hundred and almost time for lunch. Sammy reached for a fishnet next to the fish tank, dipping it into the tank and retrieving a very large fish. He took a gaff hook and hooked its mouth and held it up, grinning. He placed it on a cleaning board and went to work as deftly as any surgeon, placing the fillets in a rinsing bowl, throwing the guts, scales and bones in the fertilizer hopper. Sammy put a pot full of boiling oil next to a pot of water on to boil. He split the fish head with a sharp knife and placed the pieces in a pot of boiling water. My expression must have been hilarious for Sammy laughed loudly. "The doctor ordered you to eat lunch with me," he grinned mischievously.

"What're you going to do with that fish head?" I asked, eyeing the pot suspiciously.

"I'm making fish head soup," he said, grinning ear to ear. "Yes, sir. We have fish head soup, fried fish, shrimp, rice and salad: five-star restaurant."

Sammy threw some chopped green onion stems, soy sauce, ginger, and some herbs into the water pot. Turning the heat down, he covered the pot. He rolled the fish fillets in tempura batter and dropped them in the oil. Then he went to the tank and took another net and a five foot steel rod with a bend on the end and unhooked the screen door to the shrimp partition. Sticking his net in, he waved it around, and then folded the net over its rim to trap the shrimp. Then he closed the trap door before any fish could get inside. The tank had a screened partition on the bottom, running from end to end. It separated the shrimp from the fish, so the fish wouldn't eat them. Some of the fertilizer was lost because the shrimp did some of the tank cleaning. We liked them nonetheless, and we did turn some of the waste from cleaning the shrimp into fertilizer. After taking out the shrimp, he peeled, battered and dropped them into the oil. He turned around and produced two small salads from the refrigerator and laid them on the table.

While he tended the fish and shrimp, we talked about his life before Mars, in San Francisco, where his family owns a greenhouse and a landscaping service. It turned out his family were descendants of Tokugawa Ieyasu, who became Shogun over Japan in 1603. Sammy was quite proud of his lineage.

The soup pot was boiling when he pulled out the last of the shrimp and the fillets, and laid them on a cloth to drain. "Soup should be served first, but we got a late start, so we'll eat it last today but first next time," he explained. He put two plates on the table, and served a spoonful of rice on each plate. Next he dipped a slotted spoon into the hot grease and retrieved the shrimp and fish, fried to a golden brown crust, glistening wet with dripping grease. Their smell was like heaven to me, and my stomach growled its greeting like a tiger.

Sammy decided to set further boundaries for our meetings. "I want you to understand that I respect your religious beliefs. I am under orders to help you, not proselytize you. I do expect you to be respectful of my faith as I am yours."

"Understood."

"As you know, I am a devout Buddhist, and I have a meal chant I say before every meal." I nodded.

"First, let us reflect on our own work and the effort of those who brought us this food. Second, let us be aware of the quality of our deeds as we receive this meal. Third, what is most essential is the practice of mindfulness, which helps us to transcend greed, anger and delusion. Fourth, we appreciate this food which sustains the good health of our body and mind. Fifth, in order to continue our practice for all beings we accept this offering." He paused and I now realized it was my turn to pray.

"Lord Jesus I thank you for this food and fellowship, amen."

Sammy served the rice *Asian style*, a bit clumpy and sticky. This gave him an opportunity to teach me to eat with chopsticks. It was awkward at first, but I succeeded in hoisting a sticky clump of rice to my mouth.

"So, do you know any history of the shogun you're descended from?" I asked, in between bites of fish.

He smiled like a Cheshire cat. "Now that you mention it, I do." I suddenly realized I'd been set up. In between bites, he told me a tale of feudal Japan about emperors, feudal lords, samurai, peasants, loyalty and treacheries, battles, schemes, and fair ladies, both virtuous and unvirtuous. After we finished eating, he poured two bowls of soup. "When you can appreciate fish head soup, then you'll be truly Japanese," he said, with a glint of humor in his eyes. Even though I knew that it had been cooked, eyeballs and all, it actually wasn't that bad. In fact, I had to admit that I liked it.

We finished the soup just as the story was getting started. Sammy looked like at the clock, and announced, "Looks like you're a colonel again. I can finish this story next week. Bring your dog next time."

"Okay, I'll bring her." I arose, and noticed that the cares and worries of command had fallen off of me for a few hours. Sammy put some fish fillets and shrimp, along with some fresh vegetables in a bag, for me to cook in my quarters tonight.

"Thanks, Sammy. See you next week." He smiled and nodded in agreement and I went back to work.

Sammy introduced me to folding paper cranes, and composing Japanese Haiku poetry on my second visit. It isn't long, it doesn't rhyme, but I liked it nonetheless. It has to have exactly seventeen syllables and be three lines long. The first line has five syllables, the second seven, and the third five and conveys a poetic thought. The first one he had me do revealed I'd a bit of doom and gloom in me. It went something like this...

Winter winds, howling
Bringing forth death's icy grip
Sorrow and blackness

I remember the look on Sammy's face, when I composed that one. He flatly stated, "I see we have a lot of work to do."

I got my eagles back as promised, but it did nothing to make my world right. Over the next few months, I came to realize that I needed help. Though the greenhouse was giving me a sanctuary for a time, I needed to face my demons and get my heart right with God. Sammy and I had many discussions, but I knew the day would come when I had to speak with the chaplain. I started my own seeking, returning to prayer. For the first time since COL SEAL's death, I opened the Bible to seek wisdom. I determined that I would make a discipline out of Bible reading and daily prayer, always seeking wisdom from above. In time, I realized that I shouldn't have avoided our chaplain, and I prayed with MAJ Intercessor on several occasions. Slowly my rage gave away to reason, and though we still were at war with the Soviets, I felt my peace return. I didn't realize how much I'd missed my peace of mind. Even though my true redemption came from God alone, I continued to enjoy the Sol Jovis morning meetings with Sammy and the fellowship we had. It was actually a relief to go somewhere and not bear the responsibility of command.

The war after COL SEAL's death had been waged with fierce brutality on our part. We caught their pilots anywhere we could and killed them without mercy. We seemed to be winning the scrap reclamation, as well. Judging from our progress over time, I estimated that we could gain complete control over Mars by year's end, despite our failed siege of the Soviet post. My attitude toward the Soviets had changed somewhat, but without an accord, we were still fighting them the same way we had since COL SEAL's death. Neither the Americans nor the Soviets trusted each other enough at this point to sign a new accord. In the meantime, we had no protection or guarantee of humane treatment of our men if captured. I regretted our situation, and it weighed heavily on my conscience.

ENTER COL YURI TKACHENKO

Earth date: May 14, 1980—Martian year 197, Sol Veneris, sol 6 of the Martian Month Aries—sol of the Martian year 228

COL Tkachenko read the official summary of events that had transpired on his eight month trip to Mars. *A lot can happen in eight months,* mused the Soviet. COL SEAL was dead. Col Kiknadze was dead, LTC Matulevich was dead, and now the new American first officer was dead. Kiknadze had ordered the assassination of the Americans, succeeded at killing one of them, but spurring an all-out war with no Rules of Engagement. The new commander was thought to be insane. He had become particularly savage in his dealing with the Soviets: *probably something to do with the death of his former commander. Well, that fool Kiknadze had at least killed one of the men that Tkachenko had been ordered to kill. Now it was time to come in, calm the new American commander down a bit, get a new accord signed, kill him, and to begin the process of dominating Mars.*

On the sixth of Aires, I was in my office trying to formulate the strategy for the next few months, when I got a comm. call from MAJ Norsemun.

"Colonel, a Soviet transport has landed," he informed me.

"What's the cargo?"

"Just two passengers."

"Who?" I asked, my curiosity now in full gear.

"COL Yuri Tkachenko and LTC Vladimir Voronin," he flatly stated. LTC Menshutkin left on the same transport freighter. Suddenly the climate seemed to take on an uncharacteristic chill for this season.

I let out a low whistle. COL Tkachenko was known as the "Butcher of Titan" and the "Ukrainian Wolf." He was the man the Soviets sent to get the job done, a closer. He was tough, skilled and a brilliant strategist. The best words to describe him were *ruthlessly brilliant.* Some of his strategies were taught at the SCA Academy. As far as Soviets go, this one was the most feared, a living legend. LTC Vladimir Voronin was known as the "Lucky One." He always seemed to be at the right place at the right time, do the right thing and never makes a mistake.

"What else can you tell me?"

"Well, we decoded Soviet messages over the last six months that indicated that COL Kiknadze was falling out of favor with the SCA for losing his grip on Mars. He was being replaced before he ever launched the assassination attempt on you and COL SEAL." That got my attention.

"Assassination attempt on both of us, you said?"

"Yes, sir. The plan was to kill you both. It was supposed to be an olive branch to SCA Central Command to try to keep his command. His career had become rather lackluster since being here and he was being transferred to a desk job on Earth. Apparently he drank too much vodka toward the end, and he was desperate enough to break the treaty prohibiting the use of redfield generators. I made a call to Ganymede. We found that Tkachenko left straight for here, even though it took eight months because of the orbital alignments. In short, he was sent to replace Kiknadze before you killed him. Apparently, the Soviets didn't think that he was able to handle the American backlash for killing COL SEAL. They viewed his actions as an act of desperation."

"What do you have on Tkachenko and Voronin?" I queried him.

"I'm sending their files to you now, Norsemun out."

I opened the file on Tkachenko. Soviets serving on frontier posts used aliases as their real names were top secret. Individualism was not encouraged in their system. They didn't romanticize their call signs and did not refer to them in dealing with us. I could bet that Yuri Tkachenko was not his real name.

Subject: COL Yuri Mikhailovich Tkachenko
Approximate age: 39
Weight: 165 lbs.
Height: 5'10"
Hair: black
Eyes: brown
Place of birth: unknown
Unconfirmed widower with adult son
No data on Earth military service

Subject's first assignment, which can be confirmed, was on Luna, where he served two terms. At the rank of captain, he was transferred to Titan. After the deaths of three of his superiors over a three-year period, he was promoted to colonel and given the command of Titan. His ruthless and brilliant tactics afforded him a complete victory on Titan within two years, and there were few survivors. The ASDC Command was able to re-establish a post there, but it was a hard struggle to keep it. He was later transferred to Ganymede, where the Americans were winning. Under his command, the tide was turning in the Soviet's favor.

Personal details: Subject likes to play online chess weekly with his American counterpart. Skill level in chess ranked 1900. Physically strong and fit. Considered very dangerous and resourceful. Drinks alcohol but not considered an alcoholic. He is a highly skilled sniper, and thought possibly to have served in the Soviet Sniper Corps but unconfirmed. Tkachenko's personality was characterized as strong, calculating, with strong leadership abilities, a creative thinker, stubborn but adaptable when the situation changes and calls for it. He's warm with close friends, careful in planning but quick in execution of plans when needed. He is ruthless and merciless with his enemies but understands the importance of negotiations and diplomacy. He was reported to have made some veiled comments in the Titan accords to the American delegation that was threatening in the form of a joke. Personal DNA and dental bite pattern were acquired through dinner scraps after serving pizza to subject at Titan accord.

He was the Soviet's closer. His transfer here now meant that the SCA was desperate to dominate Mars. It was the most desirable planet in the solar system as its climate was closer to Earth's than any other. It has its own water, which makes it very, very valuable. It is close enough to Earth to be used as a refueling station and to move parts, supplies and personnel to points beyond. Sometimes the orbital alignments of the planets make it easier to ship parts, fuel and water from Mars instead of trying from Earth, though sometimes we have to wait a month or so until the orbital alignments are more favorable. Using Mars as a storage and shipping relay works very nicely. The ASDC prized this planet as well, and most officers and commanders wanted to serve here. I was anxious to talk with Tkachenko, but a good bargainer never makes the first move. I'd wait him out. Next I opened the file on Voronin.

Subject: LTC Vladimir Sergeyevich Voronin
Approximate age 30
Weight: 172 lbs.
Height: 5', 9" Hair: black
Eyes: brown
Place of birth: assumed Russia
Marital status unknown
No data on Earth military service

Personal details: Quiet, very studious in any setting, excellent pilot and sniper. He rose up the ranks on Titan and refused command of Titan when Tkachenko accepted the post on Ganymede. Considered absolutely loyal to Tkachenko and his right-hand man. Little is known of his personal life. No DNA, fingerprints or bite pattern acquired.

He was Tkachenko's right-hand man and went with him everywhere. It was a foregone conclusion that he would be his executive officer. He was a quiet man who from all reports never quit calculating his next move. His greatest attribute as an executive officer was his absolute loyalty to his commander and honesty with him. He was just as dangerous, in a different way. It seems he leaves no leftovers. He had pizza with Tkachenko at the accord on Titan and we failed to get a DNA sample or bite pattern. Unless a Soviet or American is captured, we don't give up our fingerprints. In social situations as when we sign accords, both sides are extremely careful to protect their fingerprints. We both use clear, thin plastic coverings over our fingertips so that fingerprints cannot be lifted.

We have false fingerprints impressed in those covers so even if they lift one, it matters not. The only way to get the real thing is to capture a pilot. My XO and I have never been captured, and neither have Tkachenko or Voronin. Oh, we've both been shot and hurt, but never captured.

COL TKACHENKO'S FIRST CALL

Three sols later as I was contemplating what to do next, I got a comm call from the Soviets. COL Tkachenko's image materialized on the screen, and immediately I was struck with the feeling that I was staring into the eyes of an apex predator.

The predator spoke. "I am COL Yuri Tkachenko and I would like to speak with the commanding officer."

"That would be me, COL Kahless."

"I am the new commander of the Soviet forces here. I would like to discuss the signing of a new accord."

"We weren't the ones who broke the accord first. The cowardly assassination of COL SEAL is what provoked our actions."

"That was regrettable. You will find I have no need to violate any treaties. I am capable enough to defeat you without violating any Rules of Engagement." His eyes showed the confidence of years of successful battles and his face playing host to a cold, calculating smile.

"Careful, boasting is for the one who takes off his flight suit, not the one putting it on."

Tkachenko let out a deep belly laugh, making sport of my verbal counterattack and making me feel foolish. *Typical Russian*, I thought. *Russians were loud and they laughed louder.* "What I have heard is true. You have no sense of humor. Surely you understand American trash talk. I learned from Mohammad Ali. Seriously, I do very much wish to renew the accords. I will send a copy of the old accords to you with some proposed changes." I looked him over and measured him. I didn't trust any Soviets, much less this one, but he seemed to be in earnest.

"COL Squid discussed the original accords with COL Kiknadze, halfway between our posts, at the place you Soviets refer to as the Lenin Plain." (We refer to the locale as the Eisenhower Plain, but it was an irritation to the Soviets to bring that up) "All of both side's ships were ordered to appear halfway between each post and stand-down. This is so our satellites could account for everyone and to ensure there wouldn't be a trap. If we were to talk, I'd insist on the same. Just the two of us, our first officers and one aide each would meet. We could meet tomorrow at twelve hundred. If all goes well and no treachery is found, we can negotiate a new accord like civilized men." I offered to meet at twelve hundred hours because the second Soviet satellite blackout occurs between fourteen hundred and eighteen hundred and they would never agree to a meeting then.

"Dah, very good. I hope to build trust between us."

"Colonel, I doubt I'll ever trust you, but if your word is good, I might respect you. I wish the agreement to be known as the SEAL Accords."

"This is acceptable. Oh, I have an officer of yours to bring to you tomorrow." According the old accord and the new one we proposed signing, he wouldn't have to bring him without a trade. It appeared as he was showing a measure of good faith.

"I have one of yours to bring, too." He looked surprised. He'd obviously not known that any of the pilots survived the ambush at the canyon. No more information could be extracted from the pilot. Keeping him wouldn't help any longer. He didn't trust us, and we felt he couldn't be won over. I decided that one day I'd capture one of their pilots and take my time converting him.

Tkachenko asked, "Do you play chess?"

"Yes, a little."

"Very good. I'll meet you on the plain as you asked, tomorrow at twelve hundred—and bring a chessboard. Tkachenko out."

I called LTC Killer Instinct into my office. "Jim, have a seat." I motioned to the coffee tray I had my aide bring in earlier. He accepted a cup and added cream and sugar. My mess sergeant supplied real cream at my request, not soy today, as a treat while I take the time to visit with my new executive officer. As my former wingman 1LT Dutchman, he had been good at backing my play on the battlefield and would make a fine first officer.

My new executive officer was a very good blend of all of the qualities a combat officer needed to have. A natural leader, he's very organized, hates inefficiency and incompetency, and is unquestionably loyal. A great pilot, sniper and team player, he's also quite intelligent, understands strategy, hard-working and follows through with his assignments. Men looked up to him and followed his lead. They respected his strength and courage in battle. However, it was more than that. A straight arrow, he's honest to a fault and unafraid to tell me what he thinks, but respectful enough to keep criticisms private. He cares for the men as if they were family, but is still able to make hard decisions when the need arises. LTC Ricochet was a very good leader, but our unit dynamic had improved since my new XO's promotion. I surveyed the man before me. An athletic man of medium height and build, he had reddish-blond hair and green eyes with a straight nose, a mixture of his Connecticut–Dutch descendants and his Irish national mother. "We will be meeting the new Soviet commander to renegotiate the old accord at twelve hundred tomorrow. Has the Soviet prisoner told us everything he knows?"

"I examined all the files that LTC Ricochet kept, and I talked with him before the assault. I'd say yes, I believe so," he said, taking a sip of hot coffee and then blowing it to cool.

"Inform him we will be returning him to the Soviets tomorrow and tell him if he doesn't want me to tell the Soviets what he revealed to us, he'll act like it didn't happen. And Colonel, he may tell them what he's told us. Keep any information that he told us that's changeable or damaging if they know we know, under suspicion."

I outlined how and when the meeting would take place, and he pledged his support. Dismissing him, I called 1LT Janus Dread and promoted him to captain.

On Sol Martis, the tenth day of Aries during the Martian summer, Earth year 1980, my aide, CPL Gray Eagle and LTC Killer Instinct traveled with me ahead of the others. All of our satellite reconnaissance indicated we weren't heading into a trap. My first officer, my aide and I met with our counterparts at the agreed location. We'd set up a bioshelter in the center of the Eisenhower Plain three hours before the meeting. The Soviet security officers examined it before the meeting. COL Squid signed the first accord before I arrived on Mars. Today I was the commander negotiating the Rules Of Engagement with our adversaries. I took some comfort knowing that at least I wasn't sitting across from COL Kiknadze or LTC Matulevich.

The meeting was cordial, and a certain politeness was observed, which was uncharacteristic of Russians. My long hours of being coached on how to deal with the Soviets in negotiations seemed as if it had been a waste of time. Tkachenko did none of the usual table slapping, fit-throwing, bullying and threatening to walk out that I had been warned about by my coaches. This was no ordinary Soviet. The absence of the usual Soviet antics was a sign that he was a skilled hunter, patiently taking his time to stalk his prey.

The meeting went well and there was no trap. We renewed the old accord and established the seven holidays in our agreement, May Day, October Revolution Day, USSR Constitution Day, Christmas, Thanksgiving, New Year, and the Fourth of July. On those sols, there would be no hostilities at all, and no more than two fighting vessels could travel together. Up to two ships could travel together to places outside of our territory, but they couldn't come within one hundred kilometers from the other post. This made it possible for a pair of ships to go sightseeing outside of the Tharsis Plain for pleasure during a holiday cease-fire.

The fair treatment and exchange of prisoners and a ban on all stealth weapons and protecting all of our agricultural projects were easily agreed upon. Scientific studies wouldn't need an armed escort, but archaeological digs weren't protected as we dug precious alien technology from some of them, and it was worth fighting for.

We did, however, agree that all greenhouses and food processing plants be placed no closer than three hundred meters from any military target. We had to built another greenhouse complex three hundred meters from the one we had now. The complex we moved from became a storage facility for supplies, replacement parts, equipment and machinery. No weapons could be stored in the agricultural complexes. The logic being that even if the enemy post was totally annihilated, the victor wouldn't have destroyed the food supplies.

I didn't get everything I wanted. COL Tkachenko balked at the idea of not shooting pilots in the air that ejected from their tanks when they blew. I thought about walking out of the negotiations but decided that, though we didn't get everything we wanted, it was close enough.

We exchanged 1LT Ryzhkov for 2LT Death Before Dishonor. Our man looked well, but so did the Soviet. Our prisoner looked fine, even though we had taken our liberties with him for a time. We concluded the meeting by signing the agreement, and followed with a hot pot of tea and sugar biscuits.

Afterward we played three games of chess. He bested me two games to one. We agreed to play one chess match a week via satellite uplink on Sol Saturni at nineteen hundred, unless we were in the field fighting that day or either of us lost any men in the last week. My ranking was only 1750, and I was determined to get better. One of our programmers was also a senior master with a ranking of 2450 and had created a computer chess game that would challenge me to become better. Wasting moves and bluffing were two of my faults. I broke myself of both habits. Bluffs don't fool computers and wasting moves when playing them is fatal.

I'd like to have said that the war wasn't as tough after signing the accord. But even observing SEAL's Accord by both parties, it was just as tough. The difference was that the Rules of Engagement were restored and a sense of respect had developed. Survivors breathed easier knowing they would be awarded humane treatment by their captors.

COL Tkachenko made up for the civility of the Rules of Engagement with boldness and his sense of cold calculation in planning attacks. I had my hands full; my nemesis had arrived.

GOING HOME ON LEAVE

By the Martian month Mina, Earth year 1982, my confidence in LTC Killer Instinct grew. It was time for my leave back to Earth, so I called my XO into my office. "Jim, you're soon to be in charge of this post for eight months. I'm going home on leave. I'll be leaving on the next transport freighter." He looked surprised that he would be in charge so soon.

"Yes, sir. You can depend on me, sir."

"Good, I want you to me more involved in the administrative duties here so that the transition will be smoother. You will report here tomorrow and take possession of my office and begin doing my job. If you have any questions, just call me."

Going home for a while would be good for me, I thought. It was time to start packing for my trip and moving into the post commander's quarters. I lingered over the pictures and awards that covered my wall. I stopped in front of a picture of Soke Marx presenting me my third-degree black belt in Keichu-Ryu Karate, my Louisiana College diploma, and my commission as a colonel. I dropped out of college in my second year to join the Navy, but was able to take correspondence courses through an ASDC program and get my diploma. It was not in Eugene Bordelon's name since he was officially dead. Finally, I stopped and considered my certificate telling the world I was Eagle Scout. Of all of my successes, this was my first. It set my path for everything that was to come.

It was time to move into COL Seal's old quarters. I hadn't moved in yet, even though it had been more than six months since his death and my promotion. I hadn't been fully ready yet to acknowledge his death. If I'd been a junior officer, the move would have been decided for me. As it stood, I was the only one who could command me to move. My new executive officer was waiting without a word or complaint for me to move. He was to inherit my quarters, and was extremely patient not to press the issue. My former executive officer never even asked. He sensed I had a problem with moving in. I completed moving all of my boxes into the commander's quarters and unpacked enough so I could function until I left.

I called up my executive officer. "Colonel, you can take possession of your new quarters. I got the last of my stuff out."

"Sir, very good, sir. Have a nice trip home."

I took a few of COL SEAL's Navy SEAL pictures out of archive, along with personal letters from COL SEAL to his mother and sisters and made a package for his family. Two knives and two pistols out of the collection COL SEAL left me would make nice gifts for his sister's husbands. I packed my travel gear as well as the naval officer's uniforms that the ASDC directed me to wear when visiting family of my men who had died. My uniform bore the rank of naval commander and I had the papers and ID to back it up if needed.

I stowed my gear on the *Odyssey* and called Blaze to enter. I'd packed all of Blaze's toys and her bed to make her trip less anxious. She hadn't been on the transport freighter since she was a puppy. She hesitated, but when CPT Ripsnort beckoned her to come, she entered the freighter and curled up next to the captain's chair on the bridge.

Eugene J. Bordelon, Jr. was officially dead, but I traveled as CMDR Eugene Martin on leave and also maintained pen pals with that alias. I had acquired Blaze from one of my pen pals from Missouri, an unplanned cross between his great pyrenees bitch and a wolf. She had dewclaws on the back feet that are common in wolves, but her ears stood up to a point then gave up and house, and I tips as if remembering her great pyrenees parent. The result was a snow-white female with yellow eyes, with the body and size of a wolf. This vacation was as much for her as it was for me. Blaze had not been on Earth since she was a puppy. She had never chased a rabbit, or experienced all the smells and sights of a world full of life. Where I was taking her would be teeming with life and crawling with children.

Based on the difference between Mars and Earth orbits, it could be 54 million kilometers or 227.9 million kilometers, depending on when you attempted to leave. We always scheduled our trips home so I could have the shortest trip. We had a three month trip back, and one month of liberty. The trip back would be longer, as the Martian orbit was going to swing wider out on the way back.

I brought my Bible and all the classic books that I'd never had time to read and set in for a long journey. I also packed a couple decks of cards and some cash for the inevitable poker games that would be played among the returnees.

CPT Ripsnort regarded me with the respect due my rank and didn't refer to me as one of the children. He gave the returning pilots a great deal more respect than the greenhorns. They'd all earned it if they were still alive. This was a return trip to Earth from Europa, and I was able to chat with the pilots about the welfare of COL Exit Wound. He was still as tough as boot leather and ran a tight ship, which was no surprise. I didn't envy him, though. Europa was an iced-over moon. Too high a percentage of pilots that bail out die from methane gas poisoning or freeze to death if their suit gets a tear.

I spent time with my dog, played poker and read books. CPT Ripsnort was a challenging chess player, and we got together at least once a day for a couple of games. After the often fast-paced action of the battlefield, these long trips were often boring and gave way too much time for reflection. Most men who've seen a lot of death don't want to spend a great deal of time with reflection. There was too much time to feel guilty about the ones who died and too much time to ask why you didn't.

We arrived at the ASDC Academy three months later, and both Blaze and I were more than ready. A leased Dodge pickup that I'd requested and a roadmap of the southwestern United States were waiting for me. I left the secret training facility and took an unmarked dirt road to the public road, heading east to Mexican Hat, Utah. From there I drove north until I could hit a main highway going east.

It was mid-May and not too hot yet, so I rolled the window down and let Blaze stick her head out of the window. She seemed to be on sensory overload, and was overjoyed to see hawks, rabbits, grass, sagebrush and cactus. All of the training in the world can't erase the fact that there is a wild heart in every dog that has to be able to run free every now and then. Now was that time. I stopped the truck just to let her loose. This stretch of highway was deserted anyway, so I took off her leash. I smiled and admitted to myself that the same thing that was true about dogs was true about men.

Retrieving my pistols and a couple of boxes of shells, I made a target out of an old dead mesquite branch. After firing two boxes of shells, I was satisfied that I was able to shoot in Earth's gravity and air density. Blaze looked and sniffed at everything while I walked a little and stretched my legs. She seemed to be very excited about the smells. There were no Martian life smells, except for the soldiers and some of our agricultural projects. This was absolutely making her day. After we both had spent more than an hour exploring and stretching our legs, I called Blaze to heel. This was the first time I'd ever seen her balk at a heel command. I forcefully had to pick her up and put her in the truck. After the initial whine in protest, we took off. Her mood quickly improved when she saw that she was able to stick her head out of the window again. She had the biggest doggy smile I'd ever seen that seemed to border on ecstasy.

We proceeded north until I caught an eastward highway and traveled just a few miles to Tierra Amarillo. I was hungry by then and what looked like an authentic Mexican restaurant called La Hacienda caught my attention. I couldn't bring Blaze inside, so I got a couple of steaks "to go" and we traveled about ten miles outside of town and found a place to pull over to eat.

Afterward, I took out a canteen I'd packed and watered Blaze. She was still stimulated by her surroundings, but a big, juicy steak calmed her down a bit. We continued east and arrived in Taos by fourteen hundred. I already had reservations at the San Geronimo Lodge, mostly because they had a single room where my dog was allowed. It was just south of Taos and just off HWY 64 on Witt Rd. I thought I'd go to church tonight and in the morning stop by the business operated by COL SEAL's sister's family.

The room I rented not only allowed my dog, but also had a small kitchenette with a microwave and coffeepot. After unpacking my luggage, I took Blaze for a long walk. She was still very stimulated by her surroundings, but was beginning to calm down. We hopped back in the truck and went back to town to a supermarket to pick up some groceries for our stay here. I had to lock her up in the truck and crack the window. It was a good thing it was only May and the cool of the morning. As long as my dog could stay at this hotel with a kitchenette, there was no need for a kennel. I could care for her without any assistance. However, I wouldn't be able to take Blaze to church. Upon returning, I called the main desk. They graciously arranged for one of their staff to keep her entertained until I got back.

I had long since decided where I'd go to church. I'd made a search through phone directories on our company website and made inquiries through an ASDC agent to check a couple of possibilities before I left Mars. I'd decided to go to a Baptist church in town. I had two hours until church so I made a couple of dinners for me and Blaze, took a shower and changed.

After we ate, I called the desk and requested that Blaze be picked up. A few minutes later there was a knock at my door. I answered to find an older Spanish man named Alejandro reporting to take Blaze into his care. He had a humble, gentle bearing and Blaze took to him immediately, as though she'd known him forever. I was relieved and thanked him as they left for the evening.

With Bible in hand, I left to go to the First Baptist Church of Taos. It was my first civilian church service since I was last on leave, although we do get some services via satellite. It was refreshing to worship with people that didn't have to kill their enemies as part of their job description. As I looked at these people, I was reminded for whom I was fighting for. It was enough to keep serving my country. The regulars greeted me warmly and made feel welcome. This was a friendly place, and the people were sincere. After the service, Deacon Jim Duncan invited me to have coffee and dessert at his house and I accepted. We had a fabulous time. I made a new friend and picked up a new pen pal. He invited me back to church the next time I was in Taos, and I promised I would be back.

I picked Blaze up at twenty-one thirty from Alejandro. He reported that he'd let her chase rabbits at a nearby field and take a swim at a nearby creek. She looked extremely happy. I took her back to our room and gave her a bath in the bathtub and rubbed her down with a towel, followed by a good brushing. Afterward I gave her some doggy treats and took my Bible out to read a bit. Blaze and I concluded the evening watching some old *Gunsmoke* episodes, and turned in at twenty-three hundred.

COL SEAL'S FAMILY

The desk gave me my wake-up call at zero six hundred. Blaze and I ate a breakfast of ham and eggs in our room. I polished my shoes and put on my navy dress whites to go see COL Seal's family. This was appropriate for a call like this as most of my men are either presumed by their family to be sailors or marines. Blaze looked great after her bath.

Ben's maternal grandmother, Mary Yazzie had died the previous year, and Ben's father had been dead for over five years. Uncle George's family elected to remain on the mountain. In Navajo tradition, his grandmother had owned the flocks, and when she died, what they owned was divided between her two daughters. Ben's mother Tashina decided it was time to seek the family's livelihood outside of her beloved four corners reservation. Along with the money she had saved from her husband's working for the white ranchers in Colorado and her share of the flocks, they had enough to move to Taos, NM and buy an old adobe building to open a shop to sell Navajo art, rugs, blankets, and jewelry.

We loaded up and drove to downtown Taos to an adobe building called the Taos Trading Post, which COL SEAL's family owned. Parking the truck, Blaze and I got out and picked up the footlocker I'd packed with COL SEAL's personal effects and some other things I was bringing. Closing the door behind us, the sound of a cowbell above the door clanked it report announcing that the business had new customers. The whole room was filled with Indian art, rugs, blankets, pottery, and display cases of silver and turquoise jewelry. A woman with long, black hair and dark eyes entered from a back room.

"Can I help you find something?" she asked.

"I'm looking for Tashina Begay, Victoria Tso and Jannalee Bluehorse."

"I'm Victoria Tso," she answered, studying me like a textbook the night before a test.

"I've brought the personal effects of CMDR Benjamin Begay, as well as some letters from him."

She looked evenly at me and said, "You are Cowboy, and he said that if he died you would come, in time."

I had no idea that my trip would be told to them before I even knew. I was caught off-balance, and found it useless to deny. "I go by the call sign Kahless now. Is Ben's mother, Jannalee or either of your husbands here?"

"No, I'm here alone. Jannalee took our mother and our children shopping and the men are out buying some silver. Please come to our house tonight at seven o'clock for supper. We live in the back."

"Thank you, I will."

"Bring your dog. I have children who will love her."

I took the footlocker back with me to the truck. She obviously wanted the contents opened in front of the whole family.

Blaze and I took a ride to some back roads outside of town where I was told we could take a long walk and maybe see some wildlife. We got a nice surprise right away, when Blaze flushed some grouse. Blaze went wild and tried to catch them all, but they got away. It was a beautiful day. For once, I had nothing to do but just enjoy a walk with my dog. Blaze chased a couple more jackrabbits, and we caught sight of a doe mule deer. After exploring the trail for a few hours, I was getting hungry, so we headed back.

We got back about fourteen hundred and had a light meal in our room, making sure we didn't stuff ourselves before dinner at nineteen hundred. I took one liberty, which I never did at home. After asking the front desk for a wake-up call at seventeen thirty, I stretched out for a midday nap.

The sound of the wake-up call roused me from sleep. I took the time to brush Blaze down real good. She'd gotten a few thistles and burrs in her fur during our outing. Once I had Blaze squared away, I grabbed a quick shower, dried off with a thick towel and put on my dress whites.

Since I had a little time to kill before going, I poured Blaze a bowl of milk, and made a cup of hot tea. Sipping the hot liquid, I prayed for the right words to console COL SEAL's family. COL SEAL had been officially pronounced dead many years ago, and he never visited his family here. He'd always arranged to meet them privately on the Navajo reservation. It seemed tribal members didn't care much to discuss family matters with outsiders, particularly white people. It was never a security problem to meet his family there. His mother and sisters had just moved to Taos last year, and he'd never had a chance to visit them here.

We arrived just before nineteen hundred and parked around the back. Victoria had opened the door before I had a chance to knock. Two wide-eyed children clung to her skirt, eyeing the strange white man dressed in white with a white, yellow-eyed wolfdog.

"My husband and Jannalee's husband are waiting in the living room; Ben's mother and my sister are helping me with supper." Victoria husband's name was Joseph Tso; Jannalee's husband's name was Jimmy Bluehorse. Both men rose to greet me and offered me a chair. We visited until Victoria announced dinner was ready.

A second table was placed to the side for the children. The two families had a total of seven kids: four girls and three boys ranging from ages three to fourteen. Jannalee's daughter Anna Mae fed Blaze. Jannalee seated me at the head of the table next to Ben's mother, Tashina Begay. Clearly my visit was important to the family. I was asked to say the blessing before the food was served.

Ben's mother in particular and the family in general treated me fondly, noting that I was esteemed by her beloved son as his closest friend. She was in her early fifties, erect and straight, with beautiful jet-black hair, captivating dark eyes and high cheekbones that spoke of a timeless beauty. There was none of the harshness that I was warned that some of the Navajo mother-in-laws possessed.

The matriarch thought that life was indeed very strange, for her son to die so far from the Dinétah, with a bilagaana as dear to him as any kinsman.

After grace, the women served roast mutton, fried Navajo flatbread, beans and rice with guacamole on the side. While everyone else was drinking red punch, Jannalee set before me a hot cup of black pekoe and black currant tea, with a touch of cinnamon. My favorite blend of tea must no doubt have been told them by Ben long before I came here. He must have prepared them in case I'd come to them after his death. The adults all conversed with me in warm and friendly tones, waiting patiently until I was ready to speak of the reason for my visit. We had sopapillas with honey for dessert, and my cup was filled a second time. Afterward the women cleared the table while the men sent the children to play. Blaze raised herself up, looked first at the children, and then to me with imploring eyes. I ruffled the fur on her head and laughed. "Go play." She didn't hesitate a bit. She'd never seen kids before, and she loved them. I was led back into the living room.

"So, you served with Ben?" Jimmy Bluehorse asked. I knew it was time.

"Please permit me to get his footlocker out of my truck. Many of the answers are there."

"No, I'll get it," Jimmy said. "You sit there." He left and returned with COL SEAL's footlocker. Just then the women joined us. I opened the footlocker and took out the knives and pistols.

"These are from Ben's collection. He would want you to have them." I handed the German Luger and Sgin Dubh boot knife to Jimmy Bluehorse. The Highlander Bowie and the nickel-plated Colt forty-five automatic I gave to Joseph Tso. Both men were quite pleased. I handed the personal letters from the colonel each to his mother and two sisters. Next I presented his mother with COL SEAL's dress uniform and all the medals that he had, save the Purple Heart the ASDC officer representing the Navy gave them.

Finally, Ben's mother asked the question on everyone's mind. "How did he die?"

"Five assault crafts attacked the two of us, three of them had singled out Ben, and the other two attacked me. He fought valiantly. All of the men who attacked us, as well as the one who ordered the attack, are dead. I'm not permitted to reveal any more details. I'm sorry."

The shroud of sadness lifted from Ben's mother when she reflected on his legacy. "Oral history for Navajos is very important. Do you have any stories you can tell about his courage and honor for the children?"

"You know that, as a Navy SEAL, much of what he had done and where it was done is classified. But, yes, I can eliminate the classified parts and tell of his courage."

"Good," she said and called the children.

The children all came in and sat on the floor in a row, as the adults either stood up against the wall or sat on the living room sofas and chairs, seating Ben's mother in a place of honor. "Kids, would you like to hear stories about your Uncle Ben's battles and his courage?" The children all enthusiastically said yes, their eyes gleaming with anticipation. "In a land far away in a war that cannot be spoken of with man's lips, there was a brave warrior named Benjamin Begay…" I told modified stories of his Navy SEAL career and more stories of his tours on Mars but always leaving the where and who out. It didn't matter to the children, or the adults, either, for that matter. I told stories until about twenty-two hundred. The children were getting sleepy; it was time to call it a night.

As I was about to leave, Victoria stopped me. "What's the name Kahless?"

"It is just a fictional Klingon warrior from *Star Trek*, who fought with great courage and skill."

"What does he look like?"

"He's actually quite ugly. Here's a picture." I'd kept a picture of the character because I had intended to do an oil painting of the Klingon.

"He's not ugly; he's fierce looking, like a warrior god," she said, smiling. May I have this picture?"

"Sure, why not?" I was beginning to feel as though I was being adopted.

"Can you come back again tomorrow night?" Ben's mother asked.

"Sure, I can stay in Taos another day."

I bade them all goodnight and called Blaze to heel and we drove back to the lodge. Once we were settled in, I slept like a log. I didn't leave a wake-up call and decided that if I didn't get up at the usual zero six hundred, it would be okay. The morning light streaming through the curtains woke me. It was now zero seven ten. *All too easily, I could get used to this*, I thought. Oh, well, that's what vacations were for.

Blaze and I ate breakfast and headed back out into the mid-morning sun on our nature hike. We caught sight of a prong-horned antelope but no closer than three hundred meters. The walk was something that I was already looking forward to each and every day. Some of the terrain reminded me of Mars, except here there was plant and wildlife. Blaze, as usual, investigated everything with her nose. She chased some coyotes and jackrabbits but didn't catch either. I called her to heel, but she wouldn't oblige me. It seemed that her natural urges were stronger than her training. A male gray wolf was covering her. Uh oh, I never prepared for this. She was the only dog on Mars, and I never thought to have her spayed. Oh well, it's done now.

We got hungry just before noon, and stopped at the McDonald's drive-up and got some burgers and fries. After lunch, we went downtown to an art store where I purchased some canvas, oils, brushes and other art supplies, and drove back to the lodge. Taking out the supplies, I opened the drapes widely to lighten the room. This would have to be painted entirely by memory. Putting the finishing touches on the painting at about fifteen thirty, I examined my handiwork in the light. Satisfied, I left it to dry. Nothing was interesting on TV at this hour, but I found a radio clock and listened to some music while I brushed the burrs out of Blaze's fur. I put a teakettle on to boil. Within minutes, I heard the whistling report of the teakettle, poured a cup and waited for it to steep.

After finishing my hot cup of tea, I called Soke Marx and my brother Roger. Soke Marx agreed to meet me in New Orleans as usual for three days of advanced keichu-ryu karate training. Roger and his two sons would arrive the day after my training sessions were over for some deep-sea fishing.

I'd long ago established with my brother and Soke Marx that I couldn't discuss where I was posted or what I did. They both assumed I was some kind of CIA spook or secret military adviser, but honored my request to keep the details private. Anxious to see them both, I decided that tonight would be my last night in Taos. My painting was drying nicely, and I would be able to give it to COL SEAL's mother and sisters tonight. The painting was a portrait of COL SEAL in his navy dress whites. Later that afternoon, I framed the painting and wrapped it, making sure the cloth covering didn't touch the surface. It was mostly dry, but still tacky and I didn't want to ruin it. It was time to go. Sensing that COL SEAL's family preferred me to dress in a naval uniform; I wore my khakis, not my dress whites this time.

When we arrived, I noticed six cars parked there and a lot of children in the yard. It appeared that my stories were attracting more relatives and friends, and now we had quite a gathering. I was warmly greeted by Ben's mother and noticed an additional table was set up in the living room. We ate promptly at nineteen hundred and again I had a cup of hot tea by my plate. The adults treated me warmly and spoke with me at length during supper. There were a total of twelve adults and twenty-six kids there that night. Extra kids' tables were placed outside, and the laughter from outside reminded me of a grade-school lunchroom.

After supper and some more hot tea, the table in the living room was broken down and put away. The mothers got all their children to sit down outside as there were now too many people to tell the stories indoors. The table that was in the living room was set up outside, and a small fire was placed in a barrel. The men added some dead mesquite and some scrap lumber to the fire, and a perfect mood was cast for storytelling. I wasn't ready yet and retreated to my truck and retrieved the painting. I returned and called Ben's mother and sisters over and unwrapped the painting. "This is in honor of CMDR Benjamin Begay, please accept it."

The women looked at the painting with pleasure and Victoria said, "We have something for you." She opened a leather bag and handed me a silver pendant and chain. On the pendant was an engraving of the Klingon Emperor Kahless, my namesake. "Thank you," I said as I slipped it around my neck. Ben's mother took the painting inside and placed it on the living room wall. When she returned, I spoke. "I must go see my brother tomorrow, so tonight will be the last night of my visit. I could tell there was a great deal of disappointment. "I promise I'll come to see you all every time I'm on leave. You all are like family to me now."

Ben's mother spoke, "It is a tradition of my people when one of our own has been taken away from us, to adopt one in his place. Ben was your brother, so you are now my son and our clansman. Who is your family?"

I understood what she meant. I was not going to avoid them or lie to them, so I answered their question with honesty the way they would have said it. "I'm Eugene Bordelon, born into the Douzat Clan, born for the Bordelon Clan, my maternal grandfather's mother was from the Rabalais Clan, and my paternal grandmother's was from the DuPont clan."

I hope I hadn't screwed it all up, quickly trying to convert my lineage into matrilineal terms. They didn't seem to notice if I made a mistake. It was important to declare my mother's people's entire lineage to assure that we didn't have incest in our line, not that they could tell by the names. The adults all acknowledged my lineage with respect, even though my family names weren't as colorful sounding as *Bitter Water People* or *Towering House Clan*. And that was how I got adopted into the family of Benjamin (COL SEAL) Begay.

I started the storytelling for the last time on this visit. "In a land far away in a war that cannot be spoken of with man's lips, there was a brave warrior named Benjamin Begay... I want to tell you the secret tonight of Ben Begay's courage. Ben Begay had great courage because he viewed death as being with his Lord. With this, he could live with honor and have the courage for each and every day. If you have Jesus as your lord, you can have the same courage." I sensed that many were thinking about this, and would do so for some time to come. Finally, I told them the stories they all came for. I told story after story until all the children were fast asleep. Some of the teenagers and all of the adults stayed with my storytelling until zero two hundred the next morning, and finally, I could talk no more. The ladies had kept hot tea flowing half the night and I probably wouldn't sleep when I returned to the lodge. I finally bid goodbye to all my newfound family and called Blaze to heel. Ben's mother and his sisters admonished me to bring Blaze back the next time I was on leave.

Blaze climbed into the truck, and I drove back to the lodge. I packed my navy uniforms and dress shoes away and changed into a pair of blue jeans and a t-shirt. The TV showed an after-midnight pattern complete with its irritating noise. An all-night FM radio station would have to do. I found a station playing popular music and listened to it until daylight. Blaze and I greeted the sunrise, ate breakfast, and went on one more excursion down our favorite trail before leaving town. It was a beautiful May morning in northern New Mexico. I mused that if I ever retired that I could do it here. I touched the medallion around my neck and decided that this was the most memorable trip home ever. I'd been somewhat apprehensive about coming here, not knowing if my visit would cause them more pain and sorrow. In truth, the family needed closure and wanted whatever good history they could get. Benjamin Begay was a family hero; one whom members would try to emulate and they needed the stories for inspiration. I decided I would put to pen all the stories I could remember, and send copies of them back to his family.

We reveled in our morning walk. I mentally tried to record every living plant and wildlife sighting to the smallest detail, knowing that all too soon it would be just a memory, with just red rocks and sand to call my home. Finally, I was hungry, and we went back to the lodge. I cooked the last of our steaks and beans, and we had a good meal. Suddenly too tired to pack, I fell into bed and slept soundly until twenty-one hundred.

I awoke feeling ready to turn the next page of our adventure. Since the only thing I had left in the room was tea, I decided that it was time to eat out. Calling Blaze to heel, we went to the truck and drove to Sonic Drive-In where I ordered two Sonic burgers, one plain with extra meat for Blaze, one with the works for me, and two orders of tater tots. Rested well enough to drive all night, I planned ahead. On the long stretch of road ahead across the desert, there were few if any all-night restaurants to get something "to go," and probably no drive-in's open, so I picked up some snacks and drinks at a late-night grocery store to eat along the way.

We returned back to the lodge, packed, paid my bill and checked out. Blaze seemed to sense that a new adventure was starting as we left Taos. I took HWY 68S until we got to HWY 84, and we arrived in Santa Fe, NM about twenty-three thirty. We hit I40 about zero hundred fifteen and drove south on I25 to Albuquerque. From there, we traveled east and drove through to Amarillo, Texas, where we stopped and filled up with gas and got a cup of coffee. Driving straight through, we rolled into Oklahoma City around seven fifteen. I could tell I'd gotten my schedule out of whack, and I didn't feel like driving all the way to New Orleans, LA.

We found a small, but nice hotel that let me keep Blaze, registered and unpacked. The hotel had room service, so I ordered a couple of ham and cheese omelets with biscuits and gravy for me and Blaze. I decided not to travel again until the next morning and try to adjust my body clock by not turning in until at least until twenty hundred.

After eating, I took Blaze to a park, pulled out the Frisbee, and we had a blast. We went back to the hotel where I wrote for a while in my journal and watched TV until the time for supper. After some more room service and a shower, I left instructions for a wake-up call at zero six hundred.

I slept deeply and awoke to the sound of a phone announcing my wake-up call. The last leg of the trip was 505 miles, and I took I35 South to Dallas, then I45 South to Houston. This was not the most direct route to New Orleans, but I was avoiding going through Alexandria. My hometown was Rapides Station, just north of Alexandria. ASDC officers were considered dead in their original identity and were ordered not to go back to their hometown on leave, to avoid running into people who might ask questions. I didn't want to chance breaking down or running into someone who knew me, so I never went through there.

On my first leave, my brother Roger and I met secretly in New Orleans after I called him from a pay phone. Every time I go on leave now, I send him a letter with my ETA, and he meets me in New Orleans or Baton Rouge, LA. I arrived in New Orleans at nineteen hundred and pulled into the truck stop where we always met.

Roger understood that I worked for the government, but couldn't discuss it. He seemed to understand and always accommodated my unusual rules for contact. It was a funny relationship when we met. He could talk about his life all he wanted, but I just spoke of our life together before and answered general questions about my welfare. Roger and the boys would not be here for three days.

I was to meet Soke Marx for supper at Mandina's restaurant on Canal Street. Pulling up to the restaurant, I parked my rented truck in front, on the street. Soke Marx's car pulled up and he parked behind me. Telling Blaze to stay, I cracked the window and locked the car. She had already been fed, and would probably curl up and take a nap until I got out. After Soke Karl W. Marx locked his car, I gave him a bow, which he returned, and then he hugged me. Soke Marx was an outgoing individual, given to expressions of affection and deeply committed to Christ. We went inside and were seated by the boss' daughter and manager, Cindy Mandina.

We both ordered a couple of beers while we looked over the menu. The waitress delivered the beers and left, giving us time to decide what to order. I presented my teacher with the gift I had brought him, a copy of *The Art of War.*

"Thank you. I appreciate it." He looked into my eyes. "There is something different about you this time. You have more authority in your bearing, and also sadness."

"You remember the friend I sent to you for advanced training sessions?"

238

"Yes, the Navajo known only as "Seal.""

"He was killed in action."

"You always spoke of him with such respect. I take it he was your commander as well as your friend?"

"Yes."

"So that is the reason for both your sadness and your promotion."

"Yes."

"I knew him well enough to know that he is in heaven now. You are viewing this from a temporal perspective. You must learn to see this from an eternal perspective."

"I know you are right. It will just take time."

Soke Marx looked as though something pained him. He sighed and leaned forward, his eyes as remorseful as one who had accidentally killed a friend. "I have a confession to make. I have mistakenly led you and my students down the wrong spiritual path. Now I must undo the damage, even if it is one student at a time."

"Soke?"

"The so called *spiritual disciplines* of transcendental meditation and mind-control are wrong. For years, I have been "kicking against the goads" and trying to do this *my own* way. From now on I will be doing this God's way. I apologize for leading you astray."

"Apology accepted. I will, of course, follow you as you are following Christ."

"Excellent! I want you to throw any of the old keichu-ryu patches away. I have a new one for you. This one has the sign of the dove on it, representative of the new God over Keichu-Ryu."

He handed me two patches, one for my karate gi and one for my boxing trunks. The waitress interrupted us and asked us if we were ready to order. Mandina's restaurant offered both Italian and Cajun food. Soke Marx ordered a seafood platter, and I ordered veal parmesan and spaghetti with an Italian salad. The food, as usual was exquisite, and we ate and drank our fill and departed for the evening after planning an early morning start on my training session. Blaze and I found a hotel that would allow me to keep her.

Zero six hundred came early. I arose, took a quick shower, fed Blaze and grabbed some breakfast in the diner next to the hotel I was staying in. I had to leave Blaze in the truck while I grabbed breakfast. Soke Marx did not mind my bringing her to the training session. Our training session was conducted in a small dojo which belonged to a friend of Soke Marx. I had requested training solutions to fighting in a deep sea diver's suit and using my bat'letH. A diving suit was as close to a space suit as I could manage without saying too much. I had sent ahead the design and measurements for my Klingon sword, and Soke Marx had two hardwood replicas made for practice. The boots were heavy, so kicks were basically out. My instructor made the most of close-quarters fighting in bulky equipment, focusing on using my hands and sword. It was no doubt the first time he had been asked to develop and teach a fighting technique for someone so weighed down and immobile. He probably doubted its validity as a combat application but said nothing. Three days were over more quickly than I would have liked, and my karate master bid us farewell.

At about seventeen hundred, Roger and his two sons, Mark and Andrew, rolled up in his Chevy truck, towing a trailer with my Harley and the newly installed sidecar. The sight of it gave promise of new adventures waiting for Blaze and me. His wife Barbara was visiting her sick mother and couldn't come. I surveyed my brother. Farming hadn't hurt him a bit. We both had brown hair and eyes, but he was a couple of inches shorter than me. He was fit but starting to get a slight pot belly, probably because his wife was one of the best cooks in Louisiana. Yes, my father left the farm to the right brother. We all got out and hugged each other, and I let Blaze out to meet them.

They all loved her and I explained that we couldn't eat here with Blaze, so we went to Sonic Drive-In. Jalapeno poppers were on sale and four Cajun men couldn't resist. We had a great time together and Blaze found some new friends. My family checked into the dog-friendly hotel where I was staying. Roger's twin sons had just graduated from high school. Andrew was going to LSUA in the fall and Mark was joining the Marines in July. The two boys were as different as night and day. Andrew the artist was the sensitive one, whose green eyes from his mother mirrored a soul that was thoughtful and introspective. Mark with his dark eyes and rugged good looks was a man's man, athletic, strong and aggressive, willing to take chances and driven to win. We arose early and took the drive-through to get breakfast at McDonald's as we had to accommodate Blaze.

FISHING IN THE GULF OF MEXICO

We finished breakfast and headed down to the dock to meet the captain and his two mates at zero seven hundred. We boarded with our fishing tackle and our ice chests full of food and drink. I stood at the bow of the spar deck with my hand on the gunnel, gazing toward the sunrise. The weather was fair and the sun hung low in the cloudless azure-blue sky like a Spanish doubloon, painting a ribbon of gold upon the calm, sapphire-blue sea and dividing it before me. The bow of the ship cut an ever-expanding wedge of wake lines and the cutwater below produced a clean hiss in the morning air.

Captain Thibodeaux charged me a little extra to take Blaze aboard because he thought she might be a little trouble. Our destination was the southern Chandeleur Islands in the Gulf of Mexico, where we planned to fish the islands for redfish and specs. I'd packed my waders and fly rod as I was planning to fly fish the saltwater flats. Blaze was excited and fascinated by the sights and smells of the sea. I smiled at the sight of her with both paws on the gunnel, looking out at the sea while we were moving along. With her mouth open and tongue hanging out, she was as close to being in doggy heaven as was possible on Earth. Dolphins followed our boat, probably hoping for scrap fish parts that were sometimes thrown overboard when the mates cleaned fish for their clients and Blaze barked excitedly. Breathing deeply and tasting the tang of the salt air, I wondered if I should buy a boat and retire out here someday.

The captain got us as close as possible to one of the southern Chandeleur Islands and set anchor. We loaded a skiff with our gear and my dog and headed inland. Smelling and investigating everything, Blaze wandered around the island while I fished the day away. We fished the sloughs on the southernmost island's backside flats all day and got an impressive catch of specs and some bull reds. The captain met us at sundown, and we showed him our catch.

Captain Thibodeaux told us of a place where we could catch some blackfin tuna for sure and maybe a yellowfin if we were lucky. The plan was to fish next to a natural gas platform at night. They kept lights on at night, and it attracted baitfish. And where there was baitfish, there was going to be tuna. The captain offered to supply us with heavy rigs that we needed. Since we'd fish tomorrow night away, we had tomorrow day off. We could enjoy the night and sleep in late. The mates filleted our fish and bagged and iced them for us. When I got back to the hotel, I put them all on a saltwater soak. I'd cook them when we awoke in the afternoon in the kitchenette at the hotel.

Later tonight we were going to eat all the Cajun food we wanted, listen to some genuine Cajun music, drink a few beers and spend some time together as a family. I fed Blaze some fish before we shoved off and left her with the desk clerk, but had to pay him for his trouble. We chose a New Orleans style

241

Cajun restaurant with a live band. Returning to the hotel about zero two hundred, we played poker until sunup. We laughed, carried on and had a great time. My nephew Mark asked me if he could serve with me, but changed his mind when I told him that I only set eyes upon women once every two years due to my special assignment. As much as I would like to have him with me, I was pleased to hear that. My father's family line was all here, and I didn't want him killed on Mars.

We ate breakfast in the hotel restaurant. Afterward I walked Blaze, fed her a fish and turned in for some shut-eye. I slept soundly until eleven ten and awoke to the sound of my nephew Andrew knocking on the door.

"Wake up, Uncle Gene, let's cook lunch." I let him in, and showered and trimmed my beard. When I came back, my brother and his two boys were planning to cook dinner. We had some oil in a large pot on the stove to cook fish and French fries, and it was already heating up. The refrigerator had some salad makings I'd purchased on the way here. My brother and Mark were already there when I got out of the shower and everyone was ready to eat. In Louisiana, fish are almost always cooked in cornmeal, but I convinced them to let me try tempura batter. The boys scrubbed the potatoes and cut the eyes out but didn't peel them. I preferred peel on and thick cut. The potatoes were drained of water and cut into wedges. Once the large oil pot was hot, we dropped in the battered fillets and potato wedges. The smell of the fish bubbling in the hot oil was making me hungry. After draining and cooling the rest of the fish and fries, we prayed and ate the best meal I'd had in a long time. This was not much different that my dinners made from fish we raise in our greenhouse fish tank on Mars, but this was better. This was with family, and it tasted better than ever.

We arrived at the dock promptly at fourteen hundred with enough food and drink to last us for the night. It took about four hours to reach the first offshore platform where we'd start. It was almost dark when we arrived. We had just a little daylight left to get prepared when the mate dropped anchor. In less than an hour, the sun would set, and the offshore platforms lights would come on and attract the baitfish. The rigs supplied by the captain were suitable for game fishing. I trusted his judgment as he was a professional and I was the tourist.

The idea was to catch the flying fish with a net when the rig lights came on and store the ones we weren't using right away in a live well while we fished for yellowfin tuna on the surface. Dark descended, and when we'd netted all the flying fish we thought we could use in one night, we settled down to fish. We hooked the baits in the lip and cast them between fifty to one hundred yards out, bump trolling the bait. Yellowfin tuna were predators and gave a very sporting fight, but we were all successful. When the action died down, we switched to fishing deep for blackfin tuna. Using heavy jigs, which simulated squid, we dropped them about one hundred feet deep and used a fast return. The evening was a success, taking even more fish than the first trip. I decided we'd use Captain Thibodeaux's services the next time I'm back on Earth.

All in all, we caught three yellowfins, two blackfins and a young mako shark. This would be a night to remember forever. This was almost enough to tempt me to come home for good, but not quite. The sun was rising over the gulf when we left for land, causing the surf-blue water to shine gold as the sunlight danced on its wake. Andrew knew how I felt about pictures, so he sketched charcoal drawings of us to capture the memories of the evening. He was a talented artist and had been awarded an art scholarship. He hoped to turn his love of art into a lifetime profession. My brother Roger was hoping at least one of the boys would take over the farm one day, but was going to give them their space until they decided on which path in life was their own.

The captain's mates were very experienced with processing fish. It was all cleaned, filleted and packed in barrels with dry ice. Some tuna and shark fillets I'd be taking back to Mars. Much of it was going home with Roger and a portion of mine would go to CPT Ripsnort in exchange for ignoring my weight limit back. Blaze had a ball, and I hoped it wouldn't be hard to get her back into the transport freighter home.

We returned to the hotel and got a good night's sleep in preparation to go to St. Louis to watch a Cardinals game.

In the morning, I packed my stuff and hitched the trailer with my Harley to my rented truck. I'd drive the rental pickup to St. Louis and turn it in there after the game, and go back to the Academy on my Harley. I had my portion of fish and shark steaks shipped to the Academy on dry ice.

At first light, we headed to St. Louis, MO., but it wouldn't be straight as the crow flies. I had no intention of meeting up with someone with whom I grew up with going through Alexandria. We'd take the long way around, through Mississippi, then to Little Rock, and on to St. Louis. This would also keep me from the temptation of trying to visit my parents' graves. As much as I wanted to visit their graves, it also held a sort of Tom Sawyer twist to it. I'm supposed to be buried right next to them. I didn't want someone who knew me deciding I was alive and making for a possible security leak. People seem to be full of conspiracy theories since JFK's assassination and I didn't want to fuel someone's fertile imagination. Okay, so it was a secret conspiracy of sorts, but one that they didn't need to know about. We fought hard for them, but knowledge of the war was on a *need to know* basis. The ASDC covered fine for me in most every encounter, but I had orders to stay away from my hometown.

When I retire, and my work is done on Mars, I'm sure some elaborate cover story could be made, to resurrect me so that I could go home and pay my respects to my parents.

It couldn't have been a more beautiful day in St. Louis: fluffy, cottony-white cumulus clouds were scattered across the robins-egg blue sky. The national anthem choked me with emotion and finally the umpire called "play ball."

The television camera catching me on film was a security no-no, but I wasn't concerned. My beard was full, and I was wearing a ball cap. When I'm daydreaming back on Mars, and the pressure is on, this is what I'm dreaming of. The stands were full of excited fans, there to support their hometown team. Roger and his boys grabbed an authentic baseball stadium lunch of beer, hotdogs and peanuts. On the way to our seats, I purchased two St. Louis Cardinals jerseys and two caps from the merchandise booth. I always wanted to be able to have a clean jersey when I watched the Cards on satellite TV back at home. The game was exceptionally exciting. The Cards won 6-3, driving in the winning runs with a home run in the bottom of the ninth inning.

After bidding a reluctant goodbye to Roger and the boys, I turned in my rental truck and took my Harley back to Utah. We made plans to hunt Elk in the fall on my next visit with COL SEAL's brothers-in-law. I had initially been concerned about having Blaze ride in the sidecar of my Harley, but she loved it. I put a pair of goggles on her and she didn't seem to mind at all. My dog was a sight with her tongue hanging out, and wearing goggles. I couldn't help but smile. With my probably pregnant dog in the sidecar, we hit the road. After three days of leisure driving across beautiful country, we arrived back at the ASDC Academy. I purposely shaved my beard to make sure that I was easily identified by security at the academy. I'd be stowing my bike here, and on my next trip I could pick it up directly from here when I arrived.

TEACHING AT THE ACADEMY

After clearing several security checkpoints and verifying with fingerprints and retinal scan that I was who I was supposed to be, Blaze and I were escorted to my quarters. While I was unpacking, the door buzzer announced a new cadet, checking to see if I were settled in okay.

"Cadet Wilcox reporting for duty, sir."

"At ease, Cadet. My quarters appear to be in order. I'll need my itinerary."

"Yes sir, I already have that." He unfolded a paper with my teaching schedule for the week and handed it to me. "Sir, BG Edwards wants to see you in his office right away."

BG Wilson Edwards' secretary announced me, and I walked in to find the general studying the teaching itinerary for the next week. He was once as strong as a lion, but he had paid the toll on the turnpike of time. Seventy years old now, his hair was snow white and thinning, with deepening lines in his face and liver spots on the back of his bony hands, and his pale blue eyes were not as bright as they use to be. There were pictures on the wall of children, grandchildren, and a couple of great-grandchildren. Time had wrought wounds as deep as any that my men had suffered on the battlefield with the Soviets. It was not hard to believe the rumors of his retirement.

"Come in, COL Kahless," he said, and motioned for me to sit. "I trust your leave has been restful and enjoyable?"

"Absolutely, sir. I've gotten to go deep-sea fishing, watch a Cardinals game and ride my Harley. What more could a man ask for?" He chuckled with amusement at my comment, and then measured me to see if it was truly enough.

"Still living the life of a eunuch, I see."

"Yes, sir. I'm leaving to go to Mars in one week. I just received my field command eleven months before I left. After thirteen years of military service, I don't expect to get married and retire. As I see it, that would be a conflict of interest. After all, a man who's home only one month every two years has nothing to offer. Besides, I have a dog."

He laughed good-naturedly. "And Blaze is a very special dog." He paused for a moment; a shadow of concern crossed his timeworn face like a cloud covering the sun. "I am glad that your survived your legal difficulties. I have high hopes that you will succeed me as commandant here someday. You know that I am not getting any younger. I think I will be taking my leave here in the next few years." He exhaled as if he had been holding his breath since I had been arrested, relieved as I was that it was behind me.

"Thank you, and thank you for your support."

The general smiled and nodded his head. "Now then, how is the war going?"

I spent more than an hour briefing him of our position and struggle on Mars. BG Edwards had been the first security Chief of Nuclear Command Center 4, which repaired the first alien disc. He became the commandant here when the academy first started up. This was his mission and his life's service to America, and he would do it until he retired.

I took leave of the general just as lunch was being served at the mess hall. I was scheduled to give a lecture on teamwork at thirteen hundred in the main auditorium, and all cadets were to attend. Instructors and visiting field officers were seated in one section of the mess hall; cadets were seated in another. I was able to sit next to COL Red Fangs, the commander of our post on Luna. He too, was on his last week here, though he was taking a different transport freighter home. We ate and made light talk and finally the conversation came around to Marines versus Navy.

"Now that I'm commander of our post on Mars, I think I will break the earlier tradition of *Navy only*." If I'd meant to shock him, I couldn't have done better with a stun gun. "So what changed your mind about that?" he asked, seeming very interested.

"Well, we had some jarheads come through on the way to Ganymede, and they were stranded with us for a few sols because of a meteor shower, so I put them to work. I was impressed with their *can do* attitude. I'm going to seek to add marines to my command, especially, but not limited to, security."

He looked at me with a sense of amusement, but he was clearly impressed with the compliment. He changed the subject. "I hear that your dog is rumored to be pregnant."

I couldn't believe that I finally had some leverage over this jarhead. "That's the suspicion." It was obvious that my dog had become quite a celebrity among the personnel in the solar system's various outposts, and he was quite interested in my dog's condition.

"What kind of dog is the father?"

I had a hook in his jaw, and all I had to do now was reel him in. After all these years, he was actually asking a squid for something. "The father is a gray wolf. He didn't hang around to show me his papers."

He looked as though he was pained to be in debt to a sailor. "I sure would like to have a male from that litter." This was rich! I wouldn't have missed this for the entire world. This would make a real nice story at officers' mess back home.

"What've you got to trade?"

He studied me for a moment and then he grinned. "I have a Marine Corps bomber pilot, top-notch, the best in the unit."

I couldn't believe it. He was going to transfer a marine pilot from his crew to my post—trading him for a dog, no less. Something wasn't quite right, but I just couldn't put my finger on it.

"What's his name?" I asked more to get to the bottom of this than anything else.

"CPT Luv2bomb."

I mulled it over for a moment. I'd heard of him, a very good bomber pilot, a Chinese-American. This might be good. I might someday need a pilot who could speak Chinese and maybe this one did. My curiosity was killing me, but I wanted to check out his service record before committing to anything. "If I don't hurry, I'm going to be late for class. That would set a poor example for my students. Why don't we meet later and discuss it at the o-club at beer-thirty and hoist a couple of cold ones?"

"That sounds like a plan." I hurried to class. It wouldn't provide a good example for an instructor to be late. The classroom was filled with pilots from various branches of the service, most of them with prior flight experience, some with combat experience. The ranking cadet called a crisp "Atten-shun," and after they all saluted, I addressed them.

"At ease, please be seated, gentlemen." I collected my thoughts quickly and prepared for the class. I'd requested that each cadet bring a Bible. "Please turn in your Bibles to Ecclesiastes 4:12. I read aloud from the New American Standard Bible, " 'And if one can overpower him who is alone, two can resist him. A cord of three strands isn't quickly torn apart.' "

I motioned to turn off the lights, and then the film clip started. The satellite film clip of a battle about ten years old was being displayed. Two American pilots were dogfighting with two Soviets. As the fight went on, both American ships took heavy damage, and both pilots lost their ships. The finish of the clip was a break to the memorial room of the American post on Mars. The close-up showed two plaques, CPT Thor and 2LT Chill of Death. Then the next footage started to run, showing two American tanks fighting with four Soviet tanks. The two fought hard and smart, took damage, but vanquished all four of the enemy tanks. I then signaled to turn the light back on. "Can anyone tell me the difference in the fighting styles of the two pairs of pilots?" Several hands shot up, and I picked a young cadet with a knowing look in his eyes.

"Sir, the first two fought as if they were fighting their own personal battle; the second two fought as though they were brothers."

"Well said, cadet. He's exactly right. The first two pilots had a quest for individual glory and the second became like brothers, willing to die to protect the other. In fact," I pointed to the back of the room, "Let me introduce LTC Robertson, formerly known as MAJ Chainsaw, who was the senior pilot of the second pair, as well as one of your instructors." I motioned my old friend to come to the podium. LTC Robertson took the podium and at my direction stood to speak. His speech was more polished today since he'd spent his last few years in public speaking at the academy, but his southern accent was still as strong as the day I first met him.

"One thing every senior pilot on Mars has to do is to take on a new pilot as his wingman and try to teach him enough to keep them both alive. I was assigned a young pilot fresh from Vietnam as my wingman. During orientation, I had him slip on his flight suit and put his sidearms on over his suit. I surprised him by drawing the pistol out of his holster and plugging a mannequin three times. I thought he would fill his astronaut diaper. The look on his face was priceless," he chuckled.

"My new wingman followed me everywhere except to the head. He seemed to make it his life's mission to know me, so he stuck to me like glue. He became my little brother, and we fought side-by-side as one, with one purpose. I never had such teamwork and unity of purpose with any other pilot. 2LT Cowboy was figuratively integrated with me and we were one on the battlefield, and he's still alive today." He waved his hand toward me, "I give you 2LT Cowboy."

"I was given an order by my first commander on Mars to keep that man alive. As you can see I faithfully completed that mission. It is essential that if you're to survive and win that you learn teamwork. You can learn knowledge and develop skills, but you must learn teamwork first. If you learn teamwork, we will teach you the rest, or you'll learn it with experience. I want you to try an exercise. Pair off with another cadet and share what your motivation is for serving in the ASDC. Also decide if you can put the other cadet's safety and welfare before your own. If you can't, no one will blame you if you decide to leave the ASDC now. Anyone who desires to leave the ASDC, come see me after class."

About forty cadets paired off and examined their motives. I had only two cadets who decided to leave. Boot camp did a good job of weeding out most of the ones who couldn't work as a team. I was surprised that two men were leaving, but was relieved that they were leaving before they failed their teammates. I was grateful for their honesty. I just hope there weren't others that should have left. Afterward I addressed the cadets for about forty-five minutes on the value of faithfulness and honor.

Classes were finally over for the day. Tomorrow I'd be teaching on Soviet warfare tactics. The academy had a very good officers' mess. I decided that I would have supper there, instead of trying to eat in my quarters, but first I wanted to access the PC in my quarters and pull the service record on CPT Luv2bomb. Here it was. He was twenty-nine, had an excellent service record and his re-enlistment was coming up in a month. He had a request in his file that re-enlisting was conditional on his being assigned to Mars. This was funnier than the idea of trading a pilot for a dog. He was trying to trade me something he didn't have, but then again, so was I.

1LT Powder Burns was homesick and said he wouldn't re-enlist unless he could be within sixteen hours of Earth. He preferred leave times every year. I smiled. Two can play this game, and I'll see that he takes a sailor in the process. I checked my e-mail, and LTC Killer Instinct said everything was okay, and not to worry. Like any administrator, I took the news as a mixed blessing. My post was still there, but they could do all right without me. Well, that was part of my duty, to make sure that I had good men to hold down the fort (literally) when I was not there.

Logging off of my PC, I strolled over to the officers' mess. Good, I thought. COL Red Fangs was not here and I preferred talking about this over a couple of beers. Today's special was Mexican food. My students might not appreciate that in the morning when I have to look over their shoulders in the flight simulator. I knew it was unkind, but I decided that they needed to get accustomed to hardship and ordered a double-order of beans and chilies. I got to chat with a couple of the other visiting instructors.

MAJ Skullbasher was a very accomplished pilot with a reputation for being fearless on the battlefield, but couldn't quite grasp the concept of diplomatic and negotiating courtesies that command officers must employ from time to time. To him, a Soviet was an enemy to be killed like a cockroach, not someone to drink tea with while making idle talk, smiling when you didn't mean it. His methods were a bit crude, but he always got the job done. He would never be promoted to post commander because of his inability to negotiate and observe military politeness in certain situations with the enemy that called for it. But when you wanted a killer to eradicate the enemy, he was top on my list.

LTC Chessmaster was quite different. He was a hunter of a different nature, who constantly calculates every angle, whether it is war or diplomacy. It was not hard to see him as a post commander, or even on the ASDC Central Command staff. I visited with them both and swapped war stories and general lies. COL Red Fangs didn't show up to mess, so I left. From there it was a quick trip to the Academy's vet clinic to pick up Blaze. The doctor confirmed she was indeed pregnant. She hadn't had supper, and I was due to meet COL Red Fangs at the officers' club, so I called her to heel and took her with me. This was even better. I'd have her with me when I negotiated with him about the pilot swap.

We took a leisurely stroll to the officers' club, and I observed that COL Red Fangs was already there. I took a seat on the barstool and called Blaze to heel. COL Red Fangs waved the bartender to see what I wanted. Since Blaze hadn't had supper, I ordered her a steak sandwich, plain, a glass of milk with a bowl and a beer for myself. We chatted a bit, and the subject of my morning class came up. The bartender put the steak in the deep fryer to cook, the hot grease popping its report. He opened the cooler and brought out a long-neck beer. Water droplets condensed on its neck, and a drop of moisture ran down its neck. He popped off the top, and a curl of carbonated vapor drifted out of the bottleneck like fog lifting off the damp ground on a cold morning. I accepted the bottle thirstily and took a drink.

"I heard you washed out two cadets this morning. I thought you squids were soft," he said with an amused look in his eye. I took a sip of my beer.

"They washed themselves out. I just told them that if they couldn't die for their fellow soldiers, they should look for a different job. My only concern was if some of them that should have walked, didn't." I took a long drink to accentuate my statement.

"I wish a couple of young pilots they sent me had heard your speech. You might have missed your calling, Colonel. You should have been an instructor."

I thought about that for a moment, taking another drink. "It takes an experienced soldier to teach young soldiers, and I'm not through with my experience yet."

The bartender came out with Blaze's steak sandwich and milk. I took the glass of milk and poured it into the bowl and laid the steak sandwich and bowl on the floor for her. The bartender gave me a look but said nothing. I shrugged my shoulders and told him she was pregnant, tipped him five bucks, and his mood improved somewhat.

"So it is true," said COL Red Fangs, looking very pleased at the prospect.

"I just brought her back from the vet, and yes, it is true."

"Well, how about the trade?"

"I've been thinking about it a bit, and no matter how special a dog is, to trade for a man is wrong. I'll give you pick of the litter, and if your marine wants to serve with me, I'd be honored." I knew the marine pilot would get his way in the transfer whether he said so or not. This was just a negotiating politeness. Now I'd given him something for nothing, with no strings attached. Now I was in a position to ask him a favor, and he couldn't refuse.

"I have a favor to ask you, though. I have a young pilot whose tour is up, and he's very homesick. He said he wouldn't re-enlist unless he can serve on the moon. Seems he wants to be just a few hours away from home. I need you to take him on. He's a good man."

"What's his name?"

"1LT Powder Burns."

"I've heard of him. He has an impressive record."

Suddenly it hit me. He was familiar with my crew and probably anticipated I insist on him taking a naval officer to break the lunar *Marine club*. It was obvious he'd reviewed the service records of my men and wanted to be sure he got a good man. Why shouldn't he? I checked his man out. Here I was, thinking I was one step ahead of him, when I obviously wasn't. He'd make a formidable enemy. I'm glad he's on our side.

"Sure, I'll take him. I understand homesickness. Hell, I may even make a marine out of him," he laughed. So that's how we broke the marine and naval clubs in the only two exclusive ASDC posts in the solar system. I guess Blaze getting pregnant was a good thing after all.

"By the way, Colonel, the next time I layover on the moon, I'd like to go on a patrol with you."

"I don't usually let visiting command officers put themselves in harm's way, but I'll make an exception in your case," he said, with a teasing smile.

"Thanks, I think." We shook hands over the deal. I guess I never got over being told that I was a squid and couldn't ride in his tank as a junior officer.

There was a chessboard on the end of the bar, and I'd heard he was a good player, so I invited him to play a game. In no time, we were in combat as tough as with any Soviet I'd ever fought. He was very, very good. I was right about him and glad he was on our side. We played for a half an hour, hardly speaking at all. Our concentration was intense and Blaze made her "I'm bored, and let's go home" noise.

At a point in the game where it looked as if I might be beaten soon, I began looking for one good move for a reversal. It was COL Red Fangs' move, but I lost all of my concentration.

Into the officers' club strolled a beautiful blonde-haired woman with sparkling blue eyes, finely arched eyebrows, full lips and cheekbones higher than the Kilimanjaro. She walked toward us with the grace of a cat and smiled at me, her teeth like two rows of perfect ivory. She stared at the board for a minute and said to COL Red Fangs, "May I?" Normally no chess player will let an outsider touch their board or make a move for them, but it is amazing what men will let a beautiful woman do when she smiles just right. She studied the board a little while longer and moved his queen, looked at me and said, "Check, and mate." The word mate rolled off her tongue like a private joke. She was obviously flirting with me. She turned over my king on its side, looked me right in the eyes and smiled. My heart beat like a triphammer. It took all of my discipline to get control of myself.

Then she turned and walked out, without so much as telling me her name. Her exit was even more intoxicating than her entrance. She was beautiful from all views and her perfume lingered long after she left. COL Red Fangs gave me an amused look.

"Men melt in her presence. Rumor has it the Academy assigned a cleanup crew to mop up the mess. She's LTC Yekaterina Pastukhova, an instructor here in Soviet language and culture. She's Russian born, and a former CIA analyst. She still works part time for GEN Spear's staff as an analyst. She was obviously very taken with you. You may be through with your *field experience*. I predict you'll soon be a full-time instructor."

His words struck a nerve in me. I'd fought the pull to return to Earth my entire career and sometimes having a dog for a companion wasn't enough. I was shook up, and I didn't want him to see that. I turned both palms up and spread my arms wide. "I'm still solid. There isn't a woman on Earth or elsewhere that can bring me home before my job is done," I said, not convincing either of us.

"So you say." He rolled his eyes as if he thought I was full of it.

I realized it was time to go and excuse myself and called Blaze to heel. I resolved myself to get through this week as quickly as possible and get back on that ship as scheduled. The idea of being afraid and running from a woman was beginning to gnaw on my insides like a wild beast. The whole thing was challenging my courage, and if I ran, could I in all honesty act with courage on the battlefield? I didn't need this. For all these years I'd stayed unmarried, and with a single purpose did my duty. In the back of my mind, I knew this day would come again.

Arriving at my quarters, Blaze laid down in her bed, and I checked my e-mail. Top priority was an encrypted e-mail by LTC Killer Instinct. His e-mail stated that he had a request from a *bullet sponge* to transfer in, and he wanted to know what was going on. He also said there had been a few skirmishes with the Soviets, but no major conflict and the post was still standing.

I answered back, "I'm approving the transfer of the marine and I will explain when I get back. I want you to approve the transfer for 1LT Powder Burns to Luna, and he's to leave on the next transport freighter." I knew that would raise his eyebrows, but I'd explain the whole thing when I returned. I filled out the paper work approving CPT Luv2Bomb's transfer request personally since his leave was up about the same time that mine was. I'd take him back with me.

After a hot shower, I read my Bible for a while and hit the rack. I fell into a deep sleep while the sweet smell of her perfume etched itself into my memory like an engraver's tool.

My body clock was back on schedule, and I awoke at the zero six hundred, shaved and greeted the day. After morning prayers and scripture reading, I fed and watered Blaze. Since she wasn't an officer, she wouldn't be able to eat in the officers' mess. I took Blaze out for a walk and then took her to my aide, Cadet Wilcox. Resident instructors on staff don't get an aide because they live here and their lives are pretty much settled.

After the young officer had taken Blaze, I made my way to the officers' mess, took a tray and sat down alone. COL Red Fangs spotted me and sat right next to me, much to my chagrin.

"Don't worry, she never eats here. She always takes breakfast in her quarters."

"I wasn't concerned," I replied, trying very hard to believe the lie.

"Sure," he said, dropping the subject. "Well, how many cadets are you going to wash out today?"

"Actually, today I teach Soviet warfare tactics, and that should go fairly smoothly."

"Hmmm, Soviet tactics. I hear you got COL Tkachenko from Ganymede. Are you sure you don't want to become an instructor? I hear he killed the

American commander and all the senior staff and most of the officers on Titan."

I thought on that for a moment. "I killed COL Kiknadze personally with only a sword, and I believe I'll be a formidable opponent for COL Tkachenko," I said, trying to convince myself that I was indeed Tkachenko's equal.

"Maybe, just maybe, but LTC Pastukhova looks much nicer and smells better too." He lifted an eyebrow, enjoying my discomfort again.

"Whether it is the Soviet colonel or the Russian–American lieutenant colonel, I'll meet every challenge with courage."

He raised his coffee cup as a toast. "I'll drink to that, but having courage with her may cost you your command. Personally, the only thing I'm afraid of is women. That's why I still have my command," he finished with a smile.

We parted ways after some more war stories, news and general lies. I had my first class in fifteen minutes. Yesterday's class had forty cadets; today's had thirty-eight. I made it to class on time and the senior cadet called for attention. I started the class with prayer, which would be my practice for many years to come.

"It is no secret that Soviets are smart. Never forget that. Some of the world's greatest chess players and mathematicians are Soviet and their military commanders are very good at plotting their moves in advance." I put a picture of COL Yuri Tkachenko on the screen. "This man is the single most successful Soviet in the solar system, nicknamed the "Butcher of Titan" because of his success against us on Titan. He's courageous, brilliant and especially ruthless.

When COL Kiknadze died, the Soviets transferred Tkachenko to Mars. Some of you will be engaging him in combat in a few months. Tkachenko had only been on Mars five months before I left, so I am not an expert on him. Our analysts on Titan, Ganymede, and Mars have compiled an analysis which we will discuss. From my short experience with him, I can tell you he's everything they say he is. The reason we mention him specifically is that his tactics are being taught in the SCA Academy. You'll be met with his tactical philosophies on the battlefield regardless of where you serve. Tkachenko stresses chess-like maneuvering of his opponents into position until he has his enemies exactly where he wants them. He also stresses the importance of timing, position and surprise. He makes his officers think like chess players and is unusually creative in strategy, in a country whose main system is to tell you what and how to think. His methods are catching on. He's the most famous and respected field commander the Soviets have and the SCA Central Command fawns on his every move.

This is where you come in. As young officers, you must think smarter, train harder and learn from your enemies as well as your peers. First you must know your ship and become a skilled pilot and sniper. You must also learn how the enemy thinks, how he plans and be able to know what he'll do next. If he thinks four moves ahead, you must think five. If you engage this man in combat, you must work together as a team and fight smart if you want to live to tell about it. Forget about the idea of being the most famous pilot for killing him.

A pack of wolves take down more game that a single wolf does. Oh, did I mention, his other nickname is the "Ukrainian Wolf." They don't call him that for being a Labrador Retriever." The class broke into laughter over that.

"But seriously, you'll get all the combat you can stand. Fight resourcefully, fight together, and live to fight another day." I motioned for the lights to dim and the projector to put up a set of slides. "This is Titan. The Soviets had a cave not too far from the midpoint from both of our posts. This slide shows a burned out tank, and a dead American pilot. What we didn't know is there was a cave with a mouth large enough to hold a squadron of tanks, and they'd lined the roof of it with lead. This was the trap that got the post commander of Titan, his XO and most of his senior pilots killed. When they got there to investigate the burned out tank, they were outnumbered and ran into a minefield, to boot. There's an old saying, 'curiosity killed the cat.' It works on people, too. Under your desks are copies of *The Art of War*, by Sun Tzu. He was a Chinese general who lived between three and five B.C. Men of war and businessmen have studied his principals for thousands of years. Two notable ones were Generals Patton and MacArthur. This special copy has quite a few battles over the ages critiqued in the light of Master Sun's principals, and the book has plenty of blank pages for notes. Before we reference the work itself, I have to offer one disclaimer. *The Art of War* is the definitive book of strategy for war, but not the definitive book on how we should live. That would be your Bible. To continue... concerning the tactic Tkachenko used on Titan, I'll quote from *The Art of War*. 'All warfare is based on deception...' "

I spent the rest of the morning expounding on Soviet tactics and advising that if their theater of war included the Chinese, then they would be given additional instruction in a separate class. At lunch I got my tray and COL Red Fangs moved to sit with me again. Lunch was fried chicken, corn on the cob, a salad and peach cobbler. I decided I better have an exceptionally strong cup of tea, or I'd fall asleep during afternoon class. We ate our meal and discussed the war effort, shared about students and told more war stories.

Then I noticed her and my heart skipped a beat. She was getting her tray with a salad and an ice tea. After looking around, she sat at the end of the officers' table. She never once acknowledged I was there. This was making me crazier than her obvious flirting of last night. COL Red Fangs regarded my discomfort with amusement.

"I hear she's the best analyst the ASDC has. Her specialty is negotiating with the Soviets, so she understands cat-and-mouse games. On the other hand, she probably doesn't like you at all," he said, flashing me a wide grin, enjoying my torment.

"Then, there probably isn't anything to be concerned about, is there?" I said curtly. Finished with lunch, I put my tray up. I left to go, purposely not making eye contact with her.

I was not going to be teaching this afternoon. Each pilot shipping out for points abroad had to be cleared by the flight surgeon with a physical exam, eye test and to make sure their shot records were up to date. The pilots were also required to requalify on the sniper range and in the tank. I wasn't the range officer of this class, even as a visiting command officer of higher rank. CPT Halstead was in charge here. I had to drop by and fire at least hundred rounds to requalify. Every two years this has to be done, as well as requalify on my tank. There was classroom time and I picked up some useful things I'd forgotten.

I reported as a student to the rifle range, where I shot my mandatory one hundred rounds. My scores were good enough to requalify, and high enough to qualify as a line coach. Once I'd finished, I was expected to help the instructor for the rest of the afternoon as a line coach, training the cadets.

Some of these pilots have never used a rifle outside of basic training in their original branch of service. One of the cadets, 2LT Boyer, was a former Marine Corps Scout/Sniper. He was already instructor material, but he wanted to go fight the Soviets. He was shooting picture-perfect. The instructor was pressing him hard to stay and teach, but he had his heart set on filling his kill ledger.

I took up my position as line coach over my group of four shooters, 2LT Boyer being among them. I observed and coached three of the four, but soon became aware the marine should have been coaching me. His shooting was extraordinary, like nothing I'd ever seen before. I looked over my shoulder at SGT Clark, the Block NCO over my part of the line. He usually didn't move a muscle unless the line coaches asked for help. He returned my look with a brief nod, and I knew he was impressed. The shooters continued until the end of class. Once the Block NCOs had signaled *all clear*, the range officer, CPT Halstead, turned his signal paddle to the red side facing the young private in the tower above. He, in turn, signaled all clear with his megaphone. Once we retrieved all of the targets downrange from the pit, I was even more impressed with the marine. "That's some nice shooting, son. Where was your first choice to serve?"

"Sir. Mars, sir." It wasn't a secret that I was the commander of our forces on Mars. The young marine didn't ask any special favors. He didn't need to, for his shooting had already gotten my attention. Until my agreement with COL Red Fangs, this young sniper would have gone to Luna, or one of the other posts where marines served. If word got out about his sniping ability,

COL Red Fangs would press hard to get him. He was a marine. I was a bit curious as to why his first choice was Mars.

The range officer, CPT Halstead signaled me to join him in his office, as there was a fifteen-minute break before the next class.

Once inside, CPT Halstead gave me an inside track on the best snipers, a favor for getting his brother CPT Bad Dog an assignment on Mars.

"Colonel, that marine out there isn't just good. He's so good it's phenomenal."

"I noticed."

"It's more than that. I benchmarked all of those rifles personally with a bench vice at one hundred meters and logged them with their serial numbers. The rifle that marine is shooting with has a half-inch group at one hundred meters from a bench vice. He's firing the same rifle at a quarter-inch group."

"Maybe the ammo lot he's using is better than the lot you benchmarked it with."

"I thought so, too, so I pulled five boxes out of the lot he's been using, cleaned the rifle and bench marked it again. Same results as the first time and he came back and out preformed the bench the next day. It didn't matter what I gave him to shoot. He consistently excelled on any weapon I threw at him. I've gotten him to shoot at moving targets, poor visibility, and at faster intervals and he's just simply amazing. What he can do with that rifle isn't explainable."

"It doesn't seem possible, but what I need on Mars are men who can do the impossible. Excuse me, I need to run to my quarters before my next class and fill out a request to cut orders to have him assigned to my command."

He smiled. "Better hurry."

I made a beeline for my computer terminal in my guest instructor quarters and got on line and checked 2LT Boyer's service record. He was loyal, smart, unwavering to duty, and never got into trouble. Good, I thought. This is the kind of man I'll build a stronger squadron with. I checked and so far he hadn't been assigned. I was not surprised, cadets were usually evaluated in their last week and assigned just before graduation, and we were down to the last week. After filling out a request form for assigning 2LT Boyer to Mars, I sent a communiqué to a friend in ASDC Command that owed me a favor, asking him to make sure no one else got him. Word of his sniping prowess no doubt would travel fast and I needed his orders typed right away to get him to Mars. Since I was leaving for Mars at the same time he was being assigned, we'd be traveling back together. Tkachenko was suspected to be a former sniper and one place where the Soviets beat us was with the sniper rifle.

I planned to set up a mandatory sniper class for all the pilots on Mars, with this marine as the Chief instructor. Under this phenomenal sniper's tutelage, we'd be more than a match for the Soviets. Picking up a hot cup of tea I had placed in the microwave, I headed back to class and made it with fifteen seconds to spare.

I spent the rest of the day teaching Soviet tactics. After class, I picked Blaze up from my aide, and we ran into 2LT Boyer headed for the basketball court. He was dressed in gym shoes, green shorts and t-shirt with USMC and the eagle, globe and anchor on it. The young marine brightened when he saw me.

He saluted me. "At ease, lieutenant."

"Sir, yes sir."

"Were you serious about wanting to serve on Mars?"

"Yes, sir."

"Why?"

"They say a good sniper can fill his dance card there."

"And that you can. So what call sign are you going to select, cadet?"

"Pale Rider, sir. It's from Revelations 6:8. 'And I looked, and behold a pale horse: and his name that sat on him was Death, and Hell followed with him.' "

"Very good, I believe you were going to exercise?"

"Yes, sir."

"Dismissed, then." The young man saluted me and went on his way. I had never been married, but was seriously thinking about adopting him.

LTC YEKATERINA PASTUKHOVA

Vacation has a way of upsetting my routine and getting me a little lazy. The gymnasium had a room off to the side for fencing. Since I'd not done any fencing since leaving Mars, I picked up a white fencing suit, mask, and foil from the attendant on duty. After changing, I called Blaze to heel, and we set off for the fencing room. We were the only ones there, so I commanded her to stay, and used the time to stretch and practice form.

About ten minutes into my stretching, the object of my conflicted heart arrived, threatening to disturb my status quo. LTC Pastukhova walked in, and I was caught between a feeling of elation and panic. She acknowledged me with a reserved nod, put her bag and foil aside and started stretching alone with a cool sense of detachment, which was making me even more uneasy. I remembered COL Red Fangs saying that she understands cat-and-mouse games. I was quite aware who the mouse was. In white, she appeared as the most beautiful creature I'd ever seen. I continued to stretch. When I had finished stretching, I worked through a drill alone to try to make my muscles remember the right form. I knew that at some point doing this alone was bound to become embarrassing. She appeared to be finished with her stretches.

"Would you do me the honor of drilling with me?" I asked her.

"I would like that." She put her mask back on, gave me the customary salute and assumed the en garde position.

We did simple thrusts, derobements, disengage thrusts, one twos, doubles and parries. Finally we'd drilled long enough, and it was time for a few bouts. Since we were still alone, we'd have to judge touches.

"How about five bouts, five points per bout?" she asked.

"Sure." I felt like I was playing with fire but the fire was irresistibly warm. "Yekaterina, is it?"

"I prefer to be called Katya."

She was quick and graceful as a cat, and her form was perfect. It was difficult to concentrate; her beauty was so darn distracting. She, on the other hand, obviously didn't have any problems with distraction and beat me soundly five to three in the first bout. The atmosphere was electric with excitement as fencing usually is, but there was chemistry between us that made it even more exciting.

Fencing is a sport in which it is common for women to compete with men. Size and brute strength mean less than stamina, speed and technique. I determined to concentrate and the effort paid off. The next bout I won five to four and I was beginning to see ways to score. After a hard-pressed third bout, I won again five to three.

I kept telling myself that it didn't matter whether or not a girl beat me, but on some subconscious level, I knew it mattered. I don't like being beaten by anyone, but I guess that deep down, like every man, I wanted to be looked up to by the ladies.

Bout four was a complete turnaround. She pulled out all stops and beat me five to three again. Vacation had softened me somewhat. Whereas my usual routine was to run five miles a day and lift weights in four hundred millibar air pressure, the trip over had denied me the opportunity to train so hard. In truth, I had not gotten back on my schedule since being on Earth, either. The pace was beginning to grind me down. She was as fresh as a new spirited colt while I was beginning to feel like a plow horse that was long in the tooth.

Sweat streamed down my face under the hot mask, and I was looking to end this as quickly as possible. She didn't appear to be in a hurry and attacked, parried and continued to press me for any weakness that my weary body would reveal. First touch went to her, and then the second and I rallied for the next two. She got the next touch, then I did, and back and forth until we were four to four. I had right-of-way and was pressing a particularly fast riposte. At the end of the track, I took a gamble. It took exact timing to pull off, and it had to be executed before she had the right-of-way again. As she started to move forward, I stopped. A fraction of a second before she achieved right-of-way by extending her foil, I extended mine and scored the last touch with a stop hit. She looked very surprised, but stopped, backed up, saluted and removed her mask.

"Very, very good!"

"Thank you for a good practice."

"You're very good yourself. Where did you learn?"

"My father was on the Olympic fencing team from the Soviet Union before he defected, and he taught me. I usually practice with MAJ Cheryl Garrett, but she's on vacation."

I thought about the narrow escape in our last bout for a minute. She reminded me of the girl I dated from high school who lost two out of every three bowling games to me, every time. I wondered if she threw that last touch, just to preserve my delicate male ego.

"I have a pot of rice cooked and was preparing to heat up my wok. Would you care to join me?" she asked. I was past the point of being able to resist and Mars seemed a long way away at the moment.

"Sure, but I think I need a shower first." I was sweating profusely, and she was too. Funny, I thought. With wet hair and a red face, she only looked more appealing. I wondered if being an instructor here full time wouldn't be so bad after all.

"Oh, I'll have to get a cadet to keep my dog."

"Oh, no, bring her along."

I showered and changed, and Blaze and I went to her quarters. She opened the door wearing a beautiful blue silk dress and motioned for me to sit down on the couch while she started dinner. The apartment was furnished with fine hardwood furniture and some beautiful paintings on the walls. I took a seat on the couch and one painting in particular caught my eye: an officer from czarist Russia in dress uniform astride a white horse. I noticed the signature on the bottom of the painting was K. Pastukhova. All four of the other paintings bore her signature. The one I admired most was a desert sunset colored with red and blue sky, overlooking the desert and a mountain range. My silence was broken by her voice.

"Ready in about fifteen minutes. Put on some music, will you?" She pointed the way to her stereo, and a collection of records and cassettes. I looked through her selections and found a record album that had some classical music, but qualified as easy listening mood music. While I put the record on the turntable, a picture caught my eye: an older couple on the wall, and I guessed it must be her parents. I made my way to the kitchen to move closer to her. Her sparkling eyes were the color of glacial ice, but the warmth radiating from them revealed a true paradox.

"Have a seat," she offered with a disarming smile and the wave of her hand."

"Thank you."

"Do you spend all your spare time beating women in sports?"

I laughed at her good-natured teasing. "Actually I'd call that one a narrow escape. You're very, very good, and a worthy opponent."

She made a curtsy and laughed. "Thank you sir, but I'll beat you next time."

"That's possible, even likely, though the challenge is more fun than the winning or losing. A close match is always exhilarating."

She filled a bowl for Blaze and fed her in the kitchen. After setting the table, she scooped out some rice on each plate, followed by some Broccoli Beef, my favorite Chinese dish. She poured me a hot cup of my favorite tea before pouring Darjeeling in hers. Hmm, I thought, my favorite Chinese dish, rice and my favorite drink and she never asked me anything. The girl had been doing her homework, and this meal was calculated well in advance. Her *cat-and-mouse* games were actually negotiation skills; finding out about me was nothing more than research on her part. She had resources to know everything about me. Maybe I should have felt indignant, but I was quite flattered. As much as I resisted this meeting, there was nowhere else I'd rather be. I deciding to play this hand and see where it took me. She sat down, and we prayed over our meal. It was delicious, and after I finished my plate, she filled it again. The vigorous workout had left me famished.

After I finished the second plate and concentrated on my teacup, I decided to take the bull by the horns and get this to a level of openness. I pointed at the wok and teacup. "It seems I have been the target of an intense investigation. This took some effort. I'm flattered."

"I do research and analysis for a living. I simply made a comm. call to your aide, and advised that we needed to know some of your likes and dislikes, to plan a dinner in your honor. He was very forthcoming, and he's a very nice young man."

"I'm curious about one thing. Was our meeting tonight planned?"

She giggled like a schoolgirl, and by degrees I saw my free-will slipping away, like sands in an hourglass. "The attendant was to page me if you checked in to fence, but I had a couple of alternative plans."

"Touché again. That was very nice work. I wonder if it is worth all the effort. I leave for Mars by the end of the week and will be gone for two years, plus travel time."

"I know, but relationships are difficult for me as I work on very sensitive projects for the ASDC. I don't need any civilians asking questions about where I go, or what I do for a living."

"What exactly do you do? So far all I've heard about your job is *intelligence*."

"I do analysis of how our command officers fare against their Soviet counterparts and present it to my boss. I also work on a round table think tank, with my specialty being Soviet culture, language studies and politics. My input is received as part of discussions on deciding overall strategies. I have a very high-level security clearance, so I can just about be privy to just about any company conversation. I fill out my spare time as an instructor here in Russian language and culture."

"Analysis of command officers' performance you say? I'm betting that I was being watched carefully after I went after Kiknadze."

"I'm not at liberty to say, officially. But personally, don't you ever think of doing anything like that again!" She sounded like a schoolteacher scolding a student for shooting spit wads, and I laughed a little.

"What's funny?"

"You sound like my old fourth-grade teacher in grade school when I misbehaved."

"Well, leaving the end of the week or not, I don't want to think of you dying out there. Have you ever thought of teaching at the academy full-time? BG Edwards is getting older, and someday he will retire. When he does, there will be an opening for commandant here."

"So the general has said. The thought entered my mind when you intruded on my chess game in the officers' club, but…"

"You're leaving for Mars at the end of the week," she finished.

"Exactly, I have unfinished business."

"Do you see an end in sight for this business?"

"Perhaps, but I just became post commander eleven months before leaving Mars. With the post came COL Tkachenko. I feel as if my unfinished business is with him. Who knows, he may get transferred elsewhere, or we may put an end to him."

"I just hope he doesn't put an end to you. He's a very dangerous man."

"So am I," I said, trying to convince us both that I believed it. "In any case…"

"I know, you leave for Mars by the end of the week." By now this was becoming a joke, and we both laughed.

Clearing the dishes from the table, she said, "I have something you just have to see. Being a Russian culture expert and Russian-born, I have access to some interesting things." She retrieved a VHS tape in the living room and popped it into her player. "I know you speak Russian, so sit," motioning to the couch. She set the tape up and sat close to me. We watched a Russian opera filmed in Moscow for the next hour. I put my arm around her about halfway through and she peered into my soul with blue eyes that sparkled like starlight. "You're leaving for Mars by the end of the week."

"Yes, and I believe you should walk me and my dog to the door before I act very foolishly."

She frowned. "Will I see you tomorrow night?"

"Yes, how about dinner at the officers' club, around eighteen hundred?"

"Sure," and with that she walked me to the door. I was well aware that I was leaving soon. I couldn't resist taking her into my arms; the smell of her perfume was intoxicating. When we kissed, I felt the struggle within me immediately. Part of me wanted to stay forever, and that other part of me was struggling to *stay the course*. She saw it too as our eyes met, and she whispered, "Good night."

I walked Blaze back to my quarters, and took another very hot shower, followed by a cold one for good measure, considering the company I'd kept tonight. The workout was tough, and I'd be hurting very badly tomorrow if I didn't. Sleep eventually took me, but my last thoughts were of her.

I couldn't concentrate on my classes at all the next day and avoided COL Red Fangs altogether. I knew that he would recognize the conflict within me, and tease me about it. The day seemed to drag on forever as I watched the clock, waiting for the last class to finish. My aide would be keeping Blaze for the evening. I dressed in the best dress uniform I owned and hurried to the officers' club. She wasn't there yet, so I sat down at a table as far from the door as possible for privacy, but where I could still see her come in. She showed up right on time, wearing a white evening dress with silver high heels, her blond hair hanging loosely past her shoulders. *This was going to be real difficult*, I thought. Her swaying walk, bouncing blond hair and the sound of her high heels clicking against the o-club's floor was chipping away at my will as surely as a stonemason cutting granite with a mallet and chisel. I rose, and pulled her chair back. She smiled sweetly, thanked me and sat down.

"You look absolutely stunning tonight."

"Thank you. You clean up real nice, too."

I smiled as I recounted my very serious effort to dress in the very best clothes I had, which in this case was my dress uniform. ASDC dress uniforms were distinctively black, with red trim and cords, and gold rank insignias and buttons. I could have worn civvies, but I honestly didn't own a civilian suit. I never had an opportunity that required one and blue jeans didn't seem appropriate that night.

I hardly noticed what I ate, but I knew that we did. We spent the evening telling each other stories of our youth and service. Her parents raised her in the Russian Orthodox Church, and she was a devout Christian. I felt as though my mother would approve of her and wished she were alive tonight to meet her.

"Your family name Pastukhov, is it very common?"

"Yes, *Pastukh* is the root that means shepherd. I am descended from goat and sheep herders. My father's last name is Pastukhov and mine is a feminine version of it. And your real last name is Bordelon, from the French root name *borde*, meaning farm. Your brother runs the family farm. So shepherd and farmer aren't that much different."

"No, not much difference. You have done your homework."

She spoke, and the conversation rapidly turned to more serious fare. "You've spent your entire career on Mars killing Russians, and yet here you are, having supper with one. Does this feel like a contradiction to you?"

I stopped and thought that over. "I've sent money to societies for Bibles for Russia, so I do understand the difference between the Soviet people and enemies. I fight soldiers because my duty dictates it, but the Soviet people aren't my enemies. I see no contradiction here."

She smiled. "I think you'll do, but then, you're leaving for Mars at the end of the week."

"Yes. In just two days. I'd already signed up to extend my tour. I've just barely started to serve as post commander."

"When do you think you'll have fulfilled your obligation to your duty?"

"I honestly don't know, but I have a feeling it has to do with COL Tkachenko. Who knows, I may be assigned there for "such a time as this"." She nodded at the reference from the book of "Esther."

"Yes, sometimes, God appoints people for tasks at a time and place that's a crossroad. I feel I'm about to step into that crossroad, and my destiny is intertwined with Tkachenko's."

She shuddered. "I just want to see you safely back home, and that one is dangerous."

It was getting harder than ever. I'd already signed up for another four-year tour on Mars. My next leave would be travel time back, two more years and travel time back. I was to leave in two days. I didn't want to hurt her but couldn't bear the thought of leaving her.

"I have to tell you. I'd stay here with you for the rest of my life if I had peace about my duty. I've never met anyone like you. I just don't want to sit on the front porch and look at the stars in the evening and wish I were somewhere else. It would be very unfair to ask you to wait for me."

"Promise me you'll be careful and that you'll come back for me and I'll wait." Her eyes showed that she honestly would.

"I will, under one condition. If the wait is too hard and you change your mind, just tell me and I'll release you from your vow. As for me, if I live to return, I'll marry you; that's my vow."

"I won't ask to be released."

"But you must agree that you can be released if you feel you can no longer wait."

"I agree, but I swear if we have to adopt children, I'll still wait."

"I'll be right back." There was a jukebox, and I wanted to dance with her in any case, just to hold her. I scrolled through the selection and found it. *Perfect*, I thought. I returned back to the table and extended my hand. "Shall we dance?"

"Yes."

We moved to the dance floor just as the song I put in started playing. The bittersweet words of the song were as though they were written just for us, from the movie *Romeo and Juliet*.

"A time for us, someday they'll be,
When chains are torn, by courage born,
Of a love that's free.
A time when dreams so long denied, can flourish,
As we unveil the love we now must hide.
A time for us, someday they'll be
A life worthwhile for you and for me."

We danced until the song ended. I escorted her to her quarters and kissed her goodnight. Tomorrow night was my last night on Earth. We decided to take a field trip out to the surrounding hills and watch the sunset and the next morning's sunrise.

The last day of teaching seemed to drag on forever. I went through all of the motions and finally the day was over. My brother had sent more of the shark steaks to the academy, and I'd bought thirty pounds of ribeyes to pack. I had my container of meat, tuna fillets and shark steaks on dry ice and ready to go, but my clothes, tea and other personal effects I would pack in the morning. Slinging my holster over my shoulder, I carried my backpack to meet Katya.

264

I met Katya at the officers' club, and she was thrilled see I'd brought my colts. She laughed, her blue eyes shining with excitement. "Now I have a real American cowboy to take me out!"

"Oh these, just in case we run into snakes."

We loaded up my bike's saddlebags with some provisions for the evening. I had purposely taken the sidecars off, so that she would have to wrap her arms around me on the trip. We left the box canyon that hosted the Academy and headed west about thirty klicks into the desert. Katya directed me to a hill and motioned me to head to the top. There was a dirt trail up the side with a gradual rise to it, which made it ideal for biking up. I was able to ride all the way to the top and park my bike on the mesa's flat top. It was only about eighteen thirty, and we had about an hour and a half until sunset.

We busied ourselves with gathering a wood supply before the sun went down. There were plenty of small sticks and deadwood from trees and brush nearby, and an old, dead piñon tree stump provided some pitch pine for a great fire starter. I had brought a small hatchet, a machete, and a cigarette lighter to help with the fire preparation. Making a circle of rocks, I arranged the sticks and wood into a teepee shape and shoved a couple of pine cones and some dead grass under it. Finally, I took my knife and made shavings of the pitch pine for a fire starter. Taking stock of my creation, I surveyed our wood pile and was satisfied it would make a nice fire at sundown.

I had brought a shovel, but I had forgotten to bring a flashlight, a rookie mistake for an Eagle Scout. We were of the opposite sex and trying to use the bathroom in the dark without a light to see by may prove both embarrassing and even dangerous. Quickly surveying my surroundings, I spied a small piñon tree with several branches the right size. I cut four branches about three feet long, and three inches in diameter. With my ax, I split the top nine inches, then again crossways with all four sticks, then pried the splits open and filled it with wood shavings. These would make fine torches for four trips to the mountaintop privy. The sun was beginning to set on the mountain range to the west.

Katya laid out a blanket and unpacked supper. She had some fried chicken, potato salad and apple pie. She teased me about Americans needing to eat apple pie. After praying, we ate and watched the sun slowly slip behind the mountain range. I recognized this scene. It was the same spot where the painting in her quarters was painted. The colors painted by the dying sun seemed to gain intensity and by degree became more colorful, until the sun was behind the mountain range. The clouds on the mountains had a yellow undercoating on the bottom and were fiery red and darkish purple throughout. The breaks in the clouds showed a few fluffy white clouds at the distance, with a bluish purple sky as a backdrop. The purple and red gave yield to dark black clouds higher up. This was truly magnificent. Katya had chosen to bring me here to share this precious gift. The sun finally

265

surrendered, and I lit the campfire. I knew that getting too physical alone with her tonight would be a big mistake.

"Some things are best left until a promise is fulfilled," I said, indicating a need to keep it honorable.

"Good, if I have to wait, so do you."

With the rising of the moon, we were serenaded by the mournful howl of the coyote, which seemed to be a fitting backdrop for our separation tomorrow. We talked all through the night, and I learned a lot more about the woman I was leaving behind. Katya was Russian-born, and her father was not only an Olympic fencer, but also a Soviet cryptologist. He worked for the Soviet intelligence community before he defected to the United States and started working for the CIA. She was only five when they came to America but she still loved the Russian people. It dawned on me that this was the reason why she had to know that I didn't actually hate Russians, but was simply a soldier doing my duty. Her singleness at age twenty-seven was why she had time to pursue cultural things like painting and fencing, when other women her age were too busy raising children. I still had one nagging question in the back of my mind.

"Why did you become interested in me?"

She smiled. The flickering firelight illuminated her face and showed how truly beautiful she was. "Well, you know what I do. I have to dig into the backgrounds of each command officer. I have to do security checks, which include your history, military service records and psych evals. Something between the first look at your picture and all the other things I looked at made me want to meet you. You might say I knew you long before I ever met you. Your unit has the lowest rate of transfer requests in the system. There's a list of pilots trying to transfer in. That speaks well of you. By the way, that young marine sniper has been assigned to you."

"Nice. Thanks for the head's up."

"You're welcome. I must confess the story of the cowboy who wears six guns over his space suit was larger than life. Now that I've met you, the image has been replaced by the man."

"And you're still interested?"

"Yes, I guess I still am."

It was turning cold, so she wrapped up in the blanket. We stayed close to the fire and talked all night. Sunrise was beautiful and peaceful. Gone were the fiery skies of last night, yielding to the softer colors of the early morning. The light yellow sun started to emerge on the horizon, coaxing the sky to start to turn blue. The clouds that did appear were few and far between, but they were beginning to turn white with the rising of the sun. The morning was awakening with the sounds of birds and animals beginning to stir.

We packed up all of our stuff onto my bike, and then took one last drink of our canteens before leaving. Breakfast would have to wait until we got back.

"You never showed me any shooting. How do I know if you're a real cowboy or not unless you show me some shooting?"

I dared not miss. This would break the spell cast by our perfect evening. I was accustomed to shooting in a different gravity, temperature, and atmospheric density than this. It was a good thing I shot off a couple of boxes of rounds on Earth a couple of weeks ago. Anyway, she did say she was able to accept the man over the larger than life image she once had, so I could risk failing. I pointed at her aluminum disc shaped canteen. "That will do. Throw it about twenty yards out and about twenty yards up, flat side facing me." She smiled, and tossed it up pretty close to where I asked her to, and I drew both pistols and put two holes in the canteen. I was relieved, and she was elated. She retrieved the canteen, now leaking two streams of water.

"I promise to keep it as a reminder of our date. You are a real cowboy! Maybe you can buy a ranch and raise cattle and horses when you come back for me."

"Nothing would please me more, milady." We arrived back at the academy at ten hundred. Breakfast was over in the officers' mess, but we grabbed a bite at the bar in the officers' club. After lunch, Katya excused herself to go back to her quarters and change but promised to meet me in fifteen minutes at my quarters.

Upon returning to my quarters, I had a video conference request from my XO. I made the connection, and I saw his smiling face on the video screen.

"Greetings, Colonel."

"Greetings. Is my post still standing?"

"Sir, yes sir. Are you coming back?"

"Why do you ask?"

"Rumor has it that you've taken up with a blonde-haired beauty, and may stay on Earth. In fact, a certain unnamed captain is giving odds on just that."

"What are the odds?"

"It started out four-to-one that you were coming back. Then someone got a picture of said beauty and posted it on the bulletin board. The odds dropped to two-to-one that you would remain."

"And what do you think?"

"I may just be a full-bird colonel soon."

"Well, don't count your eagles before they're hatched. I'm packing now."

"Very good, sir."

"I'm bringing back two marines with me."

"Good. So, you traded one sailor for two marines. I would have held out for three."

I didn't want to ruin it for him. "I'll tell you the whole story when I get back. Is that it?"

"That's all I got, sir. Have a nice trip."

"Thank you. Kahless out."

Katya knocked lightly on my door. She'd taken the day off as a personal day and volunteered to help me pack. After packing, we picked Blaze up from the vet. She had been treated *gently* for ticks and fleas. She was pregnant, and special care had been taken to treat her. Her bedding and bed were destroyed and replaced, and my quarters fumigated. Regulations didn't allow an animal to board a ship for points abroad without being certified free of ticks and fleas. I got her certification papers from the Academy vet and cleared her to board. We ate a late lunch at the officers' club. Blaze and I were ready to board and arrived at the launch pad at fourteen hundred.

Katya and I shared our first goodbye kiss. She handed me a chain and pendant. It was a broken heart with the words..."Mizpah. May the Lord watch between me and thee whenever we're absent one from another." She pulled the other half of the pendant and necklace out from under her shirt to show me she held the other half. I held her hand and our fingers entwined.

"When did you buy this?"

"The day after our fencing match. The Academy has a post exchange with a small jewelry counter," her voice as thin as a whisper. A single tear streamed down her cheek, and I wiped it away with my shaking hand. I felt a wave of emotion wash over me. I kissed her goodbye for the last time, reluctantly released her hand and called Blaze to heel. We boarded, and I watched Katya on the launch pad until we were commanded to strap down for lift-off.

THE MARATHON POKER GAME

I met the transport freighter with my dog and two transfers, but my heart I left behind. We were on the short end of Mars orbit in relation to Earth's location in its orbit around the sun, but not quite as short as on our trip here. It was planned that way to make my time away from the post shorter. Since my course was plotted and I was committed, I decided to settle down to the three and one-half month trip back to Mars. We play a lot of poker, and everyone reads everyone else's books on the way back, which made for a lighter travel bag. There were a lot of videotapes in the transport freighter's archive to help us pass the time. There was the inevitable Russian language class to keep us busy. The gerbil gym was only large enough for one person at a time, and we had assigned times in rotation. Sleeping arrangements are the same as a submarine, three men per bed, eight hour shifts in rotation. We had Internet access for APO e-mails and news, so we never lost contact with our country, or our post.

Blaze fared well and had six pups, six weeks into the trip to Mars. This caused no little stir. All of her pups were spoken for within hours. CPT Ripsnort wanted a pup but conceded it wouldn't be fair to the dog, being cooped up on a transport freighter in space.

Two and a half months into our trip, CPT Ripsnort got a communiqué from the transport freighter *America*. Very rarely do transport freighters pass each other and the captains and passengers take advantage of it by having a marathon poker game. Usually it lasts for about twenty-four hours, providing there's no ranking field commander in a hurry to get home. *America* locked its docking clamps to our transport freighter and CPT America, his crew and passengers came aboard. Two field commanders were on this flight, Titan's commander COL Ice Man and me. Ice Man, the former first officer from Europa, was the one the ASDC sent back to dig back in after COL Tkachenko nearly destroyed the post on Titan. He was as tenacious a fighter and leader as they came. CPT Ripsnort pulled the two of us aside to see if we'd approve the time delay.

"I'm looking forward to cleaning COL Kahless out," announced COL Ice Man, eyes boring into me like a drill as if it were personal.

"I don't have twenty-four hours. Raise the table stakes and the raise limit and make it twelve hours. You can lose a war in twelve hours."

CPT Ripsnort was undaunted. "Okay, gentlemen, it costs two thousand dollars to play. We start six to a table and play until that table is down to one man. Then when all the winners of the tables are ready, we play one last table until there's only one player left, winner take all. You won't be allowed any additional money to gamble with. When you're broke, you are eliminated. COL Kahless informs me he's in a hurry, so the opening bids are fifty dollars and raise limits are fifty dollars. If we run out of time in the final elimination, we will raise both limits again. There will be no cheating and no hard feelings. Anybody breaking these rules will be ejected from an airlock." He paused for effect. "Just kidding. But let's have fun, and keep in mind, with only one winner, the odds are that you'll lose. If you can't take that, don't play."

There were a total of twenty-four men playing today: flight mechanics, crewmembers and captains of the transport freighters, recruits, seasoned pilots, and two field commanders. Both 2LT Pale Rider and CPT Luv2bomb were in, as well as COL Ice Man and me.

I went back to my flight bag and pulled out my leather banker's cap, white shirt and armband. I may not win, but I was dressed for the part. That put me on a different table from COL Ice Man and that came with the added benefit of him not being able to put me out early. Heck, I may even not survive the first table. I may never play him at all. Both of us had fought Tkachenko and neither of us had beaten him down. I think that he wanted to beat me to prove he was the better man. We played my table for a grueling four and a half hours. I lost some, won some, going back and forth until finally one by one, players on my table were eliminated. First CPL Good Wrench, the tank mechanic from Titan, then CPT Luv2bomb, then CPT Ripsnort, and his Chief mechanic, SGT Grease Monkey.

Finally, it was down to 2LT Pale Rider, 2LT Warthog and me. It went back and forth for a while, and my sniper lost on a bluff. Three hands later I got lucky with a flush to 2LT Warthog's three kings. I'd won round one and left the room for a short walk to stretch my legs, and brewed myself a strong cup of tea. An hour later the other three tables were done, and we were down to four players. COL Ice Man had survived and was pleased I had, too. The other two winners were CPT America of the transport freighter *America* and CPL NutzNWrenches, a tank mechanic from Europa.

COL Ice Man looked at me and smiled a big, toothy grin. "Finally we play!"

"So it would seem. It is a good thing there's a wager limit, I'd hate to send you back to Earth without a shirt!"

"I assure you, I have a spare shirt. Let's play."

Three more hours passed before we eliminated another player. CPT America left in good spirits, glad to have lasted so long. CPL NutzNWrenches was an excellent poker player, who seemed able to alternately bluff us, and then come back with good hands. COL Ice Man had the best poker face I'd ever seen: his eyes revealed nothing, and he didn't seem to have any "tells."

Two more hours later, we were at a turning point. COL Ice Man was dealing. I kept three cards, all hearts. He dealt me back two nines, which matched my nine of hearts. I'd amassed a great deal of cash up to this point and lost to COL Ice Man's full house, but CPL NutzNWrenches wagered his way out of the game on a pair of tens. Now it was just COL Ice Man and me.

We played for another hour, going back and forth, back and forth. Since I was already overdue for my bunk rotation when the game started, I was hoping it would soon end. Even though I was getting sleepy, I refused to throw in the towel. It was my deal—I gave him five cards; he gave me four back and kept one. After reviewing the hand I had dealt myself, I was beginning to think this was the last hand. I kept two, both of them kings, dealt myself three cards more, and then four to him. Carefully I turned up the corners of my three new cards, an ace and two more kings. Four kings! My heart was beating like a drum, and it took all of my discipline to try to mask my body language so as not to betray my good hand. I've never in all the years I've played gotten four of anything, and the single ace I held meant he couldn't have four aces. It was unlikely he would have a straight flush or royal flush. If he had a real good hand, then I could make him bet the full amount so I could clean him out. Looking at our piles of chips, I couldn't tell who had the most. The piles looked the same.

"Let's start wrapping this up," said COL Ice Man.

I peered at him over my cards. "What do you have in mind?"

"No limit."

I could feel my grip tighten on him like the coils of an anaconda. With my four kings I could clean him out. "Okay, no limit."

"Good!"

Mostly up to now the average winner of a hand had been one pair, two pairs or three of a kind and that was with several players. It was common in a two-player hand to win with one or two pairs.

COL Ice Man counted out his chips and pushed them forward. "I raise five thousand dollars."

"I see your raise and I raise you ten thousand dollars."

COL Ice Man shoved all of his remaining chips forward. "Count them."

I counted eight thousand nine hundred and seventy-five dollars. I counted my own and I was fifty dollars short of meeting it. I suddenly realized my error in agreeing to no limit! If I didn't have as much as he did, he could wager me off the table. I looked up and knew that I'd been outfoxed. He must have been keeping track of his chips. His weren't all stacked up, and mine were. There was no doubt about it; he knew what he was doing.

"I guess you've beaten me."

"Not yet, you can still meet my raise," he said, with a crocodile smile.

"It is against the rules to bring in more money."

"It's not about money. There are no rules about adding the assignment papers of your new sniper."

He gave me a smug look, and I wanted to clean him out more than anything. I considered my four kings and realized that this young sniper was probably going to make the difference in the balance of power with the Soviets on Mars. Only two hands could beat mine, and it was highly unlikely he had either. There was one more thing. If I broke the promise to the young sniper, word would get around the ASDC that I was not to be trusted, and it would be difficult to recruit the caliber of men I was used to getting. I hated doing this, but I had no choice.

"I fold." I laid down my cards face down. COL Ice Man was unprepared for that answer. It appeared to me it wasn't about money. He'd undoubtedly lost some of his first choices to my command. And too, he was trying to appear the better man. COL Ice Man wanted to see the hand I'd folded, so he laid down his card, face up. I looked across the table, and I saw the hand he used to bid me off the table, with two black aces and a pair of eights. I stood up and let out a low whistle. "You have Wild Bill Hickok's hand, a *dead man's hand*." I knew him to be slightly superstitious, and I was enjoying the turn around. He had the look of a man who'd seen a ghost. It looked like he wasn't the complete winner he'd hoped to be.

"COL Kahless, I want to see your hand," he said, wanting to know if he truly beat me or if he just wagered me off the table.

"That would be negative, Colonel," I said, picking up my cards.

"I don't have to show them unless I play them." I turned to leave and was face to face with 2LT Pale Rider, who was looking directly and searchingly into my eyes. I slipped the cards into his shirt pocket. "Keep this to yourself."

"CPT Ripsnort, the party's over, I've got a war to fight."

"Aye sir," he replied.

CPT America, his crew and passengers of the transport freighter *America* started for the exit. COL Ice Man cashed his chips in and put the money into a fat wallet. He stopped on the way out and gave me a last look, but I smiled and went to bed.

Blaze's pups were weaned now, and since the freighter *America* was going past Luna on the way back to Earth, I sent COL Red Fangs his pup, true to my word. After a videoconference to Luna, COL Red Fangs chose his pup and CPT America agreed to deliver the young male. The rest of the pups save one were given to various passengers of the two transport freighters for transport to the new owners.

It was time for my rack rotation, and I was exhausted. I awoke after a good sleep. I had fifteen minutes to vacate before the next occupant would take possession. Through sleep filled eyes I noticed that I had company. 2LT Pale Rider was standing beside my bunk. Rubbing the sleep out of my eyes, I sat up.

"Son, did they make you the next shift in this bunk, or do you have business with me?"

"I have something to ask you. It is usually hard to talk privately on this vessel, being kind of crowded. I wanted to ask you a question or two."

The occupants of the other racks were stirring, and it looked as if we wouldn't be getting any privacy.

"Let's have our conversation in the cargo bay. Give me a minute to get dressed."

"Thank you, sir."

I rolled out of bed and got dressed, brushed my teeth and combed my hair. My sniper followed me to the cargo bay, and seeing it unoccupied, I closed the door.

"Okay, shoot."

"Colonel, you had four kings, why didn't you take his money?"

"Lieutenant, the Corps taught you about honor, right?"

"Sir, yes sir."

"Was it honorable to gamble with a man's career and break a promise? I mean, can a man be bought or sold with money?"

"No, sir. I see. So it was an honor decision for you?"

"Yes, that's correct. I refused to trade a dog for a man, and I won't gamble with a man like property, even if he's assigned to me. No, make that especially if he's assigned to me."

"I see."

"Son, you are a marine. Why was your first choice Mars? There are other posts to fill your dance card."

"There have been scores of novels about Mars going back to before Edgar Rice Burroughs wrote about John Carter of Mars. It seemed to go there would be the adventure of a lifetime. But more than that sir, I heard that honor is expected of everyone that serves there."

"That it is."

"Sir, you left forty eight thousand dollars on the table."

"Then make sure you are well worth it," I said, smiling.

He smiled in return. "Sir, yes sir."

"Son, let me catch a shower. Have you had breakfast yet?"

"Sir, no sir."

"If you wait until the regular morning breakfast shift is over, I'll pull out a couple of mako shark steaks, and we'll eat them with whatever is available for breakfast."

"Yes sir, that sounds great."

Climbing into the shower, I turned on the faucet and the water fell like warm rain. Resisting the impulse to shower for pleasure, I quickly wet down my front and then my back, turned it off, soaped up and then rinsed off. We took sailor's showers to conserve water. Even the shower water and dishwater around here is filtered and recycled. I dressed and spent a few minutes in morning prayers and read from Psalms 1.

"Blessed is the man who walks not in the counsel of the ungodly, or stands in the way of sinners, or sits in the seat of the scornful... but his delight is in the law of the Lord, and in his law does he meditate day and night."

I pulled out my sealed stainless-steel container, where I kept a portion of mako shark steaks and ribeyes to share with the other passengers on the long trip home. It had sealed sections, which contained sets of two shark or ribeye steaks, wrapped in plastic, with dry ice in each section. Generally I shared a steak with each passenger onboard during the flight. It is amazing how much networking and friends that can be made that way. Treating corporals and colonels alike, I remind them I have no real command function on this vessel, and we need not observe fraternization rules here. I haven't had a command very long, and I was experimenting with how far I could go with fraternization without damaging my ability to command. However, I'm a rarity. Most command officers don't like to let go of that dominant position, even for a little while.

I was moved when I saw a foreign president once, with an apron on, serving his soldiers Christmas dinner. It was probably a photo op, but it made a lasting impression on me. After all these years, I can't remember who that president was, but I remember what he did. This was my first leave as a commander. On these trips, I didn't intend to pay any attention to fraternization boundaries unless necessary. This is a situation on our transport freighter trips where obviously my command rank has no function on this transport. The transport freighter captain in most instances retains authority. In general, I don't play poker on Mars with enlisted men or drink socially with them, with the exception of Chief Wolverine. I reserve playing of poker and an occasional drink for my officers.

After grilling the shark steaks, I spent some time getting to know my new sniper. I outlined the plans I had for a sniper school and a sniper team, led by him, to increase our field effectiveness. He listened intently and asked a few questions but was very excited about the new idea.

I got to know my new bomber pilot and felt we were going to have a good working relationship. He turned out to be second-generation Chinese. His parents were loyal Americans, wishing nothing more than their son to serve his country honorably. He spoke Chinese fluently, and I mentally noted I might need his language skills someday. The rest of the trip was pretty much routine. We arrived exactly three and a half months to the day that we left Utah. Everything was pretty much in order, which just reaffirmed that my executive officer was indeed the man for the job. Upon arrival, we parted with the pup that looked like Blaze's great pyrenees parent. He was going to COL Exit Wound on the freighter to Europa.

HELL FROM HELLAS PLANITIA

Earth date: June 7, 1984—Martian year 199, Sol Martis, sol 3 of the Martian Month Gemini—sol of the Martian year 336

"Engine critical, twenty seconds to destruct," reported the computer's sweet sounding female voice.

"My engine is redlining and about to blow," reported LTC Killer Instinct. With that, he ejected from his doomed hovertank and drifted to safety. The American snipers were keeping the Soviet snipers busy, denying them their prize.

We're halfway around the globe, at Hellas Planitia, the largest impact basin in the solar system. The Hellas impact basin was a two kilometer deep impact crater spanning 2,300 kilometers—formed long ago before my ancestors were sticking mastodons with pointed sticks.

The Soviets and Americans have both suffered serious losses. We'd lost three pilots to snipers, the Soviets three. There were only two tanks intact, one on each side. Both were damaged heavily, and our particle beam cannons were completely discharged. Both American and Soviet rearm vehicles had been destroyed. Tkachenko and I'd both survived to the end, with our tanks intact and both realized the problem. Neither side was able to collect the scrap without cooperation from the other side. We were a long way from home, and there would be no reinforcements today. I opened up a link to the Soviet commander.

"We're at a stalemate, it seems." There was a pause from the Soviet.

"We could fight together, you and I. Whoever wins takes all of the alloy-x scrap; the other side returns with nothing. In the event of a draw, we split it all."

"I accept. I get to choose weapons. As it was your idea; I choose pistols."

"I disagree. You are an expert pistol shot from what I hear. Let us use our hands to see who is the better man."

"Agreed." Shooting him would have been my preference, but getting a chance to beat him down would be almost as enjoyable. If I beat him to death, I would be done with him forever. If I only beat him down, it would change the tone of all future interactions.

"This is COL Kahless, all Americans stand-down."

On a loudspeaker into the battlefield and on the Soviet unsecured channel, I heard, "All Soviets cease hostilities." This was said in English, for my men's benefit. The only two offensive units on the field were Tkachenko's and mine. My only concern was that one of our men might put a sniper bullet in one of us when we got out of our tanks. I must admit; shooting him would have solved a lot of problems.

"Our constructor will put up a bioshelter large enough to fight in and for all of the men to watch. First man who's down for the count of ten loses—there will be no decision or points. Bouts will be three minutes, break clean and return to your corner, and one minute's rest. We'll observe international boxing rules. We'll flip a coin to determine who the announcer is and who the referee is. Each of us may be attended in our corner by one corner man and a medic."

"Of what purpose are these rules? If the referee is Soviet or American, he will be suspected as biased. Any disqualification would be suspect, yes?"

"Will you agree, on your honor, to fight by the rules?"

"Dah. I agree, on my honor as a Soviet officer."

"I also agree on my honor as an American officer. There will be no disqualification. Each side will be allowed one armed security attachment. No other personnel can carry weapons into the bioshelter. Our security team will search your men and yours will search mine. I will have a bioshelter made with a ring, two dressing rooms and bleachers for both sides. It will take about thirty minutes to build the bioshelter."

"Agreed. We should also have thirty minutes to dress, stretch and prepare."

"Then it is agreed."

"One more thing, my men will be broadcasting fight live to Camp Lenin over satellite radio. I assume you will be doing the same." He was obviously convinced that he would win, and was looking forward to scoring a propaganda victory. If we did not broadcast the fight live to our post, it meant that I was afraid he would win.

"Absolutely, my men love a good sporting match."

"Comrade Voronin."

"Yes, comrade Colonel."

"I will be fighting the American colonel in a boxing match in one hour in a bioshelter they are building. Let them broadcast the fight to Camp Leninskaya live over the Camp intercom system."

"Comrade Colonel, what if you lose to the American? It would be very bad for morale if this was broadcasted live."

"We are fighting in front of all of our men here. We will not be able to hide anything. Besides, I will not lose. I will break his body and then his spirit."

"Yes, comrade Colonel."

LTC Voronin walked to the Soviet Constructor to use the radio. He was greeted by the constructor Chief and given access to the radio. The Soviet officer hailed his post.

"This is LTC Voronin; patch me through to tactical operations."

"Yes, comrade Sub-Colonel," answered the young radio operator and transferred the call.

"Yes, comrade Sub-Colonel?" asked MAJ Arkady Ivanov, Chief of tactical operations.

"COL Tkachenko will be fighting the American colonel in a boxing match. COL Tkachenko wants us to radio a commentary of the fight while it is occurring. You will air it over the post intercom, for all to hear."

"Yes, comrade Sub-Colonel."

"We will radio the fight live to you in about one hour."

"Yes, comrade Sub-Colonel."

LTC Voronin turned to walk out. One of the things that made him a great leader was his ability to remember details about his men. He fixed his eyes on SSGT Vasily Butkovsky. "Senior Sergeant, you were Olympic boxer, yes?"

"Yes, comrade Sub-Colonel. I was an alternate, but did not get to fight."

"Then you will make a good sports commentator. The Americans have two commentators. Choose someone to help you."

"Yes, comrade Sub-Colonel."

"Good! Bring radio equipment and report to the bioshelter that the Americans are building. You will be commenting and transmitting the fight via radio to Camp Leninskaya for a live transmission over the post intercom."

"Yes, comrade Sub-Colonel," he said as he moved quickly to gather up the equipment he would need.

MAJ Oleg Savenkov lifted an eyebrow as he heard only half of the conversation. "Comrade Major, what is going on?" MAJ Ivanov looked around the room and considered the spot he was in. He just received a direct order that the first officer passed down from the camp commander. The order was a direct concern to MAJ Savenkov, since he was the Chief political officer on the post.

"MAJ Savenkov, we should speak privately." The Chief of tactical operations led the political officer to an empty room and closed the door. "MAJ Savenkov, COL Tkachenko will be fighting the American colonel in a boxing match. He wants us to radio a commentary of the fight while it is occurring live, to air it over the post intercom for all to hear."

"What if he loses? Is he mad? No! I am the Chief political officer here, and I say no!" MAJ Savenkov thought about the other side of the issue. "But then again, if he beats the American badly, it will be very good propaganda, yes?"

"Yes, comrade Major."

"Record the fight, but do not broadcast live. We will wait until fight is over. If our colonel wins or at least fights to a draw, then we will broadcast fight over intercom. Our people here cannot tell if it is broadcast in *real time* or if it is recording."

"Yes, comrade Major."

"Are you sure you want to do this?" asked the American first officer.

"I was hoping to get to shoot him, but this will have to do."

"You let him trick you into broadcasting this live over our 1-MC."

"Yes, I know. You'll need to call the post and inform them."

"Yes, sir."

"Tkachenko tricked us concerning the live transmission. Let's return the favor. When you build the ring, loosen the ropes and canvas. He appears as though he is a little stronger than I am and I want to be able to *make like a turtle* if I need to."

"Gonna rope-a-dope, then?"

"Maybe. I just want to make my arsenal larger. I hope Tkachenko didn't see the Ali-Foreman fight in Zaire or the Ali-Frasier fight in Manila."

"Do you want me in your corner?"

"Of course."

"Okay, I'll be on my way, then." LTC Killer Instinct took a walk to the American's constructor. Chief Hardcase yielded the radio to him. "MAJ Norsemun, this is LTC Killer Instinct."

"Yes, Colonel, what can I do for you?"

"It seems our battle on the field was a draw, and COL Kahless and the Soviet colonel have agreed to duke it out over the scrap recovery."

"You're kidding!"

"No. COL Kahless has agreed to having a fight announcer radio back the fight to our post for you to broadcast live over the 1-MC."

"Do you realize what this will do to morale if COL Kahless loses?"

"Yes, I do, but that is an order, and he is not going to lose."

"Will that be all, sir?"

"That's all, Killer Instinct out."

"I need to speak with you privately in my office."

"Sir, yes sir."

"Close the door, Captain." CPT Black Ice complied. The post's security chief took the offered seat.

"What's up Major?"

"I just received an order to broadcast a live fist fight between COL Kahless and COL Tkachenko over the 1-MC."

"This is not a security issue, unless COL Kahless gets hurt or killed. However, it would be bad for morale if he lost. I wouldn't worry. The colonel teaches my karate class and he can take care of himself. You have no choice, though, right?"

"It was a direct order. I must broadcast the fight over the 1-MC live."

"Major, you don't want to do this, do you?"

"I will follow orders, of course. I will also record the fight in case of technical difficulties." CPT Black Ice wondered what kind of *technical difficulties* the major might be planning.

"Sir, yes sir."

Chief Hardcase had completed the bioshelter, bleachers, ring, two tables for the sports commentators, and two dressing rooms for the fighters. Both fighters were readying themselves for the fight.

Most of the senior American pilots were somehow involved in the fight: COL Kahless, LTC Killer Instinct, MAJ Luv2bomb, and CPT Two Horses. The American spectators comprised of four combat pilots, constructor crewmen, scavenger crewmen, and medical ambulance crewmen. The ranking American spectator sat on his side of the bleachers, flipping his challenge coin bearing his unit information between the back of his fingers, lost deep in thought. The challenge coin was typically awarded combat personnel to help identify them as *friendlies* to local civilians. Mars had no civilians, but the tradition ran deep and the men took pride in their challenge coins. CPT Janus Dread looked over at the Soviets on the other set of bleachers and addressed his men. "Look—we may not be able to get a beer here, but nothing says we can't gamble a little." He arose, and the other men followed him to the Soviet bleachers. The bleachers were each twelve feet from the ring on both sides, and the ring was twenty feet across. The Americans closed the distance of forty-four feet before security could arrive. Security from both sides moved to intercept them. They were too far away from the Americans to get there on time.

The Americans reached the Soviet bleachers and CPT Janus Dread addressed the ranking Soviet, MAJ Pavils Jankauskas. "We would like to make a friendly wager with you concerning the fight." Just then the security teams arrived.

"We are not going to have any trouble here, are we Captain?" 1SGT Justice and SSGT Zhukov tensely watched the group for signs of trouble.

"Nyet, our American hosts have come to make a friendly wager. All in the spirit of sportsmanship, yes?" asked MAJ Jankauskas. Both security teams relaxed a little.

"So what do you want to bet that our commander beats your commander?" queried the Soviet.

CPT Janus Dread realized that they probably only had script or at best, rubles. He noticed the Soviet glance at his flight watch. Time was short; the match was soon to begin. He pulled his sleeve up and showed his watch. "My watch for your watch."

"Dah, I agree," said the Soviet with a cold, mocking smile. No doubt he imagined being in possession of a genuine American pilot's watch by the end of the match.

One by one the Americans and Soviets paired off with their Soviet counterparts, and bet their time pieces against the outcome of the match. Finally, even the security teams got in on it.

Kahless put on his blue boxing trunks that bore the dove on an American flag crest of the Keichu-Ryu dojo he was affiliated with he was in high school and college. He had removed his shirt and finished stretching and getting mentally prepared for the fight.

1SGT Specialist finished wrapping Kahless' hands with tape, and he smeared a light coating of grease on the colonel's cheeks under his eyes. Finally, he took a syringe out of his medical bag and prepared a shot.

"I can't be doping up," Kahless protested.

"This is not dope. It's just a shot of vitamin C and B-12. The 'C' will keep your legs from cramping late in the fight, and the B-12 will give you some extra strength when you need it."

"Very good." Kahless' medic gave him his shot, and he was ready.

"There you go, Colonel."

"Thank you, it's good to have you in my corner."

Ring announcer MAJ Volkov and referee MAJ Luv2bomb examined the tape on COL Kahless' hands. Once satisfied, the two men went to the Soviet dressing room to perform the same inspection on the Soviet fighter.

His executive officer returned from making his call to MAJ Norsemun, and laced his gloves on his commander. The two men prayed together, and his first officer broke the silence. "Sir, it's time. You know what you have to do." He nodded and walked to the ring with his first officer and his medic.

"Camp SEAL, we are broadcasting live from Hellas Planitia. This is CPT Two Horses, and I will be your commentator for this fight, assisted by 1LT Pale Rider."

"This is MAJ Norsemun and we read you loud and clear." The major started the recording, and put the fight on the 1-MC after turning the volume control almost off. He had complied with the order, he thought. No one told him how loud to broadcast it.

"CPT Cipher."

"Sir, yes sir."

"Leave the 1-MC alone and do not fool around with the incoming transmission from the field. I am privately listening to the transmission in my office."

"Sir, yes sir."

CPT Cipher was very curious about what was going on, but the icy expression on the major's face told him to mind his own business.

"Camp SEAL, COL Kahless is approaching the ring with his second and his cut man. He looks serious. COL Tkachenko is moving toward the ring. That is one pissed-off looking Soviet."

"Camp Lenin, this is SSGT Butkovsky. We are broadcasting to you from Hellas Planitia. The fight will soon begin. Our colonel is accompanied by his first officer and a medic. He has look that would melt steel. Our colonel is left-handed, and the American will certainly have much difficulty."

"And this is JSGT Pavlov; I will be assisting the senior sergeant in this telecast. It should be a very good fight. For Soviet motherland!"

The Americans won the coin toss and the referee would be MAJ Luv2bomb and the announcer would be Soviet MAJ Mikhail Volkov.

MAJ Norsemun closed the door to his office and put the transmission on his desktop speaker. CPT Black Ice was carrying two hot sandwiches and a pair of cold near beers. "Mind if I join you for lunch, Major?"

"You do realize this makes you a co-conspirator?"

"If we divide the blame in half it will sting less if we get into trouble. Besides, I'd take a demotion to lieutenant just to listen to this match live," he said, grinning like a 'possum eating persimmons.

"Quiet, they are announcing the fight."

Chief security and political officer MAJ Oleg Savenkov had the fight routed to his office. The head of Soviet tactical operations knocked on the closed door.

"Come in, Major, they are announcing the fight." MAJ Savenkov opened his bottom desk drawer, pulled out a bottle of vodka and two glasses, poured two drinks, and handed a glass to MAJ Ivanov.

"Sit down Arkady, please."

As per agreement, all personnel except security were to remain seated while the security teams led the fighters, their seconds and their cut men to the squared ring. The American security team set up their video cassette recorders to record the fight. They usually used the recorders to document events of interest following a field engagement. If Kahless won, it would make for a great showing to the rest of the post when they got home. The Americans on their bleachers remained seated but applauded loudly while the Americans approached the ring. The American's second lifted the ropes while COL Kahless stuck his leg through and entered the ring. The American team approached the corner with a blue turnbuckle. COL Kahless was wearing his flight boots and a pair of blue trunks, with the crest of his old Keichu-Ryu dojo on the right thigh. The American was solid, lean and well-built for a man in his mid-thirties: symmetrical as a Greek god, strong arms from lifting weights and strong legs from running five miles a day. His only imperfection was his slightly crooked nose he earned in a college karate tournament. He exuded the confidence of a warrior tested in many challenges and not found wanting. He meditated on his men that Tkachenko had killed and the communist threat to his country. The stakes were very personal, both idealistically and in a practical sense. Losing the alloy-x would severely weaken his position on Mars to the point that eventually a post siege could be possible. He stretched his muscles on the ropes with a sense of cool detachment as his Soviet antagonist approached the ring.

The Soviet team followed suit. The very stoic Soviets spectators looked unmoved but were very focused on their leader's approach. Tkachenko wore his flight boots and a bright red pair of trunks with the gold hammer and sickle, the Communist symbol on the left thigh. He was the embodiment of the Soviet ideal: strong, hard and aggressive. He cut a formidable figure: strong in his loins and upper body with sledgehammer fists, not a large man in size but hard as Ukrainian maple. The nickname "Ukrainian Wolf" suited the predator who hunted the American today. He had been waiting a long time to punish the American for killing COL Kiknadze. The Soviet Central Command had high expectations when they transferred him to Mars to assume command. Part of the expectation was the killing of COL Kahless. His second likewise lifted the ropes for his man and Tkachenko stepped into the ring.

MAJ Volkov entered the center ring with a microphone. "I am MAJ Volkov, and I will be announcing this fight. He pointed to the pride of the SCA, his countenance beaming like a light beacon and his voice gushed with enthusiasm like a new strike at a Russian oil well. "In the red corner, standing at 175 centimeters, weighing in at seventy-four kilograms from Ukraine, U.S.S.R. is COL Yuri Tkachenko!" COL Tkachenko raised his hands to bask in the support of his men. The Soviets cheered for him while the Americans keep silent or booed. Professionally, but with the air of a businessman declaring some unpleasant business, he pointed to the American. "And In blue corner, standing at 176 centimeters, weighing in at seventy-six kilograms, from U.S.A., is COL Kahless." COL Kahless showed off a series of punches and raised his hands above his head for his men. The Americans cheered for their commander while Soviets observed with contempt.

MAJ Luv2bomb entered the center of the ring. He motioned to the two fighters to join him. "This is a boxing match with international rules observed by the contestants on their honor, with no disqualification. There is no set number of rounds. This match will be fought until one man is down for the count. Rounds are three minutes long and one minute's rest. If a man is down, you must return to a neutral corner while I count. At the end of each round, each fighter will break clean and return to his own corner. I have been advised that I cannot stop the fight if I think one of you is in danger of being seriously hurt. Your seconds and medics will have to throw in the towel. Watch the rabbit punches, kidney punches, and hitting below the belt; let's make it a clean fight," admonished the referee. The Soviet gave the Chinese-American referee a look of contempt, then stared at his rival. The only thing he despised worse than Americans were Chinese-Americans.

"I will beat you like curr dog!" the Soviet sneered.

"Fight first, brag later, bigmouth!"

The two fighters touched gloves together in the customary boxer's handshake. The air was filled with the expectation of the violent storm brewing. Both men returned to their corners and awaited the bell. The

American XO offered the mouth guard to his commander, and he put it in his mouth and bit down.

"Colonel, the Soviet is a southpaw; he shoots a sniper rifle left-handed. His left eye is the *dominant* one. Stay away from his left hand and try to break his ribs on his left side—close his left eye if you can. You're ambidextrous, so fight him left-handed until I tell you to switch."

COL Kahless bit down on his mouthpiece and glanced at his medic. "Any medical advice?"

"Yeah, don't let him hit you."

"Thanks, I'll keep that in mind."

"Watch the American; he is a skilled martial artist. Do not underestimate him. Draw first blood and make him doubt himself. You appear to be stronger than he is. A long fight would favor you. Wear him down and finish him off," counseled the Soviet first officer. Tkachenko nodded and bit down on his mouth guard.

"This could be the most memorable fight ever fought on Mars," noted CPT Two Horses.

"COL Tkachenko is a southpaw, and I'll bet the Soviets assume they can screw up his rhythm with a mirror image stance. Hence the old boxing idiom, 'southpaws should be drowned at birth,' " commented 1LT Pale Rider.

"Then the Soviets are in for a rude awakening. We both know that our commander is ambidextrous and is likely to fight left-handed. This will give him a stronger lead hand as well."

MAJ Savenkov adjusted the volume on his receiver to get the best compromise between loudness and being able to keep the sounds within the closed door of his office. The announcer came through in a clear voice, but not too loud. "The bell has rung, and both fighters are approaching center of ring. The winner will be rewarded by recovering the alloy-x scrap, and the loser will go home with nothing. We'll show them Kuzka's mother," said SSGT Butkovsky.

"It looks like the American is going to fight left-handed. Surely he will be at a disadvantage against a true left-hander," speculated JSGT Pavlov.

MAJ Norsemun was just finishing his sandwich when the bell rung, making him sit upright. His eyes were riveted to the radio as if staring at it would affect the outcome. "Both fighters have assumed a left-handed fighting stance and are now set. Each one is doing exploratory right jabs looking for a weakness," reported CPT Two Horses.

"What a fight! Each fighter looks about the same height and weight, both athletically built, and about the same arm length-reach, wouldn't you say, Captain?"

"From here they look like equals, but as you know, heart is what counts. We will see who has heart." CPT Black Ice moved closer to the receiver so as not to miss any details.

The Soviet was determined to show the American that he was to be feared, early in the match. His jaw was set in a resolute and menacing fashion, looking for an early win. The American was using his footwork and bobbing his head back and forth to keep from getting hit while he looked for an opening.

MAJ Ivanov drained his glass of vodka and poured another. "COL Tkachenko lunged forward with his left foot assuming right-handed stance, firing a stinging left and following by a right cross. The American side stepped the right cross by moving to his left. Our colonel turned his body right to follow his movement, left-handed stance again, and caught the American unexpectedly with a hard left cross to the mouth," reported SSGT Butkovsky.

"He appears to be bleeding. It is like American movie with James Bond, *From Russia With Love*," mocked JSGT Pavlov.

MAJ Norsemun cursed under his breath at the news of first blood going to the Soviet. "It looks as though COL Tkachenko has made a statement that he is here to fight," said CPT Two Horses.

"He certainly has, and this may be a long, hard fight," injected 1LT Pale Rider. The young sniper rolled up a piece of paper into a tube and looked at the Soviet through the hole.

"Don't worry, someday your time will come," consoled CPT Two Horses.

"So close and yet so far away," the young sniper sighed. "I've been looking for this chance ever since I got to Mars. Here is my target less than thirty feet away and I have no rifle!"

"Have patience, my young friend."

COL Kahless backed up and gave his opponent a congratulatory salute for scoring *first blood*. The two warriors continued their probing into the other's weaknesses with right jabs and an occasional left until the bell signaled the end of round one.

"He bleeds. See Yuri, he is quite human. Keep up the pressure and do not let up," counseled the Soviet first officer.

"He is stronger and faster than he looks," confessed COL Tkachenko. His medic gave him a water bottle. He rinsed his mouth out and spat into the offered bucket, then bit down on his mouth guard.

"You are more than enough to vanquish him." The colonel nodded to his first officer in agreement.

"Don't worry about it, Colonel. So he got off a lucky punch. Keep focused and keep your guard up," said the American first officer. The American rinsed his mouth out and spit into the bucket. 1SGT Specialist examined the cut on his lip and closed it.

"It wasn't a lucky punch. He is smart and very strong. He reminds me of one of the lumberjacks back home in Louisiana, not very big in size but hard as an oak. I feel like I'm hitting a tree," said Kahless.

"Then be the axe, and cut him down," encouraged his first officer. Kahless' medic put the mouthpiece back in, and Kahless bit down.

"And there is bell for round two," SSGT Butkovsky reported."

"Watching the Soviet bleachers is like studying Soviet society. When their man drew first blood, they were stoically unmoved. I guess the old saying that there is 'no sex in the Soviet Union' is true," concluded 1LT Pale Rider.

CPT Two Horses looked at his junior partner with a quizzical look. "I guess I haven't heard that expression. What are you getting at?"

"Well, if our guy had drawn first blood, what would our bleachers look like?"

"They'd be up on their feet shouting."

"Exactly my point. In the Soviet Union, they are trained to keep their thoughts to themselves. Individual expression is not encouraged. People in a repressive society bottle up their feelings and keep their emotions in check for the collective good. They are ever careful of their Soviet 'big brother'. So they watch stoically."

Being cooped up with CPT Black Ice in a closed-in space made MAJ Norsemun uneasy. It was not because he didn't like him. He did, but the major was socially ill-at-ease with people. MAJ Norsemun felt the air in his office getting tighter. MAJ Black Ice knew him well and recognized the early symptoms of a panic-attack.

He accessed the comm. "CPL Gray Eagle?"

"Sir, yes sir?"

"Please bring Blaze to MAJ Norsemun's office, and two more near beers."

"Sir, yes sir."

CPT Black Ice looked at the major and then his watch. "Corporal, make that two real beers. I'm off-duty."

"Sir, yes sir."

The major smiled at CPT Black Ice sheepishly and said, "Thank You."

The captain smiled. "Always ready to oblige, Major."

CPL Gray Eagle arrived with Blaze five minutes later and handed CPT Black Ice the beers. He directed his question to the major. "Should I leave her for a while, sir?"

"Yes, Corporal, give her a couple of hours."

"Sir, yes sir."

Major Norsemun's heart rate returned to normal with the cold wet nose of the dog pressing into his hand. He petted her and turned his attention to the fight which was already in progress in round two.

The Soviet catapulted himself from his corner like a stone from a medieval war machine hurled at his American rival. He continued to capitalize on his earlier first blood score, getting right down to business early in round two. He brought all of his fighting skill to bear on his American adversary, systematically attempting to grind and wear his opponent down. He landed two blows to each one of his opponent's, firing straight rights and an occasional punishing left. The American bade his time and waited for an opening. His opening came, with twelve seconds to spare in the second round. He launched a whipping left uppercut that lifted the Soviet off of his feet and put him on the canvas. Kahless withdrew to a neutral corner while the referee started the count.

"One—two—three," started the referee. He was acutely conscious that a fast count would cause the Soviets to cry foul. The Soviet was clawing at the canvas, trying to get to his knees, and then to his feet. His foggy brain was only conscious of the hot ring lights on his back and the canvas resin on his knees. Had the punch been one-half inch to the right and it would have been "lights out." "Four—five—six." Tkachenko's brain ascended though the fog and he was aware of his second shouting to get up. The Soviet was now on one knee, making the most of the count. "Seven—eight—nine." Tkachenko was on his feet. His American antagonist moved from the neutral corner toward the Soviet as the bell rang announcing the end of round two.

"The American got in a lucky punch. It should not affect the outcome at all," said SSGT Butkovsky. MAJ Savenkov did not like the outcome of round two, but approved of the way SSGT Butkovsky commented on the reversal. It was a very "politically correct" way for a socialist to view the round.

"And that is the end of round two!" announced CPT Two Horses. "Our colonel showed the Soviets that he is a force to be reckoned with."

"He certainly has, Captain. Now the Soviets can't assume that Tkachenko will dominate the match and do with our commander as he chooses!" exclaimed 1LT Pale Rider.

MAJ Norsemun and CPT Black Ice had nearly cheered themselves hoarse with the excitement of the knockdown. Blaze joined in and barked excitedly.

"Very, very nice, colonel. You know you can do this—and now he does, too. He is a volume puncher, but that doesn't mean anything because you're not fighting for points. Every fighter has just so many punches in him before he's punched out. You have great footwork; fight him peek-a-boo style. Keep focused and choose your shots carefully," advised the American first officer. Kahless nodded while his cut man removed his mouthpiece and washed his face with a wet sponge.

"What happened out there?!" the Soviet first officer asked. His medic took his mouthpiece and examined his face for cuts.

"He got a lucky punch in. He hits hard, and I did not expect him to be that strong. I will not overestimate him again!" His medic put his mouthpiece back in, and he bit down as the bell signaled the beginning of round three.

"The Soviet came out of his corner with guns blazing, firing six quick hard right jabs in succession at our man. COL Kahless, assuming a peek-a-boo stance has blocked half of them, deflected two more but got a stinging jab on his left jaw. Kahless stepped back, and then moved forward to get himself set," reported CPT Two Horses.

"Our commander is engaging the Soviet again, playing peek-a-boo with his adversary, keeping him from effectively scoring against his face. The Soviet is switching to working on our man's ribs," said 1LT Pale Rider.

CPT Janus Dread watched the round at the edge of his seat, crouched and leaning forward like a tiger, ready to pounce. The American bleachers were alive with excitement.

"Beat hell out of 'em, Colonel," shouted 1LT Scourge.

"Hit him, Colonel. Hit him for the U S of A," hollered CPT Boneman.

The tension of the normally stoic Soviets was like an internal pressure cooker. Though they watched in relative silence, a cauldron of Slavic passions was slowly boiling. MAJ Jankauskas watched the match, outwardly appearing to be utterly detached, but inwardly his blood pressure was climbing. To be defeated by an American was unthinkable! The Soviet military was supreme, and their commander was a great man. He absentmindedly glanced at his watch and frowned.

Majors Savenkov and Ivanov leaned forward to strain their ears for every detail. "Our commander seems to be very effective in firing punishing blows to the American's left side. The American countered with a right hook to the head—and another—and another! And there is the bell to end round three," reported SSGT Butkovsky.

"COL Tkachenko will soon start dominating the match," predicted JSGT Pavlov. He looked at his watch and over at the American commentators. He had bet his watch against 1LT Pale Rider.

If the next three rounds were scored by judges, they would have declared them a draw—each man landing punches on the other and trying to maneuver his opponent into position for a knockout punch. None came, and the bell for the end of round six sounded. Both fighters moved to their corners a little slower, with a little less bounce to their step than at the start.

CPL Gray Eagle knew something was wrong. MAJ Norsemun and CPT Black Ice were hiding something. CPT Two Horses was his father and he was COL Kahless' aide. He was worried about them both. COL Kahless maintained a mysterious godlike reputation of being everywhere—hearing and knowing everything. His aide knew the truth, and so did MAJ Norsemun and CPT Black Ice. The only common areas without listening devices were MAJ Norsemun's and CPT Black Ice's personal offices. They were both part of the technical process of the colonel's godlike mystique. CPL Gray Eagle just had to know what was going on. He slipped into his commander's office and got a small listening device out of his desk drawer, grabbed two more beers and headed to MAJ Norsemun's office. He knocked on the closed door to MAJ Norsemun's office, and the major turned the radio's volume knob off.

"Come in," said MAJ Norsemun. He was anxious to get rid of CPL Gray Eagle before round seven started. The young corporal set the two beers on the major's desk with his right hand. As he leaned over the desk, he slipped the listening device under the edge of the major's desk with his left hand. CPT Black Ice was not distracted by the beer. He had been in security for too many years to let an amateur place a bug in his presence.

"Thank you corporal. You can put that thing back in your pocket. If your daddy and your commander weren't in the field, you would be in the brig. I know you are worried. Sit! You will serve out the time for your crime in here until the fight ends," lectured CPT Black Ice. MAJ Norsemun scowled at him for the invasion but didn't say anything.

The young corporal lit up and said, "Thank you, sir." MAJ Norsemun turned the volume knob back up.

Kahless bit down on his mouthpiece as the bell announced the beginning of round seven. Sweat ran down his face, dripping down his shoulders like anointing oil, confirming him king of the blue corner and contender for the crown of Mars' squared ring. He stood ready to exercise his "divine right" to pound the king of the red corner into obeisance.

Tkachenko reminded himself that he was fighting for his socialist principals, once and for all proving that socialism was superior to capitalism. But a realization deep down in his heart was surfacing: the greater reality and with crystal clarity. The fact was this wasn't about politics at all. This was about two men, and though he would not admit it, he was fighting for himself. His reputation and pride were on the line, and he would not be disgraced by losing to a weak American.

The two gladiators squared off again and started their dance. Kahless opened up with two quick and well-timed right jabs to the left eye of the Soviet. Tkachenko flinched and then countered with a bone-jarring hard right hook to the left ribcage of the American. Kahless pulled back, painfully aware of bruised ribs. Tkachenko's vision in his left eye was not as clear as it was before the swelling started.

"Both fighters are infighting up close, avoiding being hit by blows with their opponent's whole body weight. They are working the bodies of their opponents over closely, capitalizing on the closeness with jabs to the body and uppercuts. The referee has had to break up clinches now on both sides," commented CPT Two Horses. CPL Gray Eagle leaned forward and was relieved to hear his father's voice.

"It looks as though both men are getting a little tired," observed the junior American officer.

"Yes, this looks as though this is a real test of endurance and stamina, and who has the most heart," said the senior commenter.

"And there is the bell and the end of round seven. This has been a close but exciting round!" exclaimed 1LT Pale Rider.

"It certainly was," agreed CPT Two Horses.

Tkachenko's aide was examining his left eye while sponging his face with water.

"I have been watching the American. He is tiring faster than you are. Control the pace and keep up the pressure. When he runs out, you can finish him," his first officer said.

Tkachenko nodded his agreement.

Kahless sat down in the folded chair while his medic examined his ribs.

"Tkachenko is still too fresh. Me? I'm getting tired."

His second nodded. "You remember the Jack London book, *Boxing Stories* that I loaned you?"

"Sure."

"What did the old 'un do against the stronger young 'un in "A Piece of Steak?" "

"Sorry, haven't gotten to it yet."

"Just this, he worked the end of each match, so it ended in his corner. All he had to do was sit down, while his opponent had to walk the distance each time across the ring to sit down. He got his full minute's rest and his opponent got at best, forty-five seconds. You do the same."

CPT Black Ice decided to order some more beer and some snacks. He didn't want to send CPL Gray Eagle because he might somehow reveal what was going on. Security people strongly believed that "loose lips sink ships." He called the mess hall.

"Yes sir," answered Mess SGT Gutshot.

"Sergeant, can you send one of your boys over to MAJ Norsemun's office with a six-pack of real beer and a snack for Blaze?"

"Sir, yes sir."

"What else do you have that goes with beer for us?"

"I have some roasted soy nuts seasoned with garlic and cayenne, and some sweet rolls I just pulled out of the oven."

"Sounds good, send them up."

"Sir, yes sir."

The bell sounded for round eight, and Kahless moved only one-quarter of the distance to meet Tkachenko, capitalizing on the new strategy of strength management. Tkachenko took it as a sign of weakness and launched his attack like a pair of scud missiles flying at his enemy's face. Kahless braced himself for the onslaught, blocking most of the blows. Tkachenko connected with a nasty straight right and blackened the American's other eye. Kahless shook it off and fired right-left-right combinations and backed his opponent up to the ropes. Both fighters continued with close infighting until Kahless smacked his adversary with an uppercut to the solar plexus, forcing all of the air out of his lungs. Tkachenko could not breathe and was bent over. Before he could recover, Kahless twisted his whole body weight into a devastating right hook to the Soviet's jaw, propelling him through the ropes like some discarded rag doll placed in a giveaway box for Good Will to pick up. Tkachenko landed on the padded floor at the base of the squared ring on the American's side. Security quickly moved to form a shield between the fallen fighter and the American spectators.

The referee directed Kahless to the neutral corner, and he complied. MAJ Luv2Bomb, ever conscious of a fast count being called foul, began the twenty count. "One—two—three—four—five—six—seven—eight—nine—ten," he began. Tkachenko stirred and found his way to one knee. Twice the American had surprised him, and twice had he paid for it. "Eleven—twelve—thirteen." The Soviet approached the ropes and pulled himself up. "Fourteen—fifteen—sixteen," counted the referee. Tkachenko slipped his leg through the ropes and was standing fully upright by the nineteen count.

For a man knocked completely through the ropes and onto the floor, Tkachenko didn't show it. He redoubled his efforts to regain lost momentum. He fought like a man unafraid, undaunted by the setback. Kahless was surprised by the strength and vigor his opponent still had. The American swapped blows with the Soviet and slowly *let* Tkachenko move him toward the American corner. It was slowly, artfully and carefully done, so much so as the Soviet never questioned for a minute why he was three feet from the blue corner when the bell announced the end of round eight. Kahless sat down in his chair and watched his antagonist walk the distance back to his corner. It was a small thing, but in the strategy of strength management, small things add up.

The next three rounds were a grueling exchange of body blows and head shots from both sides. Both warriors wearied themselves trying to grind their opponent down for a knockout punch, to no avail. Tkachenko's left eye went from swollen to black and blood-filled. Kahless had suffered further injury and now two of his ribs were cracked on the left side. Kahless always seemed to be at his corner at the end of the round, and despite his injuries, he slowly got his second wind while the Soviet was slowly becoming spent.

"Arkady, that is your fourth vodka. If we don't eat something soon, we may experience *time travel*. It will not go well with us if it is found that we got drunk, instead of following orders concerning the transmission."

"But of course, Oleg." MAJ Ivanov called the Mess Sergeant and ordered some food. He put the vodka bottle back in the desk drawer until they had eaten something.

MAJ Jankauskas studied the ring with interest when the bell signaled the beginning of round twelve. The internal pressure was simmering within the Slavic warriors and as the pressure increased, demanded release.

"The American is continuing that hiding technique, obviously afraid to be hit. He also looks as though he is beginning to tire before our colonel's relentless attacks. This round should be the turning point for the American's crushing defeat," predicted SSGT Butkovsky.

"I agree, Senior Sergeant. The American has attempted to clinch again, and the referee has broken it up. Both are fighting real close again; our commander is working the midsection of his enemy. The American has landed another hard right to our commander's left eye, but our colonel is continuing to press his attack, not letting up on his opponent."

MAJ Jankauskas and the Soviet pilots increasingly were becoming agitated as the fight became more intense. "The American is firing quick right jabs in rapid succession with his right hand to our colonel's left eye. Another blow from the American—our colonel blocks it and delivers a punishing overhand right, and COL Kahless' nose is gushing blood!" exclaimed JSGT Pavlov.

Kahless clinched his foe in an attempt to slow his momentum down while he could recover from the damage he'd just received. Kahless was bleeding on Tkachenko's sweaty shoulder. The Soviet shook the American to make him let go. "You are finished, give up!" he snarled.

As the referee broke the clench, with bravado he did not feel at the moment, he snapped back, "I'm just getting started."

"The American has our colonel in a clinch to avoid being hit again. The referee is breaking it up," commented JSGT Pavlov.

The internal pressure at the Soviet bleachers had finally reached critical mass, redlined and blew. MAJ Jankauskas stood up with a shout, "Destroy the American dog, Colonel!"

"Show him Kuzka's mother!" shouted 1LT Ryzhkov.

"Well, it seems that there certainly is sex in the Soviet Union," quipped CPT Two Horses.

"I stand corrected, Captain. It just appears that they are slower to arouse," answered his junior partner. "And it looks as though our colonel is about to be saved by the bell. He looks like he took a pretty hard shot to the nose."

"And there is the bell ending round twelve," said SSGT Butkovsky, not happy that it was ending with the American bleeding. He would have much preferred that COL Tkachenko capitalize on the bleeding American's weakened state. "This appears to be the turning point of the match," he reported enthusiastically.

The American medic went to work putting Kahless' nose in place and stopping the bleeding. Kahless' chest was heaving from being out of breath. His first officer sponged the parts of his sweaty brow and face that the medic wasn't working on. In between mouthfuls of blood and sweat running into his eyes, Kahless explained. "I think I'm closing his left eye. It will alter his depth perception if he can't see out of it. It is his dominant eye."

His medic looked him in the eye. "You have got to stop letting him hit you."

"I will keep that under advisement."

His cut man had the bleeding stopped in time for the bell for round thirteen. Kahless rinsed out his mouth and bit down on his mouthpiece.

MAJ Ivanov answered the door and took a tray that the Mess Sergeant had sent them. There were two steaming hot bowls of borsch with sour cream to spoon in a dollop into the hot liquid. There was bread, sausage and plenty of mayonnaise to satisfy the worst Slavic cravings. Both started to eat their fill as round thirteen started.

"The bell for round thirteen has sounded and both fighters are advancing, though the American has barely covered half the distance to the center of the ring," proclaimed SSGT Butkovsky.

"Yes, Senior Sergeant, I think the breaking of the American's nose was the turning point. It is all but over now!" the junior sergeant zealously exclaimed.

Round thirteen found two battered warriors meeting on the American's side of the ring. Gone was the bobbing and weaving and dancing. Both men were tired enough and hurt enough that they did not waste energy on fancy footwork and evasive body movements. Tkachenko took Kahless' reluctance to go all the way to the middle as a sign that he was too tired for the trip. Kahless appeared to have checked out of the fight, so intent he was to stall, clinch, and employ delaying tactics that Tkachenko was sure that victory was within his grasp. The American appeared as though he was half asleep, but every fiber of the man was waiting for his chance. Like a bear awakening from hibernation, the American suddenly propelled a lighting paw to the Soviet's jaw and he went down like a rock. The referee pointed to the neutral corner, and as Kahless complied, he began his count.

"One—two—three."

"Get up, Yuri!" his second shouted.

"Four—five—six."

Tkachenko stirred, rising to one knee, but staying down for most of the count to get the most of his rest.

"Seven—eight—nine," announced the referee.

Tkachenko was fully on both feet, and steeling himself to bring the wrath upon his rival. He made sure he got himself set, then grinned and motioned to the American to *come and get some*. Kahless moved toward him and found that the momentum he had gained was lost. The Soviet was much composed and pressed hard against him, firing right-left-right combinations, looking for an opening. Kahless subtly turned and led his opponent to his corner by ever so slowly backing up. The bell sounded the end of round thirteen. Kahless sat right down, while the Soviet walked across the ring.

"Yuri, what are you doing out there?" his second challenged.

"I can defeat him!" he exclaimed. His chest heaved with his gulping of air while he caught his breath. "In the last end of the round, he appeared slower and weaker, as if he used up a lot of his strength early in the round, hoping to end it. I can defeat him!"

Tkachenko's medic touched up the cuts on his face and looked at his eye again, shaking his head at the Soviet first officer.

"You did good, Colonel. Stay focused and make sure you keep cutting his breaks short by making him walk across the ring," the American first officer exhorted.

"I expected him to go down hard that time. I used up a lot of strength to get that knockdown, and he got back up. He doesn't seem to get the message and stay down!" grumbled Kahless.

"Keep your hands up and stay focused. If your hands are up, he can't hit you," his first officer advised.

Kahless' medic was touching up some cuts on his face. Kahless looked at him. "Yeah I know, don't let him hit me." His medic smiled as though he had just taught a child to finger-paint.

The bell sounded the beginning of round fourteen. The American let the Soviet walk most of the distance to meet him. Tkachenko was glad to oblige him. He was determined to put this American dog down for good in this round. When he collided with the American, he fired six hard rights as though they exploded from a cannon. Kahless was not ready for the assault. Tkachenko followed up with a right-left-right combination, watching Kahless' right hand drop. It was the opening Tkachenko was looking for. He put his whole body weight into a powerful twisting left hook to the American's jaw. Kahless kissed the canvas. The Soviet was directed to the neutral corner by the referee and Tkachenko complied.

"One—two—three."

Kahless stirred, trying the clear the dark clouds from his head and raise himself up.

"Four—five—six."

Kahless heard his second shouting to get up. His mind was starting to clear, but his every pore of his body and head ached and petitioned him to give up. With the heart of a warrior, he rose to one knee.

"Seven—eight—nine."

Kahless stood up, and the Soviet made a beeline to meet him. The American put up his arms peek-a-boo style and kept him from hitting his face again. Kahless evaded, stalled and clinched for the rest of the round, artfully directing his adversary to finish the round again in his corner.

"I think he is wearing out, but not enough, and my strength is almost gone," confessed the American to his first officer.

"How many rounds you got left in you?"

"One, and he's still too fresh."

"Then let him do all of the fighting. Save yourself for round sixteen."

"Time to rope-a-dope?"

"Time to rope-a dope!"

"He is mine!" he gasped, chest heaving, gulping down breathes of air. "I could feel the strength leaving him when he was in the clinch. I will take him this round!" exclaimed Tkachenko. He spit water into the bucket while the medic worked on his badly blackened left eye, which was now swollen shut.

"I've been watching him closely; he is done," concluded LTC Voronin. "Make sure you stay focused! He is sly as an old fox. Wear him down until he can't hit you and then finish him off."

Tkachenko nodded, bit down on his mouthpiece and prepared for the last battle. The bell sounded announcing the start of round fifteen.

Kahless moved slowly toward the center of the ring, making the Soviet cover more ground. He was using all the ringcraft he had to make the Soviet waste his energy reserves. The Soviet didn't seem to notice, so sure he was that the American was too weak to make the entire journey to the center of the ring. Kahless perceived that pride might be a weakness to exploit to help him with his plan to drain the strength out of the Soviet.

"Hey, you commie! Your mother is a fat pig, and she wears combat boots!" Kahless taunted, making a face at the Soviet. He was trolling for the right insult, to provoke him to anger. He'd hit pay dirt on his first attempt. Little did he know that Tkachenko's mother had died the previous year and he could not attend her funeral because he was on Mars.

"You bastard!" Tkachenko roared, his voice a blazing fire searing the air.

Kahless circled to the left and put his back to the ropes while the Soviet charged him like a mad bull. The Soviet collided with the American and pushed him hard against the ropes. Kahless put his hands up, covering his face and ribs. He peeked between his fists and said, "Fat pig." The Soviet swung hard alternately with both hands, his face set with murderous intent. The American blocked every blow, getting bruises on both arms, but was otherwise unscathed. Every time Tkachenko slowed down, Kahless insulted his mother again, which caused his to redouble his efforts to try to pound the American lifeless.

With thirty seconds left in the round, LTC Killer Instinct shouted at his commander. Kahless came off the ropes and started infighting, slowly turning the Soviet so that his own back was to his corner. Now that he was off the ropes and in position, Kahless resumed his peek-a-boo style and stopped swinging. Tkachenko pressed his attack until Kahless was nearly in his corner. At the last moment, Tkachenko swung hard around Kahless' block and stuck him with a devastating right hook to the left ribcage. Three metacarpal bones in Tkachenko's right hand broke at the same time that three of Kahless' left ribs broke. The bell announced that round fifteen was over. Both fighters were "saved by the bell." The American sat down in the folding chair, and Tkachenko walked the long journey back to his corner.

Kahless' medic's hands ran over his ribs and confirmed the bad news, three broken ribs on his left side. He pulled out a small flashlight and checked his eyes for signs of a concussion but found none. In addition to his broken nose, broken ribs, and busted lip, he was sporting two black eyes. "If we had made a jigsaw puzzle based on your likeness before the fight, your face wouldn't match the picture on the puzzle box. Seriously Colonel, you could puncture a lung if he hits you hard on this side again." He sponged his face with water and touched up some cuts on his face and eyes.

"Colonel, this has gone far enough. You could die out there," said his first officer.

"Take the towel and tie a knot in the middle," Kahless instructed. His first officer did so, and Kahless motioned to give it to him. He threw it to his former wing man, CPT Janus Dread. "Captain, no surrender!" he shouted. The Captain held it up, and the men on the bench cheered. Kahless turned to the men in his corner. "Just removing the temptation—so I won't have to kill you both."

"Okay, cover your ribs and don't let him pop you there. Switch to right-handed and end it now!" stressed his second. Kahless nodded, bit down on his mouthpiece, and went to meet his enemy. He did not tell his second that he was bone-weary, hurting so badly he wanted to quit with all of his being.

He had exhausted his strength and spent his reserves. He approached with courage the counting house of strength beyond what a man is and has, with only heart as his collateral. He would borrow strength he did not possess to finish one last round.

"He manipulated you to spend your strength fighting on the ropes," the Soviet first officer lectured. Make him fight in the center of the ring."

Tkachenko took a drink, rinsed his mouth and spit it in the bucket. He nodded, and realized in retrospect that he had been played.

Tkachenko's medic was examining his left eye, which was black and swollen shut. He shook his head at Tkachenko's second.

"I felt the bones in my right hand break when I hit him. It's useless," confessed Tkachenko.

"You are left-eye dominant. One more blow to your eye and you could be permanently blind in it and end your career as a field officer. You only have only one good hand, and one good eye. We have to throw in the towel."

Tkachenko erupted like a volcano, bolted up straight in his folding chair, and glared angrily with eyes like pools of lava at his first officer and medic. "Nyet! I will have whoever throws in the towel before a firing squad and buried at Hellas Planitia," he hotly declared as if spewing hot gases, ash, and lava. Neither man doubted it and weighed their concern for him against the threat.

Tkachenko watched as Kahless threw the towel away and proclaimed, "No surrender!"

"You see, Yuri. He will not give up! You would have to kill him before he will quit," his first officer said.

Tkachenko's smile was as cold as the East Siberian Sea in winter. "Then he will die!"

The ringing bell announced the beginning of round sixteen. Both men slowly moved to the center of the ring. The strength of both men was running out, like the sands of an hourglass. Both fighters were standing on wobbly legs, arms heavy as lead, faces swollen and hurting all over. Kahless begrudgingly offered a final boxer's handshake out of respect for the battle already fought, and Tkachenko touched his gloves against his adversary's. Blood and sweat stained the ring canvas, witness to fifteen rounds of merciless combat between two embattled warriors.

Tkachenko pointed his gloved left hand at his American antagonist. "Finish now!"

His American rival nodded his weary head. "All or nothing, leave it all out here."

Both men could stand, but barely, and they lacked the strength to keep their hands up to defend themselves. Boxing was done. What was left was a slugfest to see who would remain standing at the end and be the champion. Gone were the artful strategies of the sweet science of boxing from the earlier rounds. Primal instinct replaced training and technique. The nuclear essence of each man resembled that of cavemen with knotty clubs, beating each other senseless for their own survival and that of their tribe.

"This will probably be the last round," reported CPT Two Horses.

"They look as if they are either sleepwalking, or some undead creatures from some monster movie," added his junior partner.

Kahless switched to right-handed and kept his left down, protecting his broken ribs. Tkachenko kept his broken hand down to keep from injuring it further. Tkachenko landed a hard left cross across Kahless' chin, and Kahless momentarily stumbled but did not fall. The Soviet looked as if that took all the strength he had, and he stood there, arms down. Kahless commanded all of his strength and landed a right cross hard to the jaw of the Soviet. The punch rocked the Soviet and his legs felt like rubber, but he remained standing. Both men stood and stared, dull-eyed and slack-jawed at the other. Their seconds both shouted to get on with it. Tkachenko swung a vicious left hook with his whole body, tearing into his opponents right ribs. Kahless flinched at the impact, hesitated and delivered a hard right straight to his opponent's forehead between the eyes. The Soviet was dazed, but the American had no strength to follow up with a second punch. The fighters clinched each other, each man hoping to gain more strength than the other by the time the clinch was broken by the referee. MAJ Luv2bomb broke the clinch and Kahless wished that Tkachenko would let him take him to the ropes again.

Two hunchbacked, bleary-eyed warriors called in a loan on the last bit of borrowed strength they could summon with the force of their sheer wills. Kahless launched a hard right hook to the jaw at the same time that Tkachenko launched a left hook. Both fighters connected to the other's jaw; they both went down like two trees felled by the same axe.

The referee started the count, "One—two—three."

Kahless could not stand aright and clawed his way to the corner to get help from the ropes. The fog covered his brain like a mist and he was no longer aware of why he was trying to get up. He heard his second's voice and the voices of his men calling like the voice of many waters flowing, but he did not recognize them. He grabbed the bottom rope, raised himself to one knee, placed his hand on the second rope and then sunk into a pile of spent flesh without any conscious awareness. The American spectators were on their feet, shouting for their champion to get up.

"Four—five—six," continued the referee.

Tkachenko was no longer political, and was no longer trying to prove his pride or manhood. His descent into oblivion was complete. He was what was left of a man that was spent in animal passion trying to destroy his adversary; his shell trying to stand on his feet. With his hand on the bottom rope, he was unable to raise himself up. No amount of encouragement from the Soviet bleachers or the red corner could cause their champion to rise.

"Seven—eight—nine," continued the referee.

The counting house of both men's strength called them to account and found them both insolvent, immediately calling in all loans of strength. Both fighters were bankrupt of all endurance and vigor and could not arise by the end of the ten count.

"Ten!" MAJ Luv2bomb signaled that the fight was over and the bell tolled, calling the match to a close.

The Soviet medic broke open a vial of smelling salts and placed it under his colonel's nose. Tkachenko awoke with a start and clocked his medic with a hard left, knocking him down. The American medic took notice and put his smelling salts back into his bag. He stood back and poured a pail of water on his commander's head from a safe distance. Kahless awoke a bit startled but was not swinging. Both medics checked the eyes of their men for concussions and other damage.

Tkachenko and Kahless both slowly and with great difficulty stood unassisted to their feet as the ring announcer, MAJ Volkov stepped into the ring. He motioned to the two fighters to join him in the center of the ring. "In the fight between COL Tkachenko and COL Kahless, lasting forty-seven minutes and twenty-two seconds, neither fighter was able to stand to the count of ten. This match is hereby declared a draw. According to the agreement, both sides will divide the alloy-x material equally and return to their posts unmolested."

The men in MAJ Norsemun's office were both disappointed and proud. Though disappointed that their colonel did not defeat the Soviet, he did not lose, either. They were proud that he fought with courage and heart.

"Major, I suppose you can play the fight over the 1-MC at normal volume," concluded CPT Black Ice. MAJ Norsemun nodded and contacted CPT Cipher.

"Captain, rewind the recording of the incoming transmission to the beginning and play it on the 1-MC at normal volume."

"Sir, yes sir."

Two minutes later the recording came over the 1-MC loud and clear. "Camp SEAL, we are broadcasting live from Hellas Planitia. This is CPT Two Horses, and I will be your commentator for this fight, assisted by 1LT Pale Rider..."

"MAJ Savenkov sighed. We missed good opportunity to prove Soviet superiority today."

"It is true, Oleg, but our enemies did not get to show American superiority, either. I think we should play the recording now, yes? We can show Soviet courage in the face of adversity. It will still be good propaganda."

"Yes, yes, Arkady, by all means play it on the intercom." MAJ Ivanov rewound the recording and transmitted it "live" over the intercom. "Camp Lenin, this is SSGT Butkovsky. We are broadcasting to you from Hellas Planitia. The fight will soon begin…"

"Okay Colonel, raise both arms so I can tape up your ribs," 1SGT Specialist said. Kahless slowly and painfully raised both arms. The medic retrieved an ace bandage from his medical bag and wrapped it around Kahless' ribs. He placed tape on his patient's nose and he thought he would pass out again.

"What is that old Russian saying when somebody says they are going to beat you mercilessly to teach you a lesson?" Kahless asked.

"I will show you Kuzka's mother!" The medic smiled. "Did you see Kuzka's mother?"

"Yes."

"What did she look like?"

"Ugly! UGH-ly!"

"I'd say you must have seen her. You look like a raccoon with a broken nose and a busted lip. That is just what is visible: three of your ribs are broken and you have a boxer fracture on your right hand. If I were you I wouldn't waste any money on a Halloween mask; your face will do nicely."

"Do you know why I put up with your insolent attitude?"

1SGT Specialist smiled. "Battlefield 101, shoot the medic first. I am the highest priority target in the field and the first one to save your life if you are bleeding out."

"So I take it that you won't have a change of heart and start being more respectful?"

"I'm your surgeon. Do you want respect, or my putting my life on the line to save yours?"

"Can't I have both?"

"Just this once—good fight out there. I didn't lose my watch to the Soviet field surgeon," he said, dryly. "Do you want a painkiller?"

"I'd like nothing better, but I want my head clear until the Soviets leave."

"You don't expect be doing anything as a command officer at the moment, do you?"

"I was going to wait until the Soviets were well out of range before handing over the reins to my first officer."

"I thought so! As Chief field medical officer, I am informing you that you are temporarily relieved of your command for medical reasons. Now, hold still while I give you a shot for pain and one to sleep." 1SGT Specialist retrieved a vial and a syringe from his medical bag, took the cap off of the syringe and inserted the needle into the vial. He carefully drew the liquid into the syringe, turned it needle-point up and tapped the syringe with his finger to get all the air bubbles to float to the top. He pressed the plunger on the syringe until all of the air was gone and a single drop trickled from the needle's hole. He was doing this slowly, because Kahless hated needles worse than Soviets and he was getting a bit of perverse enjoyment out of it. Kahless' eyes grew big as he envisioned the medic as Captain Ahab looming over him with a harpoon, ready to spear the great white whale. The two were interrupted when security escorted a Soviet courier to see COL Kahless. Kahless lifted his hand to inform he was asking for a reprieve. His medic sighed and put the cap back on the syringe.

The Soviet messenger stood before the battered American at attention.

"You have a message for me?" Kahless asked the courier.

"Sir, yes sir." Normally he would refer to an officer as *comrade*, but he understood that this was how American military would be addressed. "COL Tkachenko and LTC Voronin request to meet with you and your first officer over a cup of tea, to commemorate the agreement."

Kahless hurt all over so badly that he did not want to get up. It was a matter of pride now. Tkachenko no doubt had gotten his injuries cared for and wanted to try to convey to Kahless that he was hurt less than he was. The American decided to play the game and try to pretend he was not hurt very badly. Kahless pondered it for a moment, "Tell Col Tkachenko I must get dressed first, but to meet us here in twenty minutes." The courier left him, and despite his injuries, pride took Kahless over. Kahless' wingman 1LT Janus Dread had been hovering nearby.

"Lieutenant, find my first officer and get him here ASAP."

"Sir, yes sir," he replied and headed for the exit.

"Medic! Take all of the visible tape of me ASAP! You can tape me up again later." The tape came off of his hand with little trouble. Kahless slipped on a shirt to conceal the ace bandage.

"Sorry, Colonel" he said as he carefully peeled the tape from his broken nose. Pain exploded through his nose like a fourteen pound rocket and tears fell to his shoulders like mortar fire. "You do realize that Tkachenko was present when your nose was broken? I'm sure he hasn't forgotten."

"I know. I just don't want to appear like a fugitive from the hospital."

"Officially that is what you are. Remember, I declared you relieved of duty for medical reasons and was about to treat you. You should be glad I am an understanding sort and will let you have your little tea party. As soon as it is over, I have a couple of shots for you and some bed rest."

"Understood." The medic was giving him a pathetic look. "I know what you're thinking. Am I considering taking up prize-fighting full time?"

"I wouldn't quit my day job, sir."

"Duly noted. Help me up and back to the meeting room quickly."

"Sir, yes sir."

It was a good thing Kahless had been treated in the bioshelter. The American commentator table was still up and had two chairs, so they would have tea there. Kahless did not want Tkachenko to see him walking, so he had his medic help him to the table. He fully intended to remain until the Soviet left so he could not see Kahless walk out. The battered American sat down at the table and advised the medic to keep an eye out for Tkachenko. He wanted to keep the ice pack on his face until the last possible moment. LTC Killer Instinct arrived five minutes later with Kahless' wingman in tow.

Fifteen minutes later the medic announced that Tkachenko and his first officer were coming and Kahless put the ice pack under the table. Kahless' wingman showed COL Tkachenko and LTC Voronin in. Tkachenko walked in without any difficulty it seemed, but gone was the arrogant swagger he had before the fight. With all of the discipline the American possessed, he arose and motioned for them to take a seat at the table. Tkachenko's whole face appeared swollen, sporting a black eye which was swollen shut, and a split lip. His right hand was still taped up after the fight, so Kahless assumed he'd broken it. He almost smiled at the humor of the situation; Tkachenko had damaged his hand on Kahless' ribs. Whatever other damage he'd incurred, he was no doubt concealing it to save face, the same as the American was.

Kahless' wingman did the honors and poured each man at the table a cup of tea, and retreated discreetly and stood against the wall behind his commander. Tkachenko took a sip of hot tea, and it was evident that it bothered his busted lip. "You know, you saved the lives of some of your men today, by settling it this way."

"And you saved some of yours."

"Perhaps, maybe there's some lesson to be learned here." They continued with diplomatic politeness and elevator talk until our teacups were drained. Tkachenko announced it was time to go, and Kahless nodded.

Kahless rose to satisfy diplomatic courtesy, but was using all of his discipline and strength to show no pain. He experienced a bit of difficulty as the he arose, but steeled himself to show no emotion. "It has been an honor," the American offered as the Soviets nodded in agreement. "I'll remain here and speak with my executive officer. My junior officer will show you both out."

Tkachenko looked as he had been robbed of being able to survey Kahless' walking out, but said nothing and left. The way he moved indicated Kahless was right when he thought he'd broken or cracked some of his ribs. The American made a show of sitting at the conference table with his executive officer until the Soviets left.

Kahless complied with the medic's orders, and the command was passed over to his executive officer. After the scavengers cleaned up the American half of the alloy-x, LTC Killer Instinct commandeered his commander's tank and took charge of the procession. All of the men doubled up in utility vehicles for the ride home.

When the Soviets were gone, the medic taped his commander up again. This time, Kahless submitted to a shot for pain and one to sleep. It was decided that the American commander would sleep better in the medial ambulance. Kahless wrapped up in a blanket on a stretcher in the medical ambulance and put an ice pack back on his face and one on his ribs. His medic put one of the colonel's favorite music discs in the player. The words of the song seem to summarize the day: "He was badder than old King Kong and meaner than a junkyard dog." As he fell into a deep sleep, one thing became clear to him. He had met his nemesis, and one day one of them would surely die at the hand of the other.

THE END

Turn the page for a preview of the next book of this series, entitled - Warzone: Operation Wolf Hunt.

COSTLY SKIRMISH

Earth date: December 7, 1984—Martian year 199, Sol Solis, sol 15 of the Martian Month Virgo—sol of the Martian year 515

"You are cleared for take-off, Colonel, reported MAJ Norsemun."

"First hangar airlock is open," informed Chief Wolverine. My first officer approached me as I was getting into my tank. "You sure you don't want me to bring another squad?"

"No, Jim. You get next patrol or other outing, weather permitting. I haven't been in a tank for a month because of these infernal dust storms."

"Neither have I. Have a safe trip and call us if you need us."

I visually inspected my suit and the exterior hoses, checked my air tank gauges and examined the maintenance seal, then suited up. I placed the rebreather mask on my face and turned the air valve on. The cool taste of the oxygen-nitrogen mix assured me my equipment was okay. Finally I put on my helmet. After running a preflight check on my tank, I fired my tank up and led my squad through the three transitional airlocks.

It was dust storm season. I'd grounded the entire regiment for the last month. The storms had subsided, and the dust particles had settled enough so that we were now getting our satellite views of the surface back. Our morning satellite pass revealed that the dust storm had exposed a metallic object in the Eisenhower Plain. It was possibly an alien relic, so I took a squad to the plain to investigate. I'd been going stir-crazy for the last month and welcomed the reprieve from my prison.

"A squad of Soviet tanks is crossing into the Eisenhower Plain now, sir," reported MAJ Norsemun. "Sorry sir, we didn't have a satellite view until they entered the plain. Their ETA and yours to the object is approximately sixty-three minutes."

"We'll arrive at the same time?"

"Aye, sir."

"Scramble all pilots to reinforce us."

"Aye, sir. Colonel, twenty-five Soviet tanks have just left the Soviet post and are headed your way."

"Understood."

Both our reinforcements and the Soviets' were one hour and forty-five minutes from the object. The *object of curiosity* was partially unearthed and located in the Eisenhower Plain two hundred meters on our side. The *imaginary line* dividing our turfs existed halfway between the two posts.

We coexisted with the Soviets because neither side was able to drive the other out. Engagements with the Soviets generally occurred for three reasons. The most common reason was the fight over alloy-x, either from destroyed objects turned into scrap or from meteor showers, which littered the Martian landscape with it. The second, less common but more important was to defend or attack an alien archaeological dig site. The third reason was less important than for scrap or technology, but important nonetheless. The third reason to fight was if one side had the sand to cross the imaginary line. To do so was the same as throwing down a gauntlet. If you tolerated the enemy crossing that line today, then he would cross the next line, and so forth until he was at your front door.

The economics of a fight dictated who'd recover more or most of the scrap from the destroyed vehicles and how close your reinforcements were. In today's case, there was no advantage to being closer to either post. If a Soviet patrol could make it here before our reinforcements could, they might challenge us for the dig. *This is a bad place for a dig*, I thought. This was too close to the middle of the line to be easily defendable, with no mountains here for snipers. If both sides think that this is a viable dig site, this could force us into the bloodiest conflict I'd ever witnessed here.

A Soviet patrol of five tanks was six minutes from the object; we were five. We arrived to see a piece of alloy-x metal sticking out of the sand. The Soviets were rapidly closing on our position. The Soviet commander opened a channel to me.

"COL Kahless, this is COL Tkachenko. I claim the right to salvage that object."

"Why COL Tkachenko, I didn't know we had salvage laws here."

"I will have that object. If I have to fight you for it, I will."

"You know we both have reinforcements coming, and if you choose to cross the line I'll have to fight you. Then both of our reinforcements would arrive, and they would fight which would result in many deaths on both sides. Besides, it is probably just a small piece of metal with no real importance."

I was hoping to avoid a full-scale conflict over what may or may not be a dig site of importance. I couldn't, however, afford to allow him to take the object, no matter what it was. If it was a relic with the cipher containing the cloaking technology, then the Soviets and the Chinese would both have it, and America would be at a distinct disadvantage. The Soviet colonel was also aware of this.

"If I could inspect the object, we could avoid the deaths of many of your men," the Soviet officer offered.

"No can do, Yuri. It is on our side of the line."

"I have tried to be reasonable. Prepare to die."

With that, the Soviet cut off all communications and drew his men into attack formation. With a squad of five tanks, the squad leader has the lead with his wingman close while the other three back his play.

The Soviet leader knew which tank was mine, and he led the attack against me, with his wingman close on his starboard wing. My other three tanks met the remaining enemies and a violent clash ensued. My usual wingman was on leave, and today CPT Two Horses had my six. We kicked up so much fine dust in the air with our engine jets that we were forced to fire at heat signatures. My master panel, which kept track of the GPS signals from my ships, showed we'd lost one of ours already. The air was thick with fine dust, smoke and fire. I was firing at the heat signature of COL Tkachenko's tank and estimated that I was doing some damage. His heat signature was changing, indicating his tank was on fire. My ship shook violently when I took a direct hit. Now my engine was smoldering.

"Sorry Colonel, I'm done," reported CPT Two Horses. I felt the shockwave from his tank exploding, and I prayed he was able to survive to eject. I took another direct hit.

"Engine critical, twenty seconds to destruct," reported my computer's familiar female voice. Smoke was filling the cockpit, beginning to make my control panel gauges unreadable. I turned on my rear ventilator, vented the smoke out and concentrated on the business at hand. COL Tkachenko's wingman had lost his tank the same time mine had, and the heat and radar signatures on my control panel revealed only four other tanks left. I made one last attempt to bring him down before my engine blew and fired twice with both cannons and ejected. Both our tanks blew at the same time.

The fine dust and smoke suspended in the air obscured my view as I drifted back to the ground. A brilliant flash and a loud roar signaled another tank had blown. My visibility was poor. I no longer had my ship's console to aid me in keeping track of where my pilots and their ships were.

I slung my sniper rifle over my shoulder and walked south a little to see if I could find some cover and get a better look. Another two explosions signaled what I estimated was close to the last two tanks if I counted right.

We were in trouble. All of the pilots were outside of their ships and on the ground, and a large dust devil was heading our way. I tried to radio my post on my personal communication device in my suit but got a lot of static interference. This was no small dust devil. I estimated it was one kilometer wide across the base and at least eight kilometers tall. The top six or seven kilometers of the devil consisted of a blue cloud of ice crystals. Dust devils were truly the God of War's version of wrath. There was no predicting them, just deal with them when they occur. I didn't know which was more dangerous, COL Tkachenko armed with a sniper rifle, or a dust devil coming at us with full force.

From across the battlefield, I saw the slumped figure of CPT Two Horses being picked up by the dust devil. His body was assaulted by a vortex of dark basaltic sand particles, mixed with ice crystals. The high-speed material was pinging my officer's body, arcing his form with filamentary static discharges. The dust devil pulsated with a light show within as the static charges hit my pilot over and over while carrying his body along its path down the Martian landscape. The Eisenhower Plain was mostly flat and had few rocks, but it did have a few. Bumping into a small boulder about the height of a man, my leg protested. I let out a salty epithet that sailors keep in reserve for such events. A quick examination of my suit revealed no tears or rips. It would make for a nasty bruise, but that was not my immediate concern.

After the dust devil moved away from our position, the wind had calmed, revealing no tanks left on the battlefield. I started using my sniper scope to look for enemy snipers, and I saw a Soviet sniper doing the same. His scope was moving toward line-of-sight with me, and I focused my aim on his heart. I fired at the same time that he did. The wind kicked up again and I assumed that it threw both our shots off. I felt a sharp pain in my back. The bullet had missed me cleanly from the front, but then ricocheted off the rock behind me. I'd fallen forward and was laying belly down, unable to move or even feel my legs. My suit would start decompressing in seconds. I felt around back and found the hole and pulled out a #4 hot patch and stopped the leak. I wondered if my patch job was a futile attempt; Tkachenko might still finish me off with a second shot. I pulled my spotting scope out of my suit pocket and looked for him. Incredible! He was on his back and not moving, either. I'd hit him after all! The dust storm started again, this time as violent as a Mongol horde in battle array. This was not a good day to fight out here. I accessed my remote comm. link through the static and raised my executive officer.

"LTC Killer Instinct, status of reinforcements!"

"Sir, with the dust devil in your vicinity and the storm starting again, the reinforcements on both sides won't be able to do much in this weather."

"Call the Soviet XO. Advise that his commander has been shot and we request a truce to recover our dead and wounded. Also advise that we will revisit the issue of possession of this object when the storm breaks. And Colonel?"

"Sir?"

"Please send a team to retrieve us. I need medical attention. I've been shot."

The cost of the skirmish was high. We recovered the bullets from my men's bodies, confirming that COL Tkachenko killed them all before shooting me. The ballistics of the three men killed matched a bullet we retrieved from a pilot confirmed killed by COL Tkachenko in a previous engagement.

We couldn't immediately recover CPT Two Horse's body. The dust devil had lifted and moved his body fifty kilometers west before its static energy was discharged and it dissipated. We were unable to recover his body until after the storm was over, two weeks later. The dust devil sand and ice blasted off his space suit, and peeled the skin off of his body. The only part of his spacesuit left was his helmet and boots. The nights near the equator were very cold, but the summer sols lately had been a balmy 60 °F. I could only assume that his body was freeze-dried at night, and then thawed out during the day. In the soft vacuum and low humidity, his corpse had become mummified by the time we retrieved his body. It was a gruesome sight, and we didn't let his son CPL Gray Eagle view the body. Of the squadron that I left with, only 1LT Gladiator and I survived.

MAJ Sawbones couldn't remove the bullet from my back without possibly killing or permanently paralyzing me. The swelling began to subside and little by little I recovered feeling in my feet and legs. The physical therapist here was as good as any back on Earth so I would do my rehab here. It took a month before I could walk with a walker, another to walk with a cane and was allowed to return to desk duty.

After the dust storm season was over, the object of the dispute was further uncovered. It was a piece of an old tank, nothing more. We let the Soviets inspect it, but COL Tkachenko was not present. I was still unsure of COL Tkachenko's fate until he contacted me. He looked as fit as ever. He played me a game of chess online as if nothing had ever happened; beating me two games to one. I had time during physical therapy and my restriction to desk duty to begin to process nearly dying or being confined to a wheelchair for life. I'd never retreated from a challenge before, but was beginning to wonder if it was time to pass the torch to my first officer.

GLOSSARY OF TERMS

NAVAJO TERMS

Bilagaana- Navajo word for white man.

Chindi- In Navajo religious belief, a chindi is the ghost left behind after a person dies, believed to leave the body with the deceased's last breath. It is everything that was bad about the person: the residue that man has been unable to bring into universal harmony.

Dawn boy- The sun bearer, gave gifts to the Great-Chief-of-All-Magic, and received gifts from him for all men.

Diné- Navajo people.

Hataalii- Blessing way singer, Navajo medicine man that uses sand paintings, chants, stories and songs to cure and restore the *patient* to harmony with the world.

Hozho- Navajo concept of harmony with the world.

Uncle- Uncle, the Navajo term of respect for an older man but not aged, who'd be referred to as grandfather.

Yei Bechei- Holy beings in Navajo metaphysics.

MILITARY AND OTHER TERMS

1-MC- General loudspeaker which is turned up high enough so that anyone can hear it on the naval base, used to transmit orders, alerts, or general information.

4P- Mars, fourth planet from the sun.

APO- Army Post Office.

ARVN- Army of the Republic of Vietnam (South Vietnam).

Bad bear- Phrase or expression used to indicate that a certain situation or object is difficult.

Bandits- Hostile aircraft.

Beans, bullets and bandages- Expression for things a logistician must provide his or her unit: rations, ammunition, and medical care.

BG- Brigadier general, first rank above full colonel.

Bullet sponge- pejorative term for a marine.

Cannon cockers- Artillerymen.

Chicken Plate- Bullet proof vest that the gunners wore, but the pilots often sat on.

Chief- In this story, this applies to Chief Wolverine, rank CW5, or Chief Warrant Officer, grade five.

Class A- Dress uniform.

Cooking off- (or thermally induced firing) refers to ammunition exploding prematurely due to barrel overheating due to excessive firing.

CPL- Corporal.

CAPT- Captain, U.S. Navy, equivalent to army rank of colonel.

CPT- Captain (not Navy), equivalent to navy rank of lieutenant.

CSM- Command Sergeant Major.

Dead-Man Zone- Height versus velocity curve—proper speed that should be attained before climbing or landing to avoid engine quits. Also at takeoff and decent, a helicopter is at their most vulnerable state. Dead-man zone takes on a whole new meaning with Charlie shooting at you.

Deep sixed- Throwing something overboard into the water, usually at sea, but this time in the Cua Long River.

Derobements- in fencing, an avoidance of the opponent's attempt to take the blade or beat, performed with a straight sword arm.

DEROS- Date of Estimated Return from OverSeas.

Det- Detachment, group of troops or ships - in this story, sniper detachment or Seawolf detachment.

Disengage thrusts- In fencing, a circular movement of the blade that deceives the opponent's parry, removes the blades from engagement, or changes the line of engagement.

Doc- Navy corpsman, medic attached to Navy Seal unit.

Dojo - Martial arts practice hall.

DRV- Democratic Republic of Vietnam, communist North Vietnam.

Fire bottle- Fire extinguisher on a helicopter.

Fit Rep- Fitness Report.

FTL- Fire Team Leader, the pilot of the lead bird (helicopter) in a two bird detachment.

GEN- Four Star General.

Ghillie suit- Type of camouflage clothing designed to resemble heavy foliage. The suit gives the wearer's outline a three-dimensional breakup, rather than a linear one.

Gi- Martial arts practice uniform.

Gozinaki- A traditional Georgian (East European) walnut-honey candy.

Green Faces- The name Charlie called the Navy SEALs, because of the camo makeup they wore on ops.

Gunnel- Nautical term, variant of old English gunwale, the upper edge of the side or bulwark of a vessel. The handrail about waist high on the deck.

Gunship/helicopter- Armed helicopter fitted for combat.

Hard charger- Term of endearment from a superior to a subordinate marine when he or she completes a difficult task, so named for charging through the assignment, or general toughness.

HE shells- high-explosive shells.

Huey- Bell UH-1B Iroquois attack helicopter, Bravo designating the B model.

Intel- Information, intelligence.

Jayjee- US Navy Lieutenant, Junior Grade

Joe- Coffee, so named because United States Secretary of the Navy Josephus Daniels eliminated beer and wine from naval ships, declaring nothing stronger than coffee would be allowed.

Kata- In martial arts, a kata is a detailed choreographed pattern of defense and attack movements is practiced either solo or in pairs, for exercise and practicing concentration. Sometimes it is practiced with hand held weapons, such as a knife, staff, sword, nunchuckas, or sai.

KBA- Killed by aircraft.

Kuzma's mother or **Kuzka's mother** is a part of the Russian idiomatic expression, "To show Kuzka's mother to someone" which means to teach someone a lesson, to punish someone in a brutal way.

LST- Landing Ship, Tank—naval vessels created to support amphibious operations, by carrying significant quantities of vehicles, cargo, and landing troops directly onto an unimproved shore.

Light Colonel- LTC, Lieutenant Colonel.

LT- Lieutenant.

LTG- Lieutenant General, three star general.

LTJG- in U.S. Navy- Lieutenant, Junior Grade, also Junior Lieutenant in Soviet Army.

LTSG- Senior lieutenant in Soviet Army.

Luna- Earth's moon.

LZ- landing zone.

Mag Cannon- Was outlawed by accord between the Soviets and Americans. A devastating weapon when fully charged, firing purple balls of concentrated magnetic energy. Two fully charged MAG cannon blasts will destroy a ship.

MAJ- Major

Mike boat- LCM-8 River boat and mechanized landing craft used in Vietnam.

MITS mines- Magnetic tethering snare mines.

NCOIC- Non commissioned officer in charge.

NVA- North Vietnamese Army regulars.

OIC- Officer in charge.

ONI- Office of Naval Intelligence.

Parries- In fencing, a block of the attack, made with the forte of one's own blade.

Particle Beam Cannon- A particle beam weapon uses an ultra-high energy beam of atoms or electrons (i.e., a particle beam) to damage a material target by hitting it, and thus disrupting its atomic and molecular structure, (Wikipedia reference) which is the standard energy weapon from alien technology used in Soviet and American tanks alike.

Phantom VIR- Visual Image Refractor, or phantom, makes ship invisible to satellite cameras and to the human eye, but doesn't remove the radar signature. Uses fuel while in use.

Pit- On a shooting range, the bull pit or pit is the place downrange where the targets are.

PVT- Private.

Rats- military rations, food.

Redfield Generators- Radar Echo Dampening Field, visible to satellite camera and the human eye but removes the radar signature. Uses fuel while in use.

Roger wilco- short for Roger/Understood wilco/will comply.

Ruff Puff- In Vietnam, the local militia, Regional and Popular forces, were called Ruff Puffs which occupied Ruff Puff outposts at the canal crossways, which doubled as fuel and ammo resupply points.

SEALORD- Minimally armed helicopter transport, helicopter Transport, also known as a SLC.

Seawolves- HA(L)-3, Navy Light Attack Helicopter Squadron 3, conceived, deployed and decommissioned entirely during in the Vietnam conflict.

SGT- Sergeant.

Shogun- A hereditary military dictator of Japan, the shoguns ruled Japan until the revolution of 1867–68.

Slicks- See reference SEALORD.

Soke- One who is the leader of any school or the master of a style, but it is most commonly used as a highest level Japanese title, referring to the singular leader of a school or style of martial art. In this scenario, it refers to Master Karl W. Marx, found of Keichu-Ryu Karate Do Jitsu.

Song Cua Long- Cua Lan River.

Squid- Pejorative for sailor, usually used by marines, comparing sailors to a marine animal with no backbone.

Stoner- .223/5.62mm (used linked ammo) Stoner designed AR15-M16, (light machine gun) by Eugene Stoner of Fairchild Armalite Corporation.

Stop hit- in fencing, a counterattack that hits: also a counterattack whose touch is valid by virtue of its timing.

Sub-colonel- literal Russian translation for lieutenant colonel.

Tactical Operation Center- also known as tac ops, or TOC, the command post for all security, military intelligence and planning on the post.

Tet- Vietnamese New Year.

There is no sex in the Soviet Union- The Leningrad-Boston "telemost" (TV Bridge or Space Bridge) was one of the first joint Soviet-American programs filmed live. When an American woman brought up a topic about sex, a Russian lady exclaimed to the whole world about the absence of this phenomenon in the Soviet Union by saying "There is no sex in the Soviet Union." However, the viewers only caught the first part of her response as she was interrupted by a burst of laughter. In response to the question of whether or not the Soviet media had the same amount of sexual content and violence as did the media in the US, Lyudmila Ivanova responded by saying, "There is no sex in the Soviet Union…but there is love!" This statement was mostly a commentary comparing Soviet's view of sexuality to America's sexual revolution at the time. However, in a broader sense, it also showed the Soviet government's policy of keeping their people's public expressions in check, and in control.

Thrusts- In fencing, an attack made by moving the sword parallel to its length and landing with the point.

Trail AHAC- Attack Helicopter Aircraft Commander, pilot of the trail helicopter in a two helo detachment.

VC- Viet Cong, NVA guerillas, designated by first two letters and dubbed Victor Charlie, shortened to simply *Charlie*.

War of northern aggression- This is what the South Vietnamese called the VN War.

XO- Executive officer or first officer, second-in-command.

Zoom bag- Naval Aviator's flight suit.

BOXING TERMS

Bob and weave- Bobbing moves the head laterally and beneath an incoming punch. As the opponent's punch arrives, the fighter bends the legs quickly and simultaneously shifts the body either slightly right or left.

Body Punches- It is a type of repetitive yet powerful punches commonly used to wear down the opponent. It is often delivered directly to the floating rib area of the opponent with the use of a left hook.

Bout- A boxing contest, boxing fight, or boxing match.

Boxer's Handshake- This is a part of the boxing guidelines wherein both the boxers greet each other by touching knuckles, regardless of whether they are wearing their gloves or not.

Clinch- to hold an opponent's body with one or both arms to prevent or hinder punches.

Combination- There are different punching types can be combined to form "combos," like a jab and cross combo.

Corner Man- a person who is responsible for assisting the boxer by giving him water, advises and pares down swelling or bleeding during the end of every round.

Count- The tolling of the seconds of the clock by the referee after a boxer is knocked down. If the boxer is still down at the end of ten-counts, the fight is over by a knockout.

Counterpunch- A counterattack begun immediately after an opponent throws a punch, exploiting the opening in the opponent's position.

Cross- In boxing, a cross (also commonly called a "straight") is a power-punch like the uppercut and hook. It is a punch usually thrown with the dominant hand the instant an opponent leads with his opposite hand. The blow crosses over the leading arm, hence its name.

Cut Man- A cut man is the one who deals with cuts sustained by a boxer during a bout. His job is to stop any bleeding from the face or nose and also to reduce swelling around the eyes by applying cold pressure.

Down for the Count- Knocked out for the referee's count of ten.

Fall through the Ropes- To slip or be punched through the ropes of a boxing ring. If a boxer is knocked out of the ring, he gets a count of 20 to get back in and on his feet. He cannot be assisted, or he will be considered knocked out.

Hook- A short power punch in which the boxer swings from the shoulder with his elbow bent, bringing his fist from the side toward the center. One of the most technically difficult punches to throw because it requires perfect precision, timing and coordination.

Infighting- fighting or boxing at close quarters.

Inside Fighter- An inside fighter is a very skilled boxer who can instantaneously throw a burst of punches including uppercuts and hooks, in the pursuit of ending the gap between himself and his opponent.

Jab- The jab is a quick, straight punch thrown with the lead hand. Often the most important punch in a boxer's arsenal because of its power and its ability to set up other punches. It can also be used as a way to gauge distance, to keep an opponent wary, or as a defensive move to slow an advancing opponent.

Kidney Punch- A punch to the lower back which is illegal in boxing due to the damage it can cause to the kidneys.

Kissed the canvas- Expression used to describe when a boxer is knocked down with his face facing the floor on the canvas.

Knockdown- A knockdown occurs when a boxer, after being hit by his opponent: 1) touches the ring floor with some part of his body other than the feet; 2) has any part of his body outside the ropes; 3) is hanging on the ropes helplessly; or 4) is judged to be in a semi-conscious state and unable to continue fighting. A slip or fall on the canvas by a boxer, resulting in any of the above conditions, is not a knockdown.

Knockout (KO)- A knockout occurs when an boxer is knocked down by his opponent or otherwise is down and the referee reaches the count of ten before the boxer is back on his feet.

Lucky punch- To have a lucky break.

Mouthpiece- A piece of hard, form-fitting rubber a boxer wears while fighting, primarily to prevent cuts in the mouth by the teeth, and to protect the teeth.

Neutral Corner- One of the two corners of a boxing ring not assigned to either boxer during a bout. Also referred to as a white corner in some countries: the corners of the ring where there are no chairs or members of any boxer's team. After a boxer has knocked down his opponent, he is required to go immediately to a neutral corner while the referee tolls the count.

On the Ropes- A boxer who has been knocked against the ropes and is trapped by his or her opponent's punches.

Overhand Punch- A haymaker style punch that swings up and over. It is very powerful and has been very effective.

Peek-a-Boo- A peek-a-boo defense is a style of defense created by trainer Cus D'Amato, whereby the boxer raises his two hands up high, to his forehead and extremely close to his face, to guard against punches to his face and head (but often thereby leaving his body open to attack if he does not also use his elbowed arms for protection).

Punch- Some of the basic punches are the uppercut, straight right/cross, jab and hook.

Rabbit Punch- A punch delivered by a boxer to the back of the neck of his opponent. It is illegal to use because of the potential for serious injury it can cause. The term is derived from the blow used by a rabbit hunter, to kill the animal.

Rope a Dope- Rope a dope was used by Muhammad Ali in his 1974 fight against George Foreman. It involves lying back on the ropes, shelling up and allowing your opponent to throw punches until they tire themselves out and then you exploit their defensive flaws and nail them.

Rounds- Each round lasts three minutes with have a one minute rest between rounds.

Saved by the Bell- Saved by the bell is when the bell rings signaling the end of the round before the referee finishes his count. This phrase came into being in the latter half of the 19th century.

Second- A person other than the coach who stands in a boxer's corner during a bout and gives him advice and assistance between rounds. A team of seconds is also called the boxer's corner.

Southpaw- Southpaws are left handed fighters (unorthodox). They put their right foot forward, jab with their right hand and throw power punches with their left hand (rear hand). To a "normal" right handed fighter a southpaw's punches are coming from the wrong side. When a right handed and left handed boxer fight each other their lead foot is almost on top of the other persons. Southpaws aren't always born left handed some are converted southpaws.

Southpaws should be drowned at birth- An old boxing idiom. To an orthodox right handed boxer southpaw's punches come from the opposite direction than what are trained to expect. It just feels wrong.

Stance- Stance usually refers to whether a boxer is right-handed or left-handed. If he generally hits with his right hand, with his left foot forward, he is considered an orthodox puncher. If he punches with the left hand, with the right foot forward, he is considered a southpaw. A boxer who does both is considered a switch hitter.

Straight Right- Considered as a power punch, it refers to a right handed boxer throwing a straight right punch.

Sucker Punch- A surprise punch that is used when the opponent is caught off guard.

Sweet science- Another term for the sport of boxing, created by Pierce Egan in his seminal book *Boxiana*.

Throw in the Towel- The traditional admission of defeat in boxing, where a second who feels his boxer cannot or should not continue the bout throws a towel or sponge into the ring, to end the fight by a technical knockout.

Twenty count- When a fighter has been knocked through the ropes and outside of the ring, he has to the count of twenty to be inside of the right and on his feet, ready to resume.

Upper Cut- An upwards-thrown punch designed to hit an opponent's chin, usually part of a multi-punch combination and best used when a boxer is very close to his opponent.

Proof

Made in the USA
Charleston, SC
28 March 2014